"Dance with me," he said.

Buck faced Terri and held out his hand.

Her lips parted, but she didn't speak as he drew her into his arms. She was a little stiff and self-conscious at first—Buck guessed she hadn't danced in a while. But as he pulled her close enough to be guided by his body, she softened against him, slipping into the beat of the music.

Her satiny cheek rested against his. He breathed her in, filling his senses with her sexy-clean, womanly aroma. Her curves skimmed his body, the contact hardening his arousal. There was no way she couldn't be feeling it. But she didn't pull away.

He'd made love to this woman, Buck reminded himself. He'd been inside her—and, damn it all, he ached to be there again. But that was the least of what he was feeling now.

How could he let her go after tonight? How could he watch her walk away, knowing that even if he saw her again, she would no longer be part of his life?

A LITTLE SURPRISE
FOR THE BOSS

BY
ELIZABETH LANE

First Published in Great Britain 2016
By Mills & Boon, an imprint of HarperCollins*Publishers*
1 London Bridge Street, London, SE1 9GF

© 2016 Elizabeth Lane

ISBN: 978-0-263-91868-7

51-0716

Our policy is to use papers that are natural, renewable and recyclable products and made from wood grown in sustainable forests. The logging and manufacturing processes conform to the legal environmental regulations of the country of origin.

Printed and bound in Spain
by CPI, Barcelona

Elizabeth Lane has lived and traveled in many parts of the world, including Europe, Latin America and the Far East, but her heart remains in the American West, where she was born and raised. Her idea of heaven is hiking a mountain trail on a clear autumn day. She also enjoys music, animals and dancing. You can learn more about Elizabeth by visiting her website at www.elizabethlaneauthor.com.

One

Terri Hammond dumped two aspirin into her palm and washed them down with the lukewarm coffee in her mug. The hand-thrown mug, a costly item that bore the inscription My Right-Hand Woman, had been a Christmas gift the previous December from her boss of ten years, Buck Morgan, CEO of Bucket List Enterprises. Its message, meant as a compliment, was a galling reminder of the way Buck treated her—as something that simply did whatever he asked, without requiring attention or praise. Something to be taken for granted.

To Buck's credit, he'd also given her a generous bonus. But right now, it was all Terri could do to keep from flinging the mug against the sandstone wall of her office with all her strength.

No wonder she had a headache. It was nine forty-five, the day was already turning into the Monday from hell, and Buck was nowhere to be found.

The morning had started with a voice mail from Jay Mickleson, the instructor for the resort's scheduled afternoon skydive. He'd thrown out his back over the weekend and couldn't show up for the jump that had been booked. If Terri couldn't raise one of the other instructors or find Buck, she'd have to do the job herself. She was licensed and certified, but it was just one more thing to add to an already hectic day—a day that was just getting started.

As Terri was about to check her email, a call had come from the nursing supervisor at Canyon Shadows Assisted Living. Terri's ninety-one-year-old grandmother was refusing to eat again. When the aide had tried to feed her, the old woman swore at the poor girl, knocked the plate to the floor, and demanded that somebody be called to come and drive her home.

The incident would blow over just as they always had in the past, Terri knew. But she felt duty bound to show up. It was nobody's fault that the sweet, patient woman who'd raised her after her parents died had become erratic and miserable in her old age and dementia. Her grandmother still deserved—and needed—love and attention.

While she was waiting for Bob, her young assistant, to show up and cover the calls, the phone rang again. Terri's nerves clenched as she recognized the voice of Diane, Buck's ex-wife, who, thanks to a smart divorce lawyer, owned a 20 percent share of Bucket List Enterprises.

"Terri? Put Buck on." In Terri's experience, the word *please* had never escaped the woman's collagen-enhanced lips. Neither had *thank you.*

"Sorry, Diane, he's not here."

"Well, where is he? He's not answering his cell."

"I know. I've tried to reach him. He's not answering his landline at home, either. Can I help you with something?"

"Well…" Her tongue made a little *click*. "You can pass this on. I can't drive Quinn up there this week because I'm hosting a spiritual cleansing retreat here in Sedona. If Buck wants his daughter for the summer, he's going to have to send someone to get her or come himself."

Terri bit back a snarky retort. "I'll pass that on."

"Fine. Do that." The call ended. Terri sighed as she hung up the phone. Buck's nine-year-old daughter was a little champ. But her parents relayed her back and forth like the shuttlecock in a badminton game. Neither of them seemed to have much time for the girl.

Getting Quinn here was Buck's problem, not hers. But it was her job to let him know. She picked up the phone again and punched in his cell number. She heard the recorded answer in the deep, sexy drawl that, after all these years, still raised goose bumps on the back of her neck.

Hi. You've reached Buck Morgan. I'm not available right now. Leave a message and I'll get back to you soon as I can.

Terri waited for the beep. "Blast it, Buck, where are you? Jay hurt his back. He's probably out for the week. And you need to phone Diane about picking up Quinn in Sedona—she says she can't drive her out. Call me."

Five minutes later, Bob walked in, late as usual. Dark-haired and handsome at nineteen, he was sure of himself to the point of arrogance. But when it came to actual experience or know-how to back up his ego…he had a lot to learn. Especially when it came to running things at Bucket List Enterprises. After three weeks of struggling to train him, Terri had doubts about his willingness to learn any of it. But since his father was one of Buck's partners, she was stuck with him. She sighed as he waved a greeting. What she wouldn't give for some reliable help.

After telling him where she was going and leaving him with some brief instructions, she shoved on her sunglasses and dashed out through the rustic, open-beamed lobby of the luxury hotel that was the center of Buck's business. Her vintage Jeep was parked in the employee row, next to Bob's Corvette. Piling into the driver's seat, she swung onto Porter Hollow's main street and headed for the nursing home. Her long chestnut hair, caught back in a ponytail, waved behind her as she drove.

By the time she arrived, the crisis was over. "Harriet calmed down not long after we called you," the nursing director told her. "She finally ate some breakfast and went to sleep in her lounge chair in front of the TV."

"You're not giving her anything to make her sleep, are you?" Terri demanded.

"Of course not, dear. She's just old and tired. Any little thing wears her out these days."

Terri took the stairs to the second floor, walked down the carpeted hallway and opened the door to her grandmother's tiny studio apartment. The TV was blaring a popular game show, but the old woman wasn't watching. She lay partway back in her old leather recliner, her head sagging to one side like a tired little sparrow's as she slept. She looked so small and frail that Terri had to fight back tears.

After turning off the TV, Terri left without waking her. She would come back to visit tonight after dinner. Right now she needed to check on Buck.

Worry gnawed at her as she turned onto Main Street. Buck had worked hard to build his business, and he took a hands-on approach to running it. The other side of that was that he played as hard as he worked. Oversleeping after a wild night wasn't unheard of. But it wasn't like him to drop out of sight without telling her, or at least leaving his phone on so she could reach him. Something had to be wrong.

On this warm mid-June day, Main Street was crowded with tourists. Visitors roamed the boardwalks that lined the narrow roadway, browsing the expensive boutiques and art galleries, and eating brunch in the upscale gourmet restaurants.

For generations, Porter Hollow had been a sleepy little southern Utah town, nestled amid spectacular red rock scenery but largely undiscovered by the rest of the world. Buck, who'd grown up here, had come home from the army eleven years ago burning with ideas to bring the place to life and garner the town worldwide attention.

Starting small, he'd partnered with several outdoor-adventure companies to form Bucket List Enterprises. Within a few years the town had become a magnet for high-end adventure seekers. Porter Hollow offered access to four national parks, the vast waters of Lake Powell and the Tony Award–winning Utah Shakespeare Festival in nearby Cedar City. Buck's clients could enjoy river rafting, sport fishing, hiking, biking, skydiving, four-wheeling and horseback trips into the nearby mountains. With the construction of a sprawling luxury hotel complex, featuring exclusive shops, five-star restaurants, a spa, a beauty salon and the booking office for Bucket List Adventures, Buck had forged a kingdom. As holder of a 70 percent company share, he was its absolute ruler. Even Terri could only guess how many millions of dollars he was worth.

From the main highway, Terri took a right turn onto the road that wound two miles up a vermilion-hued canyon to the gated property where Buck had built his home.

She would check there first. If she failed to find him, she would start making phone calls. Buck Morgan wasn't just her boss. The two of them went back a long way. She was genuinely concerned about him.

Growing up, Terri had known Buck as the best friend of her older brother, Steve. Buck and Steve had played football together, hunted and fished together, and double-dated the prettiest girls in school. After graduation, the two of them had joined the army and deployed in the same unit. Buck had survived Iraq and made it home without a scratch. Steve had been shot dead on patrol and come home to Porter Hollow in a flag-draped coffin. His death had devastated Terri. But Buck had tried to make sure she was all right. When, after two years of college, she'd returned home to care for her aging grandmother, he'd offered her a well-paying job as his assistant and office manager. Working side by side, her feelings for him had only grown—not that he'd ever seemed to notice. Buck had been a loyal friend to her, but it had always been clear that friendship was the only relationship he wanted with her, despite his affairs with an endless string of women.

Her grandmother's declining health, and her loyalty to Buck, had kept Terri in Porter Hollow and with Bucket List Enterprises for the past ten years. But recently she'd begun to question her future. She was thirty years old. Did she really want to spend her life looking after a man with a weakness for sexy blondes—a man who never gave her a second look, except when he needed something done?

It wasn't as if she didn't have options. As Buck's assistant, she'd gotten to know the owners of other resorts in the region. Several had expressed an interest in poaching her. Moving her grandmother shouldn't be a problem.

There had to be nice facilities in other towns—some of them better than Canyon Shadows.

She should give it some serious thought, Terri told herself as she drove up the canyon. A change of scene might be good for her. It might even help her get over the flaming crush she'd had on Buck Morgan since she was fourteen.

Pulling up to the wrought iron gate, Terri entered the code on the keypad. She felt a prickle of nervous apprehension. What would she find when she reached the house? What could explain Buck's mysterious silence?

A symphony of stone, wood and glass, the house was set amid cliffs and massive boulders like part of the landscape. The interior featured soaring cathedral ceilings and a huge stone fireplace. Buck could easily have afforded servants, but he liked his privacy. He made do with a weekly cleaning crew from the hotel to keep the place spotless.

The place looked undisturbed. As Terri pulled into the driveway, she could see Murphy, Buck's big rescue mutt, romping in the enclosed part of the yard. An imposing mix of rottweiler and pit bull, he was as playful and affectionate as he was scary-looking. He bounded up to the tall fence, tongue lolling and tail wagging, as she climbed out of the Jeep.

"Hello, boy." Terri stuck her fingers through the chain links so the dog could slurp them. The dog didn't seem upset—which he'd likely be if something was wrong. And Buck's tan Hummer was parked outside the garage, which meant he was most likely here. But if he was here, why wasn't he answering either of his phones?

The door swung open to a silent house. No TV. No sounds or smells from the kitchen. She checked the kitchen and dining room, the pantry, the den, and the downstairs bathroom. Aside from a single coffee cup and a spoon in the sink, there was no sign of life. The bedrooms, including Buck's, were upstairs. Cringing inside, Terri crept up the open staircase. What if Buck was here and he had company? If she heard telltale noises coming from his bedroom, she'd be out of the house faster than a scared jackrabbit.

From the landing, she could see that the door to Buck's room was partway open. Peeking around the door frame, she saw that the blinds were drawn, the room dim and quiet. Finally she could make out a solitary figure sprawled facedown in the rumpled king-size bed—sheets twisted around long, bare legs, a smudge of dark hair against the pillow. It was definitely Buck. But was he all right? It wasn't like him to be in bed at this hour on a workday.

Shedding her sandals in the hall, she tiptoed into the room. She could hear the deep rasp of his breathing. At least he was alive. Edging closer, she could see his shoes and work clothes scattered on the sheepskin rug, as if he'd just peeled everything off and collapsed into bed. He wasn't even wearing…

Heat rushed to Terri's face as her gaze fixed on the twin moons of his rump, nicely framed by a fold of the twisted sheet. The man wasn't wearing a stitch. What she could see of him looked damned good.

But this was no time to ogle her boss's scrumptious body. Something here wasn't right. He was either sick or drugged, maybe both.

His cell phone was on the nightstand, switched off. She also noticed an empty water glass and two plastic prescription bottles. Holding them to the light from the hall, she inspected the labels. One she recognized as a heavy-duty analgesic Buck took for his occasional migraines. The other was unfamiliar. But if Buck had taken them in combination, the side effects could have knocked him out—or worse.

She was no doctor. But one thing was certain. She couldn't just walk away and leave him like this. She needed to wake him up and make sure he was all right.

Reluctant to startle him, she nudged his bare shoulder. "Buck, wake up," she whispered.

A quiver passed through his body. He groaned, the sound muffled by the pillow.

"Wake up, Buck! Open your eyes!" She shook his shoulder again, harder this time. He moaned, twitched and rolled over onto his back. His stunning cobalt eyes were open, but they had a glazed, drowsy look.

"Hullo, pretty lady," he muttered. "You showed up just in time."

"In time for what?" Terri asked. Buck appeared to be half-asleep. He didn't even seem to recognize her. "Pretty lady" was his usual term of endearment for his conquests—he'd never called her that before.

"For this." He clasped her wrist and trailed her hand down his belly under the tangled sheet. Gently but firmly he folded her fingers around a stallion-sized erection.

Terri's heart lurched. She was no virgin—she'd had a couple of relationships in college and a short-lived fling on a trip to Hawaii. But that had been a long time ago, and this was *Buck*, not only her boss, but her friend—and the man she'd secretly pined over for years.

Clearly he wasn't in his right mind. If she was smart, she'd slap him back to his senses and leave. But the heat was already pounding through her body. Even after he released her wrist, she couldn't make her fingers let go of that warm, silky, amazing hardness.

Heaven help her, she *wanted* him.

"C'mere, you…" he said, while she was still trying to convince herself that she should, she *must* leave. Hand catching the back of her head, he pulled her down for a rough, possessive kiss that pushed every sensible logical thought out of her mind. His tongue invaded her mouth, stroking and teasing the sensitive surfaces. Desire blazed through her like the flame of a blowtorch. She could feel the wetness as her body prepared to welcome him. Common sense took flight. She wanted him so much. And it felt so incredible to believe, in this moment, that he wanted her, too.

His hands, deft and practiced, unfastened her khakis and slid them down her legs, along with her panties. Shifting on the bed, he encouraged her to straddle him, positioning her body on top of his. He slid his hand between her legs, and she could feel his grin against her lips at the wetness he found.

She leaned over him, clasped his hips with her knees and eased herself down onto his shaft. Her eyes closed as he slid upward, completely filling her. He groaned in satisfaction as her lips parted, her breath sucked inward. This was Buck inside her—the man she'd wanted from the time she'd learned what sex was all about. Even the thought was enough to trigger the delicious little spasm of her first climax.

She began to move, taking the time at first to feel every inch of him gliding in and out of her. Then, for both of them, urgency took over. His breath deepened, hips arching to meet her as she pushed harder, faster, until with a groan he rolled her onto her back, moved on top of her and took charge.

Her legs wound around his hips as he thrust into her, driving like a bull, until she burst with him, clenching around him in a climax that fulfilled fifteen years of fantasies.

With a grunt of satisfaction, he rolled off her and lay back on the pillow. For a few seconds Terri was still, basking in the afterglow. Then reality fell on her with a crash. She'd just had mindless, gasket-blowing sex with her boss. Nothing would ever be the same between them again.

Sitting up, she gazed down at him. Buck's eyes were closed, his breathing deep and even. His face wore a contented little smirk.

The man had gone back to sleep—if he'd ever actually been fully awake.

Her face burned as the truth sank home. The earth might have moved for her. But what about him? He'd roused to find a woman in his bedroom and simply reacted. She could have been anyone. When he woke up later, the odds were he'd only barely remember this encounter. She wasn't at all sure he'd remember that the woman had been her.

That would be for the best, Terri told herself as she slipped off the bed and gathered her clothes without disturbing him. If Buck didn't remember the identity of his mystery lover, there'd be no awkwardness, no embarrassing confrontations—and of course, she'd never tell him. They could go on as before, as if nothing had happened.

Or…could this be the thing she'd been looking for, to shake up her life from the rut it was in?

Dare she hope that this would change things between them? That he would look at her and see the warm, loving—and sexy, damn it—woman behind the loyal assistant who'd been at his side like a faithful hound for the past ten years?

If not, maybe it really was time to move on.

Before leaving the room, she switched on his cell phone and turned the ring volume all the way up. If Diane had something to discuss, or if there was an emergency at work, he was damned well fit to answer the call.

In the hallway, she scrambled into her clothes, cramming her shirttail into her khakis and hooking the belt with shaking hands. The memory of her time in Buck's bed already felt like some kind of crazy dream. It would be up to Buck to decide whether or not to make it real.

Downstairs, she fed the dog and changed his water. Then she left. She was no longer worried about Buck's condition. He'd given her ample proof that he was going to be fine. She would go back to work and let him sleep off whatever was in his system. Meanwhile, there were plenty of other things to demand her attention.

Twenty minutes after leaving Buck's place, she pulled into the hotel parking lot, switched off the Jeep's ignition and took a moment to compose herself. Her pulse was still racing at the memory of the time she'd spent in his bed. When she'd driven to his canyon home, the last thing she'd expected was to sleep with the man. Getting back to normal was going to be a challenge. And she couldn't repress the surge of excitement at the thought that they might be on the verge of a *new* normal.

But until then, she had to pull herself together. Glancing down, she smoothed her khaki shirt with the Bucket List logo on the front pocket, then climbed out of the vehicle and strode across the parking lot to the hotel entrance.

The hotel lobby was a showplace. Built in rustic style, like the lodges at the nearby Grand Canyon, it featured walls of red sandstone slabs, massive open-beam construction and a slate floor. At the far end, a stone fireplace rose to the ceiling. Between the entrance and the front desk, a waterfall cascaded down a face of natural rock. Exquisite Navajo rugs hung on the walls, and the gift shops sold real Native American textiles, jewelry and pottery. There was no tourist junk. Buck had insisted that everything sold here be not only authentic but of gallery quality.

Terri smiled a greeting to the clerks as she passed the front desk, then darted down a hallway to the women employees' restroom. When she checked herself in the mirror, she expected to see her usual ordinary features—the copper-flecked brown eyes and no-nonsense brows, the square chin, the straight nose sprinkled with freckles, all arranged into the businesslike expression she wore at work. But the face gazing back at her was almost a stranger's—cheeks flushed, moist lips swollen, eyes large and bright in a surprisingly sensual face. Nobody who saw her could help but notice the difference.

Good grief! Why not simply hang a sign around her neck reading I Just Had Hot Sex with the Boss?

With a shake of her head, she turned on the cold water, splashed her face and blotted it dry with a paper towel. Slicking her lips with the colored gloss she carried in her purse and smoothing her hair back with her damp hands, she called it good. Duty awaited.

The booking and management office for Bucket List Adventures was down the hall in its own wing of the hotel complex. It consisted of an open area for the staff, break and conference rooms, restrooms, a modest office for Terri, and a spacious office for Buck.

Terri breezed in from the covered hallway that connected with the hotel, trying to look as if nothing had happened. She found Bob in her office, sitting back in her chair with his boots on her desk and spilled coffee leaving a trail across the mahogany surface. A spark of annoyance flared. But she bit back a sharp comment. She'd asked the boy to cover the phones. He probably didn't know how to transfer the calls to his own desk.

"So catch me up," she said. "What's happening?"

Making no move to get out of her chair, though he did at least have the grace to drop his feet off the desk and look a bit embarrassed, he picked up a yellow notepad. At least he knew enough to write down messages. "The skydive's covered," he said. "Jay called another instructor who was willing to take it."

"That's a relief." And it was. After this morning, she was in no condition to parachute out of a plane with the seventy-year-old woman who was jumping to celebrate her birthday. "Anything else?" she asked.

"Diane called again. She wanted to know where Buck was. I told her you'd gone to look for him." He glanced up at her. "Did you have any luck?"

Terri willed her expression to freeze. "Buck isn't feeling well. He'd turned off his phone so he could get some rest, that's all."

"Well, I guess I should give you your desk back." He stood then, a gangly figure who towered over Terri by a head. "Hey, did you lose your earring?" he asked.

"Oh!" Terri's hands went to her earlobes. One earring was in place. The other was missing.

The little turquoise-inlaid silver earrings in the shape of Kokopelli, the Native American flute-playing deity, were her favorite pair. She'd received a lot of compliments on them. Even Buck had noticed them.

The missing earring could have fallen off anywhere. But it hadn't. Terri's gut feeling told her exactly how and where she'd lost it.

Buck would be sure to recognize it. And that meant

that he'd have to acknowledge what had occurred between them. Her stomach roiled in fear and anticipation.
This could be a disaster…or it could be the start of something amazing. And she had no way of knowing which
until Buck finally arrived.

Two

Buck's ringing cell phone blasted him out of a sound sleep. Cursing, he fumbled for the device on the nightstand and sent it clattering to the floor.

Damn! He could've sworn he'd turned that phone off before collapsing into bed last night. And he would *never* set the ringer up to its full, earsplitting volume. What the devil was going on?

Grabbing the phone from the floor, he pushed the answer button. "Hullo?" he mumbled.

"Where've you been, Buck?" As always, Diane's voice scraped his nerves like fingernails on a chalkboard. The worst of it was, between the daughter they shared and the chunk of his company she owned, he'd likely be hearing that shrill voice for the rest of his life.

"Sick." He forced the word through a throat that felt as if he'd swallowed glue.

"Well, get unsick. It's almost noon. Did you get my voice-mail messages? I must've left you three or four."

"Haven't checked."

"I'll save you the trouble—I need you to pick up Quinn."

His daughter's name jarred him to alertness. "Weren't you supposed to bring her here?"

"I've got people coming for a retreat. I could bring her up next week, but she's all packed and ready to go. If she has to wait, she'll be *so* disappointed."

"Fine. I'll send Evie Redfeather down in the jet to pick her up." Evie was his personal pilot. Quinn knew and liked her.

"You can't come yourself?"

"Like you, I have other commitments. Tell her Evie's coming. She'll be fine with that." Buck ended the call before Diane could think of some other way to pull his strings. This last-minute change of plans was typical. Diane would have known about her retreat for weeks and could have made arrangements for Quinn earlier. But why do that when she could create a little drama?

Diane had been a Vegas showgirl when he'd met her ten years ago. After a hot weekend in her bed, he'd flown home without giving her a second thought. But then she'd shown up pregnant on his doorstep, and he'd done the honorable thing. For a while they'd tried to make the marriage work, but it had been doomed from the first "I do." After a nightmare divorce settlement, she'd moved to Sedona, Arizona, and opened her own new age ashram.

The experience had left Buck with a bitter taste when it came to marriage. But at least he had Quinn. Quinn had been worth it all.

The phone shrilled again. Knowing it was Diane, Buck turned it off and lay back on the pillow. He'd come home last night with a pounding migraine. Feeling like roadkill, he'd taken some pills, undressed and fallen into bed, hoping to sleep through the pain. It had worked. He felt better today.

Especially after that crazy, sexy dream he'd had.

Closing his eyes, he tried to recall it in detail. He'd had erotic dreams before, plenty of them, but this one had been different. It had seemed so…*real*. The warm silkiness of skin against his body. The taste of that luscious mouth. Even the sexy aroma of her skin. He could remember everything about the woman—except her face.

Damn! He'd gulp down a whole bottle of those blasted pills if it could bring the dream back. His climax had been an explosion of sheer sensual pleasure, so powerful he'd probably drenched the bedding underneath him.

He frowned, struck by an odd notion. He should be lying in a damp spot now. But the sheet beneath him felt perfectly clean and dry.

Perplexed, he sat up, moved to one side and ran his hand across the mattress. Nothing. He shook his head, as if trying to clear out the cobwebs. What in blazes had happened here?

That was when he noticed something else—a subtle fragrance rising from the bottom sheet. Pressing his face to the fabric, he inhaled the sweet, clean aroma, trying to identify it. This wasn't the softener the hotel laundry used. And it wasn't one of the expensive perfumes his sexual partners tended to drench themselves in. It was something else, something fresh but somehow familiar. It was *her* scent, exactly as he remembered it.

There could be only one conclusion—the dream had been real. There'd been a woman in his bed, and he'd made love to her.

But how could that be? There'd been no one here when he'd gone to bed last night. The gate to the property had been locked. The house had been locked. And if the dog had barked at an intruder, he hadn't heard it.

Was he losing his mind?

He sat up. The room looked the same as usual. Nothing appeared to have been touched except—

His gaze fell on the phone.

Now that his head was clearing, he distinctly recalled turning it off before he went to sleep. But someone had not only turned it on again but adjusted the ring volume loud enough to raise the dead.

Who would play such a dirty trick on him?

Maybe he was *still* dreaming.

Sliding his legs off the bed, he pushed to his feet and stood on the sheepskin rug. His legs felt as shaky as Jell-O, probably because the pills hadn't worn off. Maybe if he went downstairs and got some coffee in his system, he'd be able to think straight.

His robe was draped over the foot of the bed. He took a step toward it, then jerked back with a grunt of pain. His bare foot had come down on something sharp—some object caught in the thick wool of the rug.

Bending over, he found it with his fingers, picked it up and held it to the light. It was a small silver earring, inlaid with turquoise and fashioned in the shape of Kokopelli, the humpbacked Native American flute player. He stared at it, recognition slamming him like a mule kick.

Terri's earring.

Buck sank onto the edge of the bed. Lord, could he have had mind-blowing sex with *Terri*, who'd always been like a kid sister to him? *Terri*, that miracle of patience and efficiency who kept the hectic world of Bucket List Enterprises running like well-oiled clockwork?

No, it was unbelievable. But it was the only possible answer. Terri would have the gate code and the security combination for the front door. The dog, who'd bark at any stranger, knew her well. Glancing at the clock, he saw how late he'd slept. That made sense, too—Terri must have come to check on him when he hadn't shown up at work.

And only Terri would have turned on his cell phone when she left and set the ringer loud enough to wake him. Knowing her, she probably would've fed the dog, too. He would remember to check when he went downstairs.

But if Terri was the answer, he still had plenty of questions. Had he really had sex with her? But the dream, which seemed less and less dreamlike the more he thought of it, left little doubt of that. He remembered waking up to a woman leaning over him, remembered pulling her into bed. Remembered her response, and the way she'd made him feel… He'd initiated the encounter, but she'd come willingly.

No way would she have joined him in that bed…unless she'd wanted to.

Holding that thought, Buck showered in the bathroom, finger-raked his hair, and pulled on sweatpants and a T-shirt. He was wide-awake now, but going back to work today wouldn't be a great idea, especially since Terri would be there. Sooner or later he'd have to face her. But before that happened, he had some serious thinking to do.

He took a minute to phone Evie Redfeather and arrange for her to pick up Quinn in Sedona. Evie, a retired air force fighter pilot, had made the short flight before and said she didn't mind going again. That taken care of, he went downstairs in his bare feet to make coffee.

With cup in hand he wandered out onto the redwood deck and leaned on the railing. His eyes traced the passing flight of a golden eagle, its wings casting a brief shadow against the sunset-hued cliffs. A downward glance into the yard confirmed that Murphy's food dish was full of kibble, his water bowl freshly filled. Terri had been here, all right. No one else would think to take care of his dog while he was sick.

But what was he going to do about her? Terri was his right-hand woman, the person he depended on for everything from booking tours and flights to hiring and firing employees to fending off Diane. But sleeping with her would change the dynamics of what had been a perfect relationship—a relationship he couldn't afford to lose. He could get a bed partner anytime he wanted one. But, damn it, Terri was irreplaceable.

Buck sipped his coffee and thought hard. This misstep would have to be dealt with. The question was, how?

He could call her into his office—no, maybe take her out to dinner, apologize profusely and promise it would never happen again. But how might Terri respond to that? At best it would create an awkward situation between them. Or she could be hurt. She could feel rejected, even angry. She could even—God forbid—quit her job and leave.

There had to be a way to put this behind them without harming their relationship.

Buck gazed down at the cooled dregs of the coffee in his cup, thinking hard. What if he were to behave as if the whole thing had never happened? After all, he'd been half-asleep. Surely Terri wouldn't be surprised if he didn't remember. She might even be relieved.

The more he thought about the idea the better it sounded. Nothing would have to change—no expectations, no awkwardness. Terri could go on working for him as always. Even if she suspected him of knowing, she'd have no proof.

His white lie would save face for both of them.

But it didn't make him feel any better about what had happened. Sex with Terri had been sensational. With any other woman, he would have been lobbying for a return engagement. But Terri was off-limits. Not only was she his employee but she was Steve's kid sister, the girl he'd promised to look after when Steve didn't make it home from Iraq.

And having half-drugged sex with her wasn't part of that promise.

At the moment Buck didn't like himself much. Between now and the next time he saw her, he had some soul-searching to do.

By the time Terri had finished her last task for the day—posting tomorrow's schedule online—it was an hour past closing time. Bob and the summer temps had gone, leaving her there alone to close up. She was about to lock the door when Quinn, trailed by Evie Redfeather, came bounding across the parking lot.

"Hi, Terri!" Blond ponytail flying, Quinn collided with Terri in an exuberant hug.

Terri hugged her back. She adored Buck's daughter. "How's my favorite girl?" she asked, meaning it.

"Great!" Quinn's blue eyes, so like her father's, sparkled.

"You're taller," Terri said.

"I know. Mom says I'm having a growth spurt. The clothes I left here won't fit. We'll have to go shopping for new ones."

Evie Redfeather had come up behind her. In her early fifties, she was a handsome, broad-faced Navajo woman. "Buck asked me to drop her off at his house, but we were two hours late getting out of Sedona." She shook her head. "That woman! Always with the drama!"

Terri didn't have to ask Evie who she meant.

"I saw your Jeep in the parking lot and realized you must still be here," Evie said. "I hope you won't mind running Quinn home. Bert and I are expecting friends for dinner. I need to get going."

"Sure." Terri stifled a groan. The last thing she wanted was to show up at Buck's house with Quinn. The conversation they needed to have couldn't happen with little ears present. "Go on, Evie. Thanks for picking her up."

"No problem. Here, I've got her bag. I'll put it in your Jeep."

Terri felt Quinn's hand slip into hers as they followed Evie's long strides to the Jeep. She fought back a rising attack of nerves. How would Buck react to what had happened? Would he treat her any differently because of it? Would he be embarrassed? Aloof? Indifferent?

But this wasn't about her and Buck, Terri reminded herself. It was about Quinn, and making the little girl's homecoming a happy occasion. She could only hope Buck would be out of bed and fit to welcome his daughter.

"Up you go." She boosted Quinn into the high seat of the Jeep. "Hang on, we'll have you there in a jiffy."

"What's a jiffy?" Quinn asked as Terri climbed into the Jeep. "You use the funniest words, Terri."

"A jiffy is a very short bit of time. I learned lots of old-fashioned words from my grandma. Maybe I should've said we'd be there in the flick of a lamb's tail. Would you have liked that better?"

Quinn giggled. Terri had kept her distance during the short duration of Buck's marriage. But after the divorce, once Quinn became old enough to spend time in Utah with her father, she'd become attached to the little girl. Maybe too attached. What if Buck were to remarry? Could she back off and let Quinn go?

But she wouldn't think about that now. Things were already complicated enough.

"Can we go out for pizza tonight?" Quinn asked. "I want lots of pepperoni on mine. Mom's vegan now, so she won't let me eat meat. She didn't even give me a choice."

"Don't they make vegan pepperoni?"

"It's yucky. So's the cheese. Has Dad got a new girlfriend yet? I didn't like the last one. She was scared of bugs and she was always fixing her makeup."

"I don't know," Terri said. "You'll have to ask him. And you can ask him about the pizza, too. He's your parent. I'm not."

"You sound mad. Are you mad, Terri?"

"At you? No way!" Terri reached across the seat and squeezed the girl's shoulder. She'd have to watch herself around Quinn. The perceptive child was wise beyond her years. If she sensed any tension where Buck was concerned, she was apt to ask awkward questions.

They'd turned off the main road and were headed up the canyon. Terri felt the knot tighten in the pit of her stomach as she realized she was still wearing her single Kokopelli earring. Had Buck found its mate in his bedroom? Or had he not yet left the bed where she'd left him, after the most explosive sexual experience of her life?

They swung up the private road to the gate, and Terri punched in the code. Buck would surely know his daughter was coming. At least he'd been awake enough to have Evie fly down and pick her up. But just to avoid an unpleasant surprise, she pushed the intercom button.

"Hi." His deep baritone went through her with the shock of memory. It made her shiver to realize she now knew exactly how that voice sounded sex-drenched and husky.

"It's me." The words emerged as nervous squeaks. "I'm bringing Quinn."

"Great. Come on up." His voice betrayed nothing. Either he was a good actor or he wasn't ready to talk about what had happened in his bedroom.

Or he didn't care. Knowing Buck, that was possible, too.

Buck stood on the front porch watching the Jeep come up the drive. Seeing Terri was a surprise. He'd asked Evie to bring Quinn here. But there must've been a change of plans.

Things could be awkward with Terri. He didn't quite know what to expect from her. But Quinn would be with them. That would make things all right—for now, at least.

The Jeep pulled up next to his Hummer and stopped. Throwing off her seat belt, Quinn bounded out of the passenger seat and raced up the steps to give him a hug. As he swung her off her feet, he could tell she'd grown since Christmas break. With her in Sedona most of the year, he was missing so much of her life. Maybe this summer he could find a way to spend more time with her.

"Hi, Daddy," she said. "I missed you."

"Me, too." He lowered her to the ground. "Are you hungry?"

"Starved."

"She told me she wanted pizza." Terri had come up the steps with Quinn's suitcase. Buck looked at her and forced a smile. Terri smiled back at him, but her eyes held a flicker of uncertainty. She was wearing one of her Kokopelli earrings. Her other earlobe was bare.

That clinched it. If Buck had had any doubt about her being in his bed this morning, it was totally gone.

He was still dealing with the reality of it. Terri was an

attractive woman—beautiful in an unassuming way. But he'd always made it a rule to keep his hands off his best friend's sister. Steve had been gone for a dozen years now, but that rule hadn't changed. Until now, he'd assumed she had the same rule. But this morning had thrown the rule book out the window, for both of them.

He forced himself up to speak. "Pizza it is. How about Giovanni's?"

"Yes!" Quinn grinned. "Their pizza's the yummiest! Can Terri come with us?"

"Terri?" He looked at her, half hoping she'd make an excuse not to come along. Terri's presence was rousing his memory and putting lustful thoughts into his head—the last thing he needed right now. Their interlude this morning had been incredible…but it could never be repeated.

"I'd better not," she said, avoiding his eyes. "I promised my grandmother I'd come and visit her tonight."

"Please, Terri!" Quinn begged. "If we go now you'll still have time to see your grandma."

"Come on, Terri." Buck remembered his resolve to act as if nothing had happened. "It won't be a party without you."

She hesitated, then sighed. "All right. I *am* getting hungry. But let me follow you in the Jeep. That way, when we're finished, I can just go from Giovanni's to Canyon Shadows."

"Okay. Let's get going." Buck put Quinn's bag inside the house and helped her into the passenger seat of the Hummer. He had to believe that in time, if he kept up the act, things would go back to normal. But right now, with the memory of Terri's lithe, lush body fresh in his mind, it was like walking a tightrope over a volcano. One slip and he'd be in big trouble.

* * *

Terri waited until the Hummer had backed down the steep driveway. Then she turned the Jeep around and followed the hulking vehicle down to the road. It wasn't too late to head off in a different direction. She could always make an excuse, call Buck's cell, apologize and say that she'd remembered an important errand. But Quinn would be disappointed if she didn't show up to share a pizza. Buck, on the other hand, didn't seem to care either way—about sharing a pizza with her now, or about sharing a bed with her this morning.

Part of her wanted to believe that this morning would make a difference, that Buck would look at her and see a warm, desirable woman. But clearly that hadn't happened. It was time for her to face the truth. No matter what happened, Buck was never going to see her the way she wanted to be seen. There was only one question left: What was she going to do about it?

Twilight was settling over the town and over the sandstone cliffs that ringed it like the setting of a jewel. Main Street glittered with streams of traffic. Shoppers and diners strolled the boardwalks. Music drifted from cafés and taverns.

This was Buck's town, but that didn't mean she had to stay here forever. She had the qualifications and the experience to get a job anywhere in the tourist industry. She'd be a fool to let loyalty keep her in a situation where she felt like a piece of furniture.

Giovanni's Pizzeria was at the far end of Main Street. When the Hummer's taillights turned into the parking lot, Terri followed and pulled into the next space. Buck and Quinn were waiting for her when she climbed out of the Jeep. "Let's go!" Quinn seized her hand and pulled her toward the entrance. "Extralarge pepperoni and giant root beer, here I come!"

Buck chuckled as he caught up with Terri. "Quinn tells me her mother's had her on nothing but wheatgrass juice and tofu," he said. "She's probably exaggerating, but it'll be a pleasure to see her enjoy real food."

Terri forced a little laugh. The hostess showed them to a booth with a traditional red-checked tablecloth and a candle melting down the outside of an empty wine bottle. They slid into the seats, Terri and Quinn on one side, Buck on the other. Their waitress came right over to take their order. The pretty blonde was a stranger to Terri, but she seemed to know Buck.

"So this is your little girl!" She flashed a toothpaste-ad smile. "What's her name?"

Buck, all charm, made the introductions. "Jennifer, this is Quinn. And this lady—" He gave Terri a nod. "This is Terri, my right-hand woman."

Terri forced a friendly smile. Inside, she was seething. Why couldn't Buck have used her job title, or just her name? Didn't he know how demeaning *right-hand woman* sounded? Obviously not, unless it was meant as hidden message to the waitress—*don't worry, she's not my girlfriend.*

Meanwhile, the waitress was looking at Buck as if she wanted to eat him alive. No doubt she'd be happy to sleep with him, if she hadn't already.

Terri brought herself up with a mental slap. Good Lord, she couldn't be jealous! Buck had never tried to hide his love life from her. She'd always accepted his shenanigans with a sisterly shrug, burying any hurt bone-deep. Even his shotgun marriage hadn't shaken her unconditional affection for the man. And she certainly hadn't expected for Buck to promise her fidelity and exclusivity after one romp in the bedroom together. But to see him now, just hours after their encounter, flirting with another woman while treating her with his usual indifference, she felt a senseless urge to leap across the table and smack Buck's handsome face.

Grow up and get over it! she told herself as the petite blonde walked away from the table with their order. Even the sway of her jeans-clad hips held an invitation. The art of seduction was one Terri had never mastered. And suddenly she felt very insecure about her performance that morning. She was hardly the alluring, experienced type of woman he usually chose as a bedmate. The sex had seemed fantastic to her…but had it been merely forgettable to him?

She had to forget what had happened. That would be the only way to survive life in Buck's magnetic aura. That—or leave.

Quinn's happy chatter was enough to fill the awkward silence while they waited for their order. Lost in her own thoughts, Terri was startled when Buck reached across the table and nudged her arm. "Hey," he said, "where have you gone to?"

She blinked herself back to the present. "Did you need something?" she asked.

He gave a shake of his head. "You're not at work now, Terri. I don't need anything. I just asked you a question. Did you know one of your earrings was missing?"

"Oh, yes." Reflexively, she brushed a hand to her bare earlobe. Was it an innocent question, or was he testing her? "Bob noticed it was gone earlier today. I'm still hoping it'll turn up somewhere."

"Too bad. I know you liked that pair." His expression was all innocence.

"Yes, I did." Terri scrambled to change the subject.

"Quinn was telling me she's growing out of her clothes. I think she needs a shopping trip."

"I'll let you off early tomorrow to take her," he said. "Take my credit card and get her anything she wants."

"Can I have an iguana?" Quinn asked.

Buck raised an eyebrow. "Now where did *that* come from?"

"My friend has one. It's really cool. I'd take care of it. Iguanas are easy. They just eat lettuce and stuff."

"Think about it a minute," Buck said. "If it eats, it poops. You'd have to clean its cage every day. Could you do that?"

"Sure. That stuff doesn't bother me."

"But what would you do with it at the end of the summer?" Terri put in. "You can't just walk away from an animal and leave it here. You'd have to take it home with you. Would your mother let you keep it?"

"If I ask her and she says yes, can I have one?"

"Ask her first. Then we'll talk about it." Buck cast Terri a grateful glance. He ran Bucket List with an iron hand, but his daughter could talk him into anything—whether it was a good idea or not.

What the little girl really wanted was his time. But it was easier for him to flash his credit card and get her whatever caught her eye. By now Terri knew the pattern. Now that she had arrived for the summer, Buck would welcome Quinn with open arms—he did love his child. But as business issues pulled him away, she'd be shunted off to riding and swimming lessons, turned over to Terri, or left to read books or play video games on her own. Maybe this summer, Terri could help her find some friends her own age in the area.

The subject of the iguana was tabled when the pizza and drinks arrived. Terri tried to ignore the way Jennifer's hip brushed Buck's shoulder as she set their order on the table. Was the woman angling for a big tip or something else? But what did it matter to her? Why should she even care?

They were all hungry. Conversation dwindled as they wolfed down the pizza. Buck had just paid the bill when Terri glanced at her watch. It was almost eight o'clock. The aides at Canyon Shadows usually came in around eight thirty to shower the residents and get them ready for bed by nine. With the facility at the far end of town from the restaurant, she would barely have time to make the promised visit to her grandmother.

She stood up, brushing the crumbs off her lap. "I've got to get going, or I won't make it."

Buck rose. "We're ready to go, too. We'll walk you out."

They trailed outside. At this hour the summer twilight was still fading. Mourning doves called from the old cottonwoods that overhung the parking lot.

"Thanks. See you tomorrow." Terri strode ahead to her Jeep, then halted with a groan. She wasn't going anywhere. The Jeep's rear tire was flat to the rim.

Three

Terri was staring at her Jeep when Buck caught up with her. "Too bad," he said. "I told you those old tires of yours needed replacing."

"Well, I can't do much about that now, can I?" Terri shook her head. Even if she left her vehicle and walked to Canyon Shadows, there was no way she'd get there in time to visit her grandmother. "Go on and take Quinn home. I know how to change a tire."

"Well, you're not doing it tonight. I've got people for that job." He whipped out his cell and, before Terri could stop him, typed out a text message before he pocketed the phone again. "Quinn and I will take you to see your grandma. I remember Harriet from the old days. She was quite the spunky little lady. I'd enjoy visiting her, too."

If Buck hadn't seen Harriet since the old days, he was in for a shock, Terri thought. Her grandmother was a different person now. "Thanks, I'd appreciate that," she said. "But you won't need to come inside. Just let me off and go. When I'm through visiting, I can walk back here and change the tire."

"You heard me—the tire will be taken care of. It's arranged. Come on." He guided her toward the Hummer with a light hand on the small of her back. The warm pressure of his palm triggered a tingle of memory that raced like flame along a fuse through her body. The feeling was sweet torture. If only she could forget what had happened between them, or at least dismiss it—as, it seemed, Buck had. But Quinn was with them now, Terri reminded herself. She wouldn't know for sure whether he was going to bring up what had happened between them until she was alone with him.

He opened the passenger door for her and helped Quinn into the backseat. The drive to Canyon Shadows took only a few minutes. "You don't have to stay—I really don't mind walking back to Giovanni's," Terri said as the Hummer pulled into the parking lot.

"Will you stop arguing with me, Terri?" Buck's voice carried a hint of reined impatience. "I told you, I'd be glad to come in and say hello to your grandmother. And Quinn won't mind coming in, either."

"I know that," Terri said. "It's just that my grandma has changed a lot since you knew her. She's ninety-one and not doing very well. She has her good days and bad. I've learned not to expect too much, but I worry that seeing her might upset Quinn."

He stopped the vehicle and laid a hand on her shoulder. "Let me be the judge of that, Terri," he said.

Buck had never been beyond the front doorway of Canyon Shadows. The rambling two-story stuccoed building was decent for a nursing home, with manicured grounds and a covered walkway leading to the front doors. Bouquets of silk roses and framed landscape prints cheered the lobby, but an air of gloom still hung over the place. Maybe that was inevitable when nobody who lived here wanted to be here.

He let Terri lead the way as they signed in at the front desk and continued on to the elevator and up to the second floor. In all the busy years she'd worked for him, he could barely recall asking her how her grandmother was doing. What had brought on this sudden interest in her life outside work?

But he knew the answer to that question, and it didn't make him feel proud of himself.

Eleven years ago, in an army medical tent, he'd knelt next to Steve's bed and promised his dying friend that he'd look after his kid sister. Buck had viewed giving Terri a job as the first step in keeping that promise. But over the years, as the pressures of building his business had closed in, she'd proven so capable and so willing that the focus had shifted. Instead of what he could do for her, it had become what *she* could do for *him*.

But that had never included her sharing his bed.

After finding her earring in his rug, his first thought had been how to avoid losing her help. But as the afternoon had worn on, his musings had deepened. He'd taken a long look at himself in the mirror and seen a first-class jerk looking back at him.

Steve, if he'd been here, would have punched him black and blue.

Somehow, he had to do a better job of keeping his promise. And he absolutely had to forget about taking her to bed again. As wonderful as it had been, he knew that a romantic relationship with Terri could never work. She was the kind of woman who would demand full honesty from her lover…and that was something he couldn't offer. Not with the secret he'd kept from her all this time.

If she knew the truth about what happened with Steve, she'd never let him touch her again—not even as a friend.

Her friendship was something he had to keep, not just for Steve's sake but for his own, too. She meant far too much to him for him to be willing to let her slip away. So that meant finding a way to make amends, to show her how much she meant to him—in a purely platonic way. But with a strong, independent woman like Terri, knowing where to start with winning her over wouldn't be easy—especially after what had happened this morning.

"Come on, Daddy!" Quinn tugged at him, and he realized he'd fallen behind. Terri had already opened a door partway down the long corridor and stepped into the room. Still holding Quinn's hand, he reached the doorway and paused on the threshold.

In the light of a single table lamp, the woman in the worn leather recliner looked as if a strong breath could blow out her life like a candle flame. Her face was as wrinkled as a walnut, her hair like white spider webbing on her ancient head. He would never have recognized feisty Harriet Cooper, Steve and Terri's maternal grandmother, who'd raised them after their parents died. Remorse crept over him. How many times in the old days had he been in her home and eaten at her table? And now—damn it all, he'd barely been aware that she was here. He certainly hadn't taken the time to visit.

"Hello, Grandma." Terri knelt next to the chair, the lamplight falling on her face. "I came by this morning but you were asleep," she said.

The old woman huffed, refusing to look at her.

"I'm sorry," Terri said. "I came as soon as I could."

"Sorry, are you?" Harriet snapped in a papery voice

that sounded so different from the warm, maternal tones he remembered. "Then take me home. They steal things here. My wedding ring—"

Terri took one bony hand and lifted it to the light. "Look, Grandma. Your ring is right here on your finger. Nobody stole it."

"Liar! That old thing isn't my ring!" The old woman snatched her hand away. "Where's Steve? He never lied to me! I want him to come and take me home!"

Still standing in the doorway, Buck felt the painful tightening in his gut. It hurt for him to watch this. But how much worse would it be for Terri, dealing with this poor woman every day?

And why couldn't Steve have been here? Why had Steve been the one to die, when it should have been him?

"Look, Grandma." Terri drew her attention toward the doorway. "You've got visitors."

"Oh?" Harriet perked up. "Who is it? Is it Steve?"

"No, it's Steve's friend Buck. And he brought his little girl. Her name's Quinn." She beckoned them over.

Quinn gripped her father's hand. Maybe Terri had been right about this experience being too much for her. But it was too late to back out now.

"Hello, Mrs. Cooper." He offered her his free hand.

Her dim eyes brightened. "Steve! It's really you! Did you come to take me home?"

Buck steeled his emotions. "I'm Buck, Mrs. Cooper. I used to come to your house with Steve."

Her grip on his hand was surprisingly strong. "You were always my favorite, Steve. More than your sister. Why'd you stay away such a long time?"

He cast a helpless glance at Terri. She was doing her best to remain smiling and composed. "This is Buck, Grandma," she said. "And here's his little girl."

"Steve's little girl." She reached out and touched Quinn's cheek. "My, but you're a pretty thing. Come give your great-grandma a kiss."

Buck could feel Quinn trembling next to him. But she stepped forward and feathered a kiss on the wrinkled cheek. Buck had never been more proud of his daughter.

The old woman fixed her cataract-blurred gaze on him. "So, why are you just standing there? Get me up and take me home."

"Grandma—" Terri began, but she was interrupted by a polite tap on the already-open door. The aides, thank heaven, had arrived to get Harriet ready for bed.

"No—I'm going home!" the old woman protested as one of the young women started unbuttoning her sweater.

"It'll be all right, Grandma. I'll see you tomorrow. We'll talk then." Terri kissed her grandmother, and the three of them made their exit down the hallway to the elevator.

"I'm sorry about the mix-up," Terri said as they walked out the front door. "She does have good days…but I'm afraid the bad ones have become a lot more common. Lately, every time I come here, she breaks my heart."

"But at least you keep coming. I've got to hand it to you, Terri. I had no idea she was so bad. Is there anything I can do to help?"

Terri shook her head. "All she wants is to go home. One of these days she will."

Quinn, usually so chatty, had fallen silent. Buck hoped he could get her to talk on the way home. She needed to process what she'd seen and heard. But meanwhile, he needed to stall Terri a little longer so she wouldn't interrupt the first part of his campaign to show her how valuable she was to him.

"Hey, how about ice cream sundaes?" he said. "The best ice cream parlor in town is right across the street!"

Quinn brightened. "Sounds yummy!"

"I really need to get back to my Jeep," Terri said, moving on. "You two go ahead and get your sundaes. It's a nice evening, and I could use the exercise of the walk back."

"Oh, come on." Buck caught her arm, his grip hard enough to stop her in her tracks. "Quinn's here. Doesn't that call for a party? We can drop you off when we're finished."

She sighed. "Okay. Ice cream does sound good."

They entered the ice cream parlor, ordered hot fudge sundaes at the counter and found a booth. The place was done in pink-and-black '50s decor with vintage rock and roll playing in the background. An elderly couple was holding hands at a corner table. The man was laughing, the woman tapping her toe to the beat. Quinn watched them a moment before she spoke.

"Do I have a grandma?" She showered her sundae with sprinkles from a canister on the table.

"Your mother's mother lives in Florida," Buck said. "She's your grandma."

"She doesn't count. She and Mom are mad at each other. They don't even send each other Christmas cards. What about your mother? How come I don't know her?"

Buck had known that sooner or later she was bound to ask. But he'd never looked forward to answering. "She died when I was in the army, before I married your mother. She had lung cancer—from smoking."

"What about your dad? He'd be my grandpa."

"I never knew him. He went away before I was born."

"And he never came back?"

"He never did. My mother raised me on her own. She

was a waitress at the old truck stop out by the main high-way. We were so poor we lived on the leftover food she brought home." Buck didn't tell her his parents had never married, or that his mother had done more than wait tables at that truck stop. Some truths were better kept in silence.

"If you were so poor, how did you get rich, Daddy?"

"Smart thinking, lots of hard work—and good help-ers like Terri."

"Is Terri rich, too?"

Buck glanced across the table at Terri. She was nib-bling her sundae, avoiding his gaze. He paid her a good salary, but after what he'd seen tonight, he was pretty sure she spent most of her money on her grandmother's care. When she didn't answer Quinn's question, he answered for her. "Terri's not nearly as rich as she deserves to be."

Guilt chewed at him, drawing blood. The old woman was Steve's grandmother, too. If Steve had lived, Terri wouldn't have had to shoulder the burden of her care alone. Nursing homes weren't cheap, but for Buck the money would be pocket change. He'd call Canyon Shad-ows tomorrow and make some arrangements. Or maybe he ought to just buy the place. It was decently maintained and would likely be a good investment.

But what was he thinking? After a day like today, he was in no frame of mind for business decisions.

His gaze wandered back to Terri. She looked irresist-ible, with tendrils of windblown hair framing her face and a little smear of chocolate fudge on her upper lip. If they'd been alone he'd have been tempted to lean over and lick it off. He'd never had thoughts like this about her before—had always viewed her strictly as a friend. But now that he knew how good it could be between them...

The memory slammed him—Terri leaning over him,

straddling his hips as he thrust deep. And this time he could visualize her face, eyes closed, lips sensually parted.

Damn!

The lady was off-limits for so many reasons. And she was driving him crazy.

After the ice cream sundaes, Terri had finally managed to convince Buck that she wanted to walk back to her Jeep. The distance wasn't far—only about seven blocks—and she truly needed to clear her head. As the Hummer drove away, she blew a last kiss to Quinn and set out.

By now it was nearly dark, but Main Street was still busy, the shops and cafés doing a bustling business. The tiny white lights that adorned the sycamores along the boardwalk had come on, their glitter creating a festive atmosphere. But Terri's mood was far from festive. From beginning to end, this had been the most emotional day in recent memory.

Quinn's presence tonight had been a godsend. She had no idea what she'd have said to Buck, or what he might have said to her, if they'd found themselves alone together. From his flirting with the waitress at dinner, it was clear that he wasn't interested in pursuing anything with Terri. She'd been foolish to even consider the possibility. Maybe she should just forget it had ever happened. Expect nothing—that was the only way to survive life with Buck.

Her thoughts shifted to their visit with her grandmother. Had it upset Buck to be mistaken for Steve? The two had been like brothers all their lives. Buck had been there in Iraq with their combat unit when Steve died. He'd never talked about it, and she'd never asked him, but Terri knew her brother's death had affected him as deeply as it had her.

She could understand why he'd insisted on ice cream tonight. He'd wanted to blur the memory and end the evening on a happy note. But the conversation with Quinn had only opened more dark windows on the past.

Terri knew about Buck's troubled childhood. And she knew how far his mother, a desperate but kindhearted woman, had gone to provide for her boy. Terri could only hope he had forgiven her.

Terri's long legs covered the seven blocks back to Giovanni's at a brisk pace. Through the deepening twilight, she could make out her Jeep at the far end of the parking lot. She felt for the keys, pulled them out of her purse and strode toward the vehicle.

Had Buck's crew fixed her flat tire, or would she have to haul out the jack and the lug wrench and do it herself? No big deal—she'd changed tires before. And at least that way, she wouldn't feel beholden to Buck. After this morning, she never wanted to feel obligated to him again. To use the old-fashioned expression, it would be too much like being paid for her favors.

She was a few yards away from the Jeep when the parking lot's overhead lights flashed on. In the sudden glare Terri saw what the shadows had hidden.

The flat tire hadn't just been changed. It had been replaced, along with the other three. Her ancient Jeep was now sporting four brand-new, top-of-the-line tires.

Terri stared at Buck's gift. What had the man been thinking? He could certainly afford to replace her tires. But why had he done it, especially without asking her? Did he think he owed her some kind of reward for her... *services*? Or had he done it out of some twisted sense of guilt for taking her to bed in the first place?

Either way, she wasn't going to let this stand.

* * *

"Daddy, why did Terri's grandma call you Steve?"

Quinn had been silent most of the way home. When she finally spoke, her question, coming out of the cab's darkness, caught Buck off guard.

"She's old," he said. "She can't see very well, and sometimes her thoughts get confused. It's sad, but it happens to some old people. That's why she's at Canyon Shadows, so the nurses can take care of her."

"But who's Steve?" Quinn persisted. "Is he somebody who looks like you?"

Buck tapped the brake as a mule deer bounded through the headlights and vanished into the brush on the far side of the road.

"Steve was Terri's brother and my best friend. He died in the war. It was a long time ago, before you were born. But his grandmother doesn't remember that."

"How did he die?"

"He was a soldier. He got shot." Buck struggled to block the images that flashed through his mind. He wished his daughter would talk about something else.

"That's sad." Quinn's profile was a dark silhouette against the side window. "Where did they bury him?"

"Right here in Porter Hollow. His grave is in the cemetery." Buck pressed the remote button to open the wrought iron gate to his property. "What would you like to do tomorrow, besides clothes shopping with Terri?"

"I want to go to the cemetery."

"What on earth for?" Buck bit back a curse as he gunned the Hummer up the steep driveway to the house. He knew Quinn was curious. But there was nothing in the cemetery he cared to show her, let alone see again himself.

"I've never been to a cemetery. I want to see what

it's like. I want to see your mother's grave—she'd be my grandma if she was alive. And I want to see where Steve is buried."

"Maybe Terri can take you after you go shopping." It was the coward's way out to dump this on Terri, but Buck really couldn't go himself. He had some wealthy clients from Dubai coming in this afternoon to raft the Grand Canyon. He wanted to greet them personally and make sure everything was up to their standard of luxury. He'd been weighing the idea of building a second resort in the southeast corner of the state, near Moab, with access to Arches and Monument Valley. So far it was just a dream, but if he decided to go ahead, a hefty infusion of Dubai cash could make it happen sooner.

If nothing else came of it, at least he'd have an excuse not to visit the cemetery and relive the past with Quinn.

"What else would you like to do?" he asked his daughter. "I can have Terri line up anything you'd like. Oh, and I've asked Mrs. Calloway to be on hand while you're here. She can take you if you want to go somewhere."

"Daddy, I'm nine years old!" Quinn stormed. "I'm not a baby, and I don't need a babysitter."

"Well, you do need to eat, and Mrs. Calloway's a good cook."

"That still doesn't mean I have to be babysat. Mrs. Calloway won't let me out of her sight. She's a nice lady, but she drives me crazy. She even sits right by the pool when I'm in the water. Last year I asked her if she could swim. She shook her head. If she had to rescue me, she'd probably drown."

"Mrs. Calloway is just doing her job," Buck said. "The agreement I have with your mother says that while you're here you have to be supervised."

"Why can't I just hang out with Terri?"

Buck ignored the slight jolt triggered by the mention of Terri's name. He wondered what she'd thought when she'd discovered the new tires on her Jeep. He'd done it in the spirit of helping her out, but would she see it that way? Maybe he should have left well enough alone.

"Terri has to work," he said. "I need her help in the office."

"Then why can't I hang out with you?" Quinn asked. "You're the boss. Nobody tells you when you have to work."

"The boss has to work the hardest of all. That's why he's the boss. I'll be busy all day tomorrow. But Terri will pick you up in the afternoon. You'll be fine."

"Sure." Quinn sighed like a deflating balloon and slumped in the seat. She was silent till the Hummer pulled into the driveway and stopped. Buck had barely switched off the engine when she opened the door, piled out of the vehicle and ran to the fence, where Murphy was waiting to welcome her with barks and whimpers of joy.

"Hi, Murphy!" She reached her small hands through the chain links to pet the huge dog, whose wagging tail could have felled a forest of small trees. "How've you been, boy? Hey, I can hang out with you, can't I? At least *somebody's* got time for me!"

Giving Buck a meaningful scowl, she stalked onto the porch and waited for her father to unlock the front door.

The next morning Terri came in early, opened the door to Buck's private office and left something on his desk. He wouldn't be happy when he found it, but she was braced for the storm. If the boss man didn't like it, he could fire her.

Minutes later, she was at her own desk, answering emails, when Buck walked in. His office had its own outside entrance, but today he came in from the hotel lobby side. Standing in the open doorway of her office, he gave her a casual smile and extended a closed fist. "Here. Hold out your hand."

Terri reached across the desk. Opening his fist, he dropped something into her palm. Even before she looked at it, she knew it was her missing earring.

Terri willed her expression to freeze into a calm mask. Did this mean he was going to tell her how he came to find it? Her pulse kicked into overdrive. After ten years, was their relationship finally about to move out of its familiar rut?

She waited for him to close her office door for more privacy. Instead he remained where he was, the same disarming smile on his face.

"The grounds crew found your earring in the parking lot," he said. "It's a lucky thing it didn't get run over."

Terri felt the sudden catch of her breath, as if she'd just been gut-punched. Instead of owning up to what had happened between them, he'd chosen to lie. The unfeeling jerk hadn't even cared enough to be honest.

It was time she faced reality. Aside from her general usefulness, Buck didn't care about her at all—and if sleeping with him hadn't changed anything, nothing ever would.

"Thanks," she said, wrapping the earring in a tissue and sliding it into her purse. "The other one's at home. It'll be nice to have the pair again."

He remained a moment, framed by the doorway. Was he waiting for some kind of confession from her? Well, the man would grow a long gray beard before he'd get one.

The standoff was broken by the first phone call of the

day. As Terri took the call, from a possible client, Buck turned away and walked back toward his office.

Terri took her time on the phone, answering questions and jotting down information. Out in the common room, the summer temps were arriving, chatting on the way to their desks. Terri hung up the phone and waited. By now, Buck would have found the check she'd written and left in an envelope on his desk. Waiting for his reaction was like waiting for the fall of an ax. But this confrontation had to happen. Her pride demanded it—especially in view of the lie he'd just told her.

It was a matter of seconds before he reappeared in her doorway. His eyes were steely, his jaw set in a grim line. "In my office, Terri," he demanded. "Now."

Four

Terri walked ahead of Buck, feeling like an errant schoolgirl being herded into the principal's office. Curious gazes followed them. Buck hadn't said another word, but his stride and his stormy expression gave off signals that somebody was in trouble.

As the door closed behind them, he turned toward his desk, picked up the check that lay next to the phone and waved it in her face. "What is this, Terri?" he demanded.

She raised her chin. "It's just what it looks like. I'm paying you back for the tires you put on my Jeep. Let me know if it isn't enough."

Terri had looked up the price of the tires online. They were top quality, almost sixteen hundred dollars for the set. Covering the payment had all but cleaned out her checking account, but she had her pride, and she wasn't about to back down.

Buck's scowl darkened. "I wanted to *give* you those tires. You needed and deserved them."

Deserved them? How? Oh—did I do something special for you?

Terri had to bite back the sarcastic retort. The fact that they'd had sex the day before was the proverbial elephant in the room. But if he wasn't going to acknowledge it, then neither was she. She'd been an impulsive fool, letting her boss pull her into bed and foolishly thinking it might actually change things between them. Right now all she wanted was to forget it had ever happened.

"I don't want your money, Terri. If you want to repay me, just take the check, say thank you and go back to work."

Terri lifted her chin higher, fixing him with a narrow-eyed gaze. "I'm your employee, not your charity case, Buck. I'm not taking that check back. If it doesn't clear the bank in the next three days, you're going to find four tires piled on your front porch. I can get perfectly decent tires for a lot less than these cost—in fact, I was planning to just that."

"Fine. You win," he snapped. "I'll cash the damned check. Just remember to drop by the vehicle department and get your wheels balanced and aligned. My crew couldn't do that in the parking lot. And no, you don't have to pay them."

Terri could feel the emotions welling—anger, embarrassment and frustration. Her throat choked off. Her eyes stung with unshed tears. "I'll take care of my own wheels, thank you," she said. "I won't be using the services of your vehicle department because…" The words were on the tip of her tongue, but she wasn't sure she could say them.

She felt light-headed. Had she gone too far? No, she had to do this. It was time.

"Because why?" he asked.

"Because I'm quitting, Buck. I'm giving you my two weeks' notice, starting right now."

Buck stared after her as she stalked out and closed the door. She hadn't meant it, of course. She was riled, that was all. Give her a little time to cool down, and she'd be fine.

I'm quitting, Buck. I'm giving you my two weeks' notice, starting right now.

Her words echoed like the memory of a bad dream. There was no way Terri could quit now, or even in two weeks—not when he needed her so much. Summer was the busy season here, with important clients coming in, and the big charity gala less than a month off. And what would he do about Quinn? She'd be devastated if Terri left.

Lord, what if she'd meant it? What if she was really going to quit?

She could do it, Buck realized. He knew of a half dozen places that would hire her in a minute. And she wouldn't have that much trouble selling her grandmother's property or relocating Harriet to a new facility. In two weeks she could have everything settled and be ready to move out of his life.

No way was he going to let that happen. He had to come up with some kind of plan. But that was easier said than done.

First off, it would help him to know why she'd been so upset. Was it because he'd bought her tires or because of what had happened in his bed? He could try talking to her about it—but he'd resolved not to show that he remembered their morning romp. Telling her the truth would only add to the complications.

Terri's check for sixteen hundred dollars lay on his

desk. He would cash it as promised, then apply the money, and more, to her grandmother's care at Canyon Shadows. Terri might not like him paying for something else behind her back, but with luck she wouldn't find out anytime soon. She was independent to a fault. But he'd promised Steve he'd take care of her. Besides, he'd discovered that he liked the way taking care of Terri made him feel.

Last night, when he'd arranged to replace her tires, he'd weighed the idea of surprising her with a brand-new vehicle. But that old Jeep had been Steve's. There was no way Terri would part with it. She would drive it till it rusted away to a pile of nuts and bolts.

Still, it didn't make sense that doing Terri a favor would push her to quit her job. There had to be more behind her reasons. Whatever was driving her away from him, he couldn't afford to lose her. He had to find a way to make her stay.

Forcing the thought aside for now, he turned on his computer and brought up his agenda for the day—the agenda Terri, as always, had prepared the day before. This morning Evie would be taking the jet, along with a flight steward, to meet the Dubai clients at the airport in Salt Lake City. The four oil-rich sheikhs would expect nothing but the best—gourmet snacks on the flight south, then a private lunch in the restaurant's dining room. Buck would be meeting the plane at the company airstrip, hosting the lunch, and taking them on a helicopter tour of Zion and Canyonlands National Parks, to be followed by an outdoor barbecue and a night's rest. Tomorrow morning, after breakfast, a helicopter would fly them to Lee's Ferry to board the raft for their three-day trip down the Colorado River, to Phantom Ranch in the canyon bottom. From there they would ride mules up the trail to the South Rim, where they could spend a night in the lodge. The next morning, Evie would fly them to Las Vegas in the jet.

Everything had been planned down to the last detail—the best guide and boat pilot available, the best food, and two camp boys who could cook and entertain as well as set up the tents and the portable latrine. He needed everything to be perfect, because if the sheikhs enjoyed the trip, they might take an interest in backing his new project.

Buck hadn't planned to go along on the river excursion. He had other things to do. And he had complete faith in the people he was sending. There was no reason not to expect a successful trip. But he'd made his plans before Terri's announcement that she was quitting. Now a sudden idea struck him.

Three days in the beautiful canyon, away from ringing phones and interruptions, might be just the ticket for talking Terri into staying around. He knew she loved this place—he just had to remind her. He'd have no trouble juggling his schedule to include himself in the trip. The challenge would be getting Terri to go along.

If he asked her, she was bound to make excuses, or even refuse to go. Rather than risk that, he would need to figure out a way to shanghai her.

Buck had hoped to free up some time for Quinn. But that would have to wait. The prospect of losing Terri was a five-alarm emergency.

After a busy morning, Terri phoned to tell Quinn she was coming to pick her up. "Is there any special place you'd like to look for clothes?" she asked.

"Anyplace away from here!" Quinn sighed. "Mrs. C.

is driving me crazy. She follows me around like she's the Secret Service."

"Well, I'm betting she could use a break, too," Terri said. "I'll see you in about twenty minutes."

Terri switched off her computer and stuck a note to the screen. She planned to come back at the end of the day to post the agenda and clean up any loose ends Bob and the temps might have left. With Buck off entertaining the Dubai clients, somebody needed to make sure everything was shipshape for tomorrow's river launch.

Quinn was waiting on the porch when Terri pulled up to the house. Like an escaping prisoner, she raced down the steps and clambered into the Jeep. "Let's go!" she said.

"Hold your horses, girl." Terri waited while the plump, middle-aged widow, dressed in a blue seersucker pantsuit, came out onto the porch. "I'll have her back here by four, Mrs. Calloway. Meanwhile, relax and enjoy some peace and quiet."

Quinn giggled as the Jeep pulled out of the driveway. "Maybe she'll take a bubble bath in Dad's Jacuzzi. God knows she needs to do something to loosen up."

"Stop that, Quinn," Terri chided the girl. "Mrs. Calloway's just doing her job. You know the woman would fight off man-eating tigers to keep you safe."

"At least it would be fun to see her do that," Quinn said. "Where are you taking me?"

"To the outlet mall at the junction. No sense spending a lot of money on clothes you'll just grow out of. Okay?"

"Sure. I just need jeans and shorts and shirts—and a jacket and a new swimsuit. Oh, and new underwear. Hey, can I get a bra?"

"You're nine." Terri glanced at the girl's flat chest. "Aren't you a little young for a bra?"

"A girl in my class has one. She showed it to me. She thinks she's *so* hot."

"I think the bra can wait till you're older." Terri swung the Jeep onto the highway. The outlet mall was ten miles down the road, a shopping mecca for the surrounding towns and farms.

"Can we get burgers and fries and shakes? Mrs. C. only feeds me healthy, balanced meals."

Terri suppressed a smile. "Okay. After we're done shopping."

Buying the clothes Quinn needed took a little less than two hours. By the time they'd finished their burgers, it was after three o'clock. "We need to get you home," Terri said as they climbed into the Jeep. "I promised to have you back by four, and I don't want Mrs. Calloway to worry."

"Daddy said you'd take me to the cemetery. I want to see where my grandma's buried."

Terri hesitated, thinking of the time. "All right. It's on the way back to town. We can stop there, but we'll only have a few minutes."

"That'll be enough," Quinn said.

"Okay. Let's go. Fasten your seat belt."

The cemetery was small and old, many of the weathered markers dating back to pioneer times. Hundred-year-old pine trees sheltered the graves. Spring grass covered the ground in patches. Among the headstones, the delicate hoofprints of mule deer etched tracery-like paths in the russet earth.

Terri knew where Buck's mother was buried. Quinn's hand crept into hers as they stood beside the grave and read the inscription on the small, plain marble slab.

Annie Morgan
July 10, 1953–August 14, 2001

"How old was she when she died?" Quinn asked.

"Not old at all, not even fifty," Terri said, thinking even that number would sound old to someone as young as Quinn.

"Was she nice?"

"She was always nice," Terri said, holding back the words *Too nice for her own good*, remembering the stories about the truck stop. Annie Morgan had been small and sad and had seemed desperately lonely—and sometimes just plain desperate—but she'd always been kind to Terri and Steve. "If she was still alive I think she'd be a good grandma to you."

"I wish I'd brought a flower or something," Quinn said.

"You can always come back."

Quinn's gaze followed the flight of a dragonfly. "Where's Steve's grave?" she asked.

"How did you know Steve was buried here?" Terri asked, mildly surprised.

"Daddy told me. He said Steve was your brother and his best friend, but that he died in the war."

"It's in the next row. I'll show you." Together they walked to the bronze plaque, set in concrete and flanked by a metal bracket where a flag could be placed on Memorial Day.

"Did he have a girlfriend?"

"He did. But after he died she married somebody else and moved away." Terri glanced at her watch. They had a few more minutes to spare. "This next grave is my grandfather's. He passed away before I was born. And this empty spot next to him is where my grandma will be buried."

Quinn had fallen silent. This talk of death was a lot for a nine-year-old to wrap her mind around. She'd likely had enough.

"Time to go." Terri led the way back to the Jeep. Twenty minutes later they pulled up to the house. Mrs. Calloway, looking relieved, was waiting on the porch.

Quinn unfastened her seat belt and leaned over the gearshift to give Terri a hug. "This was the best time ever," she said. "Can you come back again tomorrow?"

Terri hugged her back. "We'll see. That depends on what your dad needs me to do. I'll call you, okay?"

"Okay." Quinn grabbed her shopping bags and climbed out of the Jeep. With a farewell wave, Terri backed down the driveway and through the gate. There was work still waiting for her at the office.

Quinn had had such a good time today, she mused. It didn't take much to make the little girl happy, just somebody to be with her and pay attention to her—preferably without smothering her, the way Mrs. Calloway did. Maybe it would help to talk with Buck and let him know how much his daughter needed him.

A shadow darkened her thoughts as she remembered giving him her notice that morning. She was determined to go through with her plans. But leaving Quinn when the girl had so few people she could rely on would break her heart. Maybe in the time she had left, she could work on getting Buck to spend more time with his daughter—or at least help Quinn find some friends.

By the time she returned to the office, the staff was gone. The ceiling lights had been turned off, casting the common room into late-afternoon shadows. Terri was walking toward her office when she noticed Buck's door was ajar.

In her absence, it had been Bob's responsibility to make sure the place was securely locked. Evidently the young man's thoughts had been elsewhere—one more thing she would have to remind him about tomorrow.

She'd reached Buck's door and was about to lock it when she realized the room wasn't empty. Buck was sitting in the shadows, his chair turned toward the window. Terri understood him well enough to know that he was troubled. Was he upset about her quitting, or had something else gone wrong?

"Are you all right?" Terri asked softly.

"Oh, it's you." With a bitter chuckle, he swiveled the chair toward her. "How did things go with Quinn today?"

"Fine. We had a good time. But what are you doing here?"

Buck shook his head. "Sit down, Terri. I hope you're in a patient mood because I need a good listener."

"What is it?" Terri took the chair on the near side of Buck's desk. "Did everything go all right with the sheikhs?"

"Like clockwork." He paused, taking a deep breath. "Evie was there to pick them up on time, smooth flight and park tour, first-rate lunch…" His voice trailed off. "Terri, would you ever call me naive?"

She met his troubled gaze. "Why?" she asked. "What happened?"

"This would make a funny story if it wasn't so frustrating. Everything went swimmingly with the sheikhs. By the time we'd finished the tour and come back to the hotel, I was congratulating myself on money and effort well spent. Then it came time for me to see them to their rooms for a rest before the barbecue…" He gave a bitter chuckle. "I realized they were looking at me, as if expecting more. Finally the tallest one, who did most of the talking, took me aside and asked me—" Buck broke off, shaking his head.

"What?"

"He asked me, 'Where are the girls?'"

Terri's jaw dropped as the implication sank home. "Oh, Buck!"

"I should've expected this," he said. "I should have realized what they'd expect and made it clear before they even came that none of that would be happening here. I wear a lot of hats in this business, but the one thing I'm not, and won't ever be, is a damned pimp."

"So what did you tell them?"

"What could I tell them? I said that girls weren't part of the package. They were polite enough, even when I turned down the extra money they offered me, but I could tell they weren't happy about it. And something tells me they won't be offering to back my new resort."

"I'm so sorry." Terri knew how much planning and effort had gone into this venture. Buck's disappointment was evident in his tired voice and every line of his face. Terri checked the urge to move behind his chair and rub his shoulders. Two days ago she might have done it. But not now.

"What about the river trip?" she asked. "Is it still on for tomorrow?"

"Yes, they still want to go. Which reminds me, Terri, we've got a couple of the staff out sick. The equipment truck's loaded and ready to go, but I'll need you to drive it down to Lee's Ferry and bring it back here once the gear's unloaded.

Terri stifled a groan. She knew what that meant. She'd be leaving at 4:00 a.m. with the two camp boys, to be at the landing with the big trailer truck, which held the two uninflated rafts, the air pump, the food and cooking supplies, the tents, the portable latrine and the other gear. By the time the clients arrived by helicopter at eight thirty the rafts would be inflated, loaded and ready to go—one for the clients and the other for the gear. After that, she'd make the two-hour solo drive back to the resort.

"Sorry to dump this on you at the last minute," Buck said, as if reading her thoughts. "I'd drive the truck myself, but I'll be helicoptering in with the sheikhs. I've decided to guide the river trip myself. Maybe I can still salvage the situation."

Terri counted the hours the round-trip in the truck would take out of her day. Not good timing. She had a lot to do tomorrow, and she'd wanted to spend more time with Quinn—even more so now that Buck had said he'd be going on the trip with the sheikhs. With her father gone, the girl would be lonesome. "Isn't there anybody else who can haul the gear down?" she asked. "Bob, maybe?"

"He's not licensed to drive that big truck. If he has a problem, the insurance company won't pay."

"Fine." Terri sighed and shrugged. "I've done it before. No reason I can't do it again."

"Thanks. And just one more thing, Terri."

Her pulse quickened. Maybe this was the moment. Maybe he was going to ask her to stay—and not just for the job, but for *him*.

"I know you've given your two weeks' notice," he said. "But I'm hoping I can talk you into staying through the gala. It's only another week or so—and it'll be a mess without you. I'll pay you a bonus, of course. Name your price."

She should have known better. Feeling as if she'd just been slapped with a frozen fish, Terri rose from her chair. "I'll let you know after you're back from the river run. But you'll have to make it worth my time." She walked to the door, then turned. "If you don't mind a suggestion, why don't you go home and spend some quality time with your daughter before tomorrow?"

"Good idea, but I need to check the supplies for the trip and make sure everything's on the truck. By then it'll be time for the barbecue with the sheikhs. You're welcome to come if you like."

"Not on your life. They're all yours."

"See you tomorrow, then." Rising, he moved to the outside door of his office and opened it. "Thanks again for agreeing to drive the truck. I appreciate your help."

"It's my job." Her voice dripped icicles, but Buck didn't seem to notice.

He left and closed the door. Terri double-checked to make sure both doors to his office were locked, then returned to her own office and switched on her computer. The sooner she got today's work done, the sooner she could go home and rest up for an early start tomorrow. She wasn't happy about driving the truck, and even less happy about the way he'd taken her for granted yet again. She should have walked out on the spot and left him with his movie-star mouth hanging open.

Buck didn't care about her as a woman. He never had and he never would. She'd consider staying through the gala as he'd asked because she knew how much it meant to the business and she didn't want to let anyone down, but once that was over, she'd leave this place—and that man—behind for good.

The heavy trailer truck rumbled over the narrow road, swaying dangerously every time a wheel sank into a pothole. Half-blinded by the sunrise above the red-rock mesas, Terri ground the gears and wrestled with the wheel. Years ago, at Buck's suggestion, she'd learned the skills, and acquired the paperwork, to fill in for almost any job in the company. Not only could she drive the truck, she was licensed as a skydive instructor, bungee-jumping instructor and boat pilot. She was also a fair mechanic and certified in first aid and lifesaving. When Buck referred to her as his right-hand woman he wasn't just throwing out words. Anything he could do, she could do almost as well, if not better. It was a situation that backfired on her often when, like today, she was the only person on hand qualified to do an unpleasant task.

Next to her on the single bench seat, the two camp boys were catching some extra sleep. Still in their early twenties, they were both seasoned river runners. It would be their job to motor ahead in the loaded supply raft, set up camp and have everything ready when the clients arrived at the end of the day's run. At Phantom Ranch, where the adventure would end, they would put a tow on the client raft and continue all the way to Lake Mead, where both rafts would be hauled out of the water, unloaded, deflated and trucked home.

Eli Rasmussen, a local boy with freckles and red hair, was snoring, his mouth open, his head drooping to one side. George Redfeather, Evie's nephew, handsome and polite, had fallen into a quiet doze. Glancing at them, Terri smiled. Both young men were good-humored and likable. Eli could sing and play the guitar, and George was a master Native American storyteller. They'd been Buck's first choice for this trip, and she knew they would give it their all. For their sakes, Terri could only hope the four sheikhs would be generous tippers.

Up ahead, she could make out the low prefab buildings that marked Lee's Ferry, the launching point for boats running down Marble Canyon, into the Colorado River and through the Grand Canyon. She checked her watch. Time to wake the boys. With her help, they'd have a little over an hour to get everything ready before the helicopter was due.

One vital member of the team would be meeting them here. Arnie Bowles, an expert river pilot, lived in Page, the big town near the Glen Canyon Dam. He'd be dropped off by his wife, Peggy. Terri glanced around for him as she pulled the truck into the parking lot. He was nowhere to be seen.

"Maybe Arnie had car trouble." Eli had jumped out of the cab and was opening the back of the trailer.

"Maybe so. He usually gets here early." Terri began moving the food coolers out of the way while George hauled the first of two outboard motors down to the water's edge. They worked swiftly and efficiently, each one knowing exactly what needed to be done.

Half an hour later, Arnie had yet to arrive. Terri was getting concerned. He had her cell number, as did the office, but no one had called her. Maybe Buck had heard something.

At eight thirty, they heard the whirr of the approaching helicopter. Minutes later, the machine touched down, sending up clouds of red dust before the rotors slowed. Buck jumped to the ground. The four sheikhs, swarthy, handsome men dressed in rain gear for the river, climbed out behind him.

Spotting Terri, Buck beckoned her close. "There's been a change of plans," he said. "Arnie can't make it. We'll need you to take his place."

Terri's eyes went wide. "But—"

"Listen to me." His gaze drilled into her. "If you can't do the job, we'll have to cancel the whole trip."

"You can't reschedule for tomorrow?"

"No time. They're due for meetings in Vegas right after the trip." He leaned close to her. "Listen, Terri, they're already disappointed about the girls. The only way to salvage this is to give them a good river run."

"But what about the office? What about Quinn—and my grandmother?"

"It's only for three days. We can cover that. I'll make some calls."

Before Terri could protest again, he turned back to the four men. "We're good," he said. "Give us a few minutes, and we'll push off."

Terri knew better than to argue. Once Buck made up his mind there was no stopping him.

She had just a few more weeks to put up with his high-handed insensitivity. After that, Buck Morgan, the ten years she'd been at his side and that one hot encounter in his bed would be history.

Thankfully, Arnie's rain gear, needed for protection against the chilling spray of the river, had been stowed in the client boat. While Buck made his calls, she decided to get the waterproof pants and jacket, and slip the set over her clothes. But first, knowing what could happen to possessions on the river, she gave her purse to the helicopter pilot, a man she trusted, and asked him to leave it at the hotel desk for her.

To get to the waiting rafts, she had to walk between the truck and the clients, who were standing in a close group. As she passed the tallest of the four men, she felt an unexpected press on the seat of her khakis.

Terri stifled a gasp. There could be no mistaking that touch. That arrogant, billionaire jerk had just patted her on the rump.

Five

The river was swollen with spring runoff, its water choc-olate brown with silt. Calm, rippling stretches alternated with wild rapids that raced and tumbled, spraying the air with mist.

Terri knew the river like the back of her hand. She used the outboard motor to steer the raft into the spots that would make for an exhilarating but safe run, let-ting the rapids carry it downstream. The four sheikhs whooped and cheered as the flat-bottomed rubber raft bounced and slithered over the roiling water, roaring with laughter as the cold, muddy spray drenched them from head to toe.

Buck had introduced them by name—Abdul, Omar, Hassan and one more she'd already forgotten. Matching those names with faces was more than her busy mind could handle, especially when she was running on a mix of aggravation and insufficient sleep. To keep them straight in her head, she'd renamed them Eeny, Meeny, Miney and Moe—in order of their height.

Eeny was the one to watch.

Scanning the river ahead, she steered right to avoid a jutting rock. This was the easy part of her job. She could simply pilot the raft, ignored by the clients as they enjoyed the ride, and by Buck who sat in front, pointing out interesting sights and lecturing on the geologic history of the canyon. For now she could relax. But that pat on her rear had put her on high alert. Once they reached camp she would have to watch her back. She mustn't let herself be caught alone or give any hint that she might be available. Having to slap a client's face would be bad for Buck's business.

They'd be camping in the canyon three nights, then riding mules up the long, steep trail to the South Rim. She could handle the physical rigors of the journey, but between the discomfort of being the only woman and her worry about the duties she'd left behind, Terri was already anxious for the trip to end.

Buck hadn't even given her a chance to back out. As always he'd ignored her needs and taken for granted that she'd do what he wanted.

All the more reason to quit and move on.

Buck's eyes swept the sheer sandstone cliffs that rose on both sides of the river. Then his gaze shifted to the rear of the raft, where Terri sat with one hand on the tiller. Even in the oversize rain gear she wore, she looked every inch a woman. He'd seen the way the four men looked at her, especially Abdul, and he didn't like it. In their culture, an unveiled female, especially a pretty one, might easily be seen as fair game, especially since they were already paying for her services as river pilot.

He could hardly put her in a burka. But once they got to camp he would need to keep her in sight and make it clear to the men that female employees were off-limits.

Off-limits.

This trip was supposed to make Terri fall in love with the area again and choose to stay. The last thing he wanted was for her to get so fed up with ogling clients that she'd be even more determined to leave.

Besides, Abdul had no right to think of Terri as someone he was entitled to due to his money and position. Terri deserved more respect than that—and she knew it. They'd had plenty of rich men and celebrities in and out of the resort through the years, and Terri had never been dazzled or overawed by anyone. She wasn't the type to fall into a stranger's bed just because she was flattered by his attention or impressed by his wealth.

His thoughts spiraled back to that interlude in his bedroom, with Terri leaning above him, eyes closed, moist lips parted, hair hanging down to brush his face as she moved above him, pushing him deep, and deeper, into the honey of her sweet body… Instead of falling into bed with a stranger, she'd fallen into bed with him, and it had been *phenomenal*.

The raft pitched and dived, jarring him back to the present. As they plowed into another stretch of rapids, Buck grabbed the seat to keep from being flung into the water. Best keep his mind on what was happening, he scolded himself. But even then, his gaze was drawn to Terri. With her hood flung back, her wet hair streaming, her eyes bright with excitement, she was so wildly beautiful that she took his breath away.

The realization hit him like a gut punch. He'd had her once and vowed it wouldn't happen again. But right or wrong, he wanted her back—in his arms, in his bed.

Heaven help him, was he falling for his right-hand woman?

With the canyon shadows deepening, the raft crunched onto the broad sand strip below the camp. George was waiting to catch the tether line Buck tossed him and help pull the raft partway out of the water. Terri waited in the stern while the four men climbed out onto dry land— Eeny, Meeny, Miney and Moe. By now she couldn't have remembered their real names for ten thousand dollars. Her body ached from holding herself steady against the pounding current of the river. Her face, hair and rain clothes dripped with muddy water.

The sight of the glowing fire on the high, grassy bank and the aroma of grilling prime rib eye steaks reminded her that she was also hungry. The way the four sheikhs dragged their feet climbing up to the camp gave her hope that they were worn out, too.

Buck had waited for her by the raft. He gave her his hand as she climbed over the inflated bow and jumped to the ground. "Good work, Terri. Thanks for coming along."

"You didn't exactly give me a choice." She was too tired to be gracious.

"Is everything all right? You sound a little ragged around the edges."

"Just unsettled, that's all, and worried about all the things we had to leave hanging. I don't trust Bob's ability to run the office while we're both away. Quinn wanted me to come by. And I didn't even get a chance to check on my grandmother."

"I did ask Bob to call Canyon Shadows and let them know you'd be away."

"Does Quinn know where we are?"

"She was asleep when I got home last night and still asleep when I left this morning. But I spoke with Mrs. Calloway. They'll be fine."

But Quinn won't be happy. You should have at least talked to her. The words hovered on the tip of Terri's tongue, but she bit them back. There was nothing to be done now. They couldn't make phone calls from here. The rafts could communicate with each other by two-way radio. But there was no cell phone service in the canyon. Until they made it up to the South Rim, they'd have better luck calling from the moon.

Supper was eaten around the fire, sitting on camp stools and eating off sturdy paper plates. Eli and George were superb camp cooks—the prime steaks, hot buttered biscuits and roasted corn were all delicious. The three sheikhs Terri had dubbed Meeny, Miney and Moe were polite and pleasant. But Eeny—Abdul, the jerk who'd patted her rump—was already complaining.

"My grandfather lived better than this with his camel herd in the desert. Sleeping on the hard ground in a tent the size of a tabletop, no showers to wash off the mud, no laundry service—and everybody sharing that unspeakable latrine. We at least expected some kind of lodge, with beds and bathrooms."

"This canyon is one of the natural wonders of the world." Buck gazed across the fire, his voice weary but patient as he gave his stock answer. "There are rules we follow to preserve it. The most important rule is that when we leave here, nothing can be left behind. Whatever we bring in has to be brought out—the equipment, the trash, down to the last soda tab. And nothing goes in the river. Even pissing on the bank will get you slapped with a citation." He glanced around the circle of faces. "When you climb off that mule on your fourth day you'll be as tired, sore and filthy as you've ever been in your life. But you'll remember this adventure forever." Like a lawyer resting his case, he rose and walked away from the fire, back toward the tents.

Terri's pulse skittered as the realization struck her. There were six small dome tents in the camp—one for each of the clients, one to be shared by Eli and George, and another that had been packed for Buck and Arnie. But since Arnie wasn't here, she'd be sharing that one with Buck.

There was nothing to be concerned about, she told herself. They were both exhausted and would probably drop off as soon as they crawled into their sleeping bags. And judging from the glances Abdul was giving her, sharing a tent with Buck would be safer than sleeping alone. The less fuss she made over the situation the better.

Eli had picked up his guitar and was strumming the opening chords of an old Hank Williams song. He had a Hank Williams voice to go with it, and this canyon, with the river whispering and the fire glowing, was the perfect setting for the old-time music. Now, while the men were listening, would be a good time to visit the latrine, Terri thought. Screened by a canvas tarp on poles, the portable device had been set up at the end of a winding path through the willows.

She had finished and was making her way back along the trail, guided by the glow of the campfire beyond the willows, when a dark shape blocked her path.

"Ah, here you are, beautiful one."

Terri's heart sank as she recognized Abdul. She willed herself not to sound nervous. "Yes, I was just on my way

"I expect my asking price will go way down from five thousand dollars."

He stopped her with a touch on her shoulder. "You don't have to go back to the fire, Terri," he said. "You don't have to face that man again tonight."

"But I do. I need to show him that I'm all right, and that the awful things he said didn't affect me."

"Fine, but I'll come with you," he said, falling into step behind her. "I'm not letting you out of my sight."

"Of course you aren't." She pasted on a mocking smile. "After all, as you said, I'm your woman."

The night was dark, the narrowed sky above the canyon like a river of stars. By lantern light, Buck helped George and Eli stash the last of the dinner gear in the raft, douse the fire and bury the ashes. Breakfast tomorrow would be coffee heated on a propane stove, fresh fruit and pastries, so no morning fire would be needed.

Buck glanced toward Terri. She was huddled on a flat rock, hugging her knees and looking up at the sky. He knew she must be exhausted—piloting the raft was hard work, and the encounter with Abdul must have left her badly shaken. But even with the four clients zipped into their tents, he didn't want her going to bed until he was ready to go with her. Earlier, he'd taken Eli and George aside and told them what had happened. Now Terri would have three protectors looking out for her.

Terri was one tough lady. She'd be all right, Buck told himself. But he needed her to have a pleasant, relaxing experience on this trip. If she was stressed out from fending off a misbehaving client, his plan to convince her to stay wouldn't stand a chance.

Apart from Abdul, the other sheikhs were all right. They were well mannered and cooperative, and appeared to be enjoying themselves despite the rough conditions. But none of them seemed inclined to stand up to Abdul and correct his behavior. Maybe he outranked them in some way, or maybe they'd known him long enough to accept his conduct.

However, that didn't mean Buck had to put up with it. After the way Abdul had spoken to Terri, the idea of him so much as touching her made Buck want to grab the man by his shirtfront and knock out his front teeth.

Leaving the loaded raft, Buck walked over to where Terri was sitting. "How are you doing?" he asked her.

"Better. The sky makes me feel peaceful. I don't want to punch anybody anymore."

He laughed, enjoying her sense of humor. "Ready to turn in?"

"More than ready. I could go to sleep right here on this rock."

"Come on, then." He turned on his flashlight and offered his arm, which she took. Earlier he'd sensed her unease about sharing a tent. But he felt no sign of it now. They were both too tired to be tempted by anything except a good night's rest.

Reaching the tent, he unzipped the flap. The two sleeping bags had been laid out on the floor, with little more than a foot of space between them. "Go ahead," he said, holding up the flap. "I'll wait out here while you get out of your clothes and into your sleeping bag."

"Don't bother. I'm too tired to undress." She ducked inside, kicked off her sneakers and hung her damp socks from one of the tent supports. By the time Buck followed her inside, she'd crawled into her sleeping bag and pulled the top up past her ears. If she wasn't asleep yet, she was making a good show of it.

The night was pleasantly warm. Without bothering to

undress, Buck slipped off his boots and stretched out on top of his sleeping bag. He'd expected to drift right off, but his thoughts wouldn't let him rest. He remembered how Terri had felt in his arms tonight, how she'd clung to him, quivering like a small, scared animal while she cracked lame jokes to hide her fear.

She was amazing—stubborn, brave, sexy and so beautiful that Buck could scarcely believe he'd taken her for granted all these years.

When she'd looked up at him, it had been all he could do to keep from kissing her. Wisely, she'd pulled away. Kissing Terri would have been a mistake. After making love to her, and fighting the urge to do it again, a single kiss would only have left him frustrated, wanting something he could never let himself have again.

Buck was hiding a secret, one he'd kept from her since Steve's death eleven years ago. That secret alone, if it came out, would be enough to drive her away from him forever.

Buck's voice woke Terri at dawn the next morning. She opened her eyes to find him bending over her in the tent with a cup of steaming black coffee in his hand.

"Good morning." He was annoyingly bright-eyed and cheerful. "How'd you sleep?"

She sat up, finger-raking the tangles out of her hair. "Like death. Did I snore?"

"No comment." He grinned, stubble-chinned and handsome even at this ungodly hour. "Here, I brought something to wake you up." He handed her the coffee. "Careful, it's hot."

"Thanks." She took a careful sip and felt the lovely, caffeinated heat trickling down her throat. "Are our guests awake?"

"Not yet. I figured I'd give you a head start on the latrine. Ladies first."

"Thanks again. I don't suppose you have an extra toothbrush. My mouth tastes like roadkill."

"Actually, I do. I grabbed it from the gift shop when I realized I was going to have to hijack you to replace Arnie."

"I'll take it now, with toothpaste on it, please."

"Coming up."

Terri sipped her coffee, watching him as he rummaged in his dry bag. How long had it been since she was last on the river with Buck? The business had gotten so big, her own job so demanding, that she'd forgotten what it was like—the coolness of morning, bird calls blending with the sound of the current, and the first taste of fresh, hot coffee. She was rumpled, dirty and facing another strenuous day at the tiller. But right at this moment, life was good.

She would miss times like this when she left her job. But she hadn't changed her mind about going.

An hour later they were on the water. Here the canyon was narrower and deeper, its walls towering on both sides of the river. The current was swift, the rapids wild and treacherous. It took all Terri's skill to maneuver the raft through the tumbling, pitching water. Wave after wave broke over the bow, drenching everyone on board.

The four sheikhs alternately whooped with excitement and clung to the rope lines in fear for their lives. After Terri negotiated an especially challenging stretch of rapids, the men broke into applause. For a woman, especially, it was no small thing to be earning their respect. Terri caught Buck's eye. He gave her a grin and a thumbs-up.

His approval warmed her—but she'd earned it by

being good at her job, Terri reminded herself. She was Buck's right-hand woman, and loving him would never be enough to change that.

Late in the afternoon, with the sun sinking below the high canyon rim, they reached calmer water. The smell of wood smoke and barbecue, wafting upriver on the breeze, told them they were nearing their camping place.

It had been a decent day, Buck observed. And Terri had done a great job. She had to be feeling good about the way she'd impressed the clients. But would it be enough to make a difference in her plan to leave?

Twenty minutes later they dragged the raft onto the sand and stumbled—cold, hungry and exhausted—into camp. Even Abdul was subdued. Hopefully he'd be too worn out to complain or make Terri uncomfortable. If the man stepped out of line one more time, Buck wouldn't hesitate to put him in his place.

A hearty meal of barbecued beef, baked beans, potatoes and skillet cornbread revived their spirits, but by the time the meal was done and Eli had serenaded them with a couple of songs, the sheikhs were trudging off to their tents to get ready for bed.

Buck helped Eli and George clear away the meal and stash the gear. Terri had wandered off toward the river. Buck had seen Abdul go into his tent, but he still didn't like the idea of her being alone. Leaving the boys, he followed the way she'd gone.

He spotted her sitting on a rock at the river's edge, gazing out across the water. Watching her from behind, he was struck by how lonely she looked. Terri had been with him for ten years. In that time, beautiful and smart as she was, she'd never had a serious relationship with

a man. She'd been there for her work, for her grandmother—and for him.

Sensing his presence, she glanced around and saw
him. He raised his hand in silent greeting, then came
forward and took a place beside her. For a few moments they sat without speaking as the peace of the
river flowed around them. Nighthawks swooped and
darted, catching insects in the moonlight. The distant
call of a coyote echoed down the canyon. Terri's hands
fingered a pebble.

"Are you all right, Terri?" he asked her.

"Fine." She tossed the pebble into the river. "I just
needed a little time to wind down."

"Am I intruding?"

She gave a slight shake of her head. Maybe she just
wanted to be still, Buck thought. But this might be his
best chance to talk with her.

"You're so quiet," he said. "What are you thinking?"

"The same old thing. Just worrying about what
we left behind—work issues, my grandmother and
Quinn—especially Quinn." She turned toward him.
"You shouldn't have gone off and left her without saying
goodbye, Buck. Quinn adores you. She needs you more
than she lets on. Nobody can take your place, not Mrs.
Calloway, not even me."

He scuffed a foot in the sand. "I've been planning
to spend more time with her. And I will, when we get
back."

"Planning isn't the same as doing. You don't even
need to be here. You came because you wanted to interest those sheikhs in that new resort plan. Buck—" She
laid a hand on his arm. "Why on earth do you need a
new project? You're already too busy to make time for
the most important person in your life—your little girl.

And Quinn's growing up. One day she'll be on her own and it'll be too late to have a relationship with her." Her grip tightened. "You've built a great business and done a lot for the town. Why isn't that enough? Why can't you let go and make time for what really matters?"

The woman knew where to jab. Buck gazed at the river shimmering in the moonlight, knowing her question made sense but unsure of his answer. "You knew me growing up," he said. "The poorest kid in town, with a mother who waited tables and turned tricks at the truck stop. Maybe I had to work to get past that. And when I became successful, maybe I couldn't stop. It was the only thing that made me feel worth something. How's that for an answer?"

There was more, he realized. It involved making up for the way Steve had died. But he wasn't going to tell her that.

"Have you ever forgiven your mother?" she asked.

"I don't know." It was as honest an answer as he could give.

"She loved you, Buck. What she did—sacrificing her pride, her reputation—she did to keep food on the table and a roof over your head. But maybe you felt like you had to be better than where you came from."

And maybe he'd shut down emotionally because he'd felt that the mother who'd birthed and raised him hadn't deserved his love.

But then, damn it, he hadn't come out here to be psychoanalyzed.

"Don't quit, Terri," he said. "I need your help. The season, the gala and Quinn, too—I can't handle all that without you. I'll raise your salary, give you stock in the company, cover your grandmother's care, beat any offer that's out there. Name it and it's yours. Just don't go."

She stood, her face in shadow. "It's too late for that, Buck. I've already made up my mind. And now, if you'll excuse me, I'm going to sleep. Don't wake me when you come to bed."

As she turned away, the moonlight caught a glimmer of tears.

Hands thrust into his pockets, Buck watched from a distance as she disappeared inside the tent. Blast it, he'd done everything but beg on his knees, but it hadn't worked. Terri seemed more determined to go than ever.

What was he going to do without her?

The third day of the run tended to be the most taxing. Today, in the sweltering, tropical heat of the lower canyon, Terri's unwashed clothes felt sweat-glued to her body. Her hair was stiff with its dried coating of muddy water. Worse, she was nearing the time for her period to start. Since it often came early, she could only cross her fingers and hope Mother Nature would hold off her monthly visit till the party reached the lodges and shops on the rim.

The canyon here had taken on a bleak moonscape quality, with the river rushing between walls of dark gray basalt that dated from the early creation of the earth. There was no shade here, few plants, no visible animals and no refuge from the burning sun.

It was a relief when, at last, the sun went down, the canyon opened up and the raft reached the last night's campsite. Except for the usual griping from Abdul and some jokes about the canyon being hotter than Dubai, the sheikhs had borne up well. But everybody was sweaty, tired and ready for the trip to end tomorrow.

As the clients trooped up the bank to collapse in folding lawn chairs and gulp cold drinks, Terri stayed behind to help Buck pull the raft higher and secure the line to a boulder.

Buck had been his usual cheerful self, but even he seemed frayed around the edges today. Terri couldn't help wondering if she was the cause of it.

"At least we should have a calm farewell party," she said. "Nobody has enough energy to complain, not even Abdul."

"Lord, let's hope so." Buck held out his free hand to help her up the slope. "Come on. Let's get some dinner and some rest."

She took his hand and let him pull her up. It wasn't fair, she groused silently. With his mussed hair, rumpled clothes and stubbly beard, Buck still managed to look like a romance cover model. While she looked more like a drowned rat.

Dinner was grilled chicken with asparagus, roast potatoes and a bottle of alcohol-free champagne, meant for farewell toasts. But no one seemed up for toasting. The bubbly liquid was simply drunk. By the time they'd finished, it was getting dark. Clouds were rolling over the high canyon rim.

Tonight it was George's turn to entertain. In his melodious voice, accompanied by the rhythms he beat on his painted buckskin drum, he told stories of animals and how, according to legend, things had come about in the beginning of time. Most clients enjoyed George's stories. But the sheikhs were yawning before he was half-finished. In the middle of a tale, Abdul interrupted with a sharp clap of his hands.

"Enough!" he said imperiously. "How can we call this a party without a dancing girl? You, boy. Give me your drum."

George's face was expressionless, but Terri could

sense the tension in him as he hesitated, then handed the man the drum, which, Terri knew, had been in his family for generations. With his long, manicured fingers, Abdul began beating out a sensual rhythm. "Now you." His gaze fixed on Terri, who sat next to Buck. "Stand up. Dance for us."

This was too much. Terri's temper rose to the boiling point. She was about to jump up and give the man a piece of her mind when Buck rose to his feet, quivering with too-long-restrained outrage. "Terri isn't your dancing girl," he said in a glacial voice. "And that drum isn't yours to play. Here." He strode to the far side of the fire, snatched the drum away, returned it to George's hands and turned back to face Abdul. "Maybe this is how you treat people where you come from. But in this country, especially on my trips, every person has the right to be treated with respect."

Picking up a five-gallon bucket of river water, he poured it on the fire, dousing the flames. "We're done here," he said. "Go back to your tents and get ready to be on the river by sunup. We should be at Phantom Ranch before noon. From there, you can plan on a five-hour mule ride to the top.

As if to underscore his words, he took the half-empty bottle of nonalcoholic champagne and poured it on the smoking ashes. "I mean it," he said. "We're done."

Buck sat in a lawn chair next to the doused fire pit, stirring the ashes with a stick to check for live coals. As expected, he found none, but at least it gave him something to do.

Everyone else, including Terri, had gone to bed, but Buck was too wired to sleep. This would be his last night in the canyon with Terri. He'd hoped that in the peaceful

managed to drag the rafts to safety and secure the lines around the heavy boulders that littered the upper bank. It hadn't taken long. But by the time it was done, all four were drenched and exhausted.

The rain had slowed to a misty drizzle. As George and Eli headed back to their tent, Buck gave Terri his hand to help her up the slippery bank. She was soaked to the skin. Her khakis clung to her body, cold-puckered nipples showing through her shirt. Her hair framed her face in dripping strings. The night air was warm, but the river water had been frigid. She was so cold her teeth were chattering.

"Come on, let's get you warm." Buck circled her with an arm, feeling her body shiver against him. "You didn't need to come out here in the storm, Terri. I could've managed the rafts with the boys."

"Could you?" She fell into step beside him. "What if you couldn't? We might've lost a raft and everything in it. I was doing my job, just as Arnie would've done if he'd been here." She was silent for a moment, limping a little as they moved toward the tent. "What was Arnie's problem, anyway? You never told me why I had to take his place. You just said he couldn't make it."

The guilt that stabbed Buck's conscience was too sharp to ignore. He'd told Terri enough lies. She deserved the truth—about this, at least.

"I have a confession to make," he said. "I switched Arnie's schedule because I wanted *you* on this trip. You'd just told me you were quitting. I wanted some time with you before you left, away from the chaos of the office— I was hoping I could change your mind."

She'd stiffened against him, still shivering. "You know I don't like being manipulated, Buck."

"I know. But I really wanted you to have a good time."

"You could've just asked me."

"Would you have said yes?"

"Probably not. I've worried the whole three days about what I left behind." She stumbled against him, wincing.

"What's wrong? Did you hurt your foot?"

"It's just a sticker. I can get it out."

They'd reached the tent. He raised the flap for her to duck inside, then followed her. "Sit," he said, reaching for his flashlight and switching it on. "I'll have a look at that foot."

Terri didn't argue. Still dripping, she lowered herself to the space on the floor of the tent. Buck wiped the mud off her feet with a towel from his bag. It was easy to find the cactus spine that was stuck in the ball of her foot, but it was in deep. She gave a little yelp as he pulled it out.

"Are you okay?" He sponged away a drop of blood, then salved the spot with the antibiotic cream he kept in his kit.

She nodded. "Just cold."

"You can't sleep in those wet clothes. You'll need to hang them up to dry."

"I know. You, too." She hesitated. Her show of modesty was ludicrous, since he remembered the sight of her, half-naked and straddling his hips. But they both seemed to have decided not to mention that.

"Here." He switched off the flashlight, leaving the tent in darkness. "For privacy, that's the best I can do. You first. I'll give you some space."

He moved back into a corner of the tent, crouching in the cramped space as he listened to the small sounds of Terri getting undressed—the slide of a zipper, the rustle of bunching fabric, the little grunt of effort as she peeled her wet pants over her hips. The mental picture was enough to bring him to full arousal. He battled the urge to seize her in his arms for a repeat performance of that morning in his room. This wasn't the time or place. The tent was too small, its walls too thin and it was too close to neighbors. If he made love to Terri again—and the need to make that happen was driving him crazy—he wanted to do it right.

She draped her clothes on the tent frame, then snuggled down into her sleeping bag. "All clear," she said.

Buck felt chilled, too. He stripped off his clothes, hung them up and crawled into bed. They lay side by side, zipped into their sleeping bags, both of them still too charged with adrenaline to sleep. Realizing she was awake, Buck decided to take a chance.

"Should I apologize for this trip?" he asked. "I had good intentions, but I know it's been rough on you."

She rolled over to face him in the darkness. "There's no need to apologize for the trip. I enjoyed the good parts and survived the bad. What I'm unhappy about is that you lied to get me here."

"I know. But I was desperate to bring you. Since I knew you wouldn't come willingly, it was either tell a fib or tie you up and throw you on the raft."

"No comment."

Waiting for Terri to say more, Buck studied the faint outline of her face in the darkness. He remembered watching her today on the river, as the breeze fluttered a strand of chestnut hair across her sun-freckled face. Even after a third day of roughing it on the river, she was beautiful—not like the pampered women he usually dated, but strong and graceful like a wild mare or a soaring hawk. He'd always thought she was pretty. But not until this topsy-turvy week had he realized how magnificent she was.

Was it too late to stop himself from falling in love with her?

For years, he'd told himself that Terri was off-limits as anything but a friend. She was Steve's sister, and he'd promised to care for her like family. But she'd broken out of that box, and he could no longer deny the power of his growing feelings for her.

Don't go, Terri. Stay here. Give us a chance to see what might happen.

Buck knew better than to say the words. Terri deserved a better life than she'd found in Porter Hollow as his right-hand woman. If she wanted to go and find it, who was he to stop her—especially since she'd already made up her mind to leave?

She'd fallen silent. "Are you getting sleepy?" he asked.

"A little. But I'm still cold." Her teeth chattered faintly as she spoke.

"Come here." Impulsively, he grabbed a fistful of her sleeping bag and pulled her against him. Terri didn't resist. Wrapped chastely in a cocoon of nylon and synthetic down, she nestled her rump into the curve of his body and let him wrap his arms around her. Within minutes her breathing told Buck she'd drifted off to sleep.

As he lay with his arm across her shoulders, the tingle of awareness became an ache, deepening the urge to move above her and taste those soft lips. He imagined unzipping her sleeping bag, cradling a satiny breast in his palm and stroking her nipple until she moaned.

But as long as he was fantasizing, why stop there? He could imagine being someplace else, someplace private, clean and warm where he could scoop her up in his arms and carry her to bed, where they could relive their single bedroom encounter over and over till they were both deliciously sated.

Was Terri having similar dreams? She'd climbed into his bed once. Surely she wouldn't be averse to doing it a second time, and more…

Buck's thoughts had triggered his arousal again. Imagining an ice-cold shower, he brought himself under a measure of control. Tomorrow they'd be back in their familiar world, slipping into their roles as boss and employee as they counted the days till her departure. The more he thought about it, the less he looked forward to it.

How could he let her walk away without taking one last chance?

By the time they reached the South Rim tomorrow they'd be sore, hungry, tired—and within a few minutes' walk of a comfortable lodge with a good restaurant. They'd both be ready for showers, a good meal and a night's rest before driving back to Porter Hollow in the company vehicle that waited for them. The possibilities were…intriguing, to say the least.

Holding that thought and cradling Terri close, Buck drifted off to sleep.

Phantom Ranch, at the bottom of the Grand Canyon's inner gorge, was a cluster of picturesque stone cabins and a small lodge with beds that could be reserved by hikers, river runners and mule riders for a night's rest. Here Terri, Buck and the four sheikhs gathered their personal gear and left the raft to be towed downriver by George and Eli.

Terri stood on the riverbank, watching the two rafts disappear around the bend. She would ask to make sure the clients had tipped the hard-working camp boys. If not, she would suggest to Buck that he pay them a generous bonus. They'd earned it on this trip.

By the time the group had taken advantage of the

restroom and enjoyed snacks at the cantina, the mule train had arrived to take them up the winding trail to the rim. Terri had hiked that trail—a grueling eight-hour climb—several times in the past. Today she was grateful for the mule ride, which would cut the time by nearly half. She was hot, filthy and anxious to get back to her normal routine.

They mounted up and headed out at a plodding, swaying walk. There were seven big brown mules including one for the driver, who took the lead. Buck brought up the rear with Terri in front of him, and the sheikhs were strung out between. Riding single file on the narrow trail, there wouldn't be much chance to talk, which was fine. She needed some quiet time to regroup for whatever awaited her back in Porter Hollow.

She was sharply aware of Buck riding behind her, but she was too emotionally raw to turn and give him a look or a word. Last night in the canyon, he'd been so kind and protective that she'd almost believed he could care for her. But back in the real world, she knew Buck was bound to become as demanding and insensitive as ever.

The person she'd been a week ago would have patiently followed Buck's orders and accepted being taken for granted as her due. But now she knew she didn't have to be a doormat for any man—not even the high-and-mighty Buck Morgan.

The air in the deep gorge was like a sauna. By the end of the first hour, Terri was dripping. She swigged from the furnished canteen to stay hydrated. At least the higher portion of the trail would be cooler. But looking up from here, the next three hours up a steep, winding trail couldn't be over soon enough.

By the time the mule train wound its way onto the rim of the canyon, the sun was low, the air fresh and pleasant. While Buck tipped the mule driver, the four sheikhs, muddied, bone-weary and sore, climbed off their mounts and staggered toward the limousine that waited to take them to the lodge.

Terri stood with Buck at the trailhead and watched the limo drive away. "At last," Buck muttered.

"Amen," Terri echoed. "By the way, I forgot to ask. What's our plan for getting home?"

"The SUV that Kirby drove here with the sheikhs' luggage should be waiting for us behind the lodge. Since Kirby will be going as steward on the jet tomorrow, you and I will be driving the vehicle back. Are you hungry? We could have dinner before we leave, or even check in, clean up and get a good night's sleep. How does that sound to you?"

Tempting, Terri thought. She knew what would likely happen if they stayed the night. The question was, did she want another no-strings-attached romp with Buck? One that, like the last time, would lead nowhere and mean nothing?

"Let me think about that while I run to the rest-room," she said. "Maybe you should call and let somebody know we're here."

"Fine." Buck whipped out his cell phone. "It's almost five. With luck there'll still be somebody in the office. If not, at least I can pick up any messages on my landline."

"You might want to call your house, too. Quinn will want to know you're on your way back."

She left him and strode off to the nearby stone building that housed the restrooms. Before leaving, she took time to splash the dusty sweat residue from her face, neck and arms and slick back her hair. She looked like forty miles of bad road—or bad river. She didn't have a change of clothes, or even a credit card to buy something clean in the gift shop or one of the tourist boutiques. Maybe she and Buck could order room service if she agreed to stay the night.

If she agreed to stay the night? Was she really considering it? What about her pride?

Still uncertain, she walked outside to find Buck waiting for her. The look on his face stopped her in her tracks. Her pulse lurched. Something was wrong.

"What is it?" she asked. "Did you reach anybody at the office? Is everything all right?"

"I spoke with Bob. Everything at the office is fine."

"Did you call Quinn?"

"I called the house. Nobody answered so I left a message." He drew a sharp breath. "Terri—"

In the silence that hung between them, she felt cold dread crawling up her spine. "Tell me," she said.

"It's your grandmother. She passed away two days ago."

Buck watched the color fade from Terri's face. She'd loved her grandmother. The loss would cut her deeply. But even more painful, and more lasting, would be the regret that she hadn't been there to comfort the old woman in her final moments—and say goodbye.

For that, Buck had nobody to blame but himself.

She hadn't spoken a word. She didn't have to. Her anguished expression said it all. No thanks to him, she'd wasted three days on the river and, in a time of dire need, failed her beloved grandma, the woman who'd been like a mother to her.

"I'm sorry, Terri." The words fell pathetically short of what he wanted to say.

"I need to get home now. Let's go." Turning away from him, she strode off in the direction of where their vehicle would be waiting. Her spine was rigid, her shoulders painfully square.

Buck trailed a few steps behind her. If she never spoke to him again, he wouldn't blame her. But between here and Porter Hollow they had more than a two-hour drive ahead of them. Maybe he could at least get her to talk. Even railing at him, which he deserved, would be better for them both than this stony silence.

He needed to hear her words as much as she needed to say them.

The tan SUV with the Bucket List logo on the door was parked near the hotel's back entrance, its key under the mat where Kirby, the jet steward, had left it. Without a word, Terri climbed into the passenger seat, fastened her seat belt and opened one of the chilled water bottles Kirby had left in the console. She sipped the water in silence as Buck climbed into the driver's seat, buckled up and started the engine.

Twenty minutes later they'd left the park behind and were headed up Highway 89, which would take them north through the Navajo reservation to Page, across the bridge at Glen Canyon and from there over the Utah border to Porter Hollow. In the west, the sky above the desert blazed with a fiery sunset. By the time they got home it would be dark.

Buck stole a glance at Terri's stubborn profile. She was gazing out the side window, still not speaking. The two of them had had their ups and downs over the past ten years, but never a week as tumultuous as this one. Whatever came of it, good or bad, Buck sensed that their relationship would never be the same as before.

The silence between them was like rising water,

threatening to fill the breathing space and drown them both. Unable to stand it any longer, Buck spoke.

"Are you all right, Terri?"

"That depends on your definition of *all right*." She spoke without turning to look at him. "The one thing I could have done for my grandma was be there for her. I couldn't even manage that because I was *working*— trying to keep you and your billionaire clients happy."

"I know. I'm sorry." Buck knew his reply was lame, but it was all he could offer.

"How did she die?" Terri asked. "Did Bob tell you? Was she in the hospital? In her chair?"

"I don't think Bob knew. He only told me she'd passed away."

She exhaled, slumping in the seat. Outside, the darkness was closing around them. "Well, I guess I'll find out when I get home. And I guess I'll have a funeral service to plan. I hope you won't mind giving me a couple of days off."

"Take all the time you need," Buck said. "In fact, I want to pay for your grandmother's funeral. I know you've been paying for her care at Canyon Shadows. You can't have a lot of cash to spare."

There was a long pause before she spoke. "Why would you do that?" she demanded. "Do you think you owe me?"

Buck caught the cold anger in her voice. "It's my fault you missed being there for her," he said. "I'd like to make amends if I can."

"With *money*?" She jerked around to face him. "This isn't about money, Buck. It's about love and family duty. I will pay for my grandmother's funeral, and I don't want a nickel from you!"

Buck held his tongue, hoping she was finished. Maybe

it had been crass, offering to pay for the funeral. But damn it, he'd meant well. Couldn't she give him credit for that?

"You think money's the answer to everything, don't you?" The words spilled out of her like water through a broken dam. "Even with Quinn—you're too busy to spend time with her, so you whip out your credit card and buy her whatever she wants, as if that makes everything all right. As for me—you pay me the salary I earn. That's enough—all I expect. I don't need your charity for the funeral or anything else." She finished off her water and crushed the thin plastic bottle between her hands. "As long as we're on the subject, what was it that prompted you to put sixteen hundred dollars' worth of new tires on my Jeep? Was that some kind of misplaced guilt, too? For what?"

Buck felt the sting. She was cutting too close to a nerve. But he was a captive audience. He couldn't just stop the vehicle and walk away without answering.

"All right," he said. "Since you asked, I might as well tell you. When we were in Iraq, I promised Steve that if anything happened to him, I'd look after you. Lately I've realized that apart from giving you a job, I haven't done much to live up to that promise. So when you needed new tires, I wanted to help. That's all."

It wasn't all. Not by a long shot. But Terri was upset enough. For now it was as much as she could handle.

But she kept pushing him, getting under his skin. "I was in my teens when you and Steve enlisted. I'm a grown woman now. Damn it, Buck, I don't need looking after, especially when you do it all out of guilt!"

"Fine. Message received loud and clear."

Jaw set, hands gripping the wheel, Buck could feel his temper boiling over. The river run had been a lousy waste of time. He was filthy, unshaven, hungry and exhausted, and now this fool woman had not only rejected his well-meant offer of help, but she'd dismissed his motive as guilt.

What the hell, she was partially right. But that didn't mean he had to take being treated like the bad guy—not when she wasn't exactly Little Miss Innocent herself.

The words came out before he could think to stop them.

"As long as we're asking questions, tell me what the devil you were doing in my bed the morning I was sick. I remember it being a lot of fun, but not much else."

As soon as Buck heard her gasp he knew he'd made a serious mistake. He willed himself to focus his eyes on the road. There could be no taking back what he'd just said. All he could do was brazen it out and deal with the consequences.

"How dare you?" she sputtered.

"*How dare I?* Stop acting like a character out of some damned Jane Austen novel. I was half-drugged out of my mind, and you took advantage of me."

Another gasp. "*I* took advantage? I leaned over the bed to make sure you were all right. You grabbed my hand and put it on your...never mind. I've been trying to make myself believe it never happened. A gentleman would never have brought it up."

"You've known me most of your life. Have I ever claimed to be a gentleman? It happened, Terri, and I'm sick of pretending it didn't."

"Is that why you bought the tires for my Jeep? Because I slept with you?"

"Lord, no. I can't believe you'd think that."

Terri didn't reply. When he risked a glance at her, she was staring out the front window, her jaw stubbornly set.

Should he apologize? But no, she was past listening. His words would most likely set off another tirade. Besides, he was glad to have it out in the open, so he didn't have to ignore what had happened between them anymore.

But right or wrong, he'd turned a dangerous corner with Terri. Their once-comfortable relationship would never be the same. And now, especially with her grandmother gone, she'd probably be eager to leave Porter Hollow—and him.

He'd been in denial about her leaving, Buck realized. Maybe he still was. Either way, he wasn't ready to deal with losing her.

Terri watched the headlights sweep past the broken yellow lines on the highway. Here and there, in the darkness, specks of light from Navajo homes glowed like distant stars. A big double-trailer truck, roaring past in the southbound lane, left the air tinged with diesel fumes.

She willed herself not to think. Her mind was too tired to process all that had happened and come to any kind of intelligent conclusion. She knew only that the course of her life had just taken a drastic turn. She'd always counted on her grandmother, her job and Buck to provide her with stability. Now it was as if she was standing on a crumbling precipice, about to tumble into thin air.

Buck had turned on the radio, but most of the stations on the dial were nothing but static. Only an annoying call-in talk show came through clearly. After a few minutes Buck turned it off. The silence was even more oppressive than before, but it was as if they both knew talking would only do more damage. This was the first time in Terri's memory that she and Buck had nothing to say to each other.

Ahead, she could see the bright lights of Page and the Glen Canyon Dam. Buck slowed for the town. "I could use some coffee. Want something?"

At least he was talking. "No thanks," Terri said. "I think I'll just crawl into the back and try to sleep. If I'm still out when we get back to Porter Hollow, let me off at the hotel. My Jeep and my purse should be there."

"Fine." That was all he said. Terri waited till the SUV pulled up to a drive-through window. Then she crawled over the console and onto the backseat. Somebody had left a thin fleece blanket there. Curling up in it, she closed her eyes. She was too agitated to sleep, she told herself. But at least if she pretended to, she and Buck wouldn't have to worry about talking—or not talking.

The SUV pulled out of the drive-through and headed back to the highway. For all her frayed nerves, Terri was exhausted. It took only minutes for the purr of the engine and the gentle vibration beneath her body to lull her into dreamless sleep.

Seven

"Wake up, Terri. We're here."

Roused by Buck's voice, Terri pushed herself upright in the backseat. Through the side windows of the SUV, she could see the familiar lights that marked the back entrance to the hotel. As she blinked herself awake, the turmoil of the past few hours refocused in her mind. No, it hadn't been a bad dream. Her beloved grandma was gone, and Buck had finally brought up the morning they'd had sex.

Whether she was ready or not, it was time to face reality.

"Your Jeep's across the parking lot," he said. "Want me to stay until you get your keys and make sure the engine starts?"

She untangled herself from the blanket, opened the back door of the SUV and stumbled out on unsteady legs. "Don't worry about it. You need to get home. I'll fine." She closed the door hard, maybe too hard.

He rolled down the window. "I'll swing back this way after I've picked up the Hummer. If you need any help, wave."

"I said I'll be fine. I don't need you to look after me." She turned away and strode into the hotel. The hour was early, not yet nine o'clock. If the Jeep wouldn't start, there were other people she could ask for help.

The concierge had her purse, tucked into a drawer. "That must've been some trip," the woman said, looking her up and down.

Terri faked a grin. "You can't imagine. I'll tell you about it later. Thanks for keeping an eye on this." She took her purse and left the way she'd come in. Buck was gone, but her Jeep started on the first try. With a sigh of relief, she pulled out of the parking lot. All she really felt like doing was going home, stripping down for a long, hot, soapy shower and crawling into bed. But some things couldn't wait.

She would call Canyon Shadows, let them know she was back and find out everything she could about her grandmother. If they needed her to stop by in person or go to the mortuary right away, she'd drive straight there. The way she looked wasn't important.

Terri pulled the Jeep to the curb, fished in her purse and found her cell phone. She'd forgotten to turn it off before handing over her purse, and after being left on for three days without a charge, the battery was dead. With an impatient mutter, she stuffed the phone back in her purse. Never mind, she'd just go straight on to Canyon Shadows and begin the sad business of laying her grandmother to rest.

Starting the Jeep again, Terri pulled into the evening traffic. Harriet Cooper had been ready to go—no question of that. But she'd deserved better than to die alone or among cold-eyed strangers. For the rest of her life Terri would regret that she hadn't been there for the woman who'd given her so much.

Buck turned onto the road that wound up the canyon to his home. He thought about calling the house again, to let Quinn and Mrs. Calloway know he was coming. But it hardly seemed worth the trouble when he'd be there in a few minutes.

Earlier, no one had answered his call. But that had been almost three hours ago. If they'd gone out for dinner, by now they should be home. He could just walk in and surprise his daughter. Maybe, once he'd showered and changed, he could even take her out for ice cream and catch up.

Terri's Jeep had been gone when he'd driven back through the parking lot. She'd been anxious to get away from him. For that he could hardly blame her. Tonight the trust they'd built over the years had shattered. Healing, if even possible, would be long and painful, but Buck wasn't ready to give up. For now he would allow her some space, let her get through the process of grieving for her grandmother. Maybe after that he'd have a chance of winning her back.

Whatever it took, if there was any way to keep her from leaving, he had to try.

Rounding the last curve in the road, he could see his house, every window lit. Apprehension trailed a cold finger up his spine. The feeling that something was wrong became a certainty as he drove through the open gate and saw the county sheriff's brown Toyota Land Cruiser parked next to the house.

Heart pounding, Buck braked the Hummer, sprang to

the ground and raced up the porch steps. Had there been a break-in? Was Quinn all right?

Mrs. Calloway met him at the door. Her face was pale, her eyes bloodshot.

"What is it?" he asked, sick with dread.

"It's Quinn. She's gone missing."

Buck forced himself to speak past the shock. "What happened?"

"After lunch she said she was going to her room to play games on her computer. I checked on her at two. She wasn't there."

"There's no sign of her in the house and no evidence of a struggle." The sheriff, a bear of a man whose belly strained the buttons on his uniform, lumbered down the stairs to face Buck. "I'd say it looks more like a runaway than a kidnapping."

"But as my daughter, she'd be a target for kidnappers. Have you issued an Amber Alert?" Buck demanded.

The sheriff shook his head. "That's a pretty drastic measure. I don't want to do that and then find out she just wandered off."

Buck clenched his jaw, biting back an angry outburst. It wouldn't help to antagonize the man. He tried to pull himself together, forcing himself to think logically. "Did she take anything? Any food? Any clothes?" he asked.

Mrs. Calloway shook her head. "No food. I'm not sure about anything else. There's plenty of clothes left in her closet. I wouldn't know if something was missing." Her eyes welled with tears. "Oh, Lord, Mr. Morgan, I'm sorry. I don't know what happened. I watched that girl like a hawk!"

"It wasn't your fault. Just help us find her. Think—what did she do? What did she say before you missed her?"

"She said she was bored. But she was always saying that."

"What about the dog?" Buck asked the sheriff.

"The dog's here. He's fine."

"And you didn't hear him barking, Mrs. Calloway?"

"No. Didn't hear a thing all afternoon—and I was wide-awake, just watching TV."

"For now I have to assume the girl left on her own," the sheriff said. "Maybe she just went to a friend's house. Maybe you should try calling around."

Buck's patience was wearing thin. Why was everybody standing around talking when his little girl could be in danger? "She doesn't have friends here," he said. "She just came for the summer."

"What about somebody she might've met online? Like a boy? Or even somebody *pretending* to be a boy?" The implication was clear.

Buck's control snapped. "Good Lord, she's nine years old! She's not into boys yet. But if she's out there wandering around alone, anything could've happened to her! Why are we wasting time? We need to get moving and find her!"

"We're doing all we can, Mr. Morgan." The sheriff sounded like a bad imitation of a detective on a TV crime show. "I've put out an alert and given her description to my deputies. They're all watching for her. The best thing for now is sit tight and stay calm."

It was all Buck could do to keep from punching the man. "Hell, I've got a whole security team of ex-cops and ex-military at the resort. I'm calling them now to form a search party."

Buck stepped to one side and dialed Ed Clarkson, his chief of security. Clarkson, who'd once run the missing persons bureau in Tucson, promised to put every available man and woman on the search. "Most of us know your daughter, so we'll know who to look for," he said. "I'll get right on this."

"There's a school photo of Quinn in my office. You've got a key to the place. Make some copies and hand them out. And thanks, Ed." Buck paused to collect his thoughts. "I'll check her computer and call you if I find anything you need to know. Then I'll take the dog and check the canyon trails. She could've gone hiking and gotten lost or hurt."

"Good idea. I'll be in touch. Don't worry, Buck, we'll find her."

Buck ended the call, then scrolled down to Terri's number. Terri was dealing with a lot right now. But he had to bring her into this. She loved Quinn and would be concerned about her. She might even have some idea where the girl would have gone.

He tried the number. Nothing. If Terri had left her phone on during the river run, it made sense that the battery would be dead. Feeling strangely alone without her support, Buck slipped the phone back in his pocket. He'd needed Terri—needed to hear her voice, needed to share his fears with her and know she was there for him. Now all he could do was try her again later, after she'd had time to charge her phone. Right now he needed to check Quinn's computer.

Ignoring the scowl on the sheriff's face, he hurried up the stairs and down the hall to Quinn's bedroom. The sight of her ruffled bedcover and scattered cushions, her precious stuffed animals, and her fuzzy slippers tossed on the rug triggered an ache in his throat.

Pushing the emotion aside, he found Quinn's laptop on her desk and switched it on. Buck had insisted on knowing her password—thank heaven for that. He had no trouble getting into her texts and email.

He could've saved himself the trouble. Almost all of the messages and texts involved her girlfriends in Sedona. It was the usual schoolgirl chatter—nothing alarming, nothing to indicate that she'd met anyone new or was planning to go anywhere. Even her complaints about boredom and being monitored by Mrs. Calloway came as no surprise. Buck had known how she felt. The only message that caught his eye was a recent one to her mother, sent yesterday.

Hi, Mom. Daddy's gone again, this time on the river, for days. He didn't even say goodbye. He just called Mrs. C. and told her he had to go on a river run. Terri took me shopping last week, but Daddy was too busy to even look at what we bought. At least in Sedona I have my friends. I feel like a prisoner. I hate it here.

The words ripped into Buck's heart. He loved his daughter, and he'd had good intentions about spending time with her while she was in town. But good intentions weren't enough for a little girl who needed his time and affection. If anything had happened to Quinn, he'd have only himself to blame.

Lord, what was he going to tell Diane? Their marriage might have been a disaster, but she was a decent mother. If she knew her daughter was missing she'd be out of her mind with worry.

He would spare his ex-wife until he knew more, Buck resolved. Meanwhile, he'd learned all he could from Quinn's computer. It was time to get the dog and a flashlight and search the canyon. Picking up a discarded sock off the floor, he kept it to give the dog her scent. Murphy was no trained bloodhound, but he would recognize that scent as Quinn's, and he was protective of the girl. He might at least be able to hear her if she was in trouble.

Buck had never been a praying man, but as he passed the landing to go downstairs, he paused long enough to say a silent prayer for his daughter's safety. Wherever she'd gone, he vowed, he would find her.

Terri had spent half an hour at Canyon Shadows talking to the director. Her grandmother had passed away quietly, alone in her armchair with the TV blaring an old Lawrence Welk broadcast. One of the aides had discovered her when she'd gone in to bring dinner.

"There was nothing you could have done, dear." The director was an athletic fiftyish woman with glasses and dyed red hair that clashed with her purple pantsuit. "Nothing any of us could have done. It was her time. From the looks of the dear lady, I'd say she didn't suffer. We called the mortuary over in Hurricane, the one listed on the form you filled out. They've got her in their morgue, waiting for you to come make the arrangements." Her sharp gaze took in Terri's bloodshot eyes, matted hair and muddy clothes. "I'm sure that can wait till morning, dear. You look exhausted. Go home and get some rest."

Terri shook her head. "I'd rather get things settled now. Will somebody be there at this hour?"

"If you like, I can call them and find out." She reached for the phone.

An hour later, Terri was on her way back home. The funeral director had met her at the mortuary where she'd chosen a plain casket, arranged for a simple graveside service and paid with her credit card. The sad errand could have waited till tomorrow, but she hadn't wanted to leave it undone any longer. And if Buck decided to be "helpful," he'd be told that everything had been taken care of. She didn't need his guilt-driven charity.

Coming back into town, she turned off the main road and onto the narrow lane that led to her grandmother's neat little clapboard house—her house now, she supposed. It would make sense to sell it—the home wasn't worth much but it sat on an acre of choice land, prime for development.

Never mind, she could think about that later. Right now she was so tired she could barely hold her head up. All she wanted was to shower and pull on clean sweats, microwave the leftover lasagna in the fridge, open a beer and put her feet up.

Looking down the lane toward the house, Terri saw something that made her heart lurch. There were lights on inside, glowing through the kitchen and living room windows.

Had she forgotten to turn the lights off four days ago when she'd left to drive the truck to Lee's Ferry? It was possible, she conceded. It had been early, still dark outside, when she'd locked the house. And she'd been preoccupied, thinking about Buck. Still, it wasn't like her to go away and leave lights burning. She had to assume that someone had broken into the house—and that they could still be inside.

A half block from the house, she stopped the Jeep and turned off the headlights. With a dead phone, she couldn't call 911. She could always drive into town and get help. But she'd feel pretty silly if it turned out she'd left the lights on herself. She was going to need a closer look.

Taking care not to make a sound, she climbed out of the Jeep. There was a tire iron in the back. It wasn't a gun, but if she ran into trouble it would be better than no weapon at all.

She kept to the shadows as she neared the house. Nothing inside was worth stealing—the TV and her computer were old, her jewelry little more than odds and ends. But some homeless person, needing food and shelter, could have broken in. Gripping the tire iron, she tiptoed to the kitchen window and peered over the sill.

The light above the stove was on. There was no one in the room, but someone had definitely been here. A carton of milk, a bowl with a spoon in it and a box of cereal sat on the kitchen table. The cereal was a sugary brand that Terri didn't like. She'd bought it last year when Quinn slept over and hadn't touched it since.

Her hand loosened its grip on the tire iron. Acting on a hunch, Terri walked around to the back of the house. When she and Steve were kids, they'd adopted a small stray dog and had talked their grandmother into installing a pet entrance in the back door. The dog was long gone, but the swinging flap remained. The latch that held it shut would be easy to lift or break from the outside, especially for a certain little someone who had been to her house before and knew where to feel for it.

On the back porch, she crouched next to the pet door and gave it a gentle push. It swung freely. Terri began to relax.

She opened the back door with her key and walked into the kitchen. No one was there, but she could see the glow of a floor lamp in the living room. "Hello?" she called softly. No one answered.

Knowing she couldn't be too careful, she kept a grip on the tire iron as she walked into the living room. Fast asleep on the old sofa, under the crocheted afghan, was Quinn.

Terri laid the tire iron on the rug and dropped to her knees beside the sofa. Only then did she see the tearstains on Quinn's face. Buck's daughter had cried herself to sleep.

"Quinn, wake up!" Terri gave the girl's shoulder a gentle nudge.

With a little murmur, Quinn opened her eyes. "Hi, Terri," she said.

"What on earth are you doing here?" Terri was torn between hugging the girl and reading her the riot act.

Quinn sat up. "I was bored, and I wanted to see you. I thought maybe we could do something together."

"But how did you get here, Quinn? It's two or three miles, at least, from your father's house."

"I walked. I went the short way, on the old back road, but it still took me *forever*. Then you weren't here, and I was too tired to walk home. I would've called somebody to come get me, but Daddy won't let me have a phone. He says I'm not old enough."

Terri felt weak-kneed. Porter Hollow wasn't a big place, but with so many strangers around, anything could've happened to the girl. "Did you tell anybody where you were going?"

Quinn shook her head. "Mrs. C. would've stopped me. She treats me like a prisoner. Can't I stay here for a while?"

Terri rose to her feet. "Not another minute. Your dad and Mrs. Calloway will be frantic. I've got to take you home."

"Can't you just call them?" Quinn looked ready to cry again.

"I don't have a landline. My phone's dead and we don't

have time to recharge it. Come on." She took Quinn's hand and pulled her up. "Did you bring anything, like a backpack?"

Lower lip jutting, Quinn shook her head. "Aren't you at least glad to see me?"

"Oh, honey, of course I am!" Terri flung her arms around the pouting child. "I'm always glad to see you."

Quinn nestled against her. "You're not mad?"

"Not a bit. Just surprised and very glad you're okay."

"Then why can't I stay?"

"Because your dad will be looking for you. He'll be worried sick. Now come on, let's get you home."

Terri locked the house and rushed Quinn out to the Jeep. Avoiding the Main Street traffic, she took the back way to the canyon turnoff. Beside her in the passenger seat, Quinn was silent. Buck's daughter probably felt she'd been betrayed—that the one friend she'd turned to was hauling her home to be punished. Attempting to explain might be a waste of breath, but Terri knew she had to try.

"You know your father loves you, don't you, Quinn?"

"Does he? Then why does he leave me alone so much?"

Because he has a company to run and he has a lot of demands on his time. That was the first reply that popped into Terri's head. But she knew it wouldn't be enough for Quinn. She had to go deeper, to find an answer that would mean something to a lonely little girl.

"You know he's busy," she said. "But I think the real reason is that he doesn't understand how much you need him—or how much he needs you."

Quinn pondered a moment. "So how do we let him know that?"

Terri had turned the Jeep onto the canyon road. Ahead

she could see the lights of the house, blazing like a beacon in the night. "I'll give it some thought," she said, for want of a wiser answer. "You think about it, too. Maybe something will come to us."

The gate stood open. As she drove through, Terri could feel the tension flooding her body. After a cataclysmic fight and an awkward parting, she'd hoped for some private time to rest, recover and think about her future. But no such luck. Thanks to Quinn, she was about to face Buck again.

Buck had found no trace of Quinn in the canyon. Murphy had treated the whole outing as a romp, tugging at his leash, sniffing at squirrel holes and lifting his leg at every bend in the trail. After calling Quinn's name again and again, shining his flashlight over every foot of terrain, and twisting his knee when he slipped on a patch of loose rock, Buck had limped home, more worried than ever. He'd kept his cell phone on but no one had called. And he still couldn't reach Terri.

He could remember feeling this helpless only one other time in his life—that was the day Steve had been struck by a sniper's bullet and carried back to camp to die in Buck's arms.

He'd just stepped onto the porch when he spotted the familiar headlights coming up the driveway. His pulse quickened. He'd know that old Jeep anywhere. He didn't know why she was here, but maybe Terri would have some idea where Quinn might be.

As the Jeep pulled up to the house and stopped, and he saw the small figure in the passenger seat, his heart contracted with a pain that was almost physical. Rushing down the steps, he flung the Jeep's door open, unhooked her seat belt and pulled his daughter into his arms.

"Thank God you're all right," he muttered, hugging her close.

She squirmed, pulling back a little. "I'm fine, Daddy. I was just at Terri's house."

Terri came around the back of the Jeep then, still wearing the clothes she'd worn on the river. She looked tired enough to drop.

"What happened?" Buck demanded before she could open her mouth. "I've been worried sick. I've got the sheriff and my security people combing the town for her. And I've been trying to reach you for the past couple of hours. Why in hell's name didn't you call me, Terri?"

She stopped in her tracks, looking as if he'd slapped her. "Call off the search," she said in a cold voice. "Then I'll explain—that is, if you're willing to listen."

He eased Quinn to the ground. "Go tell Mrs. Calloway you're here," he said. "Have her get you some supper if you're hungry. I'll be inside in a few minutes."

As his daughter dragged her feet into the house, Buck made a couple of quick calls on his phone, letting the searchers know his daughter was safe. Then, still shaken, he turned back to Terri.

"Well?"

She told him what had happened—the dead battery in her phone and her decision to take care of her grandmother's arrangements before going home. "I walked into the house to find that Quinn had broken in through the old pet door and fixed herself some cereal. She was asleep on the sofa. I couldn't call you, so I woke her up and drove her here. And now that she's home safe, I'll be going. Forgive me, Buck, I've had a long, rough day, and you aren't making it any easier."

Turning away, she started walking back around the Jeep.

"Wait!" Buck said.

"Yes?" She turned slowly back to face him, her gaze frigid.

"I need to know this. Did Quinn say anything about why she ran away?"

"Yes, she did. It was partly because she was bored. But mostly because she doesn't believe you love her. Quinn adores you, and she wants time with her father. But except for that first night, all you've done is go off to work and leave her with Mrs. Calloway. When you left for the river you didn't even tell her goodbye. If I was your daughter, Buck Morgan, I would run away, too—fast and far!"

Terri's words stung—mostly because they were true. It had taken this scare to make Buck realize how badly he'd neglected his precious little girl. "You're right, Terri. I'm sorry," he started to say, but she cut him off.

"Don't apologize to *me*!" she snapped. "And don't stop at just an apology to Quinn. Before you know it, she'll be a young woman. If she doesn't get the attention she needs from you, she'll look for it someplace else—and find it. By then it'll be too late. Think about that when you go back in the house and start planning your week."

Her lower lip quivered. She was getting emotional. He hated it when women got emotional. "Why don't you come in and have some supper with us, Terri?" Buck said, hoping to calm her. "You must be hungry."

She shook her head. "I don't think that would be such a good idea."

"Then go on home and get some rest. Take a few days off for the funeral. Take a week, if you want. I can manage without my right-hand woman for a few days."

She sucked in her breath, looking as if she were about to explode. "You're going to have to manage a lot longer than that," she said. "Forget about the two weeks' notice I gave you. And forget about my doing the gala. I'm quitting as of right now."

Eight

Fighting tears, Terri drove down the canyon. She hadn't planned her farewell outburst. She'd wanted to leave Buck on friendly terms, not like this, in a storm of hurt and anger.

Should she apologize? Tell Buck she'd changed her mind and wanted more time to make plans? No, Terri told herself. What was done was done. The break she'd both needed and dreaded had been made. Why go back, and then have to do it again when the time came?

She'd meant to drive straight home. But her preoccupied mind hadn't been paying attention. By the time she realized where she was going, she was almost at the hotel complex that housed the Bucket List office. She slowed the Jeep, debating with herself. She was tired and she'd just made an emotional decision. She'd be wise to go home, get some rest and let things settle before taking action.

But why take the chance that she could go soft and change her mind? The office was empty now. She could let herself in, write up her resignation letter and leave it on Buck's desk. She could also go through her emails, deleting all but the most essential, and clean her personal items out of her desk. Buck would arrive in the morning to find her gone and everything in order.

She'd left the Jeep and was unlocking the office door when another wave of doubt overtook her. For the past ten years, her life had revolved around helping Buck run his business and his life. Now change was coming. She owed it to herself to let that change happen. She needed it to happen.

Still, letting go of everything familiar would be like closing her eyes and stepping off a precipice.

For almost half her life she'd been in love with Buck Morgan. She'd let her imagination build him into a romantic hero, excusing his faults and cleaning up after his mistakes. But tonight had opened her eyes and slammed her against the hard wall of reality. The man was an insensitive jerk with skewed priorities. The people who cared most about him—especially Quinn—were the ones he took most for granted. No wonder he'd never remarried after Diane. And no wonder his daughter had left the house this afternoon.

Walk away, she told herself as she turned the key in the lock. *Now, while the door's open, walk away and don't look back.*

It took her fifteen minutes to bring up her computer, compose a brief, impersonal letter of resignation and send it to the printer. It took another fifteen minutes to clean out her inbox and shut down her computer, collect a few personal items in a cardboard box, sign the letter, and leave it on Buck's desk, where he'd see it first thing tomorrow.

After securing Buck's door, she picked up the cardboard box, locked the outer office and walked to her Jeep. She'd put out some feelers a few days ago and already had a couple of job offers. After her grandmother was buried, she would make a final decision and start packing.

She was done here—finished with the job and the man. It was time to begin a new chapter in her life.

Buck arrived at work an hour early. With Terri on funeral leave—he refused to believe she'd really meant what she'd said about quitting—and with a four-day accumulation of phone messages and email to answer, the day was bound to be a busy one.

Parking the Hummer in its reserved spot, he whistled on his way to the outside door of his private office. He'd promised to take Quinn horseback riding after work. She'd given him a scare last night, but he didn't have the heart to punish her. He would show her a good time, they would forgive each other and all would be well in his world.

Stepping into the office, the first thing he noticed was the sheet of paper in the exact center of his desk. He picked it up. He read it. He swore out loud.

He read it again—the tersely worded letter of resignation, so cold, so formal. His jaw tightened. Maybe, just maybe, there was a way to end this nonsense. Striding into Terri's office, he opened the filing cabinet that held the personnel records for his employees. Since Terri had arranged the file folders in alphabetical order, finding the one he needed was easy. He took a quick look inside to make sure the folder contained what he needed. Then, clutching it in his hand, he locked the office, climbed into the Hummer and roared out of the parking lot.

Terri had returned home last night, taken a long, sudsy shower, pulled on an oversize cotton T-shirt and burrowed into bed. The next thing she knew, it was morning, and someone—or something—was pounding on her front door.

Throwing on the old blue terry cloth robe that had been Steve's, she stumbled across the living room to the door. A look though the tiny glass peephole was enough to make her wish she'd stayed in bed.

"Go away," she said loudly enough to be heard through the door. "I'm sleeping."

"I'm not going anywhere, Terri. Let me in." He sounded mad enough to kick the door down. Unhooking the chain and sliding back the bolt, she opened the door a few inches.

"Can't this wait?" she asked. "You just woke me out of the first decent sleep I've had in days."

"No, it can't wait, and I'm not leaving. So unless you want me to stand here and yell at you, you might as well let me in."

She opened the door. Spotlessly groomed and ready for the day, he stepped across the threshold like a conqueror taking possession. He'd spent a lot of time in this house when he and Steve were boys. But after his deployment, Terri couldn't remember his ever coming to visit. Had he stayed away because it held too many painful memories, or because he just never thought of it?

He glanced around the room, maybe thinking how little the place had changed. Terri noticed the personnel folder in his hand. It would be hers, of course. She should have realized this would happen. Too bad she wasn't better prepared.

He motioned toward the couch, his expression a thundercloud. "Sit down," he said. "I want to show you something."

He wasn't her boss anymore, Terri reminded herself. She didn't have to take his orders. But it wasn't worth arguing the point. She sat. He took a seat beside her, opened the folder and took out a one-page document with the Bucket List letterhead at the top.

"This is the employment contract you signed when you went to work for me," he said. "Read it. Pay special attention to paragraph three."

Terri sighed. She'd been over that document with every new hire at Bucket List. "I don't need to read it," she said. "I know what it says."

"Then you know you're *required* to give two weeks' notice."

"I did!"

"Not officially, in writing—not until last night."

"You're actually going to hold me to that?"

"You're damned right I am—even it means suing you for breach of contract."

Terri's jaw dropped. "You wouldn't dare!"

One dark eyebrow slithered upward. "Wouldn't I? Just try me, lady."

They glared at each other like two fighters going toe-to-toe. Then, abruptly, Buck exhaled and shook his head. "If you want to go, I won't stop you, Terri. But does it have to be like this, completely gone overnight, right in the heart of our busiest season? Damn it, don't you understand? I *need* you!"

If he'd raged and threatened all morning, nothing could've had as much effect as those last three words.

The only times Terri had heard them before was in connection with an order, as in *I need you to requisition more coffee.*

Unattached to anything else, the words struck Terri like a knife to the heart. But they didn't mean what she wanted them to mean, she told herself. All he really needed was her help at work.

"Two more weeks—just until the gala's over, that's all I'm asking," he said. "Give me that, and I'll give you a severance package to make your head spin—and I'll write a great recommendation to go with it."

"And if I leave now? If I don't come back at all?"

His mouth hardened. "I won't take you to court—it would be bad publicity for the company. But you walk away with nothing. Your choice."

Terri broke eye contact and gazed down at her hands. The reality was, the transition to a new job and the move to a new place would take time and money. Her grandmother's care had taken most of her savings. The funeral service would take the rest. The extra two weeks of work and the severance package Buck had promised could make all the difference for her. Pride had its price, and right now she couldn't afford it.

"When's your grandmother's service going to be?" He spoke as if he already knew he'd beaten her.

"Tomorrow—at the graveside. Just a simple ceremony. She had no living relatives except me, and most of her old friends are already gone." She met his cool gaze. "There's no reason I can't be back at work the next day. There'll be a lot to do before the gala." She gave him a steely look. "But since you brought up the subject of contracts, Buck, I want my severance terms in writing."

A look of surprise flashed across his face. Rising, he hid it quickly. "Fine. I'll write up an acceptance of your resignation and the terms of your severance and have it on your desk when you come in." He sounded like a stranger, this man she'd known since his boyhood. But that was how things would have to be from here on out.

He walked to the door, then paused. "I'm sorry about your grandmother, Terri. She was a fine lady, and she was very good to me." The door closed behind him. Seconds later Terri heard the sound of the Hummer starting up. The old Buck would have put his arms around her and given her a brotherly hug. But things had changed between them, perhaps forever.

Feeling as if he'd just been kicked by a mule, Buck drove back to the office. He'd gotten what he wanted—Terri's services for another two weeks. But the outcome of their meeting didn't feel like a victory. He could have told her how much he valued and appreciated her. Instead he'd bullied and threatened her into their agreement. He didn't like himself much right now. As Terri's late grandmother might have put it, he felt lower than a snake's belly.

When Terri came back, he would treat her right—give her the generous severance she deserved and write her a recommendation fit to win her the Nobel Prize for administrative assistants, if there was such a thing. And for the next two weeks he would be the very soul of kindness and respect. But after last night, Buck knew better than to think he could change her mind through any action on his part. And if he kept trying to manipulate her, he'd just drive her further away. Terri wanted more from life than what she'd found here in Porter Hollow. If he cared about her happiness he would ease the way for her to go.

But what was he going to do after she was gone?

Pulling into the parking lot behind the hotel, he

groaned. The big white Lincoln that Diane kept in a garage at the airstrip for her visits was parked outside his private office. Whatever had motivated his ex-wife to come all the way here, it couldn't be good.

For a moment he was tempted to turn around and leave. But no, better to get it over with, he told himself. The sooner he faced her the sooner he could finish their business and get on with the rest of his day.

Using the outside door, he walked into his office. Diane, immaculate in a white linen suit with a two-thousand-dollar designer scarf at her throat, was leaning back in his leather chair with her gold metallic Jimmy Choo sandals resting on his desktop. Her platinum hair curled softly around her face. She was showgirl tall, a woman who would have turned heads even without the surgical enhancements to her face and body.

"Hello, Buck." Her voice sounded like the growl of a tigress getting ready to pounce.

Buck remained on his feet. "This is a surprise. You could've called and let me know you were coming."

"Why should I? As part owner of this company, there's no reason I can't show up anytime I want."

"Can I order you anything, an iced tea, maybe?"

"Don't bother. This won't take long." She swung her feet to the floor and sat up. "I thought I should tell you before I went to your house. I'm here to take Quinn home."

That got his attention. "No!" He clenched his fist as her words sank in. "She's here for the summer. We have a legal agreement that says so." Even as he spoke, Buck remembered the email on Quinn's computer, telling her mother how miserable she was. Lord, how was Diane going to twist this against him?

"Legal agreements can be changed. You went off and left Quinn with the nanny for four days without even telling her goodbye. She was so unhappy that she ran away and was lost for hours."

"Who told you that?"

"Mrs. Calloway. She called me last night—said she had the child's best interest at heart."

Buck felt as if the cold jaws of a trap were closing around him—a trap he'd walked into blindly. He adored his daughter. It wasn't as if he'd wanted to leave her. But he simply hadn't paid enough attention to her needs. He'd made sure she'd be taken care of, and yet he hadn't bothered to do anything to make her *happy*. He'd set himself up for this, and now he was vulnerable. "It was an emergency," he said, realizing as he spoke how lame the excuse sounded.

"Yes, I understand." Her voice dripped sarcasm. "A business emergency. I've already called my lawyer to discuss suing for full custody, on the grounds that your work makes you unfit to be a father. He thinks we have a good chance of winning."

Buck fought down a surge of rage and panic. Leaving Quinn had been a bad decision. But he realized that now and had already resolved to change his behavior going forward. And anyway, she'd been safe and well cared for the whole time. Surely he didn't deserve to lose her for that.

"Even you wouldn't be that cruel," he said. "You know Quinn means the world to me."

"Does she?" Diane laughed. "You couldn't prove that by me, Buck."

He caught the glint of triumph in her jade-green eyes. She'd backed him into a corner, and she knew it. But something told Buck she hadn't chartered a flight and walked in here dressed to kill out of concern for Quinn. Yes, she loved her daughter—but if she truly wanted to take Quinn away from him, she'd have gone straight to his house, not to the office. Somehow, there was a business angle to this. One thing he'd learned during their brief marriage was that Diane was a master manipulator.

Eyes narrowing, he studied her. "What is it you really want, Diane?"

A smile curved her silicone-plumped lips. "That, my dear, depends on what *you* want. Maybe we can strike an agreement."

"I'll tell you what I want," Buck said. "I want you to leave Quinn here and forget this nonsense about suing for custody. You don't even want her full-time. Summers, when she's here with me, you're as free as a bird. You like it that way."

"Perhaps. But if it's in Quinn's best interest to be with me full-time…" She left the words dangling, the threat implied.

Buck struggled to cool his temper, knowing that if he exploded, the standoff would be lost. "All right," he said. "Tell me what it would take for you to back off."

Her calculating expression didn't change. "Another thousand a month in alimony might make a difference. Along with an additional two percent of the company."

Buck exhaled in disgust, knowing she'd planned this all along, and that short of giving up his daughter or going through months of legal wrangling, there was little he could do other than concede. "What the hell," he growled. "However it's split up, it'll all go to Quinn after we're gone. I'll have the papers drawn up."

"Don't bother." She unzipped her briefcase. "I have them right here. All you need to do is sign."

"You're unbelievable."

"I know." She smiled and held out a pen. Buck bent over the desk, scanned the document to make sure it held no surprises and scrawled his name. He could try to bargain her down to less, or even fight this in court if he had to, but right now all he wanted was to have her leave—without taking Quinn.

"I'll have Bob witness my signature and make a copy when he comes in, which should be any minute," he said.

"Where's Terri? Doesn't she usually handle that sort of thing?"

"Her grandmother passed away. The funeral's tomorrow."

Diane shrugged. "I suppose you can always fill her in later. She'll make sure the paperwork goes where it should. You wouldn't really trust Bob with it, surely?"

"I'm going to have to," Buck admitted through gritted teeth. "Terri will be back after the funeral, but she's put in her notice."

"Terri's leaving?" Diane's laugh was a derisive snort. "I can't even imagine that, after the way she's always mooned after you. Maybe she's finally come to her senses and realized she wasn't your type."

"What are you talking about?" Buck stared at his ex as if she'd just doused him with cold water.

Diane laughed again. "Are you blind? Don't you know the poor thing's been in love with you for years? Even when you and I were married, I could see it in the way she looked at you. I'm just surprised you haven't taken advantage and given her the thrill of a roll between the sheets." She cocked her head, gazing at him like a curious bird. "Good Lord, you haven't, have you?"

Heat flooded Buck's face. He turned away, hoping she wouldn't see the rush of color.

"Well, have you? Have you slept with that poor little plain Jane?"

Buck was tempted to put Diane and her superficial assumptions in her place. But telling her the truth would just open himself and Terri up to more ridicule. But really, Terri, a plain Jane? Not hardly.

Buck was saved from a lie by the sounds of Bob and the temps arriving for work. He opened the inside door of his office and called the young man inside to witness his signature and take the document to the copy machine.

"I'll be taking Quinn out for brunch before I leave," Diane was saying. "And maybe I'll fly in again for the gala. I'd love the chance to dress up and mingle. How would you like to be my escort?"

Buck stood in the doorway, waiting for Bob to return with the copy. "Sorry," he said, glancing back at her. "I already have a date."

"Oh, really?" Her eyes widened. "Who?"

Buck thought fast. "Terri."

Harriet Cooper's graveside funeral was sparsely attended. At ninety-one, the old woman had outlived most of her friends and family. Terri was there, of course, in a simple black knit dress and a black straw hat with a ribbon that fluttered down her slender back. Also in attendance were a couple of people from Canyon Shadows, the funeral director and the pastor of her church, who gave a eulogy and led the prayer.

Buck, who'd taken the chance and sent a spray of pink roses for the casket, had brought Quinn to the service. Since he'd dismissed Mrs. Calloway the day before and was wary of hiring anyone new who might also report back to Diane, he'd had little choice except to keep his daughter with him. Quinn, who'd never been to a funeral, had been curious enough to come along. Besides, she'd wanted to be there for Terri. Looking fresh and pretty in her white sundress, she'd stood quietly while the casket was lowered into the grave. She was bound to have questions later. Maybe they could have a good talk over lunch.

During the eulogy, Buck's gaze was drawn again and again to Terri. She stood at the graveside, hands clasped in front of her, eyes masked by her sunglasses. She looked tired and fragile, but all the same, he was struck by her beauty—a beauty of strength and integrity that went bone deep.

Are you blind? Don't you know the poor thing's been in love with you for years?

Diane's cutting words came back to him as he studied the woman who'd been at his side for more than a decade. Was that why she'd allowed herself to be lured into his bed—because she loved him?

Knowing Terri as he did, it was the only reason that made sense. Not that it could be allowed to make a difference. Whatever her feelings for him—and his for her—the past was unchangeable. Too much water under the bridge, as Harriet would have put it.

The service had ended. Terri walked toward her Jeep, then, as if remembering her manners, turned and came back toward Buck and Quinn. Buck hadn't spoken to her since their awkward parting at her house. Maybe it was time for some fence-mending. And maybe he really *should* invite her to the gala as his date. In the past she'd always worked the gala behind the scenes, making sure everything ran smoothly. This year, her last time, she deserved to put on a pretty gown and enjoy herself. Getting her to say yes might take some persuasion. But at least having Quinn here should make the asking easier.

"Thank you both for coming." She was polite, if cool. "And thank you for the flowers, Buck. You didn't have to do that, but I know grandma would have loved them. Pink roses were her favorite." Looking down at Quinn, she smiled. "You look so pretty, Quinn. Would you like a rose to keep for yourself?"

Quinn hesitated, as if thinking. "Thanks. But could I take two? I know what I want to do with them."

At Terri's nod, Quinn walked back to the grave and slipped two long-stemmed pink roses from the spray of flowers. As Buck and Terri watched, she carried them down the row of graves, paused and laid one rose next to Buck's mother's headstone. Then, crossing to the next row, she laid the other at the base of Steve's.

Buck could almost feel his heart being crushed. Terri's breath caught. Her fingers crept into his hand. He clasped them tightly as the memories slammed into him—his mother watching him walk away for the last time, and Steve, wounded and bleeding in his arms, the light fading from his eyes.

I'm sorry, Mom. And I'm sorry, Steve. Oh, God, so sorry. That should be my grave, not yours, Steve, your child, not mine. If only I could take your place now, like you took mine back then...

Before Buck could continue the thought, Quinn came dancing back to him, a smile on her face.

"That was a lovely thing to do, Quinn," Terri said, and pulled her hand away from Buck's. "Thank you for remembering my brother today—and your grandmother, too."

"Daddy told me Steve was his best friend," Quinn said.

"That's right." Biting back his emotion, Buck laid a hand on her small, suntanned shoulder and changed the subject. "Quinn and I were about to go to lunch at the Ledges. Why don't you come with us, Terri?"

He sensed a flicker in her eyes. He'd been pretty hard on her yesterday. He wouldn't blame her if she said no.

"Please come with us, Terri," Quinn begged, tugging at her hand. "It'll be lots more fun with you there!"

Quinn could be irresistible when she wanted something. Right now, Buck was grateful for it. Terri gave in with a smile. "All right. Come to think of it, I'm pretty hungry—starving, actually."

The Ledges was an upscale restaurant on the road out of town. Its floor-to-ceiling windows, as well as an outside deck, let customers enjoy a stunning panorama of towering red-and-white sandstone cliffs while they dined on organic gourmet meals. Since Buck was part owner of the place, he and his guests could expect VIP treatment.

Terri scanned the lunch menu, pondering the soup-and-salad combos. Beside her, Quinn was chattering nonstop.

"Now that Mrs. C. is gone, Daddy says that if I behave I can come to work with him and help out—run errands, keep the break room neat, stuff like that. It'll be like having a real job. Maybe I'll even get paid." She cast a plaintive look at her father.

"That's open to negotiation," Buck replied with a mock scowl.

"I can help you, too, Terri," she said. "Daddy always says you're his right-hand woman. Maybe I can be his right-hand girl."

"That sounds like a fine idea," Terri said, thinking Buck must not have told his daughter she was leaving in two weeks. How her going would affect Quinn would be one more issue to deal with—and a reason to be glad she hadn't just walked away.

The server took their orders and brought their drinks. Sitting across from Terri, Buck took a sip from his glass, then cleared his throat. "Terri, I brought you here with an ulterior motive," he said. "I have a favor to ask, and I hope you'll say yes."

Terri's instincts prickled. "That depends on what it is."

"It's about the gala," he said. "Every year you've worked behind the scenes and done a terrific job. This year I'd like you to come out front and cohost the event with me."

Terri's first reaction was a mild panic. She had her share of experience mixing with wealthy politicians and celebrities when they came to the resort as guests. But her role as part of the staff always provided a bit of a barrier. Cohosting the gala, that barrier would be gone. What if she made a fool of herself? She scrambled for excuses.

"Have you thought this through, Buck? How can I do my job if I'm out front socializing?"

"Bob can manage things if you show him what to do. You'll have two weeks to train him."

Terri shook her head. "I don't know if he can do it. Besides, I don't have anything to wear."

"That's an easy fix," Buck said. "Buy yourself an outfit. Charge it to the company. It's a legitimate work expense."

Quinn had been all ears. "Take me shopping with you, Terri! I'll help you pick out a dress! You'll be like Cinderella at the ball!"

Two against one. Terri could feel herself folding. "I still don't think it's a good idea," she said to Buck.

"You'll do fine. Now stop worrying and eat your salad." His eyes twinkled. "That's an order."

Nine

With three days to go, Terri's plans for the Seventh Annual Bucket List Gala were falling into place. The hotel's convention facilities included a large elegant ballroom where the party would be held. The restaurant staff would provide the food and drinks, an updated version of the customary gala menu that would include a few surprises. The music and entertainment had been booked more than a year in advance, the RSVP invitations mailed out six weeks earlier.

Bob had been carefully trained to coordinate everything behind the scenes. It would be a huge responsibility. Terri was already running him through his paces like an army drill sergeant. The young man was bright and capable when he put his mind to the task. She only hoped she could trust him to stay focused and do his best.

Between the gala preparations and her regular office

duties, Terri had scarcely thought of the one urgent task that remained—shopping for a gown.

It was Quinn who reminded her. "We can go today after work," Buck's daughter said, taking charge. "Can I invite Ann Marie to come with us?"

"Sure. We'll make a party of it. Ice cream for all when we're done," Terri said. Ann Marie, Evie Redfeather's nine-year-old grandniece, was visiting for the summer. She and Quinn had become fast friends. They'd be having a sleepover at Evie's the night of the gala.

When Buck heard about the plan he insisted that they leave work an hour early. They picked up Ann Marie at Evie's and headed for the outlet mall where Terri had taken Quinn earlier to buy clothes. Buck had given her carte blanche on choosing a gown, but Terri was too practical to spend a lot of money on a dress she'd wear only once. At the mall there was a discount shop that sold bridal and formal wear. With luck, it wouldn't take too long to find something suitable.

But she hadn't counted on trying to please two little fashionistas. Quinn and Ann Marie, seated on folding chairs, insisted that Terri try on and model every gown in her size.

They shook their heads when she walked out in a plain, modest black sheath that Terri might have bought if she'd been there alone. And they hooted with laughter when she showed off a purple bridesmaid dress with big puffy sleeves, followed by a strapless, ruffled pink prom gown. The next dress wasn't bad style-wise, but the lime-green color made her look ill. By the end of an entertaining hour, all three had to admit there wasn't a wearable gown in the place. Now what?

"I know," Quinn said. "There's a boutique in town where my mom likes to shop. Let's look there."

Terri suppressed a groan. She wasn't keen on anything that might look like Diane, and she could just imagine what a dress from that place might cost. But with two pairs of small hands tugging her toward the Jeep, she gave in.

Most of the gowns at the boutique, though beautiful, were too flashy for Terri's taste. But when she tried on a simple, soft teal silk that draped her body like mist, her two little critics jumped up and cheered. She'd found her perfect dress. But when she checked the price, she almost fainted. It was the most expensive gown in the exclusive shop.

She was handing it back to the saleslady to put away when Quinn gave her ribs a none-too-gentle nudge. "Go for it, Terri!" she ordered. "Daddy said you could buy anything you wanted on the company credit card. Besides, you've earned this."

Absolved of guilt, Terri reached into her purse and pulled out the plastic. She had a pair of dangly gold earrings at home that would look fine for the night. And although the dress begged for new gold sandals, she knew she'd be on her feet a lot. Covered by the long skirt, her comfy black pumps would barely show.

Terri paid for the dress and came back to find the girls whispering together. "We want to do your hair for the party," Quinn announced. "Come to Ann Marie's before you get dressed. Don't worry. We're *really* good!"

Terri had planned on going to the hotel beauty shop, or even just washing her hair and letting it hang loose. But the two little girls looked so eager and excited to play fairy godmother. What could it hurt? Why not let them have fun?

"Sure," she said. "Now let's go get ice cream."

* * *

After dropping both girls off at Evie's, Terri drove home. The day had been a long one, and for some reason, trying on all those gowns had left her exhausted. All she wanted was to curl up on the bed and go to sleep. But she still had things to do, and resting now would only keep her awake at night.

Entering the spare bedroom she'd converted to an office, she switched on her computer. Bringing up her email, she scanned the messages—mostly junk, but one jumped out at her. The managers of a big ski resort in Park City wanted to hire her. Since they needed someone right away, they wanted her to come and make arrangements at the earliest possible date.

The drive to Park City and back could be made in one very long day, or two shorter days. But there was no way she could go before the gala. She composed a reply to the message, suggesting a time early next week. It would be an ideal situation for her. Park City was a fair-sized town in a picturesque setting, with year-round social and cultural activities. She'd never skied, but she could learn.

She clicked the send button and put the computer in sleep mode. She really should finish checking her emails. But she was worn out tonight. The idea of getting into her pajamas, washing her face, brushing her teeth and watching a couple hours of mindless TV sounded like just what she needed.

Barefoot and dressed in her sweats, she pattered into the bathroom, wiped off the little makeup she wore and reached for her toothbrush. She'd thrown away the crumpled, empty toothpaste tube that morning, but she'd bought a fresh tube a couple of weeks ago and put it in the bathroom closet.

Opening the closet door, she scanned the shelves. There was the toothpaste, right next to…

Her heart dropped as her eyes fixed on the unopened box of tampons—the box she'd bought the same time as the toothpaste and expected to have needed before now. She'd never been 100 percent regular, but unless her calculations were off, her period was almost ten days overdue.

Lord have mercy, could she be pregnant with Buck's baby?

It was stress, that was all, Terri told herself as she drove to work the next day. Between the river trip, losing her grandmother, the upcoming gala and the unsettling situation at work, she was a bundle of nerves. The anxiety could have delayed her period. That, or she'd just lost track of the days and her count was off.

If she had serious concerns, she could always buy a home pregnancy test. But surely it was too soon for that. Any day now, her period would start, and she'd know she'd been worried for nothing. Meanwhile, if she could, she'd put it out of her mind. She was dealing with enough right now.

She'd arrived ahead of the staff, but the inside door to Buck's office was standing open. As she walked past, he stood, walked around his desk and motioned her inside.

"Have a seat, Terri. The restaurant just brought coffee. Let me pour you a cup." He picked up an insulated carafe from the silver tray on the credenza. "Cream with no sugar, right?"

"You should know by now." Terri settled into a chair facing the desk and took the steaming porcelain mug he offered her. The coffee was hot and good, but it failed to warm the cold spot in the pit of her stomach. In a few days' time, this job and this man would be part of her past. She should be excited at the prospect of a new life. But right now the thought of not seeing him every work-day, perhaps not seeing him ever again, made her feel as if she was lost without a compass.

One decision had been made in the dark of last night. If she really did turn out to be pregnant—which she al-most certainly wasn't—she would leave town without telling him. She'd had a front-row seat for his miser-able shotgun marriage to Diane—and she'd seen how the woman continued to manipulate him, using Quinn. For Buck to marry yet another woman out of duty to his child, a woman he didn't love, would be unthinkable, both for her and for him.

Buck sat down again. "You look a little frayed. Is ev-erything all right?"

"Fine," she lied.

"How are plans for the gala going? Quinn told me you finally bought a dress."

"Yes, I did. It's beautiful. And I've agreed to let Quinn and Ann Marie do my hair."

"You're one brave lady." A smile lit his sky-blue eyes and deepened the dimple in his cheek. If she really was pregnant, her baby had won the gene pool lottery, Terri mused, then quickly banished the thought.

"They were so excited about helping me get ready, I couldn't refuse," she said. "If my hair looks a little strange, I'll just call it a fashion statement."

"If you don't like it, you can always take it down be-fore the gala."

"No way. I'll wear it proudly."

His gaze warmed. "I can't imagine any other woman doing that," he said. "You're amazing."

He was getting to her. Terri squelched a rush of emotion. "Have you told Quinn I'm leaving?" she asked, changing the subject.

"I thought I'd let you do that."

Coward, she thought, then spoke. "Quinn might take it hard. I've always been here for her. I can tell her, but you'll want to give her some extra TLC just to make sure she's all right."

"We could always have a farewell dinner before you go, just the three of us," Buck said.

"I may not have time for that." She told him about the job offer in Park City. "They want somebody right away. If I decide to take it, I'll barely have time to pack my things and put the house on the market."

"So soon?" He looked stunned. "I'll give you a great recommendation if they ask, of course. But it's still sinking in that you're really doing this."

"For me, too," Terri said, then rose before he could strip away her fragile self-control. "I think I just heard Bob come in. Time for me to crack the whip."

Buck watched her walk out of his office, painfully aware that soon she would walk out of his life. Lord, what would he do without her? How would it feel the first time he came into work and it hit him that she was really gone?

In so many ways, Terri was irreplaceable. Where else would he find a woman who looked spectacular coated with river mud, a woman who could navigate a rapid, pack a parachute, skydive out of a plane and guide novice hikers through a slot canyon—a woman who would trust two little girls to fix her hair for a formal event where she'd want to look her best?

And what other woman would wake him out of a drug-fogged sleep with loving as tender and passionate as any he'd ever known? He would never forget the morning

Terri had stolen into his bed. But he was less sure how and when she'd also crept into his heart.

Buck backed his black Jaguar out of the garage and drove down the canyon to pick up Terri for the gala. It was raining—not a cloudburst but a fine mist that cooled the summer darkness and softened the lights along Main Street. In this desert country, rain was always welcome, even on the night of the biggest charity event of the year.

Terri had insisted that this was work, not a date. So why did Buck feel like a high school boy on prom night as he rang her doorbell and waited on the covered stoop for her to answer? He'd driven himself a little crazy trying to imagine Terri in an evening gown. In the years he'd known her, she'd worn mostly jeans or school clothes, or her khaki work uniform. Even the black dress she'd worn to her grandmother's funeral had been little more than a long T-shirt with a belt. But she was a beautiful woman. In the right dress she would look stunning.

He rang the doorbell again. There was a rustle of movement on the other side; then the door opened. Terri stood before him wearing a black nylon rain poncho with the hood covering her hair. He exhaled in disappointment. The unveiling would have to wait.

"Sorry the yard's such a muddy mess," she apologized. "You could've stayed in the car, honked me out and saved your shoes."

"I've never honked a girl out in my life," Buck said. "And I never will. You deserve better than that."

"An old-fashioned gentleman! Who'd have thought?" She flashed him a dazzling smile as she locked the door. "You look smashing in that tux, by the way."

"I'll return the compliment when I can see more of you." He ushered her into the Jag, closed the door and went around to the driver's seat. "We should get there just in time to check everything over before the guests start arriving."

She snuggled into the soft leather seat. "I just hope Bob will be all right. Otherwise, I'll have to take over and help him."

"Don't even think about it. He'll do fine. Your job tonight is to charm our guests and talk them into extra digits on their donation checks." Closing the door he gave her a sidelong glance. All he could see was the hood of her poncho and the tip of her nose just visible past the edge. "It isn't raining in the car," he said, hoping she'd take the hint.

"But it might be raining when we get to the hotel." Was she teasing him? If so, it was working. He was wild to see her out of that blasted poncho. He only hoped he could keep his hands off her.

They pulled up to the hotel's covered main entrance, where a valet was waiting to take the car and park it. Buck took Terri's hand to help her out of the car. The light grip of her fingers recalled that moment after the funeral when Quinn had placed a rose on Steve's grave. He remembered how Terri's fingers had crept into his palm, so trusting, as if seeking comfort. How he'd wanted to give her that comfort and more. But he couldn't have done that without lying to her.

He wanted this woman, damn it—wanted her in his bed and in his life. But it was useless to hope. She was already moving on, and the tragic truth he'd be honor-bound to share before he could even attempt a real relationship with her would destroy any chance of lasting happiness.

Still covered in her poncho, she crossed the hotel lobby with him. The coat check window was next to the ballroom entrance. Buck paused, turned to face her and, without a word, unfastened the snap at her throat and swept the poncho off her shoulders.

She took his breath away.

The sleeveless gown was simple perfection. The silk fabric was draped to follow the curves of her glorious body, allowing an ample glimpse of cleavage at the bodice, then clinging downward to a point above her knees, where it flared into a softly flowing skirt. Mermaid style, Diane would have called it, if Buck remembered right.

Terri wore no jewelry except a pair of shoulder-skimming golden earrings—probably not even real gold, but they were enough. Her sun-burnished skin, glowing against the deep teal silk, was all the dazzle she needed.

Her hair—he might have chosen to see it loose and flowing, but he had to admit her young stylists had done an impressive job. French braids swept her long chestnut locks back from the sides of her face to join at the nape of her neck in a single loose braid woven with strands of thin gold ribbon.

"What do you think?" She looked at him, so adorably self-conscious that Buck wanted to sweep her into his arms and show her the effect she was really having on him.

He found his voice. "You look amazing. My compliments to your hairdressers."

"They did all right, didn't they? And they had so much fun." She glanced at her wrist before she realized she wasn't wearing a watch. "Let's get busy. The doors will be opening soon."

Even looking like a goddess, she was all business. Buck trailed her through the back rooms, where she spoke with the serving, security and electrical crews, then touched base with Bob and went over his checklist.

"Wow, you look great!" the young man said.

She gave him a self-effacing smile. "Thanks, but it's just work, Bob. Everything you've done looks good, but in case you need me, I'll be right out front."

"Don't worry, he'll manage fine, Terri." Buck pulled her back down the hall toward the ballroom. "Now stop fussing and breathe. Yes, you've got a job to do, but this is your last gala. I want you to have a good time tonight."

"Is that an order, boss?"

"Absolutely." He linked his arm through hers and led her into the empty ballroom. Everything here was in readiness. The oak floor was polished to a golden gleam. The three immense crystal chandeliers blazed with light. The tables that ringed the dance floor were set with candles, crystal and silver, the buffet tables and the long antique bar at the far end fully stocked and ready.

The quartet of jazz musicians, who traveled with the legendary singer Terri had been lucky enough to book, were just warming up. Little riffs floated off the keys of the grand piano. Soft blues notes rose from the saxophone, trumpet and bass. The players in this jazz ensemble were among the best in the world. It had cost a small fortune to bring them here, fresh from a major gig in Las Vegas. But nothing was too good for the gala.

Buck could sense the tension that radiated from Terri's body as she mentally micromanaged everything. *Let it go*, he wanted to tell her. *With you on my arm, I'll be the envy of every man in the ballroom. Just relax and let me show you off.*

Struck by a sudden inspiration, he turned her toward him. "Stay right here," he said. "Don't move an inch till I get back." He strode across the floor to where the band was ending its warm-up. Stepping in close, he introduced himself and asked for a special favor.

The four musicians grinned and nodded. "Anything for the lady," the piano player said.

The music started as Buck walked back to where Terri waited. The intro began on the tinkling piano, then the bass started throbbing a sensual underbeat. The trumpet and saxophone took up the mellow strains of "At Last," and Buck faced Terri and held out his hand. "Dance with me," he said.

Her lips parted, but she didn't speak as he drew her into his arms. She was a little stiff and self-conscious at first, but as he pulled her close enough to be guided by his body, she softened against him, slipping into the beat of the music.

Her satiny cheek rested against his. He breathed her in, filling his senses with her sexy-clean, womanly aroma. Her curves skimmed his body, the contact hardening his arousal. There was no way she couldn't be feeling it. But she didn't pull away. He'd made love to this woman, Buck reminded himself. He'd been inside her—and damn it all, he ached to be there again. But that was the least of what he was feeling now. How could he let her go after tonight? How could he watch her walk away, knowing that even if he saw her again, she would no longer be part of his life?

She tilted her head to smile up at him. "I feel like Cinderella at the ball," she whispered.

Buck's arm tightened around her waist, pulling her closer. It would be heaven to hold her like this forever, he thought. But he was no prince. And like in the fairy tale, the enchantment would be fated to end when the ball was over.

Terri closed her eyes, savoring these last few moments in Buck's arms. Soon the song would end. Soon the doors to the ballroom would open and the streams of glittering guests would begin flowing in. In the hours ahead it would be her job to make sure everyone was welcomed, and to talk up the children's clinics, homeless shelters and other charities the gala supported. Tomorrow she would pack for the drive to Park City and organize the house for a possible move. But now, for this brief flicker of time, she was in his arms, and he was hers. Until the music ended and the ballroom doors opened to let in the guests, nothing else mattered.

The event started promptly at eight o'clock and ran smoothly from beginning to end. For Terri, the hours passed in a blur of greeting guests that included the governor and state officials, business and community leaders, TV and movie personalities, and a host of other wealthy donors As the party continued, she'd left Buck's side over and over again to work the floor, making sure everyone felt at home and had what they needed—a drink, a pen, directions to the restroom or a good seat for the entertainment. She'd seen enough galas to know what had to be done.

By the time the crowd was thinning out, Terri's smile felt pasted on. Her feet had gone numb, and she was so tired she could barely stand. As the last guests trickled out the door, she made her way to Buck's side. He gave her a smile, looking as fresh and energetic as when he'd walked in.

"Sit down," he said. "You look ready to drop."

"I am." She sank onto a handy chair. "Will we need to stay for the cleanup?"

"No, Bob can make sure everything's shipshape. He's done a good job tonight. Remind me to give him a raise on Monday." His expression froze as his eyes met Terri's. She could guess what he was thinking. She wouldn't be around to remind him of *anything* on Monday. She would be gone.

"Come on, we don't need to stay." He extended his hand to help her up. A word from him summoned an attendant with her poncho. He laid it gently over her shoulders as they walked out a side entrance. The black Jaguar waited in the shadows, where he must have told the valet to leave it.

"You were wonderful tonight," he said as he opened the door for her. "Thank you."

"I was just doing my job." She settled into the cushiony leather seat as he walked around the car and climbed in on the driver's side. Terri steeled herself for the drive home and what could be their final goodbye. Whatever happened, she told herself, she would not cry until he was gone.

"Your job? Was that all it was?" He touched her shoulder. "Look at me, Terri."

Despite her resolve, the tears were already welling— tears that refused to hide as she turned to face him. His cupped hand lifted her chin as he leaned in to kiss her, gently at first, then, in a release of passion that was like the bursting of a dam, he crushed her close, his mouth possessing her, stirring deep urges that were too strong to resist.

"Come home with me, Terri." His voice was a rough whisper. His lips skimmed hers as he spoke. "Come just for tonight. Let me make love to you."

Terri struggled to speak, then realized there was nothing to say. She wanted what he wanted, and he would know it without a word.

Ten

Rain drummed on the roof of the Jaguar, trickling in silver streams down the side windows as the sleek black car wound its way up the canyon. Terri sat in trembling silence, stealing glances at Buck's chiseled profile. Her pulse skittered as she remembered his words.

Come just for tonight. Let me make love to you.

At least he wasn't playing games. He'd stated his intentions and made it clear that there wouldn't be another time after this. Delicious sex with no strings attached. Wasn't that what they both wanted? After so many years together, wasn't it as good a way as any to say goodbye?

He pulled through the gate and up the driveway. A touch on the remote opened the garage. He pulled inside and closed the door behind them. From there, they entered through a door into the back hallway off the kitchen. Terri knew Buck's house well. But she'd never been here in the middle of the night, on her way to the man's bed.

She'd expected him to lead her to the stairs, but they were still in the hallway when he stopped, stripped off her poncho and pulled her to him. His kiss was pure seduction, slow, languorous and deliciously intimate. With exquisite restraint, his tongue glided along the rim of her lower lip, then, as she opened to him, slipped into her mouth to play with the tip of hers. His touch ignited a warm shimmer that flowed downward through Terri's body, heating like molten lava as it pooled in the deepest part of her. Her hands framed his head, fingers tangling in his hair as she pulled him down to deepen the kiss. Her body curled against his, hips pressing into an erection that was already big and hard.

He laughed mischievously, his lips moving down her throat to delve into the moist hollow between her breasts. "Take it easy, lady," he whispered. "We've got all night, and I plan to see that you enjoy every minute."

Not until Terri was in his arms did Buck realize how much he'd wanted her there. Something about the way her curves molded to his, her strength, her sweet, willing warmth, made him feel as if he'd come home. Holding her was as natural as breathing—coupled with a rush that was like the first few seconds of free fall in an early-morning skydive. Lord, but she felt good.

He'd made love to her once before, and it had been wonderful. But it had been nowhere near enough.

"We're in the wrong place," he murmured against the fragrant curve of her neck. "Come on, I've got a better idea."

With a rough laugh he kissed her again, then caught her in his arms, swept her through the dark living room and half carried her up the stairs. They reached the landing and stood breathless for a moment, looking out the high window at the night sky. The storm was moving east, the clouds thinning to show patches of starry sky. "It's beautiful," Terry whispered.

"So are you." He nibbled the tip of her ear. "I've been wanting you all night—no way I could've just taken you home and let you go. But now…" His gaze swept the expanse of the sky. "We've got all night if we want."

Tossing aside his tux jacket, he tugged her down beside him on the top step, where they could sit in full view of the night sky above towering canyon walls. Under different conditions, this would be a good time to talk. But he knew better than to tell her what he was feeling. The words he needed to say would spoil this moment completely. The less said the better.

Pulling her close, he kissed her, going deep with his tongue. By now his blood was pounding and his erection was threatening to burst through a seam, but he willed himself not to hurry, not even when she responded with a moan and wiggled her hips closer.

His hand reached down and slid up her leg, half expecting to find pantyhose. But Terri's sleek, tanned legs were bare. The surprise kicked his pulse into overdrive. He kissed her again, sliding his hand up to the crotch of her panties. Her breath caught as he fingered the fabric, stroking her through the thin silk.

She arched upward to meet his hand. "Touch me," she whispered. "I want you to."

"I can do more than that," he muttered. Easing her back onto the landing he knelt two steps below her, slid her panties off her legs, hiked up the narrow part of her skirt and lowered his head.

"Oh—" She gasped in wonder as his tongue found the spot. "Nobody ever…did that to me…before…" She moaned as he savored the sweet-salty taste of her, feeling the tiny nub swell beneath his touch. Her fingers tangled in his hair as she swam in the new sensation. "That feels so…so…" The words trailed off as he brought her to a shuddering climax.

"Come here, you." She seized his shoulders, drawing him up for a lingering kiss. Seeing her like this, so warm and playful and eager, tugged at his heart. He would trade anything for the chance to pamper her, make her happy and give her everything her heart desired. Reason told him that chance was already gone. But at least they had tonight. He would make the most of it.

By now, all thought of taking it slow had evaporated. He wanted her—wanted her now, cloaking his sex in her hot, tight body, meeting his thrusts with her own. Standing, he pulled her to her feet. His hands ranged hungrily over her silk-clad curves, molding her breasts, pressing her hips in hard against him. She was equally eager as she tugged his shirt open. Her urgency sent buttons clattering to the floor and bouncing down the stairs.

Searching, his fingers found the zipper tab that opened her gown down the back. He gave it a firm tug. The zipper parted about eight inches, then stuck. He pulled again, then yanked. The zipper wouldn't budge.

She gazed up at him, mischief in her eyes and a smile teasing her luscious mouth. "Rip it," she said.

They left a trail of clothes and shoes all the way down the hall to the bedroom.

Buck opened his eyes. It was early yet, with sunrise casting a rosy glow through the shutters. Lying here with Terri in his arms, he felt physical contentment to the marrow of his bones. He'd had other women, more than he cared to remember, but never one who matched his desire the way Terri did. Last night had been more than sex. It had been as if their souls were making love.

He wanted to do it again, every night for as long as he lived. He wanted to build the kind of life she was leaving him to find—to give her children who'd be brothers and sisters for Quinn, to share adventures as a family, to love and support and cherish each other for all time.

But as the dawn faded from rose to gray, he knew the odds of that dream coming true were all but hopeless. He was in love with Terri, and he sensed that she loved him, too. But the secret of his past would always stand between them. Even if he never told her, the silent lie would be there, lurking like a hidden poison—and if she were to find out what he'd kept from her, she would never forgive him.

Propping his head on one arm, he gazed down at her. She was so lovely in the soft light, her rich chestnut hair framing her face in silky tendrils, her lashes like velvet fringe against her warmly freckled cheeks. The lips that had returned his kisses with so much passion were moist and ripely swollen. He ached to lean over, capture those lips and begin again where they'd left off. But she looked so peaceful in sleep, and waking her would mean getting up out of bed, pulling on some clothes, driving her home and saying goodbye, maybe forever.

He loved her. He wanted her for keeps. There had to be a way. Why couldn't he find it?

And then, suddenly, he knew.

He had to tell her the truth.

What were the odds that she'd hate him for it? Pretty damned high. And the fact that he'd kept it from her all these years would only make things worse. She'd probably leave and never speak to him again. But if he wanted a life with her, he would have to take the chance and weather the consequences.

Terri was already aware that her brother had died from a sniper's bullet while on patrol. But telling her *why* would be one of the hardest things he'd ever done— and the biggest gamble he'd ever taken.

He would tell her this morning—but not here, in this bed, where they'd made love.

Warm and sleepy, she stirred beside him. Her eyelids fluttered open. "Hi," she murmured, smiling.

"Hi," he said. "You're a goddess when you're sleeping, did you know that?"

"Silly, how would I know?" She gave a little shake of her head as he leaned closer. "No kissing till I clean my teeth. I promise you won't like the taste of me."

He sat up. "I loved the taste of you last night. But if we start kissing, I'll never let you out of my bed, and we need to get the day started. What would you say to some breakfast?"

"Sounds good. But I don't have anything to wear."

Buck glanced down at her crumpled silk evening gown on the floor. It wouldn't be comfortable to put back on, even if he hadn't managed to break the zipper getting her out of it. "I've got some spare sweats," he said. "The bottoms have a drawstring, so they won't fall down on you—not that I'd mind."

Naked, he slipped out of bed and moved to his walk-in closet, where he found what he was looking for. Grabbing one set of sweats for himself, he tossed a second set onto the bed for her.

She laughed, watching him without a trace of embarrassment. "Oh, darn, you're getting dressed? I was just enjoying the view. Did anybody ever tell you how delectable you look from the rear?"

"You're shameless." Adoring her, he pulled on the sweatpants. He could tell she was already putting on a brave face, readying herself for the parting they both dreaded.

If nothing else, maybe what he had to tell her would make that parting easier.

"Go ahead and put yourself together," he said. "I'll be downstairs cooking you some bacon and eggs."

"And a big mug of coffee, please. I need it this morning."

"You've got it." He strolled out of the room and down the stairs, thinking how comfortable it was, being with Terri. He could be happy making breakfast for her every morning of their lives. But that wasn't something he could count on. He needed to prepare himself for the worst.

Downstairs, he went out back and checked on Murphy, giving the big mutt a morning ear scratch and refilling his water and kibble bowls. Then he came back inside, washed his hands, and started the bacon and coffee. From overhead, he could hear Terri running the guest room shower. He whistled as he worked, trying to take his mind off the urge to race upstairs and join her.

He was just adding grated cheddar to the scrambled eggs when she came downstairs, her face damp and glowing. She'd taken the braids and ribbon out of her hair, letting it hang loose around her shoulders. "All ready," he said, dishing up the eggs, then pulling out her chair. "Have a seat."

She sat. He poured coffee for both of them and took his seat across from her. She sipped her coffee, her copper-flecked eyes meeting his across the table. She looked so vulnerable, and now he was about to hurt her. Lord, how was he going to do this?

"I don't want you to leave," he said. "You know that, don't you?"

"You've made that clear." She glanced down at her breakfast, poking at her eggs as if she'd suddenly lost her appetite. "But my life hasn't changed in ten years. If I don't do something different, it never will."

"There's no reason your life couldn't change here, if you opened yourself to it." He was stumbling now, saying everything except what he'd planned to say.

"My mind's made up," she said. "If that job offer in Park City looks good, I'm taking it. It's time, Buck. I can't stay here any longer."

"Well then, I'll just have to respect your decision." He took a ragged breath, then plunged ahead. "Terri, there's something I've held back all these years because I didn't know how to tell you. Now that you're leaving, this may be my last chance to let you know how sorry I am."

She looked startled. Then her face took on a resolute expression. "I can't imagine what it would be. But if there's something you need to say, I'm listening."

"It's about Steve and how he died."

He glimpsed the look of pain that flickered across her face. Some wounds, he knew, never healed.

"You know he was shot," he said, "and you know he was carried back to camp, where he died. What you don't know is that what happened was my fault."

Her lips moved, shaping each word with effort. "What do you mean?"

Buck took a breath, then began the story he'd never told anyone before, not even Diane.

"Steve had gone on patrol the night before. He wasn't scheduled to go out the next morning. I was. But I woke up at dawn with a splitting migraine—I still get them, as you know."

"Yes, I know."

"But never as bad as the one I had that morning. I was so sick I was throwing up. I could barely see to get dressed, but I got my gear and suited up, determined to go anyway. Then somebody told our lieutenant. He looked me over and said I'd be useless out there if I couldn't see to shoot. He called for a volunteer to take my place."

"And Steve volunteered." Her voice was a whisper, drained of emotion. Her eyes were unreadable.

"That's right, and you know the rest. If I'd been in shape to go out on that patrol, or if I'd insisted on going anyway, even with a migraine, Steve would have survived that day. He'd very likely have come home, been here for you all along when your grandmother got sick, married, had children…" Buck's voice trailed off. "I could have toughed it out," he said. "I could have argued with the lieutenant, convinced him I'd be all right. Or better yet, I could have faked it and not told anybody. Maybe I would've been shot, or maybe things would've gone differently for me. Either way, Steve wouldn't have been the one to die that day."

She'd put down her fork. An eternity seemed to pass before she spoke. "You couldn't have known what would happen. Neither could Steve."

"But I knew the risks. Every time we went on patrol we were taking our lives in our hands." Buck struggled to keep the emotion out of his voice. "Later that morning, I was in camp, still wondering whether I'd done the right thing, when I heard the patrol come back. Somebody told me Steve was wounded. I got to him just in time to say goodbye."

Terri didn't speak. A single tear trickled down her face.

"Lord, Terri, I would've done anything to trade places

with him. If it were possible right now, I'd change things so that I'd be the one lying in that grave and Steve would be here with you."

Terri's silence said more than any words she could have spoken. When she finally looked up at him, the coldness in her eyes told Buck he'd already lost her.

"I understand what happened," she said, "and I don't hold you responsible. What I don't understand is why you waited all these years to tell me."

It was a tough question, and the answer didn't come easily. "The very last thing Steve asked was that I take care of you. I promised him I'd do that. When I got home and saw how you were still hurting, I knew you were going to need my help. But I was afraid that if I told you the truth, you wouldn't want anything to do with me."

Her gaze hardened. "You should have given me that choice. Instead you treated me like a child."

"I know better now. I didn't then—and as time passed, it got harder and harder to bring it up. But I was wrong. You deserved to know. Forgive me, Terri. I tried to make it up to you over the years—"

"Make it up to me?" Her fist clenched on the tabletop. "So you took me under your wing and gave me a job—out of *guilt*?" She rose, trembling. "You bought me new tires, bought flowers for my grandma and took me to the gala out of *guilt*? Did you sleep with me out of guilt, too?"

"Terri, I didn't mean—" he protested, but she cut him off.

"Never mind. Your excuses don't matter anymore. I've given you ten years of my life. That's enough. Take me home. I need to pack."

Buck knew better than to argue as he drove to her house. He'd gambled and he'd lost. Another word from him would only set loose more bottled-up anger. But as they pulled up to her house there was one thing he needed to ask.

"What should I tell Quinn?"

She looked directly at him for the first time since they'd left his house. Only then did Buck see the welling tears in her eyes. "Tell her I'm sorry, and that I'll be in touch. Maybe…" She paused, as if flustered. "Oh, never mind. Have a nice life, Buck."

Turning away, she climbed out of the vehicle. Still wearing his sweats and her muddy black pumps, she stalked into the house.

As the Hummer roared away from the house, Terri locked the door behind her, slid to the floor and buried her face against her knees. Her shoulders shook with sobs.

It was over. Really over. And after last night's lovemaking, letting go hurt even worse than she'd feared it would. She'd hoped, at least, for a sweet and tender farewell. But Buck's revelation over breakfast had made that impossible.

She could forgive him for letting Steve take his place on patrol—in fact, she already had. Steve had chosen to volunteer, and his death was a consequence of the war, a cruel twist of fate that hadn't been Buck's fault. Harder to forgive was the way he'd hidden the truth from her, keeping the secret for years, as if she were a child, incapable of understanding. But worst of all was the fact that any kindness he'd shown her had been motivated more by guilt and pity than by genuine caring. As for love…

But she wouldn't even go there. Buck had never even pretended to love her, and unrequited love was a one-way ticket to misery.

Time to move on. Terri pushed to her feet, stepped out

of her mud-stained pumps and padded into the bathroom to splash her face with water. Then she stripped off the sweats Buck had lent her, folded them neatly and put on her usual Sunday wear—jeans, sneakers and a faded T-shirt. The clean khaki uniforms she wore to work, with the Bucket List logo on the shirts, hung in her closet. Seized by an impulse, she yanked them off their hangers and tossed them on the bed. Then she folded each piece and stacked them next to the sweats. When Buck came to work Monday morning, he would find them on his desk, along with her ring of keys.

Her job interview was scheduled for Monday at ten thirty. She planned to make it a two-day trip, leaving here before noon and staying the night in Park City. Her overnight case should be enough to hold everything she needed. Packing wouldn't take long. Neither would dropping off the keys and uniforms in Buck's office. But her most important task would take more time and thought. She needed to write a letter—the most heart-wrenching letter she'd ever written.

Switching on her computer, she sat down at her desk, brought up the word processor and began to type.

Dear Quinn...

Buck had dreaded Monday morning, driving to work with Quinn, unlocking the door, knowing Terri wouldn't be there. He'd entertained the secret hope that he'd walk in and find her at her desk, her smile enough to tell him she'd changed her mind. But he should've known it wasn't to be. Stepping into his office, seeing the folded clothes and the keys she'd left for him slammed reality hard in his face.

Quinn came dragging in behind him. He'd managed to tell her last night that Terri was leaving. She wasn't taking the news well. When he handed her the envelope with her name written on the outside, she looked at it for a moment, then laid it on the desk and turned away.

"Aren't you going to open it?" he asked her.

She shook her head. "If you want to read it, you can open it yourself."

"You don't mind?" Maybe if he knew what the letter said, he could talk her into reading it. He knew she'd feel betrayed by Terri's leaving. But she wouldn't feel that way forever.

She shrugged. "Go ahead."

Buck tore open the envelope and unfolded the letter.

Dear Quinn,
I'm sorry I had to leave without saying goodbye. I should have told you sooner that I was planning to go, but I didn't want to spoil our good times together. In the end, things happened so fast that I ran out of time.

An ache tightened around Buck's heart. He'd had ten years to fall in love with Terri—ten years to win her and make her his. But he'd come to his senses too late. He, too, had run out of time. He read to the end of the letter.

I stayed in Porter Hollow to be with my grandmother. Now that she's gone, it's time for me to try new things in new places. By the time you read this, I'll be in Park City, negotiating a job there.

Thank you again, and please thank Ann Marie, too, for helping me get ready for the party. The gown and my hair looked beautiful. You'll be upset with me, I know, for leaving like this, but in time I hope you'll understand and forgive me, and that

we'll always be friends. You have my phone num-
ber and email. I'm really hoping to hear from you.
Love always,
Terri

Buck turned to his daughter. "You should read this,"
he said. "At least it might help you understand why she
went away."

Quinn took the letter, crumpled it in her small fist and
flung it in the wastepaper basket.

Terri bought the home pregnancy test kit on the way to
Park City, in a town where nobody knew her. She planned
to wait until after the job interview to take the test. If she
was pregnant, then she'd need maternity leave in a matter
of months, which might be a deal breaker. She wanted
to be as calm and as truthful as possible and, since she
wouldn't know for sure, she'd be less tempted to lie.

But she should've known her penchant for honesty
would trip her up. When the manager, a breezy, athletic
woman in her forties, confirmed her interest in hiring her
on the spot, Terri knew she had to tell the truth.

"There's a chance I may be pregnant," she said, her
stomach fluttering as she spoke the word for the first
time. "I'm not sure yet, but I wouldn't feel right about
keeping it from you."

The woman lifted off her glasses and rubbed the
bridge of her nose. "We should be able to work around
that," she said. "Assuming you are pregnant and plan to
keep the baby, I'm guessing you'd be due in the spring.
That's our slow time, between the ski season and the
summer events. Taking a couple of months off shouldn't
be a problem, especially if you're willing to do some
work from home. Just so you'll know, in the ten years

I've worked here, I've had two babies myself." She replaced her glasses and smiled. "There's a vacant apartment in the complex where I live. We'd like you to start this weekend if you can manage it. Is that okay, or do you need more time?"

Thirty minutes later, feeling a bit giddy, Terri walked out of the resort headquarters with her new employment contract in her purse. She'd done it. She'd spread her wings and, so far, managed to stay airborne. It had happened so fast, her head was still spinning.

Her motel room was in nearby Heber City, outside the pricey ski district. She'd planned to start home this afternoon, but now that she had a job, it made more sense to stay an extra day, check out the area, and either reserve the apartment or find something else.

Her thoughts churned as she drove. It was time she summoned the courage to take the pregnancy test. If the result was negative, she'd be free to move on with her life. If it was positive, if she was really carrying Buck's child—

But she'd deal with that once she knew for sure. If there really was to be a baby, two things were already settled in her mind. First, she would keep it, love it, raise it. And second, she wouldn't tell Buck. The man had done enough for her out of guilt. The last thing she wanted was a repeat of his miserable shotgun marriage to Diane.

The pregnancy test was still in her purse. Pulling up to the motel, she parked the Jeep and went into her room. In the bathroom, with shaking hands, she opened the box and followed the instructions, then waited, her eyes glued to the indicator.

She counted her heartbeats as the seconds passed. Slowly the sign emerged—a small but unmistakable plus.

She was going to be a mother.

Eleven

Hi, Terri,

I'm glad we're still Facebook friends. I missed you too much to stay mad forever. But I really wish I could see you. I'm here in Sedona with Mom, but I'll be spending Christmas vacation with Dad in Porter Hollow. Maybe you can come and visit us. Or we could come see you in Park City. It would be fun to play in the snow. Do you know how to ski yet? Maybe you could teach me. We could have so much fun. Think about it.

XOXOXOX,

Quinn

Terri sighed as she reread Quinn's message. When Buck's daughter had contacted her from Sedona in September, she'd been happy about it. She truly loved Quinn and knew that her leaving had hurt the girl. Their Facebook exchanges had been harmless enough while Quinn was with her mother. But now Quinn would be with Buck, in Porter Hollow. And she'd be pushing her father to come to Park City for a visit.

Rising from her chair, Terri reached back and massaged the strain from her lower back. The baby—a healthy little boy—wasn't due till March. But she was already showing—not too much under a jacket or coat. But in her regular clothes, there was no hiding the bump. She wasn't huge yet, but she looked unmistakably pregnant. There was no way she could let Quinn or Buck see her. Having Buck find out she was pregnant would turn her whole carefully restructured life upside down. She couldn't let it happen. She needed to nip Quinn's plans in the bud—now.

Terri sat down again. Her fingers quivered on the keys as she wrote her reply.

Dear Quinn,
I'd love to see you, but the Christmas holiday season is our busiest time here in Park City. If you and your dad were to come, I wouldn't have any time to be with you, and you'd be lucky to find a place to stay. With so much going on here, I can't get away to visit Porter Hollow. Maybe we can make it some other time.
Hugs,
Terri

She clicked the enter key with a deep sense of misgiving. Everything she'd written was true, except the one big lie of omission. If she wanted to keep her baby a secret, there could be no *some other time*. Not ever.

If she'd had the foresight to think this out, she might have gone somewhere farther away where she could have cut off all communication with her past. But there were practicalities to consider. The severance payments she'd elected to have paid out monthly were going directly to her bank account, which meant that Buck had to have some idea where she was. And some issues with the sale of her grandmother's property were still being negotiated so the Realtor needed to be in touch with her, as well.

But it struck her, in a sudden flash of insight, that there was more than practicality involved here. There was Quinn—sweet, blameless Quinn who loved her; Quinn who, if the secret was kept, would never know she had a baby brother. And there was her unborn son who would never know his father and his wonderful big sister.

The truth hit her so hard that she gasped out loud.

What gave her the right to play with these innocent children's lives—to deny them the joy and support of knowing each other—for the sake of her own pride?

Terri buried her face in her hands. What had she done? How could she fix this mess without wrecking Buck's life and her own?

It was coming up on five o'clock when Evie Redfeather dropped Quinn off at Buck's office. Alerted by a phone call, Buck was waiting outside when Evie's Buick pulled up to the curb. When the door opened, Quinn came flying out and hurtled into his arms. He grabbed her tight, swinging off her feet.

"Hey, you're getting tall!" he exclaimed, setting her down and heading for the open truck to get her suitcase.

"I know. I'm the tallest girl in my class. What're we going to do while I'm here?"

Buck waved his thanks to Evie as she pulled away and headed home. "What do you say we talk about it over pizza at Giovanni's?" he asked, hefting her suitcase and taking her hand. He'd learned some lessons about being a father last summer. Those lessons were paying off. It surprised and delighted him how much closer he and his daughter had grown.

"Can we have hot fudge sundaes afterward?" she asked, matching his stride.

"Sure." Buck remembered last summer when Terri had gone for pizza with them. The empty spot her departure had left still ached. He'd hoped to hear from her, but she hadn't called or emailed even once. He could only respect her choice and hope she was doing all right.

Even in December, the weather in Porter Hollow was mild enough for their light jackets. Stowing the suitcase in the Hummer, they walked the short distance to the restaurant. The pretty blonde waitress showed them to a booth. Her body language made it clear that she was interested. But Buck's mind was elsewhere, especially now, with his daughter along.

"So, what's new?" he asked her as they faced each other across the red-checked tablecloth.

"Oh, a few things." Quinn sipped her root beer.

"Like what?"

"Mom's got a boyfriend. He's kind of a jerk, but he's got lots of money. I think they're getting married."

"You're kidding." Diane had had plenty of men in her life since the end of their marriage, but none who could talk her into giving up that fat alimony check he put in her account every month.

"His family owns some factories in China. They make underwear or car-seat covers or something like that. Anyway, they've got this big house in Switzerland—that's where they keep all their money. He said something about being neighbors to George Clooney."

A dark weight formed in the pit of Buck's stomach. What would he do if Diane married and wanted to take their daughter out of the country, maybe put her in some snooty Swiss boarding school? Could he fight it legally and win?

"Mom wanted me to ask you something," Quinn said.

"Okay." Buck braced himself for bad news.

"If she gets married, she wants to know if I could live with you during the school year and go to school here in Porter Hollow. Then I could visit her in the summer, like I visit you now."

Buck began to breathe again. "I'd like that a lot." He hesitated. "Would you?"

"You bet I would." She grinned and held up her hand for a high five.

Soon after that their pizza arrived. Quinn wolfed down two slices, then suddenly gave her father a serious look. "What if you get married, too?" she asked. "Would you ship me off to Switzerland to be with Mom?"

"No way. We'd all be family together, or it wouldn't happen. But I don't think you have much to worry about. Do you see any women lining up to marry me?"

She stirred the ice in her root beer. "I always kind of hoped you'd marry Terri."

"To tell you the truth, I was kind of hoping the same thing. But it wasn't in the cards."

"Did you ask her?" Quinn demanded.

Buck shook his head. "I never got that far. She was mad at me when she left. I'm guessing she still is. I haven't had so much as a Tweet from her."

Quinn swirled her ice a moment before she met his gaze. "She's not mad at me, Dad. We've been emailing back and forth since this fall, when I went back to Mom's."

Buck's pulse skipped. "How is she? Is she all right?"

"She's fine. She likes her new job. She's asked me about you a couple of times."

"Asked what?"

"Oh, just stuff like whether you were okay, and had you found anybody to take her job. I told her you still just had Bob and the temps."

"Do you think she wants to come back?"

"I asked her. She said no."

"Has she met anybody? Is she dating?" Buck could've smacked the side of his own head for asking. If the answer was yes, did he really want to know?

"Not anybody that she's said. But she'd tell stuff like that to a grown-up girlfriend, not to me." Quinn gave him a thoughtful look. "You really like her, don't you, Dad?"

"I guess I do." Buck fished for his credit card to pay the check. "But I also guess it doesn't make much difference whether I like her or not. Terri's moved on. She's not coming back here."

Quinn dawdled, finishing the last of her root beer. She seemed to be holding something back.

"We could go see her," she said. "I already asked her if we could come, and she said she was too busy. But if we just showed up, she'd have to see us, wouldn't she?"

Buck signed the check and pocketed his card. "I don't know if that's a good idea," he said. "What if Terri doesn't want to see us?"

"Then we could just have some fun by ourselves and go home. At least we'd know she was all right."

"Why wouldn't she be all right?" Buck shrugged into his leather jacket. Quinn had always been a perceptive child, an old soul, as her mother called her. Maybe her instincts were telling her something. "Do you have some reason to be worried about Terri?" he asked.

Quinn walked ahead of him through the door, waiting outside for him to catch up. "I just wonder why she wouldn't want to see me. Terri's my friend. She likes me. What if something's wrong?"

"Maybe I'm the one she doesn't want to see."

Quinn had no reply for that. But as they went for sundaes and drove home, Buck couldn't stop turning the thought over in his mind. He'd tried to tell himself that letting Terri move on was the fairest thing he could do for her. But letting her go had been like ripping away a vital part of himself.

So help him, he still loved her. And now that Quinn had planted the worry in his mind, Buck knew he wouldn't rest until he saw Terri and made sure she was safe, happy and where she wanted to be.

Terri assembled the packets she'd prepared for the quarterly board of directors meeting and placed them around the table in the conference room. Her mind checked off the mental list she'd made—snacks, chilled water and sodas, napkins, pens, notepads, whiteboard markers and erasers, a computer to run the presentation on the wall-mounted TV—everything a roomful of important people would need for three hours of debate and decision making.

The meeting wouldn't start till after lunch, but there was nothing like being prepared ahead of time. Ginetta, her boss, would be running the meeting. With the setup complete, Terri's job was done. Good thing, because she was getting tired, and the baby was kicking like a little ninja.

"Everything looks great." Ginetta surveyed the room, then gave Terri a concerned glance. "You look like you could use a rest. Why don't you go in the break room and stretch out on the couch? It'll do you a world of good."

"Thanks, but it's almost noon. I won't get much rest in there, with people coming in to eat their lunch. Anyway, I promised myself I'd write up that order for cleaning supplies and send it out. As long as I can sit at my desk, I'll be fine."

"At least go get yourself a nice lunch." Ginetta slipped off her glasses and rubbed the bridge of her nose. "You've been here six months. You're doing a fine job, but all I've seen you do is work. You come in early, stay till all hours… You need to get out and make some friends. Have some fun."

"Maybe later. For now, I have the baby to think of." Terri crossed the common area to her small office and sat down at her desk. It felt good to take the weight off her feet.

Ginetta followed her to stand by the desk. "Forgive me if this is too personal, Terri. I'm just concerned. Will you have anybody to help you when the baby comes? What about your family?"

"No family. I'm the last one."

"What about your baby's father? Is he in the picture?" Terri shook her head. "He doesn't know."

"Married?" She paused, catching herself. "I'm sorry, that's none of my business."

"No, he's not married. It's…complicated."

Ginetta touched her shoulder. "Well, let me know if

there's anything I can do to help—and you really do need to take better care of yourself."

As her boss walked out of the office, Terri rested her eyes a moment, then turned to her computer and brought up the ordering form for the resort's janitorial supplies. She was lucky to have a boss as understanding as Ginetta. But until she decided how to resolve her baby's future, the fewer people she involved in her problems, the better.

She was partway down the form when her cell phone rang. She reached into her purse, grabbed the phone and, without taking time to check the ID, answered the call.

"Hi, Terri! This is Quinn!" The girlish voice sounded happy, excited. At least Terri could surmise that nothing was wrong.

"Hi, Quinn. What's up?" Terri kept her tone light and cheerful.

"I'm here in Park City, with Dad. Evie flew us in the jet. We wanted to surprise you. Wait a sec, I'll put Dad on."

Terri's heart sank like a drowning butterfly. She'd made the decision to break her news when the time was right—maybe with a well-thought-out phone call or email to Buck. But now was too soon. She needed to think things through. What could she say to Buck? And how could she explain to a nine-year-old girl how she'd come to be pregnant with her father's baby? Quinn was precocious, but surely the child wasn't ready to hear that.

"Hello, Terri." Buck's voice went through her with the hot pain of memory. "How're you doing?"

"Fine." Terri struggled to keep her voice from shaking. "I wish you'd let me know you were coming. I'm having an extremely busy day. I won't even have time to—"

"Just have lunch with us. If that's all you've got time for, we'll understand."

Terri thought fast, scrambling for an exit strategy. Now that they were here, she knew there was no way Quinn and Buck would leave without seeing her, at least for lunch. But if she kept her coat on while she was with them, maybe they wouldn't notice the change in her body.

"I guess I could manage that," she said. "On the second floor of the hotel across the street from my office, there's an outdoor restaurant with a view of the slopes. It's a nice day, and Quinn might enjoy watching the skiers while we eat. There's a stairway going up from the street. If you're close by, you can't miss it. How soon can you meet me there?"

"We're on Main Street now," Buck said. "I can see the stairway to the restaurant from here. We'll be there in a few minutes."

"I'm on my way." Heart pounding, Terri ended the call and reached for the quilted, thigh-length down parka she'd bought in town. The coat was puffy enough to camouflage her pregnancy. The tougher challenge, she knew, would be masking her emotions.

Buck ushered his excited daughter up the snow-packed stairs to the restaurant. Quinn had seen winter weather before, but not for a few years. On their way to the stairs, she'd scooped up handfuls of snow, shaping the white stuff into balls and laughing as she tossed them in the air. Once Terri would have dropped everything to play with her. Now she claimed she was too busy. Something had changed. What was it?

The restaurant was crowded, with a long waiting line, but a generous tip got Buck quickly seated at a good table with a view. Outdoor heaters, placed among the tables, warmed the air, but it was still chilly. He ordered hot cocoa for Quinn while they waited for Terri to arrive.

A few minutes later she came up the stairs, wearing a bulky dark green parka and holding tightly to the rail. Her face was flushed, her expression harried. But she smiled when she spotted Buck and Quinn, who was waving her over to their table.

Buck stood to pull out her chair. Sitting, she reached across the table and squeezed Quinn's hand. "Great to see you," she said. "How do you like the snow, Quinn?"

"I love it!" Quinn grinned. "I wish we could stay long enough for me to take ski lessons. I want to do what those people are doing." She indicated the slopes with a sweep of her hand. "Have you learned how to ski yet, Terri?"

"I've been too busy working," Terri said. "Maybe next year."

Buck studied her across the table. Terri was smiling, chatting with Quinn. But she looked tired. And the way she'd come up the stairs, gripping the rail as if pulling herself up. Was something wrong, or was worry feeding his imagination?

They ordered tuna melts and hot soup. Buck noticed how Terri picked at her food, as if too nervous to eat. Was it because he and Quinn were here, or was something else bothering her?

"Are you all right, Terri?" he asked. "You look a little frayed around the edges."

"I'm fine. Just stressed. I like my job, but this is the busy season—lots to do. And I haven't been sleeping well, probably too much coffee." She made a show of glancing at her watch. "I can't stay long—just wanted to say hello and catch up." She turned away from him. "How do you like school this year, Quinn? Tell me about your classes."

She was making small talk—avoiding him, Buck could tell. After their parting he could hardly blame her for being uncomfortable. But he was seeing more than that. This wasn't the breezy, confident Terri he remembered. She was like a wild bird, ready to take flight if he so much as reached out a hand to her.

Only one thing was solid in his mind. He loved her more deeply than ever. But he was growing more concerned by the minute. Something was troubling her. Something bigger than their unexpected visit. How could he leave her without knowing what it was?

She finished her soup, having barely nibbled the sandwich, and glanced at her watch again. "Oh, dear, I really need to be going now. I've got so much happening at work." She rose, motioning Buck to stay seated as he shifted his chair back. "Please don't bother getting up. You should stay and order some dessert. The cheesecake here is pure heaven. So good to see you both. Say hi to Evie for me, and enjoy the rest of your day."

She blew a departing kiss to Quinn, turned away and fled like an escaping prisoner toward the stairs. Buck watched her go. He needed to talk to her again—alone this time, he resolved. Maybe he could call her later, or even stay an extra day and try to see her again tonight.

His gaze followed the back of her dark green coat as she wove her way through the crowd. Something in him wanted to rush after her and stop her from leaving. He curbed the impulse. If Terri wanted to run away, he had no right to interfere.

What happened next happened fast. Two roughhousing teenage boys were wrestling each other in the waiting line. Grabbing and shoving, they stumbled hard against Terri, who'd just reached the top of the stairs and taken the first step down. The impact knocked her off balance. Arms flailing, she pitched forward, cried out and disappeared from Buck's sight.

A collective gasp went up from the watchers. Buck shot out of his seat and bulled his way through the crowd to the top of the stairs. Looking down, he could see Terri at the bottom. She lay sprawled faceup on the icy sidewalk, her eyes closed.

In an instant he was at her side. He didn't dare lift or move her, but as he touched her cheek, her eyelids fluttered open. Her lips moved as she struggled to speak.

"Get me to the hospital," she said.

"I've called nine-one-one," a man standing nearby told Buck. "They're sending an ambulance."

"Thanks." Buck held Terri's cold hand. "Lie still," he murmured. "Help's on its way, and I'm here. I love you, Terri. Do you hear me? You're going to be fine."

She didn't speak, but her fingers tightened around his.

Somehow, in the confusion, Quinn had found her way down the stairs to crouch beside him. Her eyes were huge and scared in her small, pale face.

"Will Terri be all right, Daddy?" she asked.

Buck laid his free hand on her shoulder. "Let's hope so. But if you want to say a little prayer, that couldn't hurt."

Quinn bowed her head, her lips moving in a whispered prayer. By the time she'd finished, the ambulance was pulling up to the curb. The paramedics supported Terri's neck and back, eased her onto a stretcher and loaded her into the vehicle. As it sped away, lights flashing, Buck and Quinn raced down the block to where they'd left their rental car.

Minutes later, they arrived at the hospital. By the time Buck checked at the emergency desk, Terri had been taken back to an examination room.

"Are you family?" the desk nurse asked.

"We're the closest thing to family she's got," Buck said, and realized it was true.

"Have a seat, the doctor will be out to talk to you after he's examined her." She turned away to answer a ringing phone.

Buck and Quinn settled on the couch to wait. Time crawled. Sick with worry, Buck thumbed through a stack of tattered magazines, barely aware of what he was seeing. Quinn asked for a dollar to get a soda from the vending machine. She came back and plopped down beside him. "Do you know what I think?" she asked.

"What?"

She popped the tab on her soda can. "I think you should ask Terri to marry you. We need her, and right now she needs us."

Buck smiled at her through his worry. "I think you're right. But what if she says no?"

"Then I'll talk her into it. I can talk Terri into anything."

Just then the doctor, a tall, balding man with glasses, came out into the waiting room. In an instant Buck was on his feet. He motioned the doctor into a side hall, out of Quinn's hearing. "How is she?" he asked, bracing for the worst.

"She's one very lucky lady," the doctor said. "That was a nasty fall she took. She's got a sprained wrist and some bruising, but no broken bones. And the baby appears to be fine."

"The baby?" Buck stared at the doctor, trying not to look like a fool. The last thing he'd expected was that Terri would be pregnant, but it all made sense now—the puffy coat, the nervous behavior. She hadn't wanted him to know. And it didn't take a genius to figure out why.

"We did a sonogram to make sure there was no problem," the doctor said. "Everything looked fine, but we'd like to keep her overnight for observation."

"Can I see her?"

"For a few minutes. Your little girl will have to wait out here. The nurse can keep an eye on her."

Buck thanked the doctor and walked back to where Quinn stood. "Terri's going to be all right," he said. "I'm going back to see her. You'll need to stay here. I won't be long. Okay?"

"Okay," Quinn said. "Are you going to ask her?"

"I'll see how it goes. See you in a few minutes." He turned to walk away.

"Dad—"

He glanced back at her. "What is it?"

"You can be pretty dense sometimes. Don't let her get away again."

"Got it." He flashed her a grin, which faded as he strode back through the swinging doors. Quinn's view of the situation was simple—just ask her and don't give up till she says yes. But there were things Quinn didn't know, or was too young to understand.

He found Terri sitting up in bed, dressed in a hospital gown with a flannel blanket over her legs. Her right wrist was bandaged, and an IV with a saline drip was attached to her left arm. She looked pale and shaken, but otherwise all right.

Buck's first sight of her roused a storm of emotions— relief, outrage and a love so overpowering that it left him weak in the knees. Terri was the love of his life, the mother of his child. And he was mad enough to shake her silly.

He sank onto a chair that had been left next to the bed.

"You could've told me," he said.

"I know. I'd planned to tell you eventually. But I didn't

want you thinking you had to do the right thing again. I saw what you went through with Diane, remember?"

"Blast it, Terri—" Buck bit back the rest of what wanted to be an angry outburst. That fall she'd taken could have killed both her and their child. But she was here, she was all right, and so was the baby. Anything—everything—else could be fixed.

"Listen to me." He reached across the bed and captured her hand in his. "We aren't perfect people, you and I. We've both done things that need forgiving—especially me. But damn it, I love you, Terri. Baby or no baby, I want to marry you and make a family—and Quinn wants it, too. So stop making excuses. Just say yes and make me the happiest man in the world."

Her gaze dropped to their clasped hands. He could imagine what was going through her mind. Was he proposing because of the baby? After the callous way he'd treated her in the past, could she really believe his claim that he loved her? Buck waited in an agony of hope and dread before she finally spoke.

"Do you really think we can make this work?" she asked.

Buck began to breathe again. She hadn't said no. There was still a chance. "We've been making it work for ten years," he said. "We just need to make some changes. You won't be my right-hand woman anymore. You'll be my center, my heart."

"Then, yes."

Buck wanted to shout with happiness. He wanted to turn cartwheels down the hall. But this was a hospital. He stood, leaned over her the bed and gave her a gently lingering kiss. "They're going to throw me out of here any minute," he said. "But when I come back here tomorrow I want to bring a ring and put it on your finger—or would you rather wait and pick one out yourself?"

"I have an idea," she said. "Take Quinn with you. Let her pick it out. Whatever she chooses will be perfect."

Buck barely had time for another kiss before the nurse appeared to usher him back to the waiting room. When she saw his face, Quinn broke into a wide smile.

"She said yes, didn't she, Daddy?"

"She did." Buck grabbed her hand. "Come on, young lady. You and I are going ring shopping."

Epilogue

Christmas Eve, one year later

Snow was falling, feathery light, on the big house in the canyon. Winter storms were rare in this warm country, and the snow seldom lasted long. Since this was Christmas Eve, the gentle storm added a special magic to the night.

As the clock struck eleven, Buck stood with Terri at the darkened window, watching the flakes drift down. Behind them, embers crackled in the fireplace where four stockings—one very small—hung from the mantel. A tall Christmas tree in the far corner glowed with light.

The two of them had put the children to bed and spent the past hour wrapping the last of the gifts. Now they were tired, but the peace and beauty of the snow kept them lingering at the window. Buck slid his arms around his wife, cradling her against him in the glowing darkness. Her head rested in the hollow of his throat.

"Do you think Quinn will know what her present is when she opens that big box?" Terri asked.

Buck laughed. "When she sees that saddle and bridle, she'll figure it out. It's not like we can put her horse under the Christmas tree."

Quinn had been begging for a horse for months. Buck had bought her a well-broken registered mare and arranged to board it at a nearby stable. Terri had bought her a hat and some riding boots, now wrapped in another beribboned box.

"At least Stevie's easy this year," Terri said. "I bought him some clothes and a few little toys, but he'd be just as happy playing with boxes and ribbons."

"Or climbing up the stairs," Buck added.

At nine months, young Stevie Morgan was all boy. He hadn't started walking yet, but he could crawl like a little champ, and he was into everything. His latest fascination was the staircase, which he could already climb. Buck had added gates at the foot and top of the stairs, but it took everybody's vigilance to make sure the little explorer was safe. Quinn adored her baby brother, and she'd already become his favorite person.

Buck nuzzled his wife's ear, inhaling her womanly fragrance. Desire warmed inside him. He slid his hands upward, cradling her breasts through her silky shirt. "Maybe it's time we were in bed, too," he murmured. "Santa won't come if we're awake, you know."

She made a little purring sound. "Fine. But let's check the children on our way."

Holding hands, they mounted the stairs to the second-floor landing. Quinn's room was closest. Their daughter lay curled in sleep. Her walls were decorated with horse posters. She was growing up too fast, Buck thought. In no time at all she'd be a young woman. Every day of her childhood had become precious to him.

The nursery was across the hall from the master bedroom. Stevie sprawled in his crib, restless even in his sleep. With his mother's chestnut hair and his father's blue eyes, he was the baby they'd created the very first time they'd made love. Now Buck couldn't imagine life without him.

"We should make more of those," he whispered to Terri.

"Shhh…" She drew him out into the hallway and stretched on tiptoe to kiss him. "Bedtime," she whispered. "Come on."

Content to the marrow of his bones, he followed her into their bedroom.

* * * * *

She'd imagined standing like this with him so many times, and every one of those times, he'd kissed her.

Before she knew what was happening, Carson brought her fantasy to reality by dipping his head and pressing his lips to hers. The champagne was just strong enough to mute the voices in her head that told her this was a bad idea. Instead, she gave in to his kiss, pulling him closer.

He tasted like champagne and spearmint; his touch gentle, yet firm. She could've stayed just like this forever, but eventually, Carson pulled away.

His green eyes reflected sudden panic. Her emotions came crashing back down to the ground with the reality she saw there. She had just kissed her boss. Her boss!

"Georgia, I…" he started, his voice trailing off. "I didn't mean for that to happen."

With a quick shake of her head, she dismissed his words and took a step back from him. "Don't worry about it," she said. "Excitement and champagne will make people do stupid things every time."

The problem was that it didn't feel stupid.

* * *

Saying Yes to the Boss is part of the
Dynasties: The Newports series:
Passion and chaos consume
a Chicago real estate empire

SAYING YES TO THE BOSS

BY
ANDREA LAURENCE

First Published in Great Britain 2016
By Mills & Boon, an imprint of HarperCollins*Publishers*
1 London Bridge Street, London, SE1 9GF

© 2016 Harlequin Books S.A.

Special thanks and acknowledgement are given to Andrea Laurence for her contribution to the Dynasties: The Newports series.

ISBN: 978-0-263-91868-7

51-0716

Our policy is to use papers that are natural, renewable and recyclable products and made from wood grown in sustainable forests. The logging and manufacturing processes conform to the legal environmental regulations of the country of origin.

Printed and bound in Spain
by CPI, Barcelona

Andrea Laurence is an award-winning author of contemporary romances filled with seduction and sass. She has been a lover of reading and writing stories since she was young and is thrilled to share her special blend of sensuality and dry, sarcastic humor with readers. A dedicated West Coast girl transplanted into the Deep South, she's working on her own happily-ever-after with her boyfriend and their collection of animals.

One

"I found it."

Georgia Adams eyed Carson Newport from her position in his office doorway. He looked up from the paperwork on his desk, arched one golden eyebrow in curiosity and leaned back in his chair. "You found what?"

Georgia stifled a frown of disappointment. She'd imagined this moment differently. She was carrying a chilled bottle of champagne in her purse to celebrate her discovery. Not once in her imagination had he stared at her blankly.

How could he not know that she had found *it*? The Holy Grail of real estate. The very thing they'd been searching for, for months. "I found the spot where the Newport Corporation is going to be building the Cynthia Newport Memorial Hospital for Children."

That got his attention. Carson straightened up in his leather executive chair and pinned her with his gaze. "Are you serious?"

Georgia grinned. This was more like it. "As a heart attack."

"Come in." He waved her into his office. "Tell me all about it."

She shook her head and crooked her finger to beckon him. "I think I need to show you. Come on."

Carson didn't so much as look at his calendar for conflicts before he leaped from his chair. Finding the land for their next real estate development project had been *that* hard and *that* important. There wasn't a lot of space in Chicago to do what they wanted. At least, not at a price that made any kind of financial sense.

He moved swiftly around his massive mahogany desk, buttoning the black suit coat he was wearing as he joined her in the doorway. "Lead on, Miss Adams."

Georgia spun on her heel and headed for the elevators. "We're taking your car," she reminded him as she hit the down button.

He leaned his palm against the wall and looked down at her. "You know, Georgia, you're the director of public relations at a Fortune 500 company. I think I pay you enough to get a car. I pay you enough to get a really nice car. There's even a reserved spot in the garage for you that sits open every day."

Georgia just shrugged. She didn't want the responsibility of a car. In truth, she didn't need one. Her apartment was a block away from the "L." Chicago's elevated train was efficient and cheap, and that's how she liked things. She'd never owned a car before. Public transportation was all she'd ever really known. To some people who grew up the way she had, finally getting their own car would be a milestone that showed they had made something of themselves. To her, it was an unnecessary expense. She never knew when she might need that money for something else.

"You look like a Jaguar girl to me." Carson continued to ponder aloud as they stepped out of the elevator to the employee parking deck. "Graceful, attractive and just a little bit naughty."

Georgia stopped beside Carson's pearl-white Range Rover. She brushed her loose platinum-blond hair over her shoulder and planted a hand on her hip. "Mr. Newport, am I going to have to report you to human resources?" she asked with a smile that took the teeth out of the threat.

Carson winced as he opened the door for her to get inside. "It was just a compliment. Please don't make me go to the second floor. Our HR director reminds me of my third-grade teacher. She was always mean to me."

"Were you poorly behaved?" Georgia challenged him.

Carson grinned, showcasing his bright smile. His sea-green eyes twinkled mischievously. "Maybe," he admitted before slamming the door.

She took the next ten seconds alone to take a deep breath. Being around Carson Newport was hard on Georgia's nerves. Not because he was a difficult boss—he was anything but. That was part of the problem. He was handsome, charming, smart and a miserable flirt. All the Newport brothers were that way, but only Carson made Georgia's heart race. His flattering banter was harmless. She knew that. He'd never so much as touched her in the year she'd worked for his company.

That didn't mean she didn't secretly want him to. It was a stupid fantasy, one that kept her up nights as she imagined his hands running over her bare skin. But it had to stay a fantasy. She'd worked damn hard to get into a good college and climb the corporate ladder. Landing this job at the Newport Corporation was a dream come true. She'd found a family among her co-workers here. She was good at her job. Everything had turned out just as she'd hoped. Georgia wasn't about to risk that just because she had the hots for her boss.

Carson climbed in the car and they headed out. It took about a half hour to negotiate downtown traffic and get out to the site she'd found. Once there, he pulled his Range Rover off the road and onto a patch of grass and gravel. They both got out of the car and walked a couple hundred yards into a large empty field.

If she'd known she was coming out here today before she left the house, she would've opted for a more practical outfit than a pencil skirt and heels, but she didn't get the tip on the land until she got into the office. Fortunately it hadn't rained for a while, so the ground was firm and dry. It really was an ideal plot of land. The property was fairly level without many trees that would need to be cleared. One side butted up to an inlet of Lake Michigan and another to a waterfront park.

"So…" Georgia said at last. The anticipation was killing her. She didn't know how they could find anything better than this. The property had been tied up in probate for years and the family had just now decided to sell it, or it would've long ago been turned into a shopping center or condos. If Carson didn't like it, not only was she back to the drawing board, but she also had a really expensive bottle of champagne in her purse for no reason at all. "What do you think?"

She watched Carson survey the property with his back to her for a few minutes. When he finally faced her, his winning grin was broader than ever. "It's amazing. Perfect."

Carson walked across the empty field with his hands shoved into his pants pockets. There was a casual air about him that belied how intense he could be in business affairs. Georgia had seen more than one person underestimate the youngest Newport and regret it.

"How did you ever find out about this place?"

"I know a guy," Georgia said with a smile. She'd sent out quiet feelers several weeks ago and hadn't heard anything back until today. An acquaintance from college had told her about the land. It wasn't publicly for sale, at least not yet. She'd spoken to the owners and they were entertaining bids on the whisper listing through the end of next week. She got the idea they wanted to move quickly and with as little hassle as possible. If they didn't get an offer they liked by then, they'd announce the sale. If the Newport Corporation moved fast, they could avoid the sale becoming public and competitors driving up the price of the land.

Carson turned back to her. "You know a guy? I love it."

"Shall we buy it?" Georgia asked. "We don't have a lot of time to decide. Someone will snatch it up, I'm certain."

"Yes, I think we should buy it and quickly. Let's not even wait for my brothers' opinions. Graham and Brooks will think it's great."

Georgia smiled and slipped her purse off her shoulder. The large bag could've easily accommodated enough stuff for a weekend vacation, but it was the purse that she carried every day. Anything she could ever possibly need was in that bag. Today that included an insulated bag with chilled champagne and cups. "I think this is cause for celebration," she said as she pulled out the bottle.

"You're like Mary Poppins with that thing," Carson said with a chuckle as he leaned close to peer into the abyss of her handbag. "What else do you have in there?"

Reaching back inside, Georgia pulled out two red plastic cups. "They're not lead crystal, but they'll do."

"That's perfect. I've done all my best celebrating with Solo cups." Carson took the champagne bottle and opened it. He let the cork fly across the field and then poured them both a healthy-size glass.

"To the new Cynthia Newport Memorial Hospital for Children!" Carson said, holding up his glass.

"To finally seeing your mother's dream realized!" Georgia added.

As they both took a sip, Georgia noticed the faraway look of sadness in Carson's eyes. It had been only about two months since his mother's sudden death from an aneurysm. They'd had no warning at all. She was there, and then she was gone. Their mother was all they had for family. The brothers had taken it all very hard, but Carson especially. He decided he wanted to build a children's hospital in her honor, since she'd done so much charity work with sick kids in her later years.

"I really can't believe we're making this happen." Setting down his cup, Carson wrapped Georgia in his arms and spun her around.

"Carson!" Georgia squealed and clung to his neck, but that only made him spin faster.

When he finally set her back on the ground, both of them were giggling and giddy from drinking the champagne on empty stomachs. Georgia stumbled dizzily against his chest and held to his shoulders until the world stopped moving around her.

"Thank you for finding this," he said.

"I'm happy to. I know it's important to you," she said, noting he still had his arms around her waist. Carson was the leanest of the three brothers, but his grip on her told of hard muscles hidden beneath his expensive suit.

In that moment, the giggles ceased and they were staring intently into each other's eyes. Carson's full lips were only inches from hers. She could feel his warm breath brushing over her skin. She'd imagined standing like this with him so many times, and every one of those times, he'd kissed her.

Before she knew what was happening, Carson brought her fantasy to reality by dipping his head and pressing his lips to hers. The champagne was just strong enough to mute the voices in her head that told her this was a bad idea. Instead she gave in to his kiss, pulling him closer.

He tasted like champagne and spearmint. His touch was gentle yet firm. She could've stayed just like this forever, but eventually, Carson pulled back from the kiss.

For a moment, Georgia felt light-headed. She didn't know if it was his kiss or the champagne, but she felt as though she would lift right off the ground if she let go. Then she looked up at him.

His green eyes reflected sudden panic. Her emotions came crashing back down to the ground with the reality she saw there. She had just kissed her boss. Her boss! And despite the fact that he had initiated it, he looked just as horrified by the idea.

"Georgia, I…" he started, his voice trailing off. "I didn't mean for that to happen."

With a quick shake of her head, she dismissed his words and took a step back from him. "Don't worry about it," she said. "Excitement and champagne will make people do stupid things every time."

The problem was that it didn't feel stupid. It had felt amazing. Better than any fantasy she'd ever had about Carson. But that didn't make it a good idea.

"I hope this won't make things awkward between us. I'd hate for my thoughtlessness to ruin our working relationship."

"It's fine, Carson. Please. Things happen when you work closely with someone. Besides that," she admitted reluctantly, "I wasn't exactly fighting you off."

"Georgia?"

She'd avoided his gaze once their lips parted and she saw his inevitable regret, but the pleading, husky sound of his voice as he said her name made her look back at him. The regret was gone and there was a fire in his eyes now as he looked at her. His jaw was tight. With an expression like that, she would say he desired her, but that couldn't possibly be right. That kiss was a mistake and they both knew it. Right? "Yes?"

"I—"

A hard buzz against Georgia's breast startled her. At the same time, a chirp sounded from Carson's suit pocket, interrupting what he was about to say. It was their office phones.

Georgia swallowed her disappointment, turned her back to him and reached into her blouse to retrieve her phone. She always kept it on silent, tucked away in her shirt so she would know when she got a call without interrupting business. When she looked down, the message on the screen nearly devastated her.

"Sutton Winchester has announced plans to build luxury waterfront condos here," Carson said.

Georgia clicked on the link to the news article his administrative assistant, Rebecca, had sent them both. She'd left the information on the property with Rebecca in case Brooks or Graham came in and asked where they were. Instead she'd used it to uncover their competition. The story was accompanied by an image of the fancy development they planned to build on the spot where they were standing. The article noted that Sutton's offer on the land hadn't been accepted yet, but he was confident that it would be, and he was rallying support for the project. Below the artist's rendering of the buildings was a picture of Sutton Winchester.

Georgia had no doubt Sutton must have been able to charm any woman he wanted when he was a younger man. He had quite the reputation where women were concerned even now, despite his age and longtime marriage to Celeste Van Houten. Georgia could see why. His light brown hair was mostly gray now and wrinkles lined his face, but his green eyes were still bright, and his dimpled smile exuded confidence. Fortunately Georgia knew to stay far away from the likes of Winchester. He was an underhanded bastard in business dealings. He bribed, seduced and lied to get his way, screwing over the Newport Corporation on more than one occasion and putting a handful of other companies out of business entirely.

Georgia let her phone drop to her side and turned back to face Carson. Their kiss faded into her distant memory as she focused on their next steps.

There was a steely determination set into his expression when he looked at her. "We need to move quickly. I can't—*I won't*—let that bastard Sutton steal this out from under us."

"There's no way in hell you can let Winchester have our land," Graham complained.

Carson reached over the back of his leather sofa, handed his older brother a bowl of hot buttered popcorn and rolled his eyes. He was hoping they wouldn't spend tonight talking about this, but it was clear Graham wasn't going to let it go. "You think I don't know that?"

"Has our offer gone in yet?" Graham's twin, Brooks, asked. The older brothers were identical, each a good two inches taller than Carson with shaggy blond hair and aqua eyes. It was easy for Carson to tell his brothers apart, though. Brooks's brow was always furrowed with concern and thought. He had that exact expression now as he tried to balance the three bottles of microbrew that he brought with him from the kitchen.

Carson nodded and went back through his dining room to the kitchen to grab a bag of M&M'S and a box of Twizzlers off the quartz bar. "We called and submitted the offer while we were still standing in the field. The seller's attorney was mum about other offers they'd received, including Winchester's. There's no way to know if what we've submitted is on par with the others, so all we can do is wait and see if they come back with a counteroffer before they make a final decision."

Carson settled on the couch beside his brothers. "Now, can we please let this unpleasant conversation drop so we can enjoy *The Maltese Falcon* in peace?"

"Fine," Graham muttered and shoved a handful of popcorn into his mouth.

It was the first Thursday of the month, and that meant it was movie night in the Newport family. Since they were small, they'd gathered on the couch with their mother and Gerty to watch old black-and-white movies on AMC. Gerty, a widow, had worked with their mother at a café where they waitressed together before Carson was born. When Gerty retired, she'd invited Cynthia and her boys to live with her. The apartment their mother could afford was tiny and she had three growing boys who needed room to roam. Gerty didn't like being in her big house all alone and welcomed the family.

She wasn't blood, but Gerty had been the only family they had besides each other. For reasons their mother had never wanted to discuss, their father and the rest of their family were out of the picture. As Carson and his brothers got older and pushed, Cynthia had told them only that their father was abusive and she ran away to protect them all. They were better off without him in their lives, she insisted, and she made them promise not to seek him out.

For a long time, the boys had been saddened but content with that answer. They wouldn't want to hurt their mother by seeking out a dangerous man who would only make them regret it. Besides, they had their spunky pseudo grandmother Gerty and their mother. They didn't need anyone else.

Then they lost Gerty to cancer when they were in high school. She'd left them enough money to go to college and make something of themselves. Carson and his brothers had done just that, starting the Newport Corporation and becoming wealthier than they ever imagined by developing real estate in Chicago. They couldn't have done it without Gerty, so they honored her memory by drinking beer and watching the old favorites once a month.

"Double the offer," Graham insisted as he picked up the television remote and started the film.

"We can't afford that," Brooks argued, ever the voice of reason between the twins. Without him, Graham would've gotten himself into trouble with some crazy scheme long before now.

"We can find the money somewhere," Graham said, pausing the movie before it had even begun.

Carson sighed. He knew better than to think Graham would simply shut up about it. When he got an idea in his head, he wouldn't let it go. He was like a bulldog with a bone, which made him a great attorney, but a pain as a brother. Graham was the corporate attorney for the Newport Corporation, although he spent most of his time working at his law firm,

Mayer, Mayer and Newport. Brooks was their chief operations officer but spent most days working remotely from his mansion on Lake Michigan. Carson was the CEO, running the company they'd started together, but that didn't stop his brothers from putting their two cents into every decision he made.

"Sure thing," Carson agreed. "We can start by firing our attorney and making him return his corporate car."

"Hey!" Graham complained. He shoved a sharp elbow into Carson's ribs.

Carson returned the elbow, making his brother howl and scramble to the far side of the couch. He was used to the physical and mental bullying that being the younger brother entailed, but he'd learned to fight back a long time ago. Now that they were in their thirties, it hadn't changed much. "You said to find the money. You didn't say where. Now, will you let it go so we can watch the movie?"

Graham scowled and picked up his beer from the coffee table. "Fine."

Brooks grabbed the remote from Graham and hit the play button. As the opening credits were still playing, Graham studied his bottle and said, "You know, Gerty would whup our asses for drinking this highbrow beer."

This time, Carson snorted aloud. He was right. Gerty preferred to watch her movies with a plain Hershey's bar and a can of classic Budweiser. If she'd still been alive, she'd have given them a hard time over their fancy new lives, including the small-batch artisanal brew they bought downtown.

"I miss Gerty," Brooks said, pausing the movie just

as the grainy black-and-white images of San Francisco came onto the screen.

"I miss Mom," Carson added.

The three brothers sat together in silence for a moment, acknowledging everything that they'd lost. Their mother's death had been so sudden, and their lives so busy, that they'd hardly had the time to sit and let the reality of her death hit them. They were alone now, except for each other. It was a sad thought, one Carson had tried to avoid. It sent his mind spiraling down into rabbit holes.

"When are we going to clean out her house?" Graham asked.

That was a task they'd also avoided. They'd had their mother's housekeeper throw away all the perishables and close the house up until they were able to deal with her things. Eight weeks had gone by and none of them had even set foot in their mother's home.

Brooks sighed. "We have to do it eventually. We can't leave her house sitting there like some kind of old shrine."

"I'll do it," Carson volunteered. The words slipped out so suddenly he surprised even himself. "Just let me take care of this land deal first. I have a feeling I'll have my hands full with Sutton for a while."

"Are you sure?" Brooks looked at him with his blond brows furrowed in concern. "You don't have to do it by yourself."

Carson shook his head. "You two don't have time. Besides, I want to. Maybe being around her things will make me feel less…"

"Alone?"

He turned and looked at Brooks. "Maybe."

"Do you think…" Graham began, then hesitated. "Do you think we might find something about our father among her things?"

Carson had wondered the same thing several times, but hadn't allowed himself to speak the words out loud. "Mom wouldn't want us to find him."

"Mom doesn't get a vote anymore," Brooks argued. "Our father might be the royal bastard she always told us he was, but he's not the only one out there we might find. We might have siblings, cousins, grandparents… It's possible that we have a whole family out there that would be worth the effort to track down. Don't you want to know where we come from? We would finally be able to fill out our family tree. I know Mom tried to keep us from finding out the truth, but with her gone, I don't think she'd want us to feel as isolated as we do."

"We can at least try," Graham added. "If we find something we can use, great. If not, well, at least we can say we tried. It might be a stupid move that we'll regret, but at least we'll finally know for ourselves, right?"

His brothers were right. Carson knew it. They all felt a sense of not belonging. Finding where they came from, even if they didn't get the happy family reunion they all secretly hoped for, would give them closure. They'd always wonder if they didn't find out the truth. Since their parents hadn't married and his name was left off their birth certificates, cleaning out their mother's house might be the only chance they had to uncover a clue. After that, their only leads would be in the landfill.

"I'll keep my eyes open, okay?" Carson finally

agreed. "If I find something we can use, I'll let you know."

The brothers nodded in agreement, and Brooks picked up the remote again to start the movie for the third and final time.

Two

"Mr. Newport? Miss Adams is here to see you, sir."

Carson reached out to his phone and hit the button to respond to Rebecca. "Please send her in."

The door to his office opened a minute later and Georgia stepped inside. Her platinum-blond hair was pulled back into a bun today, highlighting her high cheekbones and sharp chin. She was wearing a pewter pantsuit that very nearly matched the color of her steely gray eyes.

Carson had tried not to pay that much attention to how Georgia looked most days, but he usually failed. She was a fashionable woman who knew exactly what she should wear to highlight her outrageous curves. As her boss, he shouldn't notice she was built like a brick house. He shouldn't care that she wore a shiny lip gloss that made her pouty bottom lip call out to him.

And yet he couldn't stop himself. Kissing her in the field the other day had made it that much harder. Now he knew how those curves felt beneath his palms and that the lip gloss she wore was strawberry flavored. The feeling was ten times worse than it ever was before, and if there was a time he needed to focus on work and not on how badly he wanted his director of public relations, it was now.

"Any word?" she asked as she came across the room and settled into his guest chair.

"I spoke with the sellers directly this morning. They've still not made a decision. I told them to give us the chance to counter their offer before they choose someone else. That doesn't mean that Winchester won't do the same thing, bidding us up to well outside our top price."

"I hate this waiting game," Georgia said.

Carson sat back in his leather executive chair and brought his fingertips pensively to his lips. "Me, too. What other avenues can we pursue while we wait?"

"Well," Georgia began as she lifted her tablet and started tapping on the screen. "First, I think we should try talking to Winchester."

Carson put his coffee mug back down on his desk, happy he hadn't had a mouthful of steaming hot liquid to spit out when she made her suggestion. "Talk to Winchester? Are you serious?"

Georgia shrugged. "Why not? Surely the man can be reasoned with. This project is to help sick children. How could he possibly be against sick children?"

Carson chuckled and shook his head. "You obviously haven't met the *son of a bitch* yet. Did you know he refers to himself as the King of Chicago? A man with that kind of ego isn't going to back down for anything. Contacting him will just tip him off to the fact that we're his competition. He'll drive up the price just to watch us squirm."

"You don't think he already knows?" Georgia asked. "If we know he's bid, I'm sure he's got enough spies to know we have, as well. What he may not know is what we plan to do with the land. That might make a difference and get him to back down."

Carson put his elbows on his desk, leaned forward and gave her a wry smile. "You really are an optimist, aren't you?"

An odd expression came across her face, her brows pinching together in thought. "I guess you could say that. Sometimes there's nowhere to go but up," she responded cryptically.

He wasn't quite sure what to say to that, but he knew she was right. It couldn't hurt to call up Sutton and talk to him man-to-man. Winchester was old-school. It was possible he'd appreciate Carson manning up and calling him. It was also possible it wouldn't help, but at least he could say he'd tried to reason with him.

"Okay, you win," he said. "I'll call him, but don't get your hopes up."

Turning to his computer, he looked up Sutton's number and dialed the phone. All the while, Georgia watched him with a mix of excitement and anxiety on her face. Carson was pretty certain it would be replaced with disappointment soon enough. He didn't want to see those full lips turned down into a frown, but it probably couldn't be helped where Sutton was concerned.

A perky-sounding woman answered the phone. "Elite Industries, Mr. Winchester's office. How may I assist you?"

"Yes, this is Carson Newport. I'd like to speak with Sutton, please."

"Hold please, Mr. Newport."

An irritating instrumental music track started playing when Carson was put on hold. He tapped his fingers on the desk to the anxious rhythm in his mind as he waited. It took nearly two minutes for anyone to pick up the line again.

There was a short, muffled string of coughs. "Carson Newport," a man's voice barked into the phone. It was a deep, gravelly sound, laced with a cockiness that Carson didn't care for. "I wasn't expecting a call from you today. Tell me, what can the King of Chicago do for the Newport Corporation?"

Sit on it and rotate was the first thought that came to mind, but Carson swallowed the words. "Good afternoon, Sutton. I'm calling today to talk to you about the lakeside project you announced a few days ago."

"Won't it be splendid? Best waterfront views for miles. I've already got a list of potential buyers lined up for the best units. Are you interested in one, Carson? I'll give you the sweetest corner unit I've got. Wall-to-wall windows overlooking Lake Michigan."

Carson gritted his teeth. "That's a very kind offer, Sutton, but I'm not looking for a place to live. I'm actually looking for a place to build a new children's hospital."

There was a moment of silence on the line. "That's a very noble project," Sutton said, refusing to acknowledge what Carson was after.

"I agree. I think the Cynthia Newport Memorial Hospital for Children will be an asset to the community and a testimony to my mother's work with kids."

There was a longer silence on the line this time. Unsure of what was going through Sutton's mind, he went on. "The problem is that we were looking at the same property you've identified for those condos and put in our own bid around the time that you did."

"That's a shame."

Carson was really getting annoyed with Sutton's vagueness. He wasn't about to make it easier on Carson. He was going to make him ask for it. Beg for him to withdraw the offer. "I'm calling because I was hoping I could convince you to set the condo project aside and let us have the land to build the hospital."

"I'm afraid I can't do that, Carson. I've already got way too much money invested in this project."

"Sutton, I—"

"How about this?" Sutton interrupted. "How about tomorrow about three or so, you send that pretty little PR director of yours over here. I'll discuss it with her and see if we can't come to some kind of arrangement."

Carson looked down and realized his hand was clenched into a tight fist as though he could punch the old man through the phone line. He consciously unclenched and stretched his fingers, noticing Georgia's curious expression as she watched him across the desk.

"What is it?" she mouthed silently.

He could only shake his head and hold up a finger for her to wait. "That's not really her sandbox, Sutton."

"I don't care," Sutton snapped. "She will come here

tomorrow at three or the discussion is over. You and your sick kids can find somewhere else to convalesce."

Before Carson could respond, the line went dead. He studied the phone in his hand a moment before setting it gently onto the cradle. He was a little shell-shocked from the conversation and needed a few moments to gather his thoughts.

"What did he say?"

"No," he said. Carson wasn't about to tell her about Sutton's demands. That guy had a reputation when it came to young and beautiful women. Carson wouldn't let any females in his social circle even get close to Winchester, especially not Georgia. He felt protective of her, even though he had no real claim to her. "I told you he wouldn't budge."

"He said a hell of a lot more than no," Georgia pointed out. "What did he say? Tell me."

Carson sighed. He sat back in his chair and ran his fingers through his blond waves. "It doesn't matter what he said, Georgia. The point is that he isn't going to back down."

Georgia arched one delicate brow and leaned forward. "Tell me, or heaven help me, I'll march down this hallway and tell your brother Sutton gave you an out but you refused to take it."

He immediately straightened up in his chair. "What is this, elementary school?"

She only shrugged and sat back, casually crossing her shapely legs. She couldn't have been over five-five, but sometimes Carson was certain that at least four feet of her was leg. He'd given a lot of thought to how they'd feel wrapped around his waist.

"Carson!"

He snapped out of his mental reverie and flung his arm up in defeat. "Okay. He wants to meet with you." He spat out the words with disgust.

"With *me*? That doesn't make any sense."

Carson could only shake his head. "It makes perfect sense when we're talking about Sutton Winchester. He very specifically requested you and said he wouldn't speak to anyone else. I'm pretty sure he's interested in more than just talking to you, Georgia."

Georgia's lips formed a small O of surprise. "Wow," she said at last.

"I can't send you over there into that wolf den. Odds are that in the end, it won't make any difference. We just need to increase our offer and hope it's enough."

"No."

Carson frowned. "What do you mean, no?"

"I want to go. He's asked for me, so maybe I'm the one who can sway his decision."

"I can't risk it, Georgia. If that guy so much as lays a finger on you, I'll never forgive myself."

Georgia's lips curled into a wicked grin, highlighting today's dark burgundy lipstick. "I'm no debutante, Carson. I may have nice clothes and a good education now, but there was a time where I had to fight for survival each and every day. I can hold my own. If he gets inappropriate, I'll give him a good dose of pepper spray."

Now it was Carson's turn to look shocked. He envisioned Sutton Winchester—the King of Chicago—rolling around on the ground as he screamed and clawed at his eyes. But he'd love to hear her tell him about it.

He also couldn't forget that he'd promised his brothers that he would make this hospital project happen. Whether he liked it or not, he needed to do whatever it took, even if it meant sending Georgia right into that bastard's clutches.

"Okay, you can go," he said at last. "On one condition. You take Big Ron with you." The head of security at the Newport Corporation was a former Olympic heavy lifter. He'd once told Carson he slapped a man across the face and accidently broke his jaw. He could snap Sutton like a twig, if necessary.

Georgia considered his stipulations for a moment and then nodded. "Okay. But he stays outside the office with the secretary unless I call him."

"May I offer you something to drink?"

"No, thank you," Georgia replied. Sitting in the guest chair across from Sutton Winchester's ostentatious oak desk, she couldn't help but fiddle with the collar of her shirt. After Carson's warnings yesterday, she'd chosen a pantsuit instead of a skirt and buttoned her blouse up to her throat.

It had been a long time since she'd dressed that way. Probably not since she lived with Mrs. Anderson. She'd been a religious fanatic and swore up and down that any inch of skin Georgia showed would tempt a good man into sin. Truth be told, once Georgia blossomed into her full figure, there wasn't anything a turtleneck would do to hide it.

Even now, she could feel Sutton's eyes rake across her body. The July heat in Chicago was absolutely miserable, but at the moment she was wishing she'd worn a heavy down coat.

Sutton poured himself a drink and settled back into

his chair. Georgia noticed that the man in front of her bore little resemblance to the press picture she'd seen in the paper the other day. He was still a tall and relatively handsome man, but the green eyes watching her had a dull look. It was made more obvious by the bags under them and the wrinkles lining his brow. He looked ten years older than she'd expected, even with his wide grin and trademark dimples.

"So, Miss Adams, is it?" he asked before scooting up to the desk.

"Yes."

Sutton nodded and leaned forward to close some of the space between them. "I bet you're wondering why I asked you here today."

"Actually, yes. I'm not really the most qualified person to explain the plans the Newport Corporation has for the hospital, but I'll do the best I can. The current children's hospital is a dinosaur with outdated equipment and too few rooms and staff to provide for the number of children that need treatment. The plans we have for the new hospital will include state-of-the-art—"

Sutton held up his hand to silence her. "Actually, Miss Adams, you can stop there. To be honest, I didn't invite you here to talk about the land deal."

Georgia's brows went up in surprise. Carson had been right. She should've known better than to fall into this trap. Holding her purse tightly in her lap, she slipped one hand inside and wrapped her fingers around her trusty pepper spray. "May I ask why you did ask me here, Mr. Winchester?"

"Please, call me Sutton," he said with a smile that should've charmed her but immediately put Georgia on edge. In her years of foster care, she'd become a very good judge of character, and it took only a few minutes for her to know that she had to tread very carefully with this man.

"I saw you recently on the news speaking about the Newport Corporation's sponsorship of a charity fun run. I was impressed by you. Impressed enough that I had my people look into more of your work. You have a remarkable résumé for someone of your age."

Georgia tried not to squirm under his praise. She was very proud of how far she'd come in life. She'd worked damn hard to keep herself from becoming another sad statistic of the failing foster care system. Landing the job at Newport Corporation was the culmination of everything she had worked for. But she didn't like hearing it from Sutton's lips. Perhaps it was how he was looking at her as he said it.

"My director of public relations has recently retired. I haven't had a single applicant that could beat you out for the job."

Georgia straightened up in her seat and put on a flattered smile. "Luckily for them, I already have a job."

Sutton thoughtfully stroked his chin. "Yes, you do. But I think you can do better."

Her breath caught in her throat as Sutton pushed up from his chair and rounded the desk. He stopped just in front of her and leaned back on the edge. The hem of his pants brushed her ankle as he stretched out, causing her to tuck her legs up under the chair and out of his reach.

"What are you suggesting, Mr. Winchester?"

"I'm suggesting you come work for me, Georgia."

That wasn't going to happen. She didn't care for his cutthroat business practices. She wouldn't feel good about working for him. "And why would I do that?"

"Well," Sutton chuckled, "to start, it's the natural progression of your career. Everyone wants to work for the best, and Elite Industries is the best. Of course, there is also a generous benefits and compensation package. We offer an in-house day care, a fitness center and a month of vacation to start, plus telecommuting at least one day a week."

It sounded nice. *If* she was looking. And she wasn't.

"And then there's the signing bonus."

Georgia decided to bite. She'd done her fair share of market research to see if her earnings were on par with her peers'. If Elite Industries really was the step up he claimed it was, there should be some solid numbers behind that offer. "How much are we talking?"

"A million."

Her eyes widened as she struggled to choke down her shock. That was not at all what she was anticipating. A million dollar–signing bonus? What the hell kind of *salary* was he offering with a signing bonus like that? "That's very g-generous," she stuttered. "What's the catch?"

Sutton narrowed his green gaze at her and smiled wide. "Smart girl. Nothing is free in this world, as you are well aware, I'm sure. That said, I don't like to think of it as a catch. More as a…retainer for our mutually beneficial arrangement. You see, I'd like you to become more than just an employee to me, Georgia."

He said the words as casually as if he'd offered her a drink. It took Georgia a minute even to be certain she'd heard what she thought she did. Was he asking her to be his mistress? Carson had warned her that Sutton was a lech, but she'd never expected to be offered the opportunity to service him sexually as though it were another job opening at the company. Had his mistress retired, too?

"I'm flattered, Mr. Winchester. Really, I am. But I'm going to have to pass. On everything," she added with a pointed tone.

A flicker of disappointment danced over Sutton's worn face and then vanished just as quickly. "You don't have to decide now," he insisted. "It's a big decision. Go home and ponder what kind of opportunity I'm offering. Think about what you can do with a million dollars. When you change your mind, I'll be waiting."

Georgia wasn't going to change her mind. Not even for a million dollars. Even if Sutton wasn't old enough to be her father, he really wasn't her type. Thirty years ago, he might have attracted her at first sight, but his personality would've sunk that ship before it could sail. No amount of money or charisma would've changed that.

And even if Sutton was the most handsome, virtuous man she'd ever met, Georgia would still not be his employee. It was bad enough she'd gotten wrapped up in the moment and kissed Carson at the build site. She'd crossed the line with her boss and had regretted it ever since. Well, at least she regretted most of it. Kissing Carson had been amazing. She wanted more of him, and yet she was determined not to let that happen. Sleeping with the boss was bad news. And cliché. She refused to be cliché. She also refused to ruin the good thing she had going at the Newport Corporation.

Inappropriate relations in the workplace just led to awkwardness. Georgia was dedicated to doing her best work every day. She couldn't do that with Carson walking around, reminding her of what they did or didn't do. Things always got weird. It was bad enough she fantasized about him. Acting on it was another matter. Sutton had been a welcome distraction from what happened that day, but once the land deal was finalized, they'd both have to face what they'd done.

"I will think it over, Mr. Winchester, but my answer isn't going to change. Now, what about the children's hospital?"

Sutton sighed and crossed his arms over his chest. "My answer hasn't changed, either. We'll battle it out fair and square with the property owner and let the best—or at least the richest—man win. Unless, of course, you'd like to reconsider my offer... If you change your mind, then perhaps I might change mine, as well."

This was even worse than she'd thought. Now he was trying to twist her arm by using such a noble cause against her. What was she willing to do for sick children? A lot. But not that. She grew up with almost nothing, but she'd managed to hang on to her principles.

There was nothing else she could say, so Georgia stood up and slung her purse over her shoulder. "I guess we're done here," she said.

Sutton reached out to take her hand. He shook it for a moment, then held it longer than necessary. He ran his thumb over the back of her hand, sending a shiver of revulsion down her spine. "Consider my offer, Georgia. There are a lot of parents with sick children out there that would be willing to do anything to save their child. In the end, it isn't much of a sacrifice to help so many, is it?"

Georgia tugged her hand from his and rubbed the palm over her slacks to wipe him away from her skin. "Good afternoon, Mr. Winchester."

Three

"He *what*?"

Carson very rarely lost his temper in the office, but he could tell by Georgia's startled cringe that he'd just shouted loud enough for the people in Accounting to hear him. "I'm sorry," he said more softly. "Just please tell me I didn't hear you right."

She didn't need to answer him. He could tell by the distant look in her eye and her awkward, hunched posture with her arms crossed protectively over her chest that he'd heard her correctly. He'd always known Sutton was a bastard, but this time he'd gone too far.

"Don't make me say it again, Carson," she said softly.

He fought the protective urge to wrap his arms around her and tell her it would be okay. After the day she'd had, she probably didn't want a man touching her. Even him. Considering how quickly she'd back-pedaled from their kiss the other day, she probably didn't want Carson touching her, ever.

Looking around his office, he decided maybe they needed a change of scene for this conversation. "Buy you a drink?" he asked.

Georgia looked down at her watch and sighed. "I'm not going to get any work done, so why not?"

It wasn't an enthusiastic response, but he didn't expect one given that she'd just come here straight from Sutton's office. He grabbed his phone and escorted her to the elevator. They exited the building and crossed the street, heading down the block to an Irish pub where Carson and his brothers had spent a good bit of their time and money over the years.

Since the official business day hadn't yet come to an end, the bar wasn't crowded with the usual suits. They took a booth in a darkened corner. Carson ordered himself a Guinness and Georgia opted for a pint of hard cider. They sat quietly for a few moments with their drinks. He didn't want to push her, but he needed the whole story. Brooks and Graham would be very interested in just how low Winchester had stooped today.

Georgia took a long sip of her drink and sighed heavily. "Well, the punch line is that he isn't going to back down on the land. He doesn't care if we're building a children's hospital or homes for one-legged orphan refugees. Well, actually that's not entirely true," she noted. "He said he might reconsider his position if I was willing to seriously consider his *generous* offer."

Carson's grip on his glass was so tight he worried he might crush the drink in his hand. "What was the offer?"

"First, he offered me a job as his director of public relations with a million-dollar signing bonus."

That didn't surprise him. Sutton was constantly cherry-picking employees from his competitors. They'd lost several high performers due to his below-the-belt tactics. But who offered a seven-figure bonus? "I never knew he was such a generous man," he said with a flat tone.

"I wouldn't call him that," she chuckled. "It came with some very important fine print. I was also to become his mistress. Then, and only then, would he consider backing down on the land project."

"Did he touch you inappropriately?" Carson hated to ask, but if Sutton crossed a line, Georgia could bring charges. She wasn't his employee yet, but at the very least they could file a civil suit and drag his name through the mud.

"Not really." Georgia rubbed her palms together thoughtfully. "He held my hand longer than I wanted him to, but it could've been a lot worse."

"Thank goodness," Carson said in a rush of breath he'd been holding. Just the thought of that old pervert laying a hand on Georgia made him want to punch his fist through the drywall. He felt bad enough about letting her go over there against his better judgment. If Sutton had gotten physically aggressive, Carson never would've forgiven himself. "I'm so sorry about all this. He's an even bigger pig than I expected. Where was Ron during all of this? I told you he had to escort you over there."

"He did. I just left him sitting in the waiting room as I told you I would."

"You didn't call for him when Sutton got inappropriate?"

"No. Like I said, he didn't really touch me. He just made me an offer I didn't accept," Georgia said with a guilty look. She held up her hand to silence him. "I know, I know. But I had it under control. My finger was on the trigger of my pepper spray the whole time. Sutton is bold, and certainly arrogant, but he's also smart. He's not going to have a woman run screaming from his office. It would hurt business."

That was probably true. The only thing Sutton Winchester liked more than women was money. He wasn't about to ruin his business and jeopardize his cash flow. It didn't make Carson feel any better. Georgia was confident in her ability to protect herself, but he had his doubts.

She was a petite woman. Curvy, but small. With her platinum waves and knockout body, she drew men's eyes wherever she went. She had certainly drawn his gaze the first moment they met. A part of him hadn't wanted to hire her just so he could ask her out to dinner instead. In the end, his brain had overridden his erection. She was smart, experienced and the perfect candidate for the position.

"Georgia," he began, "I need to apologize to you."

"You just apologized. Really, Carson, it's not your fault. You warned me about what he was like. I just never dreamed he'd be that bold."

Carson shook his head. "I'm certainly sorry about what happened today, but that's not what I was apologizing for. I actually was talking about that kiss by the lake."

Georgia's soft, friendly expression hardened. He

could tell she was uncomfortable with his bringing it up. "Carson, I—"

"No, let me say this," he interrupted. "In the moment, it felt like the right thing to do. But after what happened today, I realize just how inappropriate it was. If I don't recognize that, I'm just as bad as he is."

Georgia reached across the table and took Carson's hand. "You will never, ever be anything like that man. Don't even think that for a second."

Carson looked into her gray eyes, noting the touch of olive green that radiated from the center. It was an unusual color, one he'd never seen before. Her gaze seemed to penetrate him, as if she were seeing inside him in a way that made him uncomfortable. He looked down at their hands, which were still clasped atop the polished wood table.

It was only then that he allowed himself to notice how soft her skin felt against his. As he grasped her fingers, the blood started to hum in his veins. He remembered the sensation from the field, knew how long it would take him to recover from the reaction she stirred in him.

He didn't understand it. Georgia was beautiful, but Carson had touched his fair share of beautiful women. She was smart and funny, and he'd been around women like that, too. But never, not once since he broke the seal on his manhood in high school, had a woman affected him the way Georgia did. Lately all it took was the lingering scent of her perfume in the hallways at work, and he was consumed with thoughts of her.

Carson hated Sutton for putting the moves on Georgia, but he understood fully why he had done it. She had the power to enchant a man without even trying. A million dollars was chump change to Sutton, especially when it was a corporate write-off, but it was still a significant offer. If it came to it, what would Carson be willing to pay to keep her with him?

All that and more.

Looking up, he realized Georgia's expression had changed. She was no longer softly consoling him. Now her brow was lined with concern, and he realized it was because he was still holding her hand as though he might be repelled from the face of the earth if he didn't cling to her.

He immediately let her hand go and buried his own beneath the table. "I'm sorry. That probably just made it worse. I...I don't know why I have such a hard time maintaining a professional distance when I'm around you, Georgia. I've never had this problem before."

She nodded curtly and took another large drink, finishing off her glass without meeting his gaze. "I understand. We're both human, after all. We work together a lot, so the temptation is there. But we're strong, smart people. We can fight it."

Georgia said the words, but as he looked at her, he wasn't entirely sure she believed them. For the first time, the pieces started to click together in Carson's mind. She'd said "we," as in she was attracted to him, as well. That would certainly explain her flushed cheeks when he greeted her in the hallway and her more than enthusiastic response to his kiss. It was one thing for him to be attracted to her, but knowing the feeling was mutual would make this all ten times harder.

They needed to focus on work. That was what they

were good at, what offered the best distraction. Going over their conversation about Sutton in his mind, he decided to talk strategy going forward. "So what is our next step?" he asked. "We've got to secure that land no matter what Sutton wants."

A sly smile spread across Georgia's face. There was a twinkle of mischief in her gray eyes as she looked at him and said, "Next, we play dirty."

Smile. Look into the camera. Focus.

"I'd like to thank you all for coming today," Georgia began, ignoring the camera flashes and microphones in her face. Because she was PR director, press conferences fell into her job description, but she was always filled with nerves in front of the camera. Especially today. This was her moment to turn the tide with the land deal, and she couldn't screw it up.

"The Newport Corporation is a family company. It was founded by brothers Brooks, Graham and Carson Newport as a small real estate venture that turned into much more. CEO Carson Newport once told me that he knew they were a success when they were able to buy their mother, Cynthia Newport, a home and let her retire early.

"The love these three men had for their mother is why I've asked you to be here today. With her newfound free time, Cynthia discovered a purpose in working with sick children at the local hospital. She spent hours there reading stories, playing games and helping children forget—if for just a short time—about the pain and fear they lived with each day."

Georgia looked down at her notes and confirmed her next point. "The entire Newport Corporation was extremely saddened to hear about the sudden loss of Cynthia Newport two months ago. Without warning, she was stricken with a brain aneurysm, and there was nothing that could be done. She was only fifty-five years old.

"Cynthia's sons have decided that the best way to honor their mother's memory is to put their resources and expertise into the cause that was so dear to her heart. Ladies and gentleman," she said, reaching for the easel beside her, "I give you the plans for the Cynthia Newport Memorial Hospital for Children."

She removed a blank placard and revealed the artist's rendering of the hospital underneath. Georgia waited a moment for the cameras to stop flashing before she continued. "Newport Memorial will be the most sophisticated facility for children in the US. They will provide cutting-edge technology, the best treatment and the most skilled staff available."

Georgia spied Carson standing near the back of the crowd of reporters. Quite a few had showed up today for the press conference, huddling in a semicircle in the garden courtyard of the Newport building. Even then, he was easy to spot, especially with his brother, Brooks, beside him. The COO was almost always the tallest man in the room unless Graham was in the office. The two of them were like Norse gods in expensive suits.

Carson was like a demigod, half man, half immortal. Just real enough for her to feel like she could stand a chance with him, but enough of a fantasy to keep her pessimistic feet firmly planted on the ground.

Losing her place in the speech, she tore her gaze away and flicked over the neatly printed lines of the press statement. "After an exhaustive search, the Newport Corporation has identified an ideal spot for the hospital overlooking Lake Michigan. Unfortunately, we are not the only company with our eyes on the land. Recently, Elite Industries has announced, perhaps prematurely, their plans to build luxury condominiums along the water.

"It is our hope that with enough community support, we can make the Newport Memorial Hospital a reality, no matter how much money our competitors might try to throw around. The community needs this facility for our children far more than we need additional fancy housing for Chicago's wealthy."

She reached for the artist's rendering and set it aside to display a graphic of their social media campaign. "Show your support by posting on social media using the hashtag *#NewportMemorial4Kids* and letting the community know how you feel. Together, we can make this dream a reality. Now, I'll be taking any questions."

Georgia fielded about ten questions from the reporters about the project before ending the press conference. "Thank you," she said as she gathered up her note cards and slipped away from the podium. Moving through the crowd packing up their equipment, she found Carson and Brooks at the back where they'd been standing earlier. "How'd I do?" she asked.

"Amazing," Carson said with a pleased grin.

"There's no way Winchester's offer stands a chance with the seller after that." Brooks held up his cell phone. "Two of the stations aired this live, and there have already been over two hundred tweets under our hashtag. When this re-airs during the evening news, it will explode."

Georgia gave a heavy sigh of relief. She hoped this worked. If the owners were more interested in money, Winchester could still win them over.

After the press cleared out, they headed back upstairs to the executive floor. Brooks followed Carson into his office, where they poured a celebratory glass of scotch.

"Would you care for a drink, Georgia?" Brooks asked. "You certainly earned it."

"Actually, I think I'll pass," she said. The adrenaline that had gotten her though the press conference was fading, and she was ready to crash. "If you two don't mind, I think I'd like to catch an early train home and watch our segment on the news on the couch with some takeout."

She dismissed the flicker of disappointment on Carson's face. "Understandable," he said. "Keep the phone nearby, though. If the seller accepts our offer, you'll be the first person I call."

Georgia gave them a wave and slipped down the hallway to her office. She quickly gathered her things. If she could get to the "L" platform in the next ten minutes, she'd catch the express train.

She found herself at her building about a half hour later. Once she reached her apartment door, she gave a heavy sigh of relief. Georgia loved her loft. It was the first thing she'd bought when she secured her first real executive position with a major company. She could barely afford it at the time but she had been desperate to be able finally to have a home of her own.

She hadn't had the easiest time growing up. Her

mother had been a teenage runaway when she was born. Georgia didn't remember much about those early years, but her caseworker, Sheila, had told her when she was older that her mother had developed a heroin addiction and was working as a prostitute for drugs. Georgia had been taken away and placed in foster care when she was only three.

From there, she'd become a Ping-Pong ball, bouncing from place to place. She never lived anywhere longer than a year, and none of those places ever felt like home. She tried not to let her mind dwell too much on her childhood in Detroit, but she'd let enough of the dirty homes, strict or even abusive foster parents and secondhand everything through to let her appreciate what she had now.

This loft, with its floor-to-ceiling windows and modern, industrial elements, was everything she'd ever wanted. The walls were painted in warm, inviting colors and the plush furniture was overflowing with pillows. The kitchen was state-of-the-art despite the fact that she never cooked. She could swim in her master bathtub and have a party in the shower. She had a service come in to clean once a week, so the place was always spotless.

It was wonderful. The perfect escape from the world. Even the longest, hardest day at the office couldn't keep the smile from her face when she walked in the door each evening.

Tonight she went through her nightly ritual. She set down her purse and disappeared into the bedroom to change. She reemerged ten minutes later with her blond hair in a knot on the top of her head, her face scrubbed free of makeup and her favorite pair of pajamas on. She poured herself a glass of pinot grigio and grabbed her favorite Chinese delivery menu before she collapsed on her suede sofa.

The delivery man arrived with her dinner with just minutes to spare before the evening newscast. The segment on the Newport Corporation was in the second news block when she was about halfway through her kung pao chicken. She didn't like watching herself on camera, but she forced herself to do it anyway. Her speech professor had made all the students do it. It was the only way to truly see the nervous ticks and language crutches she used when she spoke in public.

All in all, not bad. Her voice was sultry, like a phone sex operator, but there was nothing she could do about it. She'd tried a million times to alter it, but it sounded fake. On the upside, she used the word "uh" only twice and she didn't use "like" at all. Professor Kline would be very proud of her.

At the end of the segment, the news station flashed the campaign hashtag on the screen and encouraged viewers to use it to show their support. Georgia reached for her phone to check on the response. There were thousands of posts on Twitter with even more on other platforms. They were even trending.

Georgia chewed nervously at her thumbnail as she watched the posts scroll down the screen. This might actually work. She really, truly hoped so. The idea of Winchester taking that land and building condos on it made her stomach turn. She knew from experience that things weren't always fair or just in life, but she certainly hoped she was about to outsmart the system.

The rest of the newscast dragged on. She sat in front of the TV, idly chewing her dinner and not listening to anything. She was waiting for that phone to ring. It just had to ring.

She was on her second glass of wine when the news ended, and still no call. Georgia paced anxiously across the concrete floor, gazing out at her view of the city. The sun was just setting, making the Chicago skyline a stark silhouette against the golden glow of the sky. Lights were starting to turn on around town, slowly transforming the hard, industrial shapes of downtown into a sparkling constellation.

Georgia was so lost in her thoughts that when the phone rang, she jumped nearly six inches off the ground. Turning on her heel, she ran back to the kitchen and snatched her phone off the countertop. It was Carson.

She held her breath in anticipation as she picked up. "Yes?" she answered.

"Our offer has been accepted!" he announced triumphantly. "They said it was the highest and in the end, they decided to accept it and not start a bidding war because of the newscast. We got it, Georgia, and it's all because of your hard work."

"Thanks," she said, dismissing his compliment. "It's not hard to get behind a project like this when the lives of sick children are at stake. It made my work pretty easy, I have to say. I'm very happy our project can go forward."

"It will. Once the paperwork is signed, I want to have a grand groundbreaking ceremony. Your group will be heading up that effort. But first, we're going to kick off the project with a cocktail party on Friday night to celebrate. Rebecca is putting it together as we speak. Wear your dancing shoes."

Four

The sale was really happening. The lawyers were handling the details and it was off Georgia's plate. At least for now. Once the land was officially the property of the Newport Corporation, she would start the groundbreaking-ceremony preparation. After that, she had no doubt there would be charity fund-raiser events and a million other tasks on her plate to handle.

But tonight was for celebration, not work.

Carson's assistant had rented out a chic little bistro on the Magnificent Mile for the party. Wine was flowing like water, a jazz band was playing at a tasteful level in the corner and everyone was mingling and laughing. Every employee, from the janitor to the executives, had loved Cynthia. They knew how important this was to the brothers and were excited about this being the next new project on the agenda.

Folks had put on their fanciest cocktail attire for the night. At least, the women had. There was a rainbow of slinky and sparkly dresses in the room. Georgia herself had opted for a muted gold snakeskin cocktail dress by Tom Ford. It was a little showy, but with a high, scooped neck and long sleeves, it was also very modest, which she liked. The gold complemented her skin tone and brought out the darker tones of her platinum hair. The dress also didn't really need any jewelry to enhance it, so she'd been able to wear a simple pair of diamond stud earrings.

As usual, the men fell back on their arsenal of suits, although Georgia didn't mind a bit. She enjoyed the look of a man in a nice suit, especially the Newport brothers. Theirs were custom fitted to their broad shoulders and narrow hips. All three of them were milling around the room, drinks in hand. They were a ridiculously handsome trio, and every single woman in the room was eyeing the bachelors with interest. Except Georgia.

She turned away from them and glanced self-consciously around the room. She knew she should have been socializing, but she was happy to loiter at her cocktail table in the corner, watching the action. She loved working at the Newport Corporation. The people here were the family she'd never had. But at the same time, she wasn't really great with this kind of social setting. Perhaps it was a handicap of her childhood. She'd moved too much to make friends and never had family she could count on. She watched the world go by from the fringe.

"Good evening, Georgia."

At the sound of a man's voice, Georgia turned to

her left, startled. She was shocked to find Sutton Winchester standing so near her that they nearly brushed shoulders.

Biting down her irritation with him from earlier in the week, she smiled. "Good evening, Mr. Winchester." After all, she'd won the battle. She should have been happy to see him and gloat about her victory.

He held up a glass of white wine. "I got you a refill," he said.

Georgia looked down and noticed she had only half a sip left in her own glass. She set it on the table and accepted the fresh drink. "That was very thoughtful of you."

"I'm not a complete bastard," he said with a wry smile as he turned to look at the crowd she'd been eyeing a moment before.

"The jury is still out on that one."

Sutton chuckled heartily before it disintegrated into a string of harsh coughs. "Pardon me," he said, clearing his throat.

"So, what brings you to our little celebration tonight, Mr. Winchester? You don't have any pig's blood stashed in the rafters or anything, do you?"

"Not at all. I was actually invited," Sutton said with emphasis. "I'm sure the Newport boys want to rub their victory in my face. I'm happy to drink wine on their tab while they do it. Besides that, I wanted to talk to you."

"Me?" Georgia turned to him with her brow lifted in surprise.

"Yes. I saw your press conference the other day. I wanted to tell you what a good job you did with it.

You worked the press and the social media outlets beautifully. The owner had no real choice but to sell to Newport after that. I underestimated your talent, Georgia. You're much more than just a pretty face. Knowing that makes me want you on my team even more. Come work for me. I'll bump that bonus up to 1.2 million dollars if you'll consider it."

Georgia couldn't believe the nerve of him to come into their celebration and proposition her again. "That's very generous of you, but I'm sorry, Mr. Winchester. The answer is still no." She glanced around the crowd, looking for an escape, but everyone seemed involved in other conversations.

He nodded, sipping his drink and pursing his lips in thought. "I understand you feel a sense of loyalty to the Newports, but this offer doesn't have to be a package deal. What about the *other* position we discussed?"

The other position? As his mistress? Every muscle in Georgia's body tensed as she felt the older man take in every inch of her. She hadn't been expecting to see Sutton tonight. She was dressed quite differently than she had at his office. Her gold dress covered all the necessary skin, but it was clingy. And short. And the back was completely bare to contrast with the chaste front. She wished she was wearing a caftan instead. Or that she could dump her wine on him and tell the pervert to go to hell. But that was unprofessional. She would hold it together and get away from him as soon as she was able.

"I'm not interested in *any* of the offers," she said as forcefully as she could. "It doesn't matter how much money is involved."

Sutton narrowed his gaze at her. He looked a bit befuddled, as though he didn't quite understand what she was saying to him. He was a man used to getting his way, and Georgia wasn't playing by his rules. "May I ask why?"

Georgia searched her brain for a reason with which he couldn't argue. He was a shrewd businessman who could likely destroy any argument as surely as an attorney during cross-examination. She didn't want to leave any room for hope on his part.

"Georgia?" Sutton pressed.

"Fine," she said as the idea suddenly crystallized in her mind. Good or bad, it was all she had. "I'm not going to be your mistress because I already have a lover."

He looked shocked. Georgia wasn't certain if she should be insulted by his response. "Who?" he asked.

"Carson Newport." The words slipped from her lips before she could stop them, surprising even herself.

She wasn't the only one. Sutton's eyes were wide. He turned his head, and Georgia followed his gaze to where Carson was standing only a few feet away. He must have seen Sutton with her, because it looked as though he was on his way to rescue her from Winchester's clutches. Her words had stopped Carson cold. He was frozen in place, his drink clutched in his hand.

"Carson Newport is your lover?" Sutton asked with an incredulous tone.

Was it so unbelievable that a man like Carson would be interested in her? She didn't know what to say to his question. Georgia thought she might be caught in a lie. She hadn't expected Carson to overhear all of this. Now his reaction was key to selling her story. Before she could respond, Carson sidled up beside her and wrapped his arm around her waist.

"Surprised, Sutton?"

The old man turned to him and shrugged. "To be honest, I didn't think you had it in you, Carson."

Carson leaned in to nuzzle Georgia's ear and plant a searing kiss on the sensitive skin on her neck. "Go with it," he whispered softly.

She tried to do as he said and not tense in his arms, even as a thrill of arousal ran through her body. Leaning into his touch, she let her eyes flutter closed for a moment. If she was being honest with herself, it wasn't hard to feign interest in him. Such a simple touch had lit up her nerves like Christmas lights.

She opened her eyes in time to see Carson turn back to Sutton with a grin. "You're not having the best week, are you? You were after waterfront property and a woman, and I bested you on both. You must be losing your touch, old man."

With a clenched jaw, Sutton looked over both of them and slammed back the last of his drink. "I'm not the kind of man who gives up that easily, Carson. Enjoy her while you can," he suggested before turning on his heel and stomping through the crowd to the exit.

Once he was gone, Georgia took a step away from Carson and covered her mouth with her hand to smother her embarrassment. "Oh, Carson," she said. "I am so sorry. He put me on the spot and it just came out."

Carson put a reassuring hand on her shoulder and shook his head. "Not to worry. It did the trick, for now, at least. I wouldn't count on him letting it go entirely. Like he said, he's not that kind of man. Then again, who would want to compete with me for a woman's affections?"

At that, Georgia giggled, and the tension of the moment slipped away. Thank goodness he hadn't read more into her naming him as her lover. "Hopefully no one was listening in on the conversation. I'd hate for rumors to start about us."

"Oh, I'd say half the room heard you blurt out my name, but don't worry about the rumors. Your boss knows it isn't true, and he's the only one who can fire you."

"I'm relieved to hear that. The last thing I want to do is put my position at the Newport Corporation in jeopardy."

"Well, if nothing else, I hear Sutton has a position open," he said with laughter lighting his eyes. "Come on," Carson said, slipping a comforting arm around her shoulder to guide her into the crowd. "No more hiding in the corner. This is your party, too. Let's celebrate."

Carson never went into the office on a Saturday if he could avoid it. He always tried to make the most of his time away from work so he could have a life. Or at least, so he'd have the time to have a life when he actually decided to get around to it.

The Newport brothers passed that same work-life balance philosophy on to their employees. That was why Carson was so surprised to see a light on when he walked down the hallway. It was Georgia's office.

Curious, he paused in the doorway, hoping not to scare her. She was working intently at her computer, probably not expecting anyone to appear suddenly.

He took the quiet moment to admire her without her knowing it. There was just something so appealing about Georgia. Of course, she was the blonde bombshell that most men desired, but even the little things drew him to her. At the moment, he found the crease between her eyebrows as she concentrated on her work appealing.

Today her hair was in a casual ponytail, something she would never wear to the office on an average workday. She was wearing a tight-fitting T-shirt and jeans. Carson realized in that moment that he'd never seen Georgia look like this before. She was always so professional and put together, even on a casual Friday. He appreciated that about her, but she looked so much younger and more easygoing today.

"You know, it's rude to stare."

Busted. Carson grinned wide and met Georgia's amused gaze. "I wasn't expecting to see anyone here today. Nor did I think I'd find you in jeans."

Georgia looked down self-consciously at herself. "Is that okay? I didn't think anyone would see me. I'm usually here alone on the weekends."

"It's absolutely fine," he said, although he was concerned by the rest of her response. "Are you here most weekends?"

"Yes. I like the quiet of the office. It lets me catch up on things and focus without calls or people coming by. I know the company is big on spending time with family, but I don't have a family."

Carson tried not to frown. He didn't know much about Georgia. She was all work during business hours, so they hadn't spent much time socializing. Her office was tidy and well decorated, but there weren't any photos of family or friends on her desk or bookshelves. Now he knew why.

"What about you?" she asked. "Why are you in today? I thought after all that champagne last night that most people would be laid out until noon at least."

He had woken with a slight headache, but nothing he couldn't handle. As for why he was here, that was a good question. He'd gotten into his car, fully intending to drive to his mother's home and make good on his promise to clean out the house. The next thing he knew, he was at work. "I thought I'd come in and check on some things."

Georgia wrinkled her nose. "You're avoiding something," she said without a touch of doubt in her voice.

He sighed and slumped against her door frame. Was he that transparent? "I guess I am."

"Anything I can help you with?"

Whereas he hadn't been looking to drag anyone into the slog of work, he realized that he didn't dread the task so much when he envisioned Georgia there with him. "No, no. You've probably got better things to do," he argued.

"No, tell me," Georgia insisted.

"I'm supposed to be cleaning out my mother's house. I told Brooks and Graham that I'd go through everything and start getting it ready to sell. That's where I intended to go today, but I ended up here instead. I don't know why."

"I can imagine that would be difficult," she said. "Would you like me to go with you? I'd be happy to lend a hand. At the very least, I can offer moral support."

It sounded great, but he still felt anxious about it.

"Are you sure? Her house is about a half hour from here, up in Kenilworth."

Georgia closed her laptop and stood up. She picked up her massive black purse and slung it over her arm. "I'm sure. Let's go."

He wasn't going to argue with her. Without even making it as far as his own office, they turned around and headed back to the elevator.

They were on the expressway north before they spoke again. "So tell me," Georgia began, "what's going on here? I mean, if you don't mind. I get the feeling this is about more than just sorting through your mother's things."

Carson gripped the leather-wrapped steering wheel and focused his gaze intently on the traffic ahead of him. "Do you really want to know my tragic life story?"

Georgia snorted delicately. "I think I can trump you on tragic life stories."

"Tell me about you, then." Carson was far more interested in Georgia's life than he was in rehashing his own.

She shook her head adamantly. "Nope. I asked you first. And besides, this trip is about you. I need to know if I'm treading into a mine field here."

His brothers wanted him to dig up the truth about their father. If she was going to be there helping him, she needed to know. "Okay," he relented. "My mother is the only real family we ever had. Our aunt Gerty died a long time ago, and she wasn't really related to us. Losing Mom, we lost any connection we have to our roots. It's been a difficult realization for us all."

"I understand what that can be like," Georgia said

without elaborating. "Did your mother ever speak about her family or your father to you?"

"Rarely, and when we pushed her, nothing she said was good. She insisted that our father was abusive and she ran away from him in the middle of the night when we were still babies. She never would tell us where we lived before, his name or anything about the past. She made it very clear that she didn't want us to find him when we were older."

"That must be frustrating for you all," Georgia noted. "Wanting to belong, yet having that fear that the truth would be worse than being alone."

"Exactly," Carson said with surprise in his voice. He didn't expect her to be able to understand it all so easily. "Brooks and Graham want me to look for clues in the house. They seem convinced that the answers are hidden away somewhere. I'm not so sure, but I told them I would look. It's our last chance at the truth. The rest died with Mom."

That was probably the hardest part. Carson had gotten the feeling that maybe one day their mother might tell them the rest of the story. They weren't children anymore. She had nothing to fear from her past because the boys could protect her, no matter what. Cynthia probably thought she had time to share the whole tale about where they came from, and then it was stolen away in an instant.

"I'll help you find out the truth," Georgia said.

As Carson exited the expressway and headed toward the house in Kenilworth, he found himself nearly overwhelmed with gratitude that she was here with him. That she understood. "Thank you" was all he could verbalize.

"I don't know my real family, either," she offered. "I grew up in the Detroit foster care system because my mother was a teenage runaway. She got into drugs and a lot of other nasty things and they took me away. I have no idea who my father is or anything about my family. My father's name was left off the birth certificate. I don't even know for certain that my last name is really Adams. She could've just picked that name out of the sky. Not having that link to your past and where you come from can make you feel like discarded paper drifting on the wind."

Carson was surprised by her confession, but it made a lot of the pieces of the Georgia puzzle fall into place. Maybe that's why he was so drawn to her. They were both lost, anchorless. "Have you kept contact with your mother at all over the years?"

"No," she said, shaking her head and looking down into her hands folded in her lap. "I haven't seen her since I was three and social services came for me. I wouldn't really even know what she looked like if my caseworker, Sheila, hadn't given me an old photo of her. I keep it in my purse." Georgia reached for her bag and pulled out the photo.

Carson turned in to his mother's driveway just as she handed over the picture. He put the car in Park and studied the worn photograph. The blonde girl in the picture was holding a towheaded toddler. She looked very young, not more than fifteen or sixteen. The late '80s influences were evident in her big hair and heavy makeup, which didn't hide the dark circles under her eyes or the hollowed-out cheeks. There were purple track marks on the girl's arm.

"I think she looked a lot like me, but thinner.

Harder. There wasn't much life in her eyes by that point. Aside from that, I don't have any memories of her that really stayed with me. I just remember the homes."

In that moment, Carson was extremely thankful to his mother for everything she'd done for him and his brothers. They hadn't had much, but she'd done all she could to keep them safe and healthy. Georgia hadn't been so lucky. He handed the photo back to her. "Did you move around a lot?"

Georgia chuckled bitterly as she put the picture away. "You could say that. It was a blessing and a curse. If the family was horrible, I had the solace of knowing I wouldn't be there long. If they were amazing and kind, I would cry every night knowing that eventually I would have to leave. The only constant in my life was Sheila. In a way, she became my family. She's the one that helped me get into college by helping me write a million scholarship essays. She insisted that I make something of myself."

"That was my aunt Gerty for us. She took us in after her husband died and made us her family. When she passed away, she left enough money for my brothers and me to go to college and start our business. Our mother insisted that we become the best version of ourselves we could possibly be. Without that kick start, I'm not sure what would've become of us. Everything we are is because of my mother and Gerty."

Georgia reached out in that moment and took his hand. Her touch was warm and enveloping, like a comforting blanket. They sat for a moment in the driveway, silently acknowledging all that they'd shared.

His mother's home stood like a monolith in front of

them. Inside were all the memories, secrets and emotions of her life. Going inside felt like disturbing her grave somehow.

"Are you ready?" Georgia prompted him after a few minutes.

"No, but let's go inside anyway."

They climbed from his Range Rover and walked together toward the front door. Carson unlocked it and they stepped into the tile foyer. The house had always seemed so warm and welcoming before, but now it was cold and silent like a tomb. His mother had given it life.

"Where should we start?"

Carson looked around and pointed toward the staircase. "Let's focus on her bedroom. If she was keeping any kind of secrets, I think that's where they'd be."

"Okay." Georgia started for the stairs, but paused and turned back when Carson didn't follow her. Her gray eyes questioned him.

Thank goodness she was here. He wouldn't even have made it this far without her prompting. It was better this way. Get it done, get it over with. If Carson didn't find anything about their family history, so be it. At least he and his brothers could move on with their lives. "I'm coming."

Georgia reached out her hand to him until he took it. "My past may be buried forever, but we're going to find your family, Carson. I can feel it."

Five

Carson was getting discouraged. They'd gone through almost everything in his mother's bedroom. Drawer by drawer, box by box, they'd sorted through for any personal effects and then bagged the remaining items up. Some clothes and accessories were for donation, some things were for the dump, and others, like her jewelry, were to be split up among the brothers.

Hours had gone by without a single discovery of interest. No skeletons under the bed, no dark secrets hidden away in the underwear drawer. They'd checked the pocket of every coat and the contents of each old purse. Nothing but used tubes of lipstick and some faded receipts. All that was left was a collection of shoe boxes on the very top shelf of the closet.

Carson eyed the boxes with dismay. They were likely to find nothing but shoes in them. Most of the boxes seemed like fairly new acquisitions from her life after he and his brothers had made their fortune— Stuart Weitzman, Jimmy Choo, Christian Louboutin… But one box caught his eye. On the very top of the stack, in the far back corner, was a ratty old box with a faded and curling Hush Puppies label on it. There was no doubt that box had been around in his mother's closet for a very long time. Maybe even thirty years or so…

"There's a shoe box in the very back corner that looks promising," Carson said. Looking around, he was annoyed to find that it was out of his reach even with his height and long arms. "How can my mother not own a stepladder or something? I guess I'll run downstairs and get a chair."

"No," Georgia insisted. "I'm sure I can reach it. I just need you to give me a boost."

Carson looked at her with concern. "A boost?"

"Yes, just make a step for me to put my foot in your hands and boost me up. I'll be able to reach it."

It would be just as easy to go get a chair, but he wasn't going to argue with her. He wanted into that box as soon as possible. Crouching over, Carson laced his fingers together and made a steady perch for Georgia's shoe.

"One, two, three," she counted, hoisting herself up.

Carson held her up and patiently waited for news. "Can you reach it?"

"It's just beyond me. Hold on. Wait… I've…almost… got it!" A moment later, it came tumbling off the top shelf along with several others. Georgia lost her balance and dropped from his hands, colliding with his chest.

"Whoa there," he said, catching her before she could bounce off him and hit the floor. He'd instinctively wrapped his arms around her, holding her body tight against his own. The contact sent a surge of need through his veins, making him hyperaware of her breasts molded to his chest. Every muscle in his body tightened, his pulse quickening in his throat as he held her. "Are you okay?" he asked as he swallowed hard.

She looked up at him with momentarily dazed eyes. "Yeah...I mean *yes*. I wasn't expecting it to all rain down at once." She pressed gently but insistently against his chest. Carson relinquished his hold and she took a step back. He breathed in deeply to cool his arousal and tried to focus on their discovery instead.

Georgia looked down at the floor of the closet and the mess they'd made. There were several pairs of shoes scattered around the floor. The shoe box they'd sought out, the oldest one in the bunch with the peeling Hush Puppies label, had come open, too. As expected, there was not a thirty-year-old pair of shoes in it. Instead the paper contents had scattered everywhere, making the closet look as if a blizzard had struck.

They both crouched down and started sorting through the mess. Carson found a few pictures bundled together with a piece of twine. He untied them and sifted through the images. A couple were of him and his brothers when they were small. Things like Christmas morning and school pageants. There was one of his mother when she was very young, maybe even a teenager. After that were a few with his mother and some other people he didn't recognize. He flipped the pictures over, but there was no writing on the back, no clue as to whether the other people were family or friends.

Setting them aside, he picked up some old newspaper clippings. Most of the pieces were about a missing girl named Amy Jo Turner. He scanned one of the articles looking for clues about his mother, but all it talked about was the circumstances surrounding the teenager's disappearance and how the authorities presumed the worst. Her boat had been found drifting empty in a lake. A single shoe and the sweater she was last seen in had washed up a mile away about a week later.

The header was for a paper in Houston, Texas, and the dates were all in the early '80s before Brooks and Graham were born. Their mother had never mentioned Houston, much less that she might have lived there at some point. Who was Amy Jo Turner? What did any of this have to do with his mother? It was important enough for her to keep the clippings for thirty years, but he didn't understand why.

"Carson," Georgia said, drawing his eye from the photos. "Look at this."

He took a discolored envelope from her hand and unfolded the letter inside it. It was a handwritten letter addressed to his mother. Impatient, he skimmed through the words to the bottom where it was signed "Yours always, S." Returning to the top, he read through it again, looking for clues to the identity of the writer that he might have missed the first time.

Dearest Cynthia,
You don't know how hard it's been to be away from you. I know that I've put myself in this po-

sition, and I can't apologize enough. I seem to destroy everything that I love. You and the boys are probably better off without me. I hope that one day you can forgive me for what I've done to you. Know that no matter how much time has passed, my feelings for you will never fade. You have been, and always will be, the one true love of my life.

Yours always, S

That was totally and completely useless. All Carson got from it was an initial. He flipped over the envelope to look at the postmark. The date sent a sudden surge of adrenaline through him. It was a Chicago postmark dated seven months before he was born. *That* meant something. Could this lover, this "S," actually be his father? Why couldn't the man have written his name and made it easier on them all?

"What do you think?" Georgia asked tentatively after a few minutes.

Turning the letter over in his hand, Carson ran his gaze over the words one last time. "I think the person who wrote this letter is my father. It's the biggest lead I've ever had and yet somehow, I don't feel like I'm any closer to finding out his identity than I was before. What good is one initial?"

"It's more than you had before," she said in an upbeat tone.

Carson wasn't feeling quite as optimistic. "Anything else interesting?" he asked.

Georgia shuffled through some more envelopes that were bound together with a rubber band. "These are old pay stubs. She's kept them going back for years and years. Other than that, not much, sorry."

Carson nodded and started putting everything back into the shoe box. "That's okay. We found something. That should make my brothers happy. I'll hand this over to them and let them analyze to their hearts' content. Let's pack up the last of these shoes and call it a day."

They slowly gathered up all the bags and boxes and hauled them downstairs to the foyer. When he looked down at his watch, Carson realized he'd kept Georgia here far longer than he'd expected to. "Wow, it's late. I'm sorry about that. I hijacked your whole Saturday."

Georgia set down a bag of clothes and shrugged. "I would've spent it working anyway. I told you I'd help. I didn't put a time limit on it."

"Well, thank you. I got through that faster with you here. I might have given up long before I found that box. There's still more to go through, but I think what I was looking for is right here," he said, holding the old shoe box. "I'd like to make it up to you. May I buy you dinner?"

Georgia studied his face for a moment, her pert nose wrinkling as she thought it over. Finally she said, "How do you feel about Chinese takeout?"

"Can you pass me the carton of fried rice?"

Georgia accepted the container and used some chopsticks to shovel a pile out onto her plate beside her sesame chicken and spring roll. The Chinese place a block from her loft was the best in town. She ate there at least three times a week. Carson hadn't seemed too convinced about her dinner suggestion at first. He must have wanted to take her someplace nice with linen napkins or something, but she'd insisted.

They drove back downtown to her place, then walked up the street together to procure a big paper bag full of yum and grab a six-pack of hard cider from the corner store. That was her idea, too. Lobster and expensive wine were nice, but honestly, nothing topped a couple of cartons of Jade Palace delicacies eaten around the coffee table.

"Wow," Carson said after taking a bite of beef and broccoli. "This is really good."

"I told you. It's all amazing. And really, you have to eat it while you sit on the floor. It adds to the experience."

Carson chuckled at her and returned to his food. She'd expected him to turn his nose up at eating on the floor around her coffee table, but he'd gone with it. She had a dining room table, but she almost never ate there. It was the place where she worked on her laptop, not ate.

"I lived with a family for a while that ate every meal around the coffee table," Georgia explained. "They didn't watch television or anything. It was just where they liked to be together. There were about six of us who would crowd around it and eat every night, talking and laughing. I really enjoyed that."

"Those moments are the best ones," Carson agreed. "There are some days when I'd give up every penny I've ever earned to be a kid again, watching old movies and eating popcorn with Aunt Gerty and Mom. My brothers and I get together and do it every few weeks, but it's not the same."

Georgia watched her boss's face softly crumble into

muted sadness as he stared down at his plate, shoveled some chicken into his mouth and chewed absentmindedly. She knew what it was like to miss people that you could never have back in your life. She'd always consoled herself with the idea that there was something better in her future. "You'll make new moments," she reassured him. "And one day when you have a family of your own, your children will treasure the little things you share with them just the same."

"That feels like it won't happen for decades. Honestly, just the idea of a family of my own seems impossible. I work so much. And even if I found the perfect woman, I'd feel like a fraud somehow. How can I be a father when I don't know what it's like to have one?"

"You'll figure it out. Just start by being there and you'll already have both our fathers beat. You're a good guy, Carson. I have no doubt that it will come naturally to you."

"What about you? You're not going to have a family of your own while you spend all your free time at work."

Georgia knew that. A part of her counted on it. What good was starting a relationship when it was just going to end? People always left her—life had proven that much—so she kept her relationships casual and avoided more disappointment. "Right now, the Newport Corporation and its employees are my family. The only family I've ever had. For now, that's enough for me."

"So you're not dating anyone?" Carson asked.

Georgia's gaze met his with curiosity. Was he really fishing for information or just being polite? "Haven't you heard? Carson Newport is my lover." She punctuated the sentence by popping the last bite of food into her mouth and putting her chopsticks across the plate in disgust. She could really put her foot in her mouth sometimes.

Carson chuckled and set aside his own utensils. Leaning onto his hand, he looked at her over the coffee table and said, "Can I ask you something?"

"Why not?" she said. They'd already covered their painful childhoods. What could be worse than that?

"Why did you tell Sutton I was your lover last night?"

That. That could be worse. "I, uh…" Georgia started, but couldn't think of anything else to say. "It just popped into my head," she said as she got up and carried a few dishes into the kitchen.

Carson didn't let her escape. He followed her with the last of their dinner and set it on the counter beside her. "That's it?" he asked as he leaned his hip against the counter. He was so near to her that her senses were flooded with the scent of his cologne and the heat of his body.

With a sigh, Georgia turned to face him. This wasn't junior high; she needed to be a grown-up about this. The movement put her so close to him that they almost touched, but she felt childish taking a step back. "It was just wishful thinking," she said, letting her gaze fall to the collar of his shirt.

Carson's hand came to rest at her waist. "Georgia?" he asked softly.

She almost couldn't answer with him touching her. The hem of her T-shirt just barely brushed the waistband of her jeans, and his fingers had come to rest in part on her bare skin. It was a simple touch, and yet it made her heart stutter in her chest and her breath catch in her throat. "Yes?"

He hooked his finger under her chin and tilted her head up until she had no choice but to look at him. She felt her cheeks flush with embarrassment and a touch of excitement as her gaze met his. His sea-green eyes searched her face as his lips tipped upward in a smile of encouragement. "I was hoping you'd say that."

Georgia almost couldn't hear him for the blood rushing in her ears. Had that kiss the other day been more than just excitement and champagne? "Why?"

Carson slid his hand around to her lower back, pulling her body flush against his own. "Because I lie in bed at night and think about that kiss we shared. I've fantasized about holding you in my arms again. I know that I shouldn't because you work for me, but I can't help it. And now that you've announced to half the company that we're lovers and the world didn't end... I don't have any reason to hold back any longer."

The longer he spoke, the more she fell under his spell. He was right. Their work relationship could survive this if they handled it like adults. They were attracted to each other. A little indulgence couldn't hurt. It wouldn't turn into anything serious and impact their business dealings. No one else seemed to care except Sutton.

"Then don't," she said, boldly meeting his gaze.

He took her at her word. Carson's lips met hers without hesitation. His kiss was powerful yet not overwhelming. Georgia stood on tiptoe to wrap her arms around his neck and draw herself closer to him. When his tongue sought her out, she opened to him and melted into his touch.

She had thought the kiss at the hospital property was amazing, but that was nothing, nothing like this. This kiss was like a lightning bolt to her core. As his hands rubbed her back and his fingers pressed into her flesh, all she could think about was how badly she needed Carson.

"I want you," she whispered against his lips.

Carson broke away from her mouth and trailed kisses along her jawline to the sensitive hollow of her neck. "You're going to have me," he said in a low growl at her ear.

His mouth returned to hers, hungrier than before. This was no longer just a simple kiss. It was officially foreplay. Without breaking the kiss, he walked them backward through the kitchen until her legs met with the dining room table. Georgia eased up onto it until she was sitting on it with Carson nestled snugly between her denim-clad thighs. She could feel his desire pressing against her, sending a shiver of need down her spine.

Carson slipped his hand beneath her shirt to stroke the smooth skin of her back and press her even closer to him. He gripped the hem and in one fluid move pulled her T-shirt up and over her head, throwing it to the floor. He took in the overflowing cups of her bra before he reached over his shoulder to tug his own shirt off.

His mouth moved quickly to her collarbone, traveling lower to taste her breasts. Georgia unfastened her bra and slipped it off her arms. She didn't want anything else between them. This was the skin-on-skin contact she'd craved, and she wanted it now.

Carson groaned at the sight of her before he covered

both her breasts with his hands. She felt her nipples tighten as his palms grazed over them. He moved his lips and tongue over her skin, tasting every inch of her exposed flesh before he drew one tight bud into his mouth.

"Carson!" she cried out as the sharp stab of pleasure shot straight to her inner core. She arched her back, pressing herself closer to him and to the touch she desperately craved.

"I can't believe this is really happening," she gasped as she looked up at the ceiling.

He planted a kiss on her sternum. "Believe it, beautiful."

Georgia closed her eyes and gave in to the sensations he was eliciting from her body. Just when she thought she couldn't take any more of his pleasurable torture, she felt his hand slide down her stomach to her jeans. She lifted her hips as he slid them and her panties down her legs.

As he stood, his eyes devoured her naked body. Reaching into his pants pocket, he pulled out a condom and set it on the table beside her. He kissed her again and let his hand wander over her bare thigh as he did. Carson dipped his fingers between her legs, brushing over her sensitive skin and sending a shiver through her whole body.

He did it again, harder, and this time Georgia cried aloud when he made contact. "Do you like that?" he asked.

"Oh yeah," she said.

Encouraged by her response, he stroked again and again until she was panting and squirming at the edge of the table. He built up the release inside her so quickly, she could hardly believe it until it was almost too late.

"Stop," she gasped, gripping his wrist with her hand. "Not yet. I want you inside me."

"Very well," Carson agreed. His gaze never left hers as he unfastened his pants and sheathed himself quickly. He settled back between her legs, and Georgia felt him press against her.

"Yesss," she hissed as he slowly sank into her.

Carson hooked his hands around the backs of her knees and tugged her to the very edge of the table. If he let go, she'd fall, so she wrapped her legs around his rib cage and drew him in deeper. Judging by his sharp intake of breath, he wasn't going anywhere.

He gripped her hips, holding her steady as he started to move in her. Every stroke set off fire bursts beneath her eyelids as they fluttered closed. Georgia arched her back and braced her hands on the table as their movements became more desperate.

How had she even gotten here? This morning, she'd gone into work with few expectations for the day. By nightfall, she was fulfilling her biggest fantasy with Carson and on the verge of an amazing orgasm. She could feel it building inside her. He coaxed the response from her body so easily, as though they were longtime lovers.

"So close," she said between ragged breaths.

Carson seemed to know just what to do to push her over the edge. Rolling his hips forward, he thrust harder, striking her sensitive core with each advance. In seconds, Georgia was tensing up in anticipation of her undoing.

Then it hit. It radiated through her body like a nuclear blast. She clung to Carson's shoulders as the shockwaves of pleasure made every muscle tremble and quiver. They rode though it together. With her final gasp, her head dropped back and her body went limp in his arms.

"Georgia," he groaned, thrusting hard into her. He surged forward and gasped against the curve of her throat as he poured into her.

Georgia cradled him against her bare chest as he recovered. Thoughts swirled through her mind as the sexual haze faded away and she realized she'd just had sex with her boss on the dining room table.

Before she could say anything, Carson straightened up and wrapped his arms around her waist. He lifted her from the table and carried her through the living room. "Bedroom?" he asked.

"Upstairs," she said.

"Of course it is."

With a smile, he carried her upstairs to the master suite that overlooked the downstairs. He placed her gently on the bed and moved quickly to strip off his remaining clothes before crawling onto the mattress beside her. He tugged her back against him and wrapped his arms around her waist.

Georgia was surprised to find him ready for her so quickly. "Again?" she asked.

"Oh yes. And this time, it will be in a proper bed."

"At least I can say I used the dining room table this year," she said with a wicked grin.

Six

"You won't believe what I've dug up!"

Brooks and Carson were talking business in Carson's office when Graham charged in with his bold declaration. Carson had been waiting for this moment since he turned over the shoe box to his older brothers. It had been nearly a week since the discovery and his encounter with Georgia.

After giving Graham the box of paperwork, Carson had returned his focus to Georgia. Work had sucked up the majority of their time, as usual, but he was looking forward to the weekend and having another chance to meet up with her outside the office. At work, she was too tense. Despite the fact that he didn't care if anyone knew they were seeing one another, she still wasn't comfortable with it.

The contents of the shoe box had slipped his mind

as the final paperwork on the hospital property went through and the finishing touches were put on the plans. Then Graham burst through his office door and it all came back to him.

Graham flopped into a chair at the table where Brooks and Carson were sitting. There was a light of excitement in his blue eyes, like he'd get when he had a breakthrough in a legal case. They'd given him the box because sorting through paperwork and finding clues was his specialty as a lawyer. Carson would've fallen asleep before he found anything important.

"Well?" Brooks prompted after several moments of silence.

"Well," Graham began, "as I went through everything, I was surprised to find a few months' worth of pay stubs from Elite Industries. Apparently Mom went to work there right before Brooks and I were born and stayed until seven months before she had you, Carson."

Carson frowned. She'd never mentioned that, not once in all those years. Not even when they complained about their competitor around the dinner table. "I thought she worked as a waitress at the café with Gerty."

"She did until she was in the third trimester of her pregnancy with Brooks and me. She went back to the diner again after her time with Elite. It looks as though she was laid off from her job after six months, although I don't know why. The paperwork I found showed she was given a very generous severance package and a glowing letter of reference from her boss when she left. Guess who she worked for at Elite? Starts with an S…"

Carson's stomach started to ache. He didn't really want to know where this was headed.

"Sutton Winchester?" Brooks guessed with as much dread in his voice as Carson was feeling.

"Yep," Graham confirmed, nearly boiling over with excitement. "She was his executive assistant."

Carson pushed up from his chair and shook his head. "I need a drink. Anyone else?"

"I think we all could use one," Brooks said.

Carson busied himself pouring them each a finger of scotch over ice. He carried the three short tumblers to the conference table and flopped back down into his chair with a sigh of disgust. Without waiting on his brothers, he took a large sip of the scotch, savoring the burn as it rushed down his throat into his empty stomach.

"So Mom was his executive assistant? That's a big leap from a coffee shop waitress," Brooks noted with a frown as he picked up his own glass.

It was. How could she have possibly qualified for a job like that? Knowing what Carson knew about Sutton, the answer wasn't one he wanted to consider. Would his mother really have accepted that sleaze's secretarial position when it came with sexual duties? Especially when she was seven months pregnant with twins? Or was she already his lover long before she went to work for him?

"Carson?" Graham said with concern in his voice. "Are you okay? You look a little pale."

He understood why. He could feel the blood draining from his face as the reality of their past solidified in his mind. He hadn't had enough scotch to handle this. No wonder their mother didn't want them to know

the truth. No wonder she said their father was a horrible person. He was. Still, he had trouble believing it
could be true. It just couldn't be. And yet…he knew
the truth almost instinctively.

"He's our father," Carson blurted out.

Brooks narrowed his gaze suspiciously at Carson.
"How can you be so sure?"

"The letter I showed you guys the other day from
the box. It talks about hurting her, missing her terribly
and how sorry he was about everything that happened.
How she and the boys would be better off without him.
It's signed 'S.'"

"That's still a bit of a stretch," Brooks argued.
"There are a lot of people with a first name starting
with *S* in the world."

"Yes, but we're talking about Sutton Winchester
here. I don't know if I told both of you, but when he
demanded that Georgia meet with him, he offered her
quite a sweet deal to come work for Elite Industries.
The job came with a million-dollar signing bonus and
the role of his mistress."

Graham's mouth dropped open, his glass of scotch
hanging in his hand midair. "Are you serious? That
old dog!"

Carson nodded gravely. "If that's how Sutton re-
cruits employees *and* lovers, it all makes sense. Say
he met Mom at the diner and they started an affair.
When she ends up pregnant, he offers her the job as
his assistant so she would have medical benefits and
maternity leave. Being on her feet all day carrying
twins had to be rough on her. I can see why she would
accept the offer, especially if she was put on bed rest
or something until you two were born."

Brooks looked at him thoughtfully. "If he went to all that trouble when she was pregnant the first time, why would he fire her when she was pregnant with you? It seems inconsistent."

Carson shook his head. "I don't know why. But I think it all goes back to the letter I found in the shoe box. It sounds to me like it might not have been Sutton's decision to let her go."

"Well," Graham said, "he was married at the time. Do you think his wife found out about his family on the side and made him put an end to all of it?"

Brooks chuckled. "Have you *met* Celeste Van Houten? She's one icy-cold woman. I wouldn't put it past her."

"We need proof," Graham argued and ran his fingers through his blond hair. "If we want to know the truth, once and for all, we'll need a paternity test. I doubt the old man will just go along with it to be nice, especially when it would mean we'd be eligible for a chunk of that multimillion-dollar estate of his when he dies. There's no way I can compel a paternity test just on the basis of our mother having been his employee at the time of Carson's conception. We need something that shows they actually had an affair."

"Who would know aside from the two of them?" Brooks asked.

"That's a tough one. Sutton wasn't likely to broadcast what he was doing, even though it looks obvious to us."

"Someone would have to know," Carson insisted. "Maybe someone who worked for Sutton at the time at his office or his house."

"That's someplace we can start," Graham agreed.

"I'll do some more digging and see what I can find. Maybe we'll luck out and find someone who still remembers that far back. It's been thirty years."

Carson knew Graham was trying to be upbeat, but he could hear the discouragement in his voice. The odds of finding someone who knew about their mother's relationship were pretty low. Most of Sutton's employees were probably paid handsomely to keep their mouths shut. But if anyone could track them down, Graham could.

"It's more than we knew a week ago," Brooks said.

"That's true," Carson agreed. "I just wonder what the point of it would be."

"What do you mean?" Graham asked.

"Well, we take the paternity test and we find out he's our father. Then what? I don't see this ending well."

"It won't, at least not for Sutton," Brooks said. "We're going to make him pay for what he did to our mother and to us."

"How?" Carson asked. "The man has no conscience."

"That's true," Brooks agreed. "But he does have a multimillion-dollar estate and we would be rightful heirs to it as well as his three legitimate daughters with Celeste. We go in and demand our share as his penance. I don't care if we blow it all in a year, as long as we pry it from his cold, dead hands."

"Wouldn't most of the estate go to his wife?"

Graham shook his head. "Celeste is his ex-wife now and has been for a couple years. Her lawyers have already seized her share. The rest of his estate most likely goes to his daughters. No matter what, Sutton can change the will to include us if he wants to. We just have to give him a little encouragement."

Carson tried not to frown. It all made sense. Sutton deserved it. He just didn't like it. "Okay," he said. "We find a way to push for a test, then go after the estate. There's just one downside to all of this."

"What's that?"

"If we're right, it means that Sutton Winchester is our father. Mom warned us up one side and down the other to stay away from our father. She said he was dangerous and we were far better off without him in our lives. I always thought that maybe she had exaggerated and that when we met him, we'd find he was a better man that we expected. But if it *is* Sutton…I worry that our worst fears about our father are about to come true."

"Georgia?"

Georgia looked up from her barely touched dinner and found Carson looking at her with concern. She was lost in her thoughts and he'd caught her not listening.

After fantasizing about time alone with Carson for so long, she was letting it slip through her fingers. Tonight he'd insisted on taking her out to dinner someplace nice. He was wearing her favorite navy pinstripe suit. For some reason, that color against his tan skin made his green eyes pop. He was looking so handsome and yet she could barely focus on a word he said.

"Yes?"

"Are you okay? You seem…distracted tonight. Are you having second thoughts about the two of us being seen together publicly?"

Georgia shook her head. She had a lot on her mind, but surprisingly, the budding romance between her and Carson was not one of her worries. "No, no. I'm sorry. I've just got a lot on my mind tonight."

Carson nodded and picked up his wine. His plate was empty and the server came by to take it away. Georgia let him take hers, as well. She didn't have much of an appetite and hadn't since she'd gotten that phone call. The universe had basically ground to a halt at that moment, but no one seemed to notice but her.

"Want to talk about it? I'm all ears," he said, taking a sip of his wine.

She was almost afraid to talk about what had happened out loud, but she did want to share it with someone. Carson was the only person she'd told about her past, and he might really understand what was going on and how important it was. The only other person she could tell was her former caseworker, Sheila. She'd avoided that call, however. Somehow she worried Sheila wouldn't think this was a great development.

"Okay," she agreed. "Well, yesterday evening, I got a phone call. From my mother."

Carson perked up in his seat. "Your mother? Really?"

Georgia nodded. "I could hardly believe it myself. I've gone twenty-six years without her in my life, and then all of a sudden, she calls me out of nowhere. She said she saw my news conference about the hospital last week and hunted down my number to get in contact with me."

"That must've been quite a shock."

"You have no idea." She'd actually been in tears. She held it together as long as she could, but once she hung up the phone, she'd bawled like a baby for twenty minutes. It was so surreal to pick up the phone and hear the voice of someone claiming to be her mother. She didn't even remember what her mother's voice sounded like, but it didn't take long to figure out she really was talking to Misty Lynn Adams.

"What did she say?"

"Well, it wasn't a long call, but she said she was getting her life back together and wanted to reconnect with me. I get the feeling this is part of a recovery program she's in to stay clean and sober. She wants to come to Chicago and see me."

"Wow," Carson said, reaching across the table to take Georgia's hand. "That's really great. How do you feel about all this?"

That was the difference between telling this story to someone who grew up with both parents and telling someone like Carson, who knew what it was like to live without knowing your past. Anyone else would've asked if she was excited and happy. Those weren't quite the words for it. Cautious was more like it. Hopeful, but not too much. Being hurt as many times as she had made her loath to jump in with both feet, but she was going to try.

"It's a mix of emotions," she admitted. "I want to see her and ask her some questions, but I don't think we're about to be best friends or anything. That's going to take time, if it's even possible. My mother is pretty messed up. I don't know how long she's had her act together, but if she relapses, I don't want to get caught in it."

Carson nodded sympathetically. "I understand. You want to know your family and have that relationship, but there's a reason why they haven't been in your life. Sometimes you wonder if it isn't for the best."

"Exactly. But I'm going to meet with her. I sent her some money to take the bus here from Detroit and she's going to stay with me for a few days. We'll see what happens."

At her words, Carson frowned. He was silent as he watched her face for a moment. "Georgia," he said at last, "is giving her money a good idea? And letting her stay with you? She's a virtual stranger."

She tugged her hand from his and buried it under the table. "I've thought of all that. It was only a hundred dollars for the bus ticket. If she blows it on drugs and never shows up, it was a relatively cheap lesson learned. But I have to have a little bit of faith if this is going to work."

"But staying with you," he pressed. "I don't think that's a good idea."

What little enthusiasm Georgia had about this development with her mother was starting to wane in the face of Carson's skepticism. What did he want Georgia to do? Hide the good silver? She didn't have good silver. Most of her money had gone into her loft and that was one thing her mother couldn't take, no matter how hard she tried.

"What are my choices? If she can't afford a bus ticket, she can't afford a hotel. I'd have to pay for it, too. It's only for a few days, Carson. If I feel remotely uncomfortable having her there, or leaving her there alone, I'll get her a room somewhere, okay?"

Carson flinched at her sharp, defensive tone. "Listen, I'm sorry to be such a pessimist, Georgia, but I guess it's just a by-product of how I grew up. I just don't want you to get hurt."

"I won't," she insisted. "I know I have to tread carefully with Misty, but I could use your support. I've encouraged your search for your father, and I'd really appreciate your support as I look into my own past."

Carson got up from his side of the restaurant booth and sat down beside her. He wrapped her in a hug and kissed her sweetly on the cheek. "I support you one hundred percent. Don't ever doubt that. I'm just worried about you, is all."

Georgia eased into his embrace, letting her anxieties fade away in his arms. She supposed he was right to feel cautious about the whole thing. There wasn't much point in jumping to Misty's defense when she knew nothing about her. "Well, thank you. I'm not used to anyone worrying about me."

"You'd better get used to it, although I'll admit I could be just a little on edge after what Graham found. My mom had warned us that our father was a terrible person, but I never could've imagined that it could be Sutton Winchester. Of all the men in Chicago…"

Georgia had been quite stunned to hear the news herself. After he told her the rest of the story, it had made sense. Carson had Sutton's mischievous green eyes, but she didn't want to tell him that. At this point, she got the feeling he didn't want to have anything in common with Sutton, especially common genetics. "What are you guys going to do?"

"Graham is going to try to track down someone who might remember the two of them being together back then. If we're successful, we'll push for a paternity test to know once and for all."

Georgia nodded absently as he described their plans, but she could tell the brothers had little idea what they would do with the truth. "So if he is your father, then what?"

As she predicted, Carson frowned slightly. "I don't know. I doubt we'll be invited over for Thanksgiving dinner with his other children. If we play any role in his life, we're going to have to fight for it. I think Graham and Brooks are more willing to battle than I am. I just keep thinking of my mother's warnings. She kept him out of our lives for a reason. All things considered, do you really want him in my life?"

Georgia nodded. "I know I'm taking a risk by letting my mother come see me. It might work out, or she might be the same junkie who abandoned me. I've done pretty well without her. At the same time, I won't let myself give up on her. With your parents, you stand there and let yourself get kicked in the teeth again and again in the hope that they will finally stand up and be the people you always dreamed of. That child in you is always craving that love and acceptance you didn't get. If you give up on that, what's left?"

"Everything else," Carson argued. "Your mother was a broke, messed up kid who had no business taking care of a baby, but Sutton is the richest guy in Chicago. What's his excuse? Sutton knows that we're his kids. He hasn't once sought us out in all these years. No birthday cards, no child support, not even a little lenience in business dealings. Why would I want a man like that in my life?"

"You won't know for sure until you get to know him better."

"I've never had a father, Georgia. I don't know

whether it's better to have a lousy one and know the truth than to never have one and always wonder."

"I understand. With the truth come things you may not want to know. I'm giving my mother this chance, but considering my father impregnated a teenage runaway with a drug problem, I think I'll go with never knowing him. That way I can keep the fantasy father in my mind. I'd rather not know than find out he was her customer, or her drug dealer, or that he raped a young girl with no one to turn to."

Carson carefully considered her words and then took the final sip of his wine. "Well, in the end I don't get to make the decision, because there's more than just me in the equation. My brothers want to see this through no matter what. Like it or not, I will know if Sutton is my father. As for what comes after that…I guess that all depends on dear old Dad."

Georgia nodded and finished her drink. They were both in limbo when it came to their parents. She hated that feeling. For years, as she bounced from one foster home to the next, she had both hoped and worried that her mother would get her act together and take her home for good.

She had been excited about her mother seeking her out. She had made the first step, which is something Georgia had been adamant about. It wouldn't have taken much to track down her mother, but she didn't want to. Knowing that her mother had gone to the trouble of finding her felt good. Still, she was scared. And after talking to Carson about Misty's visit, she wasn't feeling as optimistic.

Georgia could already tell that she would spend all night lying in bed worrying about this. Her mother was due to arrive on Friday, so that meant days of anxiety until she knew for certain. She needed a distraction. Something to keep her mind off the situation. Work wouldn't do it, but leaning into Carson's chest and resting her head on his shoulder gave her a good idea of what might.

"Are you ready to get out of here?" she asked.

"I thought you wanted dessert."

Reaching up to caress his stubble-covered jaw, Georgia turned his head until his full lips met with hers. She drank him in, letting her tongue curl along his as she gave a soft moan of approval. A sizzle of awareness traveled down her spine, making her suddenly warm and flush in the previously cold restaurant. All thoughts of Misty and Sutton faded away with his touch.

She was right. Losing herself in a night of passion with Carson was just what she needed. What they both needed. "I do," she said as she pulled away and looked into his eyes with wicked intention.

"Then let's go." Carson smiled wide and scanned the bill the waiter had brought. He tossed some cash on the table for it and slipped out of the booth with Georgia's hand in his own.

Seven

"Rebecca, what is this three o'clock on my calendar today?" Carson waited impatiently for his assistant to answer him as he studied his computer screen. He hadn't made this appointment, and he had no real clue who the woman was that he and his brothers were scheduled to meet in just a few minutes' time.

Rebecca appeared in the doorway and shook her head. "I'm not really sure, sir. Graham called this morning and told me to add it. Did he not speak with you?"

No, he had not. But Carson didn't want to worry Rebecca. "He may have and I just forgot. Thank you."

Rebecca slipped back out of his office, leaving him to ponder the appointment. He didn't have long to wait. Brooks showed up a few minutes later, eyeing his smart phone with dismay. "What's the three o'clock about?"

Carson shrugged. "It's Graham's doing. He didn't tell you, either?"

"Why would he do something like that?" Brooks flopped down into Carson's guest chair and frowned. "Who is Tammy Ross? I've never heard of her."

"She is Sutton Winchester's retired housekeeper." Graham appeared in the doorway with a smug grin on his face.

That was the last thing Carson expected. Why would they be meeting with Sutton's old housekeeper, unless... "Does she know anything about Sutton's relationship with our mother?"

Graham strolled at an obnoxiously slow pace across the Moroccan rug and sat down in the other chair. "She does."

"Why not just tell us what she had to say? Why bring her here?"

"Because," Graham insisted, "she wanted to talk to all of us in person. Apparently she feels bad about how it all went down back then. She's a sentimental older lady who knew and liked our mother. Indulge her a little."

"Mr. Newport," Carson's assistant chirped through the speaker phone. "Mrs. Ross is here to see you."

"Right on time," Graham said with a smile. He got up from his chair and went to the reception area. A moment later he returned with a petite older woman with short gray hair and a pleasant smile.

Carson and Brooks both stood to greet their guest. "Mrs. Ross," Carson said, reaching out to shake her hand. "Please have a seat." He gestured over to his conference table and followed the others there as they took their seats.

"Thank you for seeing me today. When Graham contacted me and I realized I was talking to one of the twins all grown up—" the woman's dark eyes grew a little misty "—well, I knew I had to tell you everything I knew. My loyalty to the Winchesters ended with the paychecks."

"I contacted the agency that Sutton hires household staff through," Graham explained. "I was able to talk to someone and they passed along my number to her."

"I read about your mother's passing in the paper," she said. "It was hard to believe that the vibrant young girl I knew was gone. Or that the babies I remembered were full-grown men."

"How did you know about our mother?" Brooks asked.

"At first I knew Cynthia as Mr. Sutton's secretary. She would call the house from time to time relaying his requests for dinner or telling me what shirt he wanted starched for the next day. She was sweet and we chatted some. She was very excited about her pregnancy, and having two children of my own, I relayed plenty of advice. After the twins—*you*—were born, I volunteered to babysit a couple of nights while she went out. I didn't realize at the time who she was going out with or whose babies I was watching."

"So our mother *was* seeing Sutton on the side?"

"Yes. From what I gathered, they were together long before she started working at Elite Industries. It wasn't surprising, though. Your mother was a lovely young woman, just the kind Sutton liked. I think his marriage to Celeste Van Houten was more business than pleasure, so he was always on the prowl for... extracurricular entertainment."

Carson's stomach ached to think of his mother as just one in a line of women who had marched in and out of Sutton Winchester's bedroom. She deserved better. A real love with a man who wanted to marry her and give her all the happiness in the world. Instead she'd raised his three children alone on a waitress's salary. Carson wasn't sure what their mother would've done without Gerty's help.

"Finding out about you was the biggest shock," Mrs. Ross said, looking at Carson. "Your mother must have left the company so soon into her second pregnancy that I didn't even know she was expecting again. I'm sure that was part of Mr. Winchester's plan. Mrs. Winchester was already beside herself over the relationship. I don't think she knew about the twins, and I'm sure Mr. Winchester didn't want anyone to know about you, either."

"If he was so secretive, how do you know about all of this?"

The older woman smiled. "There are different kinds of rich people and in my day, I worked for them all. The Winchesters are the kind of rich people who see their employees as a lesser species. Sometimes Mrs. Winchester pretended I wasn't even there. Or maybe she wasn't pretending. Maybe I just wasn't important enough for her notice. It was annoying, but sometimes it was useful.

"I remember one night Mr. and Mrs. Winchester really got into a row. She was pregnant with Nora at the time. Mrs. Winchester didn't yell much, but it was a glass-breaking night. They went into the bedroom and closed the door, but it didn't matter. You could hear them yelling from anywhere in the house, and the house is a mansion. I was in the hallway, sweeping up a glass vase she'd thrown at him, when I heard her mention Cynthia's name. She told him she wasn't just going to sit by and let him parade around with his secretary while she was suffering through another difficult pregnancy to have his child. She threatened to divorce him and clean him out. She told him he'd never see Eve or the new baby again. I had no doubt she could do it. Her brother was one of the most ruthless divorce attorneys in Illinois. She told him he would end it, or she would end him.

"It was then I realized that the twins had to be his. I couldn't imagine Mr. Winchester taking care of a woman with another man's children the way he did. A week later, a lady called the house claiming to be Mr. Winchester's secretary. When I asked what happened to Cynthia, she told me that she was no longer with the company. That's the last I heard of her, or of any of you. She disappeared after that."

"You can't be certain that I'm Sutton's child, though," Carson said. "She could've gotten pregnant by someone else after she left Elite."

The older woman reached across the table and patted his hand. "You are Sutton Winchester's boy, no doubt in my mind. Your brothers take more after Cynthia, but you, you're the spitting image of your father when he was younger."

Carson swallowed hard. He'd always known he looked different from his brothers and likely took after their father while they favored their mother, but he didn't want to be the spitting *anything* of Sutton Winchester.

"Mrs. Ross, would you be willing to testify to a

judge about what you told us today?" Graham asked. "Odds are that it won't be necessary for us to compel the paternity test, but the judge might ask to speak with you."

"Absolutely. I think I've stayed quiet about all this long enough. Mr. Winchester needs to do right by his children. It's never too late for that."

"Thank you for coming to speak with us today," Carson said, shaking the woman's hand.

She took it, standing up and clutching her bag to her side. "It was no trouble. I've wondered for years what happened to Cynthia's babies. Now I know. She would be so proud of you three. I'm sure of it."

Graham escorted the woman out of the office, returning about ten minutes later. "So? What do you think?"

"I think you're the luckiest bastard in the world," Brooks said. "I can't fathom how you managed to find her."

"Luck has nothing to do with it," he said, dropping into a chair. "Law school is brutal, but it teaches you how to find the information you need to sway the court in your favor. My research skills are second to none. It wasn't easy, I assure you. I called every damn employment agency in town before I struck gold. If that hadn't worked, I was going to try to smooth-talk his accountant into finding past employment records. Thankfully, this worked."

"So now what?" Carson asked.

"I've got the paperwork all ready to submit to the judge," Graham said. "Once he issues the order for the paternity test, we'll deliver it to Sutton. When we're certain he's our father, we'll make our bid to be included in his estate, sit back and watch the fireworks."

"I knew you'd be back."

Georgia ignored Sutton's smug expression. It was far more unnerving to look him in the eye now that she recognized that those green eyes were so much like Carson's. Knowing this man was likely Carson's father was hard to stomach, especially when his gaze raked over her with poorly masked desire.

"Does Newport know you're here?"

"No, he doesn't." Georgia hadn't told him because she knew Carson wouldn't let her do this. She wanted to keep the door open to Sutton. Not because she wanted the job, but because she wanted information. If Carson and his brothers ended up taking Sutton to court, anything she came up with could be helpful. And if she could get some money for the hospital from him, more the better.

"So have you come to your senses and decided to accept my offer? Finally figure out Newport isn't man enough for you?"

She tried not to roll her eyes. She needed to play along, at least for a little bit, if she was going to get what she wanted out of this meeting. Georgia knew it was dangerous to waltz back into the lion's den, but it was the only way to get the information she was after.

"A girl has to keep her options open."

Sutton's chuckle was punctuated with a long bout of coughing. He pulled the pocket square from his suit coat and held it over his mouth. She couldn't help but notice as she watched him that he didn't look well. His suit was hanging off him. His face was slightly sunken in, emphasizing his cheekbones and the gray circles beneath his eyes. He seemed to have deteriorated pretty rapidly since she saw him at the party about a week ago.

When he finished coughing and pulled the handkerchief away, Georgia noticed a few small droplets of blood on the fabric. Sutton was seriously ill. He didn't need a mistress. He needed a doctor.

"I think I could use a drink." Sutton cleared his throat, pushed up from his desk and walked over to the minibar in the corner. "Can I get you something?"

"Sure." Standing up, she followed Sutton to where he was dropping ice cubes into two crystal tumblers. She leaned against the edge of the conference room table and watched as he poured himself some scotch, and then made her a vodka gimlet. It was her favorite drink, although she had no idea how he could possibly know that.

Finally he held up her glass to her. "Here you go, my dear. What shall we drink to?"

Georgia eyed the glass until she came up with an answer. "To keeping our options open," she said with a smile.

"Indeed." He clinked his crystal against hers and took a sip. He watched her as she drank some of her drink, then set his glass down on the edge of the table beside her. "So what is it that I can do for you today, Georgia? Are you ready to accept my generous offer?"

"Not yet."

"Well, 'not yet' is better than the no you gave me last time. I'm making progress."

Georgia was willing to let a sickly old man believe

that if it made him feel better. "It's a woman's preroga-
tive to change her mind."

"Never were truer words spoken." Sutton took a
step toward her, crowding into her space and leaning close. "What would convince you to accept my
offer, Georgia? Just name it. More money? Jewelry?
A nice high-rise penthouse? I can give you anything
you want if you'll give yourself to me right now." His
hand rested on her thigh as he gazed intently at her.
She got the feeling he meant it. But there was no way
she would accept.

"I'll have to think on that," she said as she picked
up his hand and moved it off her leg. "But there are
some things you could do that might sway my final
decision."

"A negotiator, eh? I'll bite." He scooped up his
drink, although he didn't move away. They were
nearly touching. "Like what?"

"I'd like Elite Industries to make a donation to the
Newport children's hospital project."

He narrowed his gaze at her as he sipped his scotch.
"And why would I want to do that?"

"Well, I happen to know that you don't have a public relations director at the moment. If I were heading
up your PR department, that is exactly what I would
recommend. People know that you were competing
for the land where the hospital will be built. Some may
think that Elite should've backed down on the condo
project to support a worthy cause. I think donating to
the hospital would be good damage control."

"I don't need damage control. I run this town."

"That may be," she continued, "but you wouldn't
want to look like a poor sport for losing to Newport,

would you? I know you're not used to losing, so you might not know how to handle it."

"Losing…" Sutton muttered. "If I had wanted that land, I would've gotten it."

He could tell himself that, but he'd passed along his stubbornness to Carson along with his eyes. "Sure you would've," she agreed. "But what better way to bless the project you let happen than by supporting it? Come on, Sutton. Just cut a check."

Sutton leaned into her, forcing Georgia to lean farther back on the conference room table. "And aside from good PR, what will my check get me?"

Georgia placed a hand on Sutton's chest to keep him from moving any closer. "That depends on how big the check is."

A wide grin spread across the older man's face, suddenly reminding her so much of Carson that her chest ached. "You're a feisty one. I love that about you. You win. I'll write a check to Newport for whatever you want."

"Write it for however much you think I'm worth."

"Mr. Winchester? Georgia?" A sharp, startled voice sounded from the other side of the office.

Georgia snapped her head to the door of Sutton's office, where Graham was standing. His face showed a mix of surprise and anger as he looked at the two of them together. Hovering over his shoulder was Eve Winchester, the oldest of Sutton's three daughters and corporate heir apparent. Both of them looked quite stunned to walk in on Sutton nearly manhandling Georgia.

"I'm sorry, Daddy," Eve said. "I couldn't stop him."

Georgia pressed harder against Sutton's chest and

he finally backed away. With a sigh, he turned away from Georgia to address the interlopers in his office. "It's no problem. I've got Newport employees all over the place today. Come in, come in."

Sutton strolled back over to his desk, and Georgia tried to pull herself back together. She was hardly misbehaving, but she didn't like the look on Graham's face. He obviously thought he was walking in on something. Georgia avoided his gaze, holding her position near the conference room table.

"What can I do for you, Graham? Or are you Brooks? Damn it, I can never tell you two apart."

That made Graham angry. His jaw tightened and the edges of his ears reddened as he stared Sutton down. "You'd think that a father would be able to tell his own children apart."

Sutton barely reacted to the accusation. He leaned back in his chair and laced his fingers together over his stomach. "A father *would*, but I'm not sure I like what you're implying, Mr. Newport."

"I'm implying nothing. I'm saying it straight up, *Dad*."

Georgia held her breath as she watched the two men speak. The tension in the room was thick. Her gaze drifted over to Eve. She'd followed Graham into the office and seemed to be the only one in the room stunned by Graham's accusations. And if Georgia was reading her correctly, Eve looked a bit disappointed, too. She supposed any red-blooded woman in Chicago would feel the same way if she found out the handsome and rich Newport boys were her half brothers.

"I am not your father." Sutton didn't hesitate to shoot down Graham.

"Are you denying you had a relationship with my mother?"

Sutton pursed his lips, considering his response. "I did have a relationship with Cynthia. She was a lovely woman. You take after her, I have to admit. But I am not your father. Your mother was already pregnant when we met."

Graham laid an envelope on Sutton's desk. "We'll see about that."

Sutton opened the envelope and pulled out the paperwork inside. "A subpoena for a paternity test? That's cute. Very well," he said, setting the paperwork aside. "I will comply with the court order. But don't get cocky thinking you've won some kind of battle here, Graham. In the end, you won't like the results, because I am not your father."

Graham started down Sutton without flinching. "I wouldn't expect a man like you to say anything else."

Graham turned his attention to Georgia on the far side of the room. "Do you need a ride back to the office?" His tone was pointed, but she wasn't surprised.

"I do." She'd gotten what she wanted out of Sutton for now. Staying behind after this incident would be nothing but awkward for them both.

Moving quickly, she scooped up her big black purse and slung it over her shoulder. Not wanting to let things unravel with Sutton, she gave him one last smile before she followed Graham out of the office. "Can you have that check for the hospital sent by courier over to our offices?"

The irritation faded from Sutton's eyes as he focused on her again. "I'll have it taken care of."

Turning, she caught Graham and Eve sharing a

meaningful look. Interesting. She brushed past a stunned Eve on her way to meet Graham in the doorway. They were halfway to his car before he said anything to her.

"What was that about?" he asked.

She didn't like the way he was addressing her, as though he'd caught her beneath Sutton's desk. "I've got a better question," she said, deflecting the discussion. "What exactly was that just now between you and Eve Winchester?"

Graham's jaw stiffened, but he didn't turn to look at her. Instead he held open the door to the parking garage. "That was nothing."

Georgia laughed. She didn't work much with Graham since he spent so much time at his law firm, but she knew enough to know he was lying. "Tell that to someone who believes you. Eve was watching you like a tasty meal. At least until you started calling her father 'Dad.'"

Graham took a deep breath and pulled his keys from his pocket. "If Sutton is our father, then it doesn't matter what you think you saw. This isn't a V.C. Andrews novel. The odds are that Eve is my half sister, so end of story."

He opened the car door and Georgia slipped inside. Once he got in and started the engine, she said, "Sutton seemed pretty adamant that he wasn't your father."

"Yes, well, did you expect otherwise?"

Georgia hesitated for a moment. That didn't sound like Sutton's style. Maybe he would lie by omission, but the way he insisted he wasn't Graham's father made her believe him. Her interactions with him had always been very direct. "I don't know. I've never known him to lie. He usually gets his way without stooping to deceit."

"You know him so well now, do you? How much time have you been spending here with him behind Carson's back? He told me about the dirty old man's offer. Have you changed your mind about accepting it?"

"No, I haven't. We were talking business." She refused to elaborate any further. It was none of his damn business what she was doing there anyway.

"I bet," he snapped before shooting into traffic and tearing down the street. "Let me give you a word of advice about Carson. He doesn't get involved with women very often. His last real relationship ended when the woman dumped him for a richer guy."

Georgia didn't know that. They hadn't really discussed their dating history in depth. "Really?"

"Yes. He and Candy were even engaged when she decided to run off with some billionaire tech innovator. It was really hard on him."

"Well, Carson and I are just—"

"I don't care what you two are or aren't," Graham interrupted. "I just want you to know so you think long and hard about putting Carson through the same thing again."

Georgia bit her tongue. She was about as far from leaving Carson for Sutton as she was from leaving him for Prince Harry. She wasn't going to argue that point with Graham. She'd tell Carson what she was up to, but she didn't think Graham could be trusted. Judging by the body language between him and Eve, he was compromised. Especially if Sutton wasn't their father.

If either of them was going to be sleeping with the enemy, it was Graham.

Eight

"Can we talk?" Carson caught Georgia as she went past him in the hallway.

"Let me grab something off the printer," she said, "and then I'll come by."

Carson returned to his office. He was filled with nervous energy that wouldn't let him sit. Instead he stood and looked out the window at the sprawling sights of downtown Chicago. The view he loved did little to soothe him. He'd been tied up in knots inside since Graham left his office earlier.

His brother's tale of the meeting with Sutton and Georgia's unexpected presence had left him with a number of questions. He wasn't sure he would like the answers. The dread in his stomach felt so familiar. He didn't want to believe what Graham implied about Georgia, and he fought to reserve judgment no matter how badly his instincts wanted to react. Then again, he'd felt the same way when he'd started hearing the rumors about his ex-fiancée, Candy, stepping out with another man. He hadn't wanted to believe it at first and yet the nagging ache in his gut couldn't be ignored.

Breaking off their engagement hadn't really bothered him. If Carson were honest with himself, he hadn't been in love with Candy Stratton. She had been convenient—everything he thought a good wife should be. He didn't have the time to look around forever, so he'd decided to move forward with her.

What had gutted him, though, was why Candy left him. He'd done well for himself. He and his brothers had crawled their way up from an unremarkable start in life to be some of the wealthiest and most successful businessmen in Chicago. Carson was painfully aware that he wasn't from a good family. That he was a bastard, unclaimed by his father. He already had a daily battle shoring up his feelings of self-worth and adequacy.

What he didn't need was a woman ditching him for a man who had all the things he lacked. For a while he'd wondered if he'd ever be enough. He had a ton of money, but not enough for Candy. He was very successful, but not successful enough for his father to be proud and step forward to claim his son. No matter how hard he worked, it never seemed like enough.

He'd hoped he could be enough for Georgia. A lot had changed since his engagement—he was wiser, older and even more successful. And yet it felt the same. Would it be that much worse if Georgia ditched him for his own father?

"You wanted to speak with me?"

Carson turned to find Georgia at the threshold. "Yes. Please come in. Shut the door and have a seat."

Georgia narrowed her gaze at him for a moment before complying. "Is this about yesterday?" she asked, sitting down.

Carson took a seat behind his desk and sighed. "Maybe. I had a discussion with Graham this morning that wasn't very encouraging, but I'd like to hear your version of events."

"It's not a version of events. Graham has no idea what he walked in on."

"What did he walk in on?" After the way his brother described it, he wasn't entirely sure he wanted to hear it from her own lips. The thought of her getting involved with his father was enough to make him want to punch a hole through his office wall.

"Nothing more than a little corporate espionage."

Carson's brow shot up. "What?"

"Listen," Georgia said, sitting forward in her seat. "With everything going on between Newport Corporation and Elite Industries, I decided it was a good idea to keep the lines of communication open. If Sutton thought I was still considering his offer, I might be able to get some information from him that could help you. There's nothing more to it than that."

Carson breathed a deep sigh of relief. He hadn't realized he'd been holding his breath for so long. He tried to suppress the doubts in his mind that Candy had left behind. There was no real reason to doubt Georgia. He needed to at least try to hear her out and see if he could trust her. "Really?"

Georgia got up from her seat. She rounded his desk

and settled into his lap. She ran her fingers through his hair and looked down at him with her pale gray eyes. "Yes, really. Would you like to know what I've found out so far?"

She already had information? That was faster than he expected. At the same time, the weight of her firm, round behind in his lap was sending his thoughts in another direction. He settled for resting a hand on her bare knee and stroking her soft skin. "Sure, tell me."

"Well, first I secured a large donation from Elite for the children's hospital. Sutton will be having a check sent over by courier this week."

Carson couldn't help the smile that spread across his face. He wrapped his arms around Georgia and pulled her soft body tight against his own. She was an amazing woman, and for some reason, she wanted to be with him. "Really?"

"Yep. I don't think his pride will let him donate less than seven figures so he can always have top billing on the list of corporate sponsors. I also have some interesting personal information about Sutton that you and your brothers might need to know."

Personal information? "Like what?" he asked.

"Graham wasn't there long enough to notice this, but I was. I think Sutton is sick."

"Sick? That old bastard is too mean to get sick. The germs are repelled by him."

Georgia didn't smile at his joke. "I'm serious, Carson. I'm not talking about him having a cold here. He was coughing up blood. He's lost weight. He looks terrible. He does a good job trying to hide it, but I really think something is wrong with him."

If what she said was true, it wasn't public knowledge. The failing health of the King of Chicago would start wild speculation. Who would take over Elite Industries? Who were the beneficiaries of his will? How many of his mistresses would show up at the funeral?

Ideally, those paternity-test results would come through quickly. They were running short on time if Graham and Brooks were dead set on getting their piece of the Winchester pie. Sooner was better than later. If they *were* Sutton's children, pushing their way into the will once he announced he was ill would look really bad. While Carson didn't care much for appearances, the last thing he wanted was for people to think he was a ruthless chip off the old block.

That was just his luck, though. He'd gone over thirty years wondering who his father was. Within days of finding a solid candidate, the man got sick. If Georgia was right and this was a serious illness, just how long would he have with dear ol' Dad before he died? Not long enough, although Carson doubted they'd have a touching, father-son bonding moment even if Sutton lived for another decade.

"Carson? Are you okay?" Georgia asked.

He realized he hadn't responded to her revelations. "I'm fine. I guess I was trying to think through what all that would mean for us. Do you really think he's seriously ill?"

Georgia shrugged. "I'm no doctor, but he looked bad to me. This wasn't the flu or a passing stomach bug. Whatever has hit him, has hit him hard and taken a physical toll quickly."

"Well, the man does have a reputation for hard living. Perhaps it's catching up with him."

Georgia studied his face for a moment, and then

ran her finger along his jaw. "Are you still mad at me for going over to meet with Sutton?"

"No, I'm not mad. I'm actually pleased by your underhandedness."

"Do you want me to stop going over there?"

Carson considered her question. He should say yes, but she was right. There was valuable information to be had. "No. Keep visiting him if you think it's useful and you feel comfortable around him. Just be careful. That guy can't be trusted."

"I think he's more talk than action these days, but I promise to tell you if I go back. But you know you don't have to worry about me leaving you for him, right? It doesn't matter what he offers. I'm not going to run off with Winchester."

She looked at Carson with her big gray eyes and he had no choice but to believe her. She wasn't Candy and despite what Graham thought he saw, nothing was happening with Sutton. If she'd wanted to leave him for the old man, she would've done it when he first offered the job. Instead she was here, sitting in Carson's lap, telling him she wasn't going anywhere. That was the sexiest thing she could've said to him.

"I'd like to think so," he said, "but we've only been together a little less than two weeks. We're hardly serious enough for me to start making demands on you."

"You can make a few demands," she said coyly. "I like a man who's in charge. At least in the bedroom."

Georgia shifted on his lap, and all thoughts of his potential father's potential illness vanished. He wanted to hike up the hem of her skirt, brush his fingertips across her bare thighs and take her on his desk. The fantasy played out so vividly in his mind that he had to squirm uncomfortably beneath her to avoid his building arousal pressing inappropriately into her. He was breaking a pretty sensible rule by having a relationship with one of his employees. He wasn't going to compound the problem and blur the lines by making love to Georgia here.

Instead he palmed the curve of her rear end through her pencil skirt and gave her a wicked look. "Is it time to go home yet?"

She smiled and looked at his desk clock. "It's only three thirty."

"Yes, but I'm the boss. When the boss says you can go home early, you can go home early."

Leaning in, Georgia pressed her lips to his, lighting the fire in his belly that quickly rushed through his veins. "Whatever you say, Mr. Newport."

Georgia stood waiting anxiously outside the bus station. Tonight was the night her mother was arriving from Detroit. She had texted to let her know she made her connection and would be arriving at six thirty. A steady stream of people had started coming out of the station. Glancing down at her phone, Georgia confirmed it was almost 6:45. Her mother could be the next person to step out the door.

Her nerves were getting the best of her. This was a big moment for her. She didn't know how it was going to go. Carson's skepticism had planted seeds of doubt in her mind, but she was trying hard not to cultivate them. She was too scared to have big dreams about her fantasy mother and their new relationship, but she desperately wanted something with her.

Just then, a woman came out the front door. She

was a blonde, in her early forties. She had a backpack slung over one shoulder and a small duffel bag in one hand. Her hair was pulled back in a ponytail and her clothes were wrinkled from hours traveling on a bus.

When their eyes met, Georgia knew that it was her mother. She was surprised to find she looked so young. Misty had been a teenager when she had Georgia, but in her mind, she had envisioned her mother being older somehow.

"Georgia?" the woman asked, stopping a few feet away.

"Hi, Mom." She didn't know what else to say.

The woman approached her cautiously. It seemed both of them were at a loss for how to handle this momentous event. Finally she dropped her duffel bag on the ground and lunged forward to wrap her daughter in a hug.

Georgia buried her face in her mother's neck and hung on. She could feel the sting of tears in her eyes and hid them by letting them spill onto her mother's sweater.

"Oh, my li'l Peaches," her mother whispered as they continued to embrace. "Let me get a good look at you."

They separated so Misty could study her daughter's face. Georgia tried not to squirm under the scrutiny, focusing instead on the realization that her mother was really here.

"You turned out to be so beautiful," Misty said. "I was a pretty girl, but you…you are the most stunning woman I've ever seen in real life. Like a movie star."

"Hardly," Georgia said, awkwardly dismissing her praise.

"And you've done so well for yourself. Such nice clothes, so well-groomed. Seeing you on the news working for that big real estate development company...I was so proud."

"Thank you." Georgia was never comfortable with how she looked, but she'd worked hard for her success and would accept those compliments while she dismissed others. "Are you hungry? I thought maybe we could get some dinner."

"You know, I'm really just tired from all the traveling. Would you mind too much if we just went back to your place and got some food delivered?"

Georgia smiled. Perhaps she had gotten her love of takeout from her mother without knowing it. "That would be fine. There's a great Chinese place near my house, or an Italian eatery around the block."

"I love Chinese," Misty said with a smile and picked up her duffel bag.

That must be genetic, too.

"So, where are you parked?" Misty asked, looking around the parking lot.

"Oh, I don't have a car. I stay in the city, so I usually ride the train." Misty's disappointed expression caught her off guard. Georgia quickly realized that she was probably tired and not really interested in navigating any more public transportation today. "But I can get a taxi," she added.

The smile returned to Misty's face. "That would be wonderful. I got hit by a drunk driver a few years ago and shattered my pelvis," she said, shuffling from one foot to the other. "I can't stay on my feet for too long or it aches."

Georgia's eyes widened. She didn't even know how

to respond. Instead she called for a taxi, and they rode back to her apartment in relative silence. Once they stepped out of the cab, she could tell that Misty was in a state of awe. She looked up at the tall building Georgia called home as though they were about to step into a lush European castle. They walked through the nicely appointed lobby with Misty seeming unsure quite where to look. The marble floors? The shining brass elevator doors? The giant floral arrangement at the front desk?

"I don't think I've ever been anyplace this nice before," Misty said as they entered Georgia's apartment. Her gaze ran over the pieces of art on the walls and the entire wall of windows on the one side that overlooked the Chicago cityscape. "I'm afraid to touch anything," she said, clutching anxiously at her backpack.

"There's nothing to worry about. Just put down your things and relax." Georgia took her duffel bag and set it in the living room by the couch. "Unfortunately I don't have a guest room. I've never actually had a guest, so we'll have to make up the sofa bed for you."

"Okay. It's nice of you to let me stay with you at all. Hopefully it doesn't aggravate my back condition."

"What happened to your back?"

Misty sighed. "Honey, after the life I've lived, there's something wrong with every part of me. You don't want to hear my sob stories. You've got plenty of your own, thanks to me, I'm sure."

"No, really," Georgia pressed. It was hard not knowing anything about her mother aside from what was in her file. "What happened?"

She put her backpack on the ground and crossed

her arms protectively over her chest. The movement pushed up the sleeves of her shirt, exposing a sad collage of scars across her pale skin. "About ten years ago my dealer had his thugs come for me because I owed him money. They pushed me down the stairs at my apartment complex. They had to put some screws and pins in my spine, so I have trouble sleeping sometimes."

"That's terrible."

Misty just shrugged it away. "Like I said, you don't want to hear about my life. I'm sure there's a part of you that hates me, and I don't blame you for that. But being taken away from me was probably the best thing that ever happened to you. I'm pretty sure that anyone else would've been a better parent than I was. That's why I never..." She hesitated, her face flushing red with emotion. "That's why I never tried to get you back. I thought you were better off without me. And I was right. Just look at you now. You'd be a mess like me if I'd fought to get you back. That's why I let all of you go."

Georgia swallowed hard. She had grown up thinking her mother had never cared for her. From the sound of it, the opposite was true. Her mother had stayed out of her life *because* she cared. Part of what she'd said confused her, though. "What do you mean, all of us?"

Misty's gaze dropped to the floor. "You have a younger brother and a sister, Georgia. I should've told you that before."

Georgia was nearly blown off her feet. A brother and a sister? All this time she'd thought she was alone in the world, and now she found out she had siblings she never knew about? "Where? Tell me about them."

"There's not much I can tell you. I'm sorry. I was so drug addicted by then that they took the babies from me right after each of them was born. They were both adopted, so I don't know their names or where they ended up. I might have been messed up, but by then I knew giving up my rights would allow them to have a real family and not end up in the foster system like you. I should've done the same for you, but they told me it was harder to place an older child. By then you were five or six. I've got a lot of sins to pay for," Misty said.

Georgia's knees grew weak beneath her, and she slipped down into the nearby armchair before she fell. She'd known she would learn a lot about her mother and her early years with her, but somehow she hadn't anticipated this.

"I'm sorry for that, Peaches. I'm sorry for all of this. That's why I wanted to come here, to see you. To tell you how bad I feel about everything that happened in your life. It's a part of my recovery, one step at a time. I don't expect you to forgive me, but I needed to come anyway."

"I think we've got a lot of talking to do while you're here," Georgia managed.

"That we do." Turning away, Misty patted the cushions of the couch. "I think this will be comfortable enough. It's a really nice couch. It's got to be better than the cot at the shelter."

Georgia felt a pang of guilt for putting her mother on the couch. She got to sleep in a nice bed every night; she should let her mother do it while she was here. "You know what, Mom? Why don't you take my bed upstairs? It's a nice memory foam bed, so you'll be comfortable. I can sleep down here."

"Oh no," Misty argued. "I didn't tell you all that to make you feel bad."

"Really. It's not a problem. Let's take your things upstairs and I can show you around."

Her mother followed her upstairs to the loft bedroom that overlooked the living room. The large bed took up the center of the space with a luxurious en suite bath. Georgia set her bag down on the foot of the bed. "Hopefully you'll be comfortable up here."

Misty looked around and slipped out of her sweater. That exposed even more scars, blended in with a swirl of tattoos that disappeared beneath her short-sleeved shirt. "They're track marks," she said, noticing Georgia looking. "Well, not all of them. Some of them are leftover from my cutting phase."

Georgia knew her mother had a heroin problem, but she hadn't heard about the cutting. "You cut yourself?"

She nodded. "Yes. That was from my younger years. I was a messed-up kid. Cutting myself made me feel better. It was my only release. At least until I found drugs and sex." She shook her head and ran her palms over her bare arms. "I should've stuck with the cutting. I didn't hurt anyone but myself."

Georgia couldn't help giving her mother another hug. She was the parent, the one who should be comforting her daughter, but in reality, Misty was just a lost child. Georgia wasn't sure she wanted to know about what set her down this path of self-destruction, but she knew she wanted to help her make a different life for herself.

"You're turning things around," she said. "You've got plenty of time to live a different life."

"Do you think so?" Misty asked. Her gray eyes, exactly like Georgia's, were red and brimming with tears.

"I know so."

Nine

"The results are back."

Carson had opened the front door of his loft expecting to see Georgia, but instead he found Graham and Brooks standing there. Graham was holding a large envelope. All thoughts of his dinner plans with her evaporated when he realized what it was. He had been awaiting and dreading this moment all week.

"Have you looked at the results yet?"

"No," Graham said. "I practiced an amazing amount of restraint because I thought it was best that we all look at it together."

"With alcohol," Brooks added, holding up an expensive bottle of tequila in one hand and a bag of limes in the other.

"That's probably wise," Carson noted.

Stepping back, he let his brothers in. He expected

them to want to rush to the results, considering how hard they'd worked to uncover the truth and how long they'd waited. But they took their time. Graham poured shots while Brooks sliced up a few limes. Carson just watched anxiously, tapping his fingers on the quartz countertops while he waited.

There was something final about reading the lab report, like the end of an era. For their whole lives, their father had been a mystery to them. Carson was certain that each of them had entertained private fantasies about what their father was really like and what he would say to them if they ever came face-to-face. It was possible that this envelope could shatter those fantasies once and for all. If the test results came back positive, the mystery was over and they were left with the cold, hard reality of Sutton Winchester being their father.

If the results were negative, they had to start back at square one. This time with no leads to follow. The only evidence they'd found pointed to Sutton. If he wasn't the answer, Carson was at a loss for where to look next.

As he looked down at the envelope, their mother's words echoed through his mind. *You're better off without your father in your life,* she'd said. What if she was right? This was their last chance to change their minds.

"Are you guys sure you want to do this?" Carson asked.

"Are you serious?" Graham asked.

"Yes, I'm serious." Carson picked up the envelope and held it up. "Once we open this thing, there's no going back. Mom kept our father out of our lives for a reason. Maybe it was the right decision."

"Maybe, but we've come too far to turn back now," Brooks argued. "Besides, Sutton will have the results, too. It's too late to change our minds. We're going to find out one way or another."

"You're right," Carson admitted and tossed the envelope back onto the counter. And it was true. They were past the point of no return.

Graham handed a shot out to each of them. "Let's do one to take the edge off before we open the results. What shall we drink to?"

"The truth," Carson offered. Good or bad, at least they'd finally have that.

"The truth," his brothers repeated in unison. Together they all drank their shots of smooth tequila, not even needing the limes when they were through. They sat their shot glasses down and one by one, their gazes returned to the unopened envelope.

"Hurry up and open it," Brooks said at last. "The suspense is killing me."

"Who wants to read it aloud?" Graham asked as he slid his finger beneath the seal and opened the envelope.

"You do it," Carson said. "You're the one who made this happen."

Graham pulled out two sheets of paper, one with Carson's results and one with the twins' results. "Okay. Let's start with Carson." His gaze danced back and forth across the paper for a moment, making Carson's stomach tangle into knots as he waited. Not even the tequila could tame it.

"The alleged father, Sutton Winchester, *cannot* be excluded as the biological father of the child, Carson Newport, since they share genetic markers. Using the above systems, the probability of paternity is 99.99%, as compared to an untested, unrelated man of the Caucasian population."

"We were right," Brooks said.

Carson didn't know how to react to the news. He'd braced himself for this moment, part of him hoping Sutton wasn't his father and part of him hoping he was, just so he'd have the answer at last. Well, now he had it. He was that old bastard's son. He'd known in his heart that he was, but having the official confirmation just sealed it in his mind.

The man he'd been looking for his whole life, the one his mother warned him about, had been right under his nose the whole time. Sutton had always treated him like a nuisance. The Newport Corporation and its owners were just an annoying fly buzzing around the King of Chicago's crown. He'd never once treated them like anything else, certainly not like his own children. It was one thing not to be able to publicly acknowledge your illegitimate sons, but to deliberately handle them like pebbles in his shoe their whole lives...

"Carson, are you okay?" Brooks asked.

He realized that he'd been holding his breath and let it out in one big burst. "Yes." He reached for the tequila bottle and did another shot without them. "Let's read yours and get this over with."

Graham shuffled the papers in his hands until he could read the second report. "The alleged father, Sutton Winchester, cannot be excluded *or* confirmed as the biological father of the children, Graham and Brooks Newport. The children's samples were tainted or mishandled, containing foreign contaminants, and must be recollected and retested for final results."

"Mishandled?" Brooks exclaimed. "Are you kidding me? After all this?" Now it was his turn to reach for the bottle and take a shot.

Graham just shook his head. "I guess we need to go back tomorrow and get swabbed again."

"And while we wait for those results, we can plan how we want to move forward," Carson said, trying to distract his brothers from their disappointment. "We know at the very least that I'm his son, so we can do some contingency planning."

"No," Brooks says. "We can't wait. We need to jump on these results, especially if he's as sick as Georgia makes him sound. Sutton has gone long enough without receiving his comeuppance. He needs to pay for abandoning us. He needs to pay for using and tossing our mother aside. He may be our father, but this is war. It's best to attack while the opposing side isn't expecting it."

Graham gave a curt nod in agreement, making Carson's stomach start to ache again. "Let's set up a meeting with the Winchesters for tomorrow."

Georgia was surprised to brush past the Newport twins as they got off the elevator in Carson's building and she was getting on. They gave her a polite wave but didn't stop to say hello. They both had a cold, calculating look in their eyes that worried her. What had happened? She got the feeling her date with Carson would be different from what they'd planned.

She waited patiently after ringing the doorbell. When Carson finally answered, the expression on his face worried her even more than his brothers' scheming scowls. He looked heartbroken. His mouth was drawn down into an uncharacteristic frown and his face was flushed. His eyes looked a little red and his brow was furrowed in thought.

"Hey, Georgia," he said in a flat tone. "I have to apologize in advance. I'm not going to be very good company tonight. Do you mind if we don't go out?"

"We can stay in," Georgia said and pushed past him into his apartment. She got the feeling he wanted to turn her away, and she wouldn't let him. He needed someone to talk to, and she was going to be the one whether he liked it or not.

She set her purse down on the counter beside a half-empty bottle of tequila and three shot glasses. That explained the flushed face and red eyes. Then her gaze ran across the paperwork and the lab logo across the top. He'd gotten the results of the paternity test.

Georgia didn't need to read the papers. She could tell by the look on Carson's face that Sutton was the father he'd never wanted. Turning to face him, she wrapped her arms around his waist and looked up into his green eyes. "Are you going to be okay?"

"Eventually. I just have to forget about everything I know to be true and adjust to a world where a man like Sutton could produce a man like me."

"Sutton didn't produce a man like you, Carson. If he had been in your life, you'd be a completely different person and likely one I wouldn't date. He might be your genetic contributor, but you were produced by the loving environment your mother raised you in. That's what's important. You're nothing like him."

"Oh really?" He pulled away and wandered into the

living room, where he dropped down onto the couch. "I'm more of a cutthroat bastard than you might think. We're going to destroy him, you know."

Georgia's eyes widened. "What do you mean?"

"Graham and Brooks want to go after his estate. No holds barred. They think we're owed something after years of neglect and now is their chance to make Sutton pay the piper."

Georgia sat down on the couch beside him and rested her hand on his knee. "You don't agree with their plans?"

"I do and I don't. I mean, I want him to suffer. I want him to spend the rest of his life regretting what he did to my mother and to us. But at the same time, I guess I just don't have the killer instinct. That's the one thing I wish I had inherited from him."

"Don't wish that. It's your conscientiousness that I'm drawn to."

Carson looked at her with some of his previous sparkle in his eyes. "You mean it's not my dashing good looks and rock-hard abs?"

Georgia smiled wide. She was happy to see a glimmer of her Carson beneath the gloom. "Those certainly don't hurt."

He wrapped his arm around her shoulders, and Georgia snuggled in against his chest. "I'm glad you came over tonight. If I was alone, I'd probably stew all evening and finish off that bottle of tequila."

"You'd regret it tomorrow."

"I usually do. But enough of my parental drama. I don't want to waste our night together talking about that. But I do have to ask how it's going with your mom. Hopefully better news than on my end."

"Good. Better than I ever could've expected or hoped," Georgia said. She knew that Carson was feeling down, but she was filled with more optimism than she'd felt in years. Maybe even her whole life. The last few days had been amazing. She'd gotten answers to questions she'd never even thought to ask. "We've spent hours talking. I've learned so much about her and my family that I've never met. Did you know I have a brother and sister somewhere?"

"Really?" He chuckled and slowly shook his head. "That seems to be going around lately. I've suddenly got more siblings than I know what to do with."

"The hardest part, though, is hearing about her life. I mean, I thought I had it rough growing up in the foster care system, but it's nothing compared to what she went through. I'm not surprised she turned to drugs. I don't even know how she gets out of bed every morning."

"Where is she now? We could've rescheduled tonight until after she went back to Michigan."

"No, that's okay. It actually worked out perfectly. I helped her find a local Alcoholics Anonymous support group that meets tonight. It's just a few blocks from my place in a church, so I gave her enough money to get herself some authentic Chicago-style deep-dish pizza from a place across the street from it. That will keep her busy for a few hours."

"Are you okay leaving her alone in your apartment?"

This again. "She's been alone all day while I've been at the office and there hasn't been a problem. I appreciate your concern, Carson, but I think it will be okay. If I was worried, I wouldn't be here with you."

"Okay. You can smack me for being overcautious. I know I'm being selfish, but I'd much rather you be here with me, anyway. I just wish I was better company." Carson gave her a weak smile. "I figured I wouldn't get to see you after work hours until Misty had left."

Georgia didn't want to wait that long to spend time with Carson. At the office, it just wasn't the same. They kept things distant and professional, the way they should have. Their conversations were about business—planning the charity gala for the hospital was the big task of the moment. She didn't get to snuggle against his chest and feel his arms around her the way she wanted them to be.

"Well, I miss you," she said. Georgia didn't like the way it felt to admit vulnerability like that, but it was true. Whether or not this fling of theirs lasted through the month, she'd found herself getting increasingly attached to Carson. She wanted to tell him about how things were going with her mom. She wanted to be there to soothe him when he got bad news. "And I'm glad I came over. I wouldn't want you to be home alone tonight."

"You make me not want to be home alone any night."

Leaning into her, he pressed his lips against hers. The soft touch rapidly intensified as the taste of tequila and emotion mixed together on her tongue. She drank in his sadness, doing whatever she could to make him feel better tonight. She would use her body like a bandage to cover the wounds his father left without ever realizing it.

Pulling away from Carson's mouth, she smiled coyly at him. "I know what will make you feel better."

He lifted a curious eyebrow but didn't question her. Instead he waited for her to reveal her answer. Without speaking, she slipped off the couch onto the floor in front of him. On her knees, she eased between his legs. Her gaze stayed fixed on his as she slowly unbuttoned his shirt.

Carson didn't argue. He just took a deep breath and let her do as she pleased. Georgia tugged the shirt out of his waistband, unbuttoning the last of the buttons and opening it to expose his chest. Leaning in, she planted a line of kisses starting at his collarbone and moving down. She noticed how the hair on his belly thickened as she traveled lower, planting one last kiss above his belt and drawing in the warm scent of his skin before she sat back to unbuckle it. Her fingers moved deftly to unbutton his pants and zip his fly open. She could feel the heat of his desire pressing against her hand through the cotton of his underwear.

Georgia let her palm glide over it ever so slowly before she gathered the waistbands and tugged both his pants and underwear down his thighs. With nothing left in her way, she curled her fingers around the length of him and gave a little squeeze until he hissed and squirmed on the sofa. She let her hot breath blow across his skin before she bent her head and took him into her mouth.

Her tongue glided along his smooth skin as her lips pressed farther and farther down. Carson's whole body tensed the lower she moved. He didn't even breathe until she eased back.

"Oh, Georgia," he groaned, threading his fingers through her blond waves and holding tight. His grip didn't hurt, but the intensity urged her on. "Damn, you feel good, baby."

She worked into a slow, tortuous rhythm between her mouth and her hands. Carson's fingertips massaged her scalp, never forcing her movements, but going along with them. She could feel every muscle in his body tighten as she sped up, then slowed down to tease him.

"I don't think I can take much more of this," he managed through gritted teeth.

"I'm just getting started."

"Yeah, well, so am I. Come here," he said. Reaching out, he took her hand and tugged her up until she was straddling him. He took a moment to slip on a condom, and then pushed the hem of her pencil skirt up to her hips, brushing over the lace tops of her thigh-high hosiery. His hands slipped beneath her legs, feeling at the insignificant scrap of fabric that separated them. His fingers pushed the lace aside, allowing the length of him to seek out her opening.

Georgia took it from there. She slowly lowered her hips, taking in every inch of him until she was fully seated on his lap. He reached for her blouse, unbuttoning the silk fabric and slipping it off her shoulders to the floor. His palms covered the cream lace bra, molding the full globes of her breasts in his hands and pinching at the hardened nipples that strained against the rough material.

Closing her eyes, Georgia rolled her hips, moving him inside her. A low growl sounded from Carson's throat as she eased up and slid down the length of him again. She bit her bottom lip as the movements started to generate a liquid heat in her belly.

"Why did I wait so long to touch you?" Carson wondered aloud. "You could've been in my arms all this time."

The same thought had crossed Georgia's mind in the last week. She'd been at the Newport Corporation for over a year now. A year when she'd gone home each night fantasizing about her boss and never believing she could have him. A year of loneliness that could've been spent with him if she had thought for a moment that she deserved a man like him.

She still wasn't entirely sure she was good enough, but she'd savor every moment she could share with him. Georgia had never let herself get truly close to someone, but she felt Carson getting past all her barriers. He was the first man even to try, and the stone walls just tumbled at his slightest touch. Her heart swelled at the thought of him, and her body craved him.

She wasn't entirely sure she knew what love felt like. She'd read about it in books and seen examples in movies, but she'd never felt it herself. But now, here with Carson, she thought she might finally know for sure. It was more than like, more than just need or desire. He consumed her, body and soul, and she never wanted to let him go.

Georgia was falling in love with him.

The rush of emotions spilled from her heart, and the pleasurable coil inside her grew that much tighter. As the sensations grew more intense, Carson shifted his hands to grip her hips. His fingertips pressed into her flesh. Her thighs started to burn as she moved faster, coaxing the release from deep inside her. Soft cries and whimpers of anticipation escaped her lips as her climax grew nearer and nearer.

"Yeah," Carson whispered in soft encouragement. "Let go, Georgia."

She didn't have any choice in the matter. Her orgasm exploded inside her, the shockwaves radiating through her whole body. He steadied her hips and she braced herself against his shoulders as she writhed and cried out. Her muscles clamped down around him, fluttering and pulsing as the final throbs of pleasure echoed and then finally faded away. When she opened her eyes, she found Carson watching her.

"You are so beautiful," he said. "And you're even more amazing when you come undone. I love to watch you let go and just feel."

Georgia felt a blush rise to her cheeks. "Well, now it's your turn," she said, clamping her inner muscles down hard around him.

He groaned as his hands slid up from her hips until they were wrapped around her back. He pulled her torso toward him until she was hunched over him with her face buried in his neck. Keeping a tight grip on her, he started moving beneath her.

Georgia gasped and clung to him as her overstimulated nerves tried to absorb more pleasure. Her lips danced across the salty skin of his neck and shoulder, tasting and nipping at him. As he tensed and his moves became more frantic, she whispered a few provocative and erotic things into his ear.

It wasn't what she wanted to say. In the moment, overflowing with emotions and sensations, she wanted to whisper that she was falling in love with him, but it wasn't the right time or place. She'd never said the words before, and when she did, she wanted it to be special. She wanted him to respond in kind. That, she feared, would take more time.

What she *did* say was just right, however. Carson's fingers dug into her flesh as he thrust hard and poured into her with a satisfied roar. Georgia rode through the waves, planting a soft kiss on his lips once he stilled beneath her.

"You know what?" he said when he caught his breath.

"What?"

"You were right. I do feel better."

Ten

Carson had trouble sleeping that night after Georgia went home. He didn't know if it was his ever-evolving feelings for her or his nerves about his meeting at Elite Industries the next day, but by the time he and his brothers arrived at Sutton's offices that afternoon, he felt very unprepared.

"This isn't the way to Sutton's office," Graham said as the assistant took the three brothers down the hallway.

"Yes, sir. This is the way to Miss Winchester's office. Mr. Winchester isn't in today."

"That bastard stood us up," Brooks grumbled. "He got the results the same as we did and he was too big a coward to show his face."

"Actually," Eve Winchester said from just ahead of them, "he's quite ill."

Carson narrowed his gaze at Eve, Sutton's oldest daughter. Based on what Tammy had said, Eve was already born when his parents split up, so that meant Eve was his older sister. It was hard enough to think about Sutton as his father, but the shockwaves that radiated through the family were equally difficult. His sister. He ran his fingers through his hair and shook his head. He wasn't going to adjust to this easily.

"I'm sure he is feeling poorly," Brooks said, "after being caught in such a big lie."

Eve's thin frame tensed at Brooks's words. Instead of responding, she waved them past her into her office to sit at the conference room table.

Looking down the table, Carson noticed Brooks was wound tight and ready to fight. Graham was uncharacteristically silent, but his eyes never left Eve. She sat down across from them. A moment later, another woman arrived. She was tinier than Eve with lighter blond hair. They both had the same green eyes, though. Sutton's eyes. Carson's eyes.

"This is my youngest sister, Grace."

"Where's Nora?" Brooks asked. "I believe we requested to meet with everyone today."

"Nora lives in Colorado and has a small child. Since you demanded this meeting take place today, you'll understand that it was impossible for her to make it."

"And Sutton?" Graham said at last. "Is he really sick or just sick at the thought of more of his money being funneled away?"

Carson watched the Winchester women as they reacted to Graham's cutting words. He could see the worry in Grace's eyes. He knew then that Sutton truly was ill. "What's wrong with him?" he asked. He was his father, after all.

"We don't know," Grace replied. "He's seeing the doctor today."

"Let's cut to the chase, gentlemen." Eve stared all of them down, her cold, businesslike demeanor reminding Carson very much of their father. "I can run this business and this family just as well as my father, so I see no reason why we can't proceed without him."

"Well," Carson began, "we presume that your father received the results of the paternity tests and has informed you of what they revealed."

"He did. You are our half brother," Eve said matter-of-factly. Turning to the twins, she added, "You two are to be determined."

"I'm pretty sure the results will turn out positive this time," Brooks said. "So we wanted to get the process started."

"The process of what?" Grace asked.

"The process of ensuring that we get our share of the Winchester estate."

"Our father is sick, not dead. There's no estate to have yet."

"There will be one day. He won't live forever, even with all his money. We're not about to wait until he's six feet under to start contesting the will. We intend to make sure we get what's coming to us, fair and square."

Carson sat uncomfortably as his brothers and sisters argued back and forth.

"And how do you propose this miracle will happen?" Eve asked. "It doesn't matter if you're biologically Winchesters or not. Our father doesn't have to include anyone in his will he doesn't want to."

"That's true," Graham said. "He can leave us out. But if he does, I can guarantee that you and your sisters will never see a penny of your inheritances. We will sue and tie the estate up in court for years. You won't get a thing until it's settled by the judge, and by then, half of it might have been drained away in legal fees."

Grace swallowed hard. "And what is our alternative?"

"It's fairly simple," Brooks said. "If your father voluntarily updates his will now, we'll have no problem. We've already gone our entire lives being ignored. Our mother raised us alone without receiving a dime in child support from our father. I don't think it's too much to ask that we get our share once he's gone. We think you ladies can help make that happen."

"Us?" Eve asked.

"You're daddy's little girls, right? Encourage your father to update the will to include us with even distribution among all the biological children. Tell him that you don't want to fight family in court over the estate. Certainly he'll listen to you."

"Have you met our father?" Eve asked.

At that, Carson had to chuckle. All four of his siblings looked over at him with venom in their expressions. Now was not the time to find amusement in the situation. He opted to try diffusing the tension instead.

"Eve, Grace," he said, "try to see this from our point of view. You had your father in your life. You had everything you've ever wanted. We were equally deserving, but we were shut out. We had to fight for everything we have, and we're not going to stop now. Our father owes us this, for our mother's sake and for the sake of the children he abandoned."

"I am very sorry for the way you all grew up. I'm sorry that you felt unloved and had a difficult life. But you do understand that this has nothing to do with us girls? Have you given any consideration to how we feel about all of this?" Eve looked at Carson as she said the words, making him feel like the bully in the situation. "We suddenly have brothers? Or, at least, one for certain. We are faced with the knowledge that our father not only cheated on our mother but also did it in such a reckless way. You're not punishing Sutton with this proposal of yours. You're punishing us."

"I hate that's the way it has to be," Graham said, with a touch of sadness in his voice that Carson didn't expect. He was used to Graham being a shark in this kind of negotiation. Perhaps he wasn't as enthusiastic about using his sharp teeth on his own sister.

"But you and I both know that there's only one way to get to Sutton Winchester," Graham continued, "and that's through his wallet. We're not going to get a tearful reunion out of him. Hell, we'll be lucky to get him to acknowledge us privately, much less publicly. I'm sorry that we have to rob your trust funds to make it happen, but money is all we're going to get out of our father, so you'd better be damn sure that we're going to get it."

The room was awkwardly silent for a moment as all the potential siblings sized one another up. "Very well," Eve said at last. "I'll have a discussion with Father about the will. When the new DNA test results are ready, perhaps he will be willing to move forward with updates. But not until then."

"Fair enough," Graham answered.

"Well, then, if there's nothing else, I'm sure we all

have businesses to run." Eve pushed up from her chair, and everyone else followed suit.

"We'll see ourselves out," Carson said as they spilled out into the hallway. He was certain the sisters had plenty of talking to do among themselves. As did the brothers.

They moved silently through the offices until they climbed into Brooks's car and slammed the doors shut.

"Now what?" Carson asked.

"I think that went well," Graham said. "I think we wait on the results and see what they do next."

"You were too soft on them," Brooks complained to Graham. "That Eve woman is just your type. She had you eating from her hand."

"That Eve woman might be our sister, man. That's gross."

"Well, either way, she's your type and you didn't go in for the kill."

"There wasn't need to. We got our point across. Like she said, they're being punished for their father's actions. I'm not going to push harder until we have to."

Carson listened to the twins argue. He wasn't sure how he felt about their plans to get revenge against Sutton. "I don't know about all this," he said.

Both brothers turned toward the backseat to look at him. "What do you mean?" Brooks asked.

"I mean…what's the point? We don't need the money. We're not going to get a dad out of this. We're just going to make our sisters hate us, and when Sutton is gone, they might be all we have left."

"He dumped our mother, Carson. He left her pregnant with infant twins to care for. He needs to be punished. Tell me another way to do it and I'll do it," Graham offered.

There wasn't another way and he knew it. "I don't know."

Brooks's expression softened as he looked at Carson. "This isn't the kind of thing Mom raised us to do, I know, but her memory demands vengeance. If you don't want our mother's blood money, funnel it into the hospital. Buy equipment that will save children's lives, if that's what helps you sleep at night. But it's happening and you need to get used to the idea. We're going to get our pound of flesh from Winchester."

Georgia was surprised by a voice mail from Sutton at the office when she returned from lunch. She thought that he was meeting with the Newport brothers today, but the message indicated he was calling her from home. He wanted to speak with her and give her his donation check personally. If she was available, he would send a car to pick her up.

She had no idea where the Winchester home was, but she was pretty sure the "L" didn't go there, so she made arrangements with his secretary to be picked up within the hour.

She knew she'd made a promise to Carson that she would tell him when she went to see Sutton, but it would have to wait until tomorrow. He would be tied up with his brothers and their scheming, she had no doubt, and tonight she was spending time with her mother. She was leaving in the morning for Detroit, and Georgia was planning to make a special dinner.

It took quite a while to get out to Sutton's estate, but when she arrived, she was stunned by the extravagance of it all. Large iron gates protected the winding driveway that led to the giant gray mansion. It sprawled on forever, easily housing twenty people or more instead of the five Winchesters she knew about.

The driver circled the courtyard fountain and pulled up to the front steps. He opened the door and let Georgia out. An older man in a suit was waiting for her at the entrance.

"Miss Adams," he greeted her with a polite smile. "I am Christopher, the butler. Mr. Winchester is expecting you."

"I thought Mr. Winchester would be in the office today," she said.

"Normally he would be, but he's not feeling well."

Georgia followed Christopher up the marble staircase to the second floor of the mansion. They headed toward a set of double doors at the end of the hallway. "Are we going to his office?" she asked.

"No, ma'am. He's not well enough to leave his bed today. You'll be meeting with him in the master suite." Christopher pushed open the double doors and moved ahead.

She wasn't too keen on the idea of being in Sutton Winchester's bedroom, but it was too late to do anything about it. As she looked around, it hardly seemed like a bedroom anyway. It was almost like an apartment in itself with its own seating area, dressing area, a desk and a wall of French doors that led out to a private balcony overlooking the pool and tennis courts. Up ahead, another set of doors led to the bedroom itself.

Christopher opened the second set of doors. "Mr. Winchester, Miss Adams is here to see you."

"Good, send her in. And have some tea sent up."

Christopher disappeared, leaving Georgia alone in Sutton's bedroom. The minute she laid eyes on him, however, all her worries disappeared. This was not a man luring her here for seduction.

He looked even more sunken and thin than he had a few days ago. The circles under his eyes were darker. There was an IV in his hand and some medical equipment tracking his heart rate and other vital signs nearby. An oxygen tube was inserted into his nose and wrapped around his ears.

"I'm afraid I'm going to have to rescind my offer to be your lover, Georgia." He said the words with a smile, but there was no twinkle of amusement in his familiar green eyes.

She couldn't help her gaze from widening at the sight of him propped up in his bed. "They said you were sick, but this is more than just sick, isn't it?"

"Unfortunately. Please, have a seat." Sutton gestured to a chair at his bedside.

"I thought you were meeting with the Newport boys today to talk about the test results."

"That was the plan, but this damn cancer has other ideas. Eve is handling it."

"Cancer?"

"That's what they tell me," he said with a defeated tone. "Stage IV lung cancer. They haven't tested yet, but they're pretty sure it's spread. Probably to my lymph nodes. My doctor will be trying some things, but this is basically a death sentence. Some people would say it's long overdue."

"Does your family know yet?"

Sutton shook his head. "No. The girls know I'm

ill, but not to what extent. I'm going to meet with the children in a few days to tell them everything once the plans are finalized. This is a very delicate situation, Georgia, and I need you to promise to keep my illness a secret. You can't tell anyone, especially Carson. I need to tell them all this in my own way, in my own time."

Georgia could only nod. Her heart was breaking on the inside for Carson. He'd only learned about his father the day before, and now he was going to lose him before he'd even gotten to know him. It didn't seem fair that she was getting a second chance with her long-lost parent and he wouldn't have the same.

A woman arrived in the room with a silver tea service just then. She laid everything out on the nearby nightstand, pouring them both a delicate china cup of hot black tea. She quickly prepared Sutton's tea as he liked it, then handed him the cup and saucer with a buttery piece of shortbread on the edge.

"How do you take your tea, miss?" she asked.

"One sugar and a splash of cream, please."

The woman handed her a cup. "Is there anything else I can get you, Mr. Winchester?"

"No, thank you. That will be all."

The woman nodded and disappeared as quickly as she had arrived.

Georgia studied her tea, taking a tentative sip as she thought over everything Sutton had told her. "Why are you telling me before anyone else? Why did you ask me here today?" She hated being burdened with this knowledge, knowing how it would affect Carson and his brothers.

"Because I like you, Georgia. You're smart. You're

attractive. You've got a great head for business. If I was twenty years younger, you would be in trouble." He sighed wistfully and shook his head. "But my mind and my body don't really cooperate the way I'd like them to anymore. I asked you here today because I wanted to tell you this in person so you'd understand where I was coming from. Since you and Carson are together, I thought maybe you could help him process it all."

Georgia was surprised by Sutton's thoughtfulness. Despite his physical and emotional distance from his son, he seemed to know that this would be hard on Carson. And not only that, but he knew, too, that Carson wouldn't turn to him for comfort—he would go to Georgia.

"I also wanted to give you something."

Sutton reached over to his nightstand and pulled out a sealed envelope from the top drawer. It had Carson's name written on the front in his handwriting. "This is the check I promised you for the hospital. I wanted to give it to you personally. Please see to it that Carson gets this when you see him next."

Georgia took the envelope from him and slipped it into her purse. "I will."

"He hates me, you know?" Sutton said matter-of-factly. "I've given him every reason to. I doubt that check will help, but it's all I can offer. Cindy was a bright spot in my life. When I lost her, I gave in to the darkness once and for all. Honoring her memory by contributing to the children's hospital is the least I can do."

Georgia couldn't help but notice the soft, sentimental expression on Sutton's face when he talked about

Carson's mother and how he referred to her as Cindy.
Was there more between them than just one more of
his dalliances? She and Carson would probably never
know. But she did understand how Carson felt.

"He doesn't hate you," Georgia argued. "He hates
how you treated his mother."

At that, Sutton laughed. "I bet Cindy told the boys
quite the tale to keep them away from me. She probably did it to protect me. That's why she left the company," he said. "My wife at the time was threatening
all sorts of chaos if I didn't break it off with Cindy. I
couldn't do it, though. I didn't care if she ruined me.
But Cindy cared. She said she wouldn't let me give
up everything for her, and she left. All I could do was
give her a severance package to ease the loss. She told
me not to look for her. She made me promise, so I kept
my word. I wish every day that I hadn't. I would've
known about Carson if I'd searched for her."

Georgia perked up in her seat. "You didn't know
about Carson?"

Sutton shook his head. "No. I knew about the twins,
of course, but they weren't mine. When they started
their business and became my main competitors, I
knew who they were. I started to contact Cindy, then
thought better of it. It had been a long time and she
probably didn't want me interrupting her life. When
I realized there was a younger Newport boy, I figured he was the child of Cindy's next lover. It never
occurred to me…"

There was a sadness in Sutton's eyes that she didn't
expect to see there. "I'd always wanted a son. I love
my girls more than anything, but it pains me greatly
to know that I had a child out there all these years and

I didn't know it. And now—" he gestured toward the medical equipment next to the bed "—it's too late."

This was a side of Sutton that Georgia had never expected to see. He wasn't a saint by any stretch of the imagination, but he wasn't the monster he'd been painted to be, either. She felt a genuine pain coming from him as he spoke about his regrets. Perhaps she was right and his relationship with Carson's mother had been more than just a sleazy affair. It sounded like love to her. She knew how that felt, and how much she was willing to do for Carson because she cared. Was Cynthia willing to go to such great lengths to protect Sutton from financial and corporate ruin?

"It's not too late," Georgia said. "You and Carson can still have a relationship. You just have to convince him to give you a chance. If all those things his mother told him about you aren't true, he needs to know that."

Sutton listened to her thoughtfully, then shook his head. "He won't listen to me. Maybe he'll listen to you."

Eleven

"Mom?"

Georgia pushed her way through the front door of her loft, her arms filled with groceries. It was late enough when she'd left the Winchester estate that she'd had the car drop her at her neighborhood grocery store instead of returning to the office. She'd picked up a few things her mother liked, and got what she needed to make her famous lasagna for dinner. Misty had been asleep when she got home from Carson's the night before, so Georgia had planned a nice evening for them to spend together before her mother took the bus back to Detroit.

She'd been feeling quite sentimental since she left Sutton. If there was hope for his relationship with Carson, perhaps there was hope for her relationship with Misty. Things had gone well so far.

She dropped the bags onto the dining room table and listened for sounds of Misty in the house. The last few days, she'd returned home to find her curled up on the couch reading one of her books or watching television. But there was no murmur of voices coming from the TV set or the radio.

"Mom?" she said again, but there was no answer.

Frowning, Georgia made her way through the living room. Everything seemed to be in place. The book her mother had been reading was sitting on the coffee table where she'd left it. The lamp was on nearby. Perhaps she'd gone upstairs for something.

She climbed up the stairs to her bedroom loft and stopped short when her eyes took in the sight. There it seemed like a tornado had flown around the room. All her drawers were open with clothes cast to the ground, her closet door was ajar, and her jewelry armoire had its now-empty trays tossed onto the floor.

Her first reaction was to be scared and worried for Misty. She ran into the closet, half expecting to find her crumpled, beaten body there. Nothing. Then she went into the bathroom, once again hoping her mother hadn't been attacked when her apartment was robbed. Nothing there, either. Then she noticed among the chaos that her mother's backpack and duffel bag were gone.

Along with Georgia's nicer things.

She didn't have much in the way of expensive jewelry, but she had some. At least, before now she had. Everything had been cleaned out of her jewelry armoire, even the cheap costume pieces. In her closet, several pairs of expensive shoes were missing with the empty boxes left lying on the ground. Her new iPad she'd left charging on the dresser was gone, too.

There was only one thing left that was worth anything. She always kept an envelope of cash and an emergency credit card between her mattress and box springs. It was an old habit, one that would allow her to disappear at a moment's notice. With that money and the items in her purse, she could walk away and never come back. It was a remnant of her nomadic life as a foster child.

Georgia crouched down and thrust her hand beneath the mattress. She felt around, but her fingertips didn't make contact with the envelope. Finally she lifted the whole mattress up, but that just confirmed her suspicions. The money was gone. Along with her mother.

She sunk down onto the bed, her chest tight with emotions she wasn't ready to face. It had happened. Everything Carson had warned her about had happened. She'd hoped that Misty was ready to be a mother, that she'd cleaned up her act, but Georgia had been wrong. Instead Misty had gained Georgia's trust and abused it. How could she have been so naive?

Pushing herself up from the bed as the tears began to flow, she rushed into the bathroom. She turned on the cold water and splashed her flushed, heated face. The water stung as it mixed with her angry tears and dripped back into the sink.

Georgia braced her hands on the counter and hovered there. She wasn't sure what to do now. Should she call the cops on her mother? She knew she should, but a part of her couldn't do it. Even though she was heartbroken. Even though she felt like an abandoned child sitting in an unfamiliar foster home again.

She'd come to like her mother over the past few days, and even this hadn't erased those memories. Somehow she couldn't turn her mother in to the police. The things she'd taken might've been a lot to Misty, but they weren't important to Georgia. They were all replaceable. Unlike their relationship. If they even had one.

As she stood up, her gaze fell on the nearby wastebasket. A small clear baggie with residue and a used hypodermic needle were in there among the tissue. Her mother was using again. That explained the sudden change. Had she taken the pizza money and decided to get high instead of going to AA? When she'd come home last night, was her mother passed out instead of sleeping? Probably so. Misty had let her addiction get the best of her and ruined what they'd started to build together.

Georgia was so disappointed. In her mother. In herself. She needed to talk to someone. Going back downstairs, she picked up her phone from where she'd left it on the dining room table. She quickly dialed Carson.

"Hey, Georgia," he answered. "I wasn't expecting to hear from you tonight."

"Can I come over?" The minute she opened her mouth to speak, the tears threatened again. She fought to keep them from her voice. If she was going to break down again, it would be in his arms, and not before.

"Uh, sure. I'll warn you that I'm not very good company, but you're welcome to come by. I thought you were with your mom tonight."

Georgia swallowed the lump that had lodged in her throat. "Change of plans."

"I'll be here. See you soon."

She hung up the phone and set it back on the table. She conscientiously put all the perishable groceries away, leaving the pantry goods in the bag. Then she armed her home security system in case her mother returned for more, and headed to Carson's place. Tonight she couldn't face the "L," so she hailed a cab instead.

"Come on in, Georgia," he called as she knocked on the door. She slipped inside and closed the door behind her. "I'm in the exercise room!" he said just as she wondered where he was.

Georgia hadn't known he had an exercise room, but she followed the sound of his voice down the hallway. There she found him in nothing but a pair of shorts and some boxing gloves. He was covered in sweat and wailing angrily on a punching bag hung from the ceiling.

She watched him for a few minutes. She kept expecting him to stop since she was here. To ask what was wrong. To console her. But he kept punching until exhaustion took over and his forehead dropped against the bag.

"Are you okay?" she asked.

"We were supposed to meet with Sutton and his daughters today," he explained as he ripped the Velcro open to pull off his gloves. "He stood us up."

She knew that wasn't entirely true, but she couldn't tell him that. She had to pretend that she didn't know. "Sutton wasn't there?"

"No," he said, throwing the gloves into the corner. "They said he was sick, which just confirms what you told me. But how sick could he be? He met with you the other day hoping for a piece of tail, but when he's supposed to meet with his own sons, he can't do it?"

Sutton had deteriorated pretty quickly. He was sicker than anyone could've guessed. "I'm not surprised. I told you he looked terrible."

"Don't defend him," Carson snapped.

Georgia flinched at his sharp criticism. Carson was completely spun up. She'd never seen him like this before. He was always fairly calm and collected, but the news about Sutton really seemed to have rattled him. "Did you meet with Eve?"

He nodded. "Eve and Grace. They weren't very receptive to our plan, but I didn't expect them to be. They weren't very receptive to me being their brother, either, as though I'd wrecked their parents' marriage by existing. Like I had anything to do with it! I just… I think this whole thing is going to blow up in our faces. Mom was right. We were better off without having our father in our lives. He was a bastard then and he's a bastard now. Nothing has changed on that front."

Georgia didn't have much to add on that note. She could tell that beneath all the blustering, he was really disappointed. The little boy deep inside had hoped his father and sisters would welcome him, just as she'd hoped her mother would be there for her. For all the good it did them. "You should give Sutton a chance to be your father. Maybe you'll be surprised by how it turns out."

Carson snatched a towel off the folded stack nearby and rubbed his face with it. "I sincerely doubt that. The man can't be trusted. I don't want you meeting with him anymore," he said.

"What? Why? I thought you wanted me to continue getting information for you."

"No. It isn't worth it. I don't want you anywhere near him. I don't want to be anywhere near him, either. I just can't believe this." Carson dropped down onto the weight bench and shook his head. "I never should've dug through my mother's things. I was better off not knowing the truth."

"You can't go back and change the past. All you can do is make the most of what's done."

Carson made an annoyed *hrmph* sound and slung the towel around his neck as he stood up. "If you don't mind, I'd rather not talk about this anymore. It will ruin the whole evening." He walked up to Georgia and gave her a kiss as he wrapped his arms around her waist. "What's going on with you? You said you were going to be with your mom tonight."

Georgia's gaze dropped to his bare chest as she nodded. "Yeah, that was the plan. But when I got home from work, I found that my mom is gone."

Carson's brow furrowed into a frown. "You mean she left early?"

"You could say that. You could also say that while I was at work, she robbed me to buy drugs and ran off."

Carson eased back so he could look her in the eye. Certainly he hadn't heard her right. "What?"

Georgia just shook her head as he pulled her tightly into his arms. "You were right all along," she said as she started to sob against his bare skin. "I thought she really wanted to be a part of my life, but she was just using me. I feel so stupid for falling for this."

Carson stroked her hair as he held her close. "I'm

sorry, Georgia. I didn't want to be right. I'd hoped I was wrong. Are you sure that she wasn't just out somewhere? Maybe she went to another AA meeting?"

"Yes, I'm sure. There was no need for her to take my iPad, emergency cash and all my jewelry for an AA meeting. She destroyed my bedroom looking for stuff she could sell. She's not coming back. And if she did, I'd turn her away."

All Carson could do was hold her. He couldn't make her mother a better person or erase what she'd done to her daughter. He could only be here for her now.

Georgia finally pulled away, rubbing the tears away from her cheeks and creating black streaks of mascara across her pale skin. "I'm sorry to just fall apart like that. Excuse me for a minute. I've cried all my mascara off. I'm going to run to the restroom and clean up a bit."

Carson nodded. "Okay. How about I pour us some wine and order a pizza? I think we both need a little alcohol and cheese tonight."

"That sounds great. Thanks."

He watched her disappear down the hallway to the powder room. Then he went to the kitchen to open some wine and dig out the pizza-delivery flyer. Georgia's giant purse was sitting on the stack of papers he needed to search through. Since the day she'd interviewed, he'd been curious about what she had in that thing. His life fit in a wallet. What could she possibly need to carry around with her all the time?

When he lifted the straps to move the bag aside, curiosity got the best of him, and he leaned forward to peek at what she kept in there. It was hard to make out much, but he did see a white envelope with his name written on it. He knew he shouldn't do it, but he reached inside and pulled it out. When he opened the envelope, he found a check inside from Sutton. For twenty million dollars. It was made out to the Cynthia Newport Memorial Hospital for Children fund. Carson almost couldn't believe what he was looking at.

"What kind of pizz—?" Georgia stopped when she saw what was in his hand. "Did you snoop in my bag?"

"I picked it up to move it and saw this envelope with my name on it. What the hell is this about?"

"It's a check for the hospital," she said, snatching her purse from his hands. "I told you that Sutton was going to make a donation."

Carson scanned the check again and shook his head. Why had he given so much? And how long had she been holding on to it? "When did Sutton give you this check?"

Georgia frowned and her gaze dropped from his to the check in his hands. "This afternoon."

"Wait…you saw Sutton today? After he stood us all up for our meeting?"

She nodded. "He asked me to come out to his home to pick it up."

"And you didn't think to mention that to me before? You were supposed to tell me when you were going to see him. Going to his house isn't very safe, Georgia."

"You weren't around to tell. Anyway, I was going to give you that as soon as I saw you next, but I completely forgot about it with everything that happened with my mother. So here you go. He asked me to give that to you."

He wouldn't even meet his own son face-to-face, but he'd asked Georgia to come all the way out to his mansion just to give her a check? Something didn't seem right with any of this. "What did you guys talk about?"

"You, mostly."

Carson chuckled bitterly. "So he'd rather talk about me with you than actually see me or spend time with me now that he knows I'm his son?"

Georgia looked genuinely pained by his words. "You know, I don't think he's the villain you've made him out to be. All you know about him is what your mother told you and what you've learned from your cutthroat business dealings. I really think you need to spend time with him and form your own opinion."

"Why?"

"Because he's your father, Carson. You should at least give him a chance to be one to you."

"Yes, because that plan worked out so well for you and your mother." Carson snapped. It was a low blow, but he didn't care. She didn't understand what she was asking of him.

"I don't regret it, though. Yes, it didn't turn out the way I'd hoped, but at least I tried. I learned more about my past and my family—things I never would've known if I hadn't taken the chance. Yes, it cost me some personal belongings and some emotional pain, but it was worth it. You won't even give Sutton the chance."

After everything that had happened with her mother, and after Georgia had been at his side through all the drama with Sutton, Carson couldn't fathom why she would encourage him to spend time with his father. "I don't understand why you're pushing so hard for this. Whose side are you on, anyway?"

"I'm on your side, of course. Your situation with Sutton is different from mine with my mother. You've got a better shot at making this work. I would just hate for you to miss the opportunity to have a relationship with your father. That's what you've always wanted, right? You've lost so much time already. Every moment you can have with him is precious."

Sutton had said something to her. He'd woven some sob story to lure her over to his side, because she'd never stood up for him like this before. Did twenty million buy her loyalties? "What did he say to you today? What's changed?"

Georgia looked at him with conflict lining her eyes. "I can't tell you."

"You can't or you just won't? Where do your loyalties lie, Georgia? It sounds like you're choosing Sutton over me."

She gave him an indignant frown and crossed her arms over her chest. "I am not choosing Sutton over you. I want you. I only want you. I just care for you very much, and I know how important this is."

"If you cared for me, you'd tell me what he said," Carson stated.

"I can't. I gave my word that I wouldn't tell anyone before he got to talk to everyone, including you. I'm telling you this much because I care and I don't want you to do something you'll regret later. You're going to have to trust me on this."

"Trust you? How can I trust you when you've been spending so much time with him under the guise of being a spy? When my corporate rival sends me a check for twenty million dollars with you as the only courier he trusts? Am I not right to get a little suspicious?"

Georgia's eyes widened. "Twenty million dollars?"

Was she really surprised? "What? You didn't know how much he'd written it for? Certainly he didn't give me this much out of the kindness of his heart. This had to be some kind of payment, like you've earned every penny on your back."

Georgia gasped, her mouth dropping open in surprise. "That's a hateful thing to say, Carson. My dedication to your mother's charity only goes so far. I have not, nor would I ever, have something to do with Sutton outside business."

"Why else would he give me that much? Does he have a sudden fondness for sick children?" He shook his head and put the check on the counter. "I guess I should give you a raise for going above and beyond for the company. Not everyone at the Newport Corporation has that much dedication to their job."

Georgia stumbled back as though he'd struck her. It truly felt as though he had. She reached out for the counter to stabilize herself and gather her wits. "You can take that raise and shove it, along with the job, *Mr. Newport*. I thought we really had something, but I was being naive. You've spent your whole life thinking you aren't good enough and didn't deserve a woman's love, so you wouldn't know it if it bit you. You'd rather push me away, so fine. Your wish is granted. If you can't trust me, then we don't have anything. I didn't go behind your back and I didn't sleep with your father. I don't want to be with someone, or work for someone, who could ever think otherwise."

His brow raised in surprise. "You're quitting?"

"Yes. I think I am."

Carson crossed his arms defensively over his chest. "Are you going to run back to Sutton and beg for that job he offered you?"

"I'm not going to dignify that with an answer. I knew it was a bad idea to get involved with you. I shouldn't have let my emotions rule my head. Lesson learned."

Turning on her heel, she marched out of Carson's apartment. Angry tears streamed down her cheeks as she exited the building and stopped at the street corner to wait for the light. She pulled a tissue out of her purse and blew her nose. She was getting tired of crying.

The day had started out so well. She'd been basking in her newly discovered love for Carson and her budding relationship with her mother. And now, only twelve hours later, she had nothing—including a reason to stay around Chicago. She needed a break from this town.

Raising her arm to hail a taxi, she climbed inside one as it stopped at the curb.

"Where to?" he asked.

"O'Hare Airport."

Georgia wanted someone who would listen to her. She couldn't count on her mother or her lover for that. The only person she could count on, the only person she'd ever been truly able to trust, was her old social worker, Sheila. She gave the best advice in the world and maybe, just maybe, she could help Georgia sort her way out of his mess.

Twelve

Carson sat on his couch, staring at his silent cell phone. It had been three days since Georgia walked out, and there hadn't been the slightest sign of her. He didn't think she would call, not really. After everything that had happened that night, he expected her to tuck her tail and go running back to Sutton. He did, however, expect her to at least show up at work to pack up her things.

So far, her office remained dark and untouched. He could've had Rebecca pack it for her, but frankly, he was hoping she would change her mind about quitting. They had no business dating, but she was still a damn good PR person, and it would be hard to replace her. He needed to remind himself of this exact moment if he ever looked at another employee with interest again.

He was just about to set his phone back on the coffee table when it rang in his hand. It was Graham's ringtone, not Georgia's.

"Yes?" he answered.

"I have news," Graham said. "Sutton has called a meeting for tomorrow. We're all to be there, but he didn't elaborate on why."

"I suppose he'll show up for his own meeting," Carson said bitterly. As he said it, he was reminded of what Georgia had said to him—that Sutton was waiting to make some kind of announcement that she couldn't share with him. This must be it, although Carson couldn't fathom what it could be about. Bringing all the kids together seemed like a recipe for disaster. "Do you think Eve was able to talk him into changing the will?"

"I have no idea. If she did, I've underestimated her, because she's worked a miracle in days."

"Will we get the test results back before we meet with them?" The paternity test on the twins was being run a second time, and they expected to hear from the lab any day now.

"Who knows? Maybe that's what Sutton is anticipating. If he knows we're his sons and the test is just a formality, he may be tired of fighting and ready to just accept us even without the results back. I'll let Rebecca know to put it on our calendars for tomorrow."

If Sutton was about to deliver the news that Georgia had hinted at, it would be big. Big enough that she couldn't tell him despite how many times he demanded she do it. "Okay," he replied after an extended silence.

The line was quiet for a moment. "Carson, what's wrong?"

Carson had deliberately not mentioned the blowup

with Georgia to his brothers. They had enough to
worry about with Sutton. They didn't need his relationship drama on top of the task of finding a new PR
director to handle the hospital promotions.

"Is it Georgia?" Graham pressed. "I noticed she
wasn't in the office today. She hasn't quit to go work
for Sutton, has she?"

Carson couldn't avoid the topic any longer. "She
has quit, but I don't know where's she's gone."

"What happened?"

"This crap with Sutton happened, and when she
said some things I didn't like, I lashed out at her. Then
she quit."

"Sorry, man. I guess that's why you don't date co-
workers. When you break up, it impacts everything
else. Should I have HR open a requisition for a new
PR person?"

"Not yet," Carson said, although he really didn't
know why. The odds were that Georgia was not coming back. He certainly wouldn't after what was said
between them. "Give it a few days," he suggested.
"Let's deal with Sutton's meeting and the fallout from
that first."

One fire at a time.

"Here you go, sweetie."

Georgia looked up and took the cup of hot tea from
her friend and former social worker, Sheila. "Thank
you," she said. "And thank you for taking me in for a
few days. I just didn't know where else to go."

Sheila took her own cup of tea with her to sit in the
wingback chair beside the couch where Georgia was
lounging with a blanket. She'd called from O'Hare,

and when she showed up on Sheila's doorstep in Detroit at nearly midnight without so much as a change of clothes, she was welcomed like family.

She supposed that was what Sheila was to her. The only family she'd ever had. She'd been there for her since she was assigned her case when Georgia was ten. Sheila did her best to place Georgia in the most stable, safe homes she could, but there weren't always a lot of options, so she tried to help in other ways. She assisted Georgia with her college and scholarship applications. She encouraged her to go to Northwestern and make something of herself. She'd also counseled her that finding her real family wasn't always the best decision.

Sheila hit the nail on the head with that advice.

"I'll help around the house while I'm here," Georgia added. As a new foster child in a home, she always found she was accepted more readily if she became useful. "I don't want you spoiling me like a houseguest."

"You've had a pretty rough week," Sheila said. "And even if you hadn't, I'd still spoil you because you deserve it. You can help if you want to, but there's really no need. I doubt two grown women will make much of a mess to worry about."

Georgia accepted her words and sipped at her tea. It was hot but not too hot, with the perfect splash of cream and sugar like the cup she'd had at Sutton's estate. How had everything in her life fallen apart since that day? She'd fallen in love, had a breakthrough with Sutton and was really getting somewhere with Misty, and the hospital project was coming along so well. Now she was single, motherless and unemployed.

"Do you have any plans while you're in Detroit?"

"Not really. I fled here before I really had a game plan. I just knew I had to get out of Chicago. But now that I'm here, I'm starting to wonder if I should go back at all."

"Why would you say that?"

"There's nothing for me there. I can unload my loft pretty easily and have my things shipped here. I don't have a job or friends there. My whole life was about my work. A fresh start in Detroit might be just what I need."

Sheila didn't bother to mask her frown. "You're talking nonsense, honey. For the work you do, Chicago is where you need to be. You love your apartment. You don't need a car like you would here. You may think there isn't much for you in Chicago, but there's certainly more than there is here. All you have in Detroit are bad memories."

"That's not true," Georgia said. "Misty said that I have a brother and sister here in Detroit that she gave up for adoption. I thought I might be able to track them down. Do you think you could help me do that?"

"That's a tricky thing to do. It depends a lot on how the adoption was done. They might not even know they were adopted if their parents didn't tell them. I'll do what I can within the limits of my job, but you might not find what you're looking for with them, either."

"What am I looking for?" Georgia asked.

"A family. You didn't get what you wanted with your mother, and I don't think it will pan out with your siblings, either. I've been doing this work for a long time, and there aren't a lot of happy endings. If I were you, instead of working so hard and focusing on the past, I'd focus on your future and having a family of your own."

A family of her own?

Honestly, that was something that had never really taken root in her mind. Her fleeting time with Carson, such as it was, was the closest thing she'd had to a serious relationship. The idea of marriage and commitment was an alien concept, and after her breakup with Carson, it seemed to be that much further away. She didn't seem to have good judgment when it came to men. Perhaps steering clear for a while was the best idea.

And while the occasional thought of *one day when I have kids* would pop up from time to time, that day never seemed to arrive. She still had plenty of childbearing years ahead of her, but it already seemed like a lost cause unless she got brave enough to buy sperm and go it alone. That would be a terrible decision. She'd never had a mother, so how would she know how to be one? The last thing she wanted to do was fail at something that important the way her mother had.

"I don't need a family of my own," Georgia argued. "I have you."

Sheila set her tea down on the coffee table and moved over to the couch beside Georgia. She put her arm around her shoulder and hugged her close. "Yes, you do. But you don't have to be in Detroit for that. You'll have me wherever you are, Georgia. I know you've had a lot of bad things happen all at once, but you can't just give up on everything you've worked for. You could always take the job at Elite Industries, couldn't you?"

That offer was technically still on the table. If she

accepted the position, it would be minus the mistress part, of course. But even if she did feel like she'd had some kind of breakthrough with Sutton, he wouldn't be around long. She didn't know Eve well enough, and she wouldn't want her presumptions about their professional relationship to get her canned again in a few months. "I'm not sure that's a very good idea."

"Well, that's the beauty of a town like Chicago. There is nothing but opportunity there."

"You're right," Georgia agreed. She knew Sheila was right. It just seemed easier to run away than to deal with the mess she'd left behind. In Detroit, she'd never have to worry about running into Carson, and then maybe she could ignore the heartbreak. She felt the prickle of tears sting her eyes again.

"Are you going to be okay, Georgia?"

She shrugged as she looked at her only friend and fought back the tears. "You know, a part of me was always expecting my mother to do what she did. Whether I can blame her or her addiction, it just seemed like I was waiting for the other shoe to drop. The thing with Carson is that much harder. I thought what we had was… I don't know. The things he said to me were just so cruel, so unlike the man I knew. He lashed out at me like an abused dog."

"In that case, do you blame the dog or the owner that abused her?" Sheila asked.

"Carson is too old to blame anyone but himself. But I could tell that I'd hit his hot buttons. It caught me so off guard, you know? He's handsome, successful, rich, powerful…and yet he seemed to just be waiting for me to turn on him."

"Sometimes the more successful you are, the more

people are waiting around to knock you off your pedestal. Everyone has their issues. His knee-jerk reflex was stronger than most, but it sounds like a pretty hard-wired defense mechanism. Here's a question for you, though. If he realizes he's made a mistake and apologizes, would you take him back?"

Georgia had pondered that question since she got to Detroit. "I probably would," she admitted. "I've given everyone else in my life a second chance, even when they didn't deserve it and I regretted it in the end. Maybe this time will be different. Or not. But either way, I love him. I might be a fool, but I do."

"Okay," Sheila said. "So when he has this miraculous revelation and rushes to tell you he's sorry and how much he loves you, how the heck is he supposed to find you here?"

The six potential and confirmed children of Sutton Winchester were gathered silently around the old man's conference room table. No one seemed very keen to chat; they just glared across the table at one another.

The middle sister, Nora, had come from Colorado today. Carson had never seen her before. Since she'd left Chicago, he didn't run into her at any industry events the way he tended to bump into Eve. She'd gotten out and he didn't blame her. She was probably the smartest one of them all.

A moment later, the door opened and Sutton came in with a woman at his side. Carson hoped it wasn't another mistress. His father didn't need any more women in his life, and he certainly didn't need to be flaunting one in front of his kids. Of course, she didn't really look like his type. This lady was very buttoned up, almost studious looking. She was wearing a light gray suit, and her wheat-blond hair was pulled back into a tight bun.

Sutton pulled back the chair for the woman to take the seat beside him, and he sat at the head of the table. Carson noted a slight tremble in the old man's hand as he moved. He did look thinner than the last time he'd seen him. Sutton looked like hell, frankly. Georgia had been right: this wasn't just a stomach bug.

"I'm sure that all of you are curious about why I called you here today," Sutton began. "If I had time to waste, I'd prolong the suspense, but I don't, so I'll get right to the point. I'm dying."

Carson didn't react. Instead he turned to watch his three newfound sisters gasp in shock and horror. Nora's hand flew to cover her mouth, and Grace's eyes started to well up with tears.

"What?" Eve asked. "Dying? Are you sure?"

"Yes. This is Dr. Wilde," he said, gesturing to the prim woman beside him. "She'll be treating me at the Midwest Regional Medical Center for my stage IV lung cancer—not that there's much that can be done. We'll try a few things because I hate just lying down and letting cancer win, but I've already come to terms with the fact that I won't see the new year."

Stage IV. Cancer. Dead before the new year. The words flew around in Carson's brain as he tried to process it all. Finally he turned to Brooks, and they exchanged a meaningful glance. They'd gone into this thinking they had plenty of time to achieve their goals. Even if Sutton was stubborn, they knew they would eventually convince him to change his will and include them. But now…the clock was ticking. The father they'd just gained would be gone before they knew it.

"I'm getting things in order, and then I'll be going to the hospital. I'm not sure when I'll be discharged, if ever," he continued.

"We're going to be trying some experimental treatments," Dr. Wilde said. "At this point, we don't have anything to lose, and we have everything to gain. But really, all we're buying your father is time. Eventually he will succumb."

"Oh, Daddy!" Grace leaped up from her seat and rushed to give her father a hug.

Carson watched with a twinge of jealousy as Sutton gently stroked his daughter's hair and held her close. He doubted his father would ever hug him like that. They wouldn't get to that point even if Sutton had decades to live instead of months.

"Don't you worry about me, Gracie. I've lived three lifetimes while I've been on this earth."

"How am I going to handle all of this without you?" Eve said with a startled look in her eye. The pressure of taking over Elite Industries seemed to be weighing as heavily on her shoulders as the loss of her father.

"Oh, please, Eve," Sutton said with a dismissive tone. "You're smart and capable. You practically run the company now. You'll be fine. You will all be just fine without me. I think some of you might even be better off," Sutton said, pointedly looking at Carson.

It was the first time they'd made eye contact since the truth came out about Carson's paternity. The first hint of acknowledgment.

"All that said, we have some other business to tend

to today." Sutton held up a package with a logo that Carson recognized from the lab. "It seems we've received the test results for Graham and Brooks. Would one of you care to do the honors?"

Brooks took the folder and quickly opened it. Carson just watched Sutton. There was a smugness on his face that convinced him that Sutton had been telling the truth all along. He didn't need the test results to know the twins weren't his children. But how could he know for certain?

"Sutton Winchester is not our father," Brooks said after scanning the document for what seemed like a lifetime.

Sutton sat back in his chair and folded his hands casually over his stomach. There was a small curl of amusement on his lips as he watched Graham and Brooks reel from the news.

Carson wasn't taking it well, either. He'd spent his whole life feeling different, feeling separated from his brothers. He'd convinced himself that it was just because they were twins and had an extraordinarily close relationship. He'd ignored the fact that he looked different. But now the variations were glaringly obvious.

It just left one question. If Sutton wasn't their father, then who the hell was? They were back at the drawing board with his brothers' paternity.

"Well," Graham said as he turned to Sutton, "now that this is settled, I believe we can move forward with the requested changes to the will."

"You don't still expect to be included, do you?" Eve asked.

"No," Graham said. "Since I am not your half brother, Brooks and I have no claim. But Carson still does. The only difference is that the estate should be divided by four instead of six."

"This is ridiculous!" one of the sisters shouted.

Carson didn't bother to look up and see which one it was. Everyone at the table started yelling all at once. He didn't bother to open his mouth. He let them carry on.

In that moment, none of it really mattered to him. Yes, he was still angry with his father, but it sounded like cancer would get his revenge faster and more thoroughly than Carson ever would. If he got any money out of the estate, he would put it toward the hospital along with the twenty million Sutton had already donated. The children's hospital built in his mother's name would be amazing.

And on the day it opened, there would be a different PR director by his side. It seemed wrong that any of it could happen without Georgia. She had been with him since—

The thought was interrupted as a sudden realization hit Carson like a punch to the gut.

She *knew.*

Georgia knew that Sutton was dying. He didn't know why Sutton had decided to tell her before he even told his own children, but it had to be the secret she couldn't share. In an instant, all the pieces of that horrible evening started to fit together. That's why she was encouraging him to get to know his father, damn near pushing him into it. She knew that he wouldn't have much time with Sutton.

And perhaps his pending mortality was why Sutton had written such a big check to the foundation. It wasn't as though he could take it with him, despite his best efforts. Was it possible it had nothing to do with Georgia's relationship with Sutton at all?

As quickly as it all came together, a final thought entered Carson's mind—he was a royal jerk. He'd accused her of taking sides, being disloyal to the company and to him, and even suggested she'd been sleeping with Sutton. All this after he'd encouraged her to keep seeing Sutton so Carson could use her for information.

Without thinking, Carson stood suddenly. The whole table stopped squabbling and looked at him in anticipation.

"I have to go."

Graham reached out and grabbed his arm. "What do you mean, you have to go?"

"I've got to find Georgia and apologize."

Both twins looked at him with aqua eyes that reflected their concern that he'd gone mad. "We're kind of in the middle of something important. Do you have to go right now?" Brooks asked.

"Absolutely, right now," Sutton agreed, backing him up in a way Carson hadn't expected. "Don't let a jewel like that get away, son." He winked and gave him a small smile.

Son? A lump formed in Carson's throat. He couldn't respond to his brothers or his father. He knew he just had to get out of there. Without another word, he stepped away from the table and made his way out of the office. He had more important issues to tend to.

He had to track Georgia down.

Thirteen

Carson blew into the Newport building like a tornado. The elevator couldn't move fast enough for him as it raced to the top floor, where their executive offices were.

"Rebecca!" he shouted almost the moment the doors started to part. "Rebecca, I need you!"

By the time he reached his assistant's desk outside his office, Rebecca's eyes were wide with surprise and panic. "What is it, sir? Is everything okay?"

"Yes and no," he said, making a beeline for his door. "Please come in and bring your tablet."

He settled in at his desk and turned to face Rebecca, who was at the ready, as always. "I need you to help me find Georgia."

"She's not in today, Mr. Newport. I actually haven't seen her this week."

"Yes, I know. That's because she quit."

"Oh no," she gasped. "When? I hadn't heard any-thing about it."

"A few days ago."

Rebecca studied him for a moment. "What did you do, sir?"

Carson looked up in surprise. She'd been his as-sistant for five years now. Apparently she knew him better than he gave her credit for. "Well, you know we were dating, right?"

"Everyone knew, sir."

"Okay, then. As expected, I put my foot so far into my mouth, I crapped my shoe. It's all my fault, and I know it. I'm not sure she'll ever forgive me for being such a jerk, but I'm going to try."

"Are you in love with her?"

He'd never really had a personal conversation like this with Rebecca. Typically their discussions were work related, or they exchanged casual pleasantries about her kids and how her weekend was. They usu-ally didn't talk about Carson's personal life. Of course, Carson hadn't really had much of a personal life until recently. At a time like this, he needed all the help he could get, especially if it came in the form of femi-nine relationship wisdom.

Did he love her? "Yes. Absolutely." He knew that much was true when Georgia's presumed betrayal had hurt so badly. He'd let himself fall for her only to have her drop him for a bigger fish just like Candy had, only this one hurt ten times worse because he loved her. Realizing she hadn't done any of the things he'd accused her of only made it that much more painful.

"That's refreshing to hear," Rebecca said. "Does she love you?"

That he wasn't sure about. Because of her tears and
anger, he was certain his accusations cut deep. She'd
never said she was in love with him, but it was early.
No one wanted to be first. To get her back, he would
shout it from the rooftops. "I don't know. I hope so."

Rebecca nodded thoughtfully. "And what big gesture are you planning to woo her back?"

Big gesture? "I haven't really thought that far yet.
First we've got to find her."

"We'll find her, sir. I have no worries about that.
But when we do, it's crucial you know what you're
going to say. Screw that up and we might as well save
ourselves the time of tracking her down."

Carson swallowed hard. She was right. This was
one of the most important things he would ever do, and
he couldn't wing it. Georgia deserved better. "What
do you suggest?"

"For one, apologize. No caveats, no justifications.
Just apologize. Two, give her flowers. It's a cliché,
but that's because it works. My husband can make me
absolutely insane and then walk in with a handful of
lilies and I melt. Do you know what kind she likes?"

"No."

Rebecca twisted her lips in thought. "When you get
to the florist, pick some that remind you of her. You
can't go wrong with that tactic. Then tell her you love
her and see what happens. From there, it's up to her."

"That's it?" That sounded far too easy.

"Well, it depends." Rebecca arched a curious eyebrow at him before she laid down her challenge. "Are
you wanting to go all the way? Pull out all the stops?"

Yes. Yes, he did want to go all the way, and he knew
exactly where to take it from there. "You're right. All

the way it is. I'll take care of that part this afternoon. Now we've got to get her back, you and I. The problem is, she's vanished. We've got to figure out where she's gone. I just went by her building and her doorman says she's got a hold on her mail with no expected return date. That's not a good sign."

"Does she have family nearby or friends she would stay with?"

"I don't think so, at least not family. I'm not so sure about friends."

"Would you like me to look in her office? Maybe she had an address book or something? I could also get the IT department to log into her laptop, and we can see who's in her contact lists."

Alarm bells started going off in Carson's head. Yes, that was probably the smartest, most direct choice, but he remembered the look in Georgia's eyes when she realized he's looked into her purse. She had very strong personal boundaries, and understandably so. Technically her office was company property and he could do what he liked, especially since she'd quit, but if he could avoid that, he wanted to.

"Let's start with talking to her assistant and co-workers first to see if they have any ideas. Maybe we can strike gold without digging too far into her personal things. I know she doesn't like that. Let me know the minute you find anything."

Rebecca stood up, tapping at her screen. She was almost to the door when a name popped into Carson's mind.

"Rebecca? Let me know if you find any references to a Sheila. That's the only person she's ever mentioned. She probably lives, or at least lived, in Detroit."

"Sheila. Got it." With that, she disappeared to start the hunt.

With her on Georgia's trail, Carson started on the next task—going all the way. He called to make an appointment at Tiffany and Co. and headed there about an hour later. By the time he returned to the office with a tiny blue bag and a stomach full of nerves, Rebecca was sitting at her desk with a bright smile. "What?"

She handed over a piece of paper with a name, a phone number and a Detroit address for Sheila. "Georgia's assistant had this information. Apparently she sent flowers to her on Mother's Day. That sounds like the place to start."

"You're amazing," Carson said with a wide grin. "I'm going to give her a call right now."

Carson went into his office and shut the door. He had a feeling that Sheila would know where Georgia had run off to. He'd follow her anywhere she'd gone. He just needed to know what flight to take.

The phone rang for what felt like a lifetime. "Hello?" a woman's voice finally answered.

"Hello. Is this Sheila?"

"Yes, it is. Who's this?"

"My name is Carson Newport. I'm—"

"Hold on a second," Sheila said, interrupting him. He sat waiting silently, his heart pounding in his throat as he heard her shuffling around and then doing something that sounded like closing a door. "Okay, that's better. I don't want her to hear us talking."

Her? "Is Georgia there with you?"

"She is. She's been here a few days."

He'd hit the jackpot on the first try. *Thank you, Re-*

becca. She was getting a raise. "Thank goodness," he said. "I didn't know where else to look if you didn't know where she'd gone. I've got to get her back."

"I'm glad to hear that. She doesn't have many places to go, Carson. Georgia never really had a home or a family. I'm just her social worker, but I'm the only person she has. Except for you. Does she still have you?"

"Yes, she absolutely still has me. I don't want her to ever feel like she has to run away. I want her to run *to* me from here on out."

"You sound very confident, Carson, but Georgia is very hurt. You crossed a line with her. She's not the kind that trusts easily to begin with, so it's going to take a lot more than a smile and a casual 'I'm sorry' to earn her trust back."

"I know that. She deserves far more than that," Carson answered. "She deserves a man she can trust. One who makes her feel safe and loved, and I want to be that man. I love her and I feel like a fool for letting my past issues color the situation. I—"

"Honey, save it for her," Sheila interrupted. "How soon can you get to Detroit?"

Carson looked down at his watch. It wasn't a long flight, but the logistics of the airport, even with a private flight, would take time. "By dinnertime."

"Good. I'll keep her distracted and at the house until you get here. She was talking about going out to eat, but I'm going to insist on cooking something special that she can't refuse. You've got my address on Mayflower?"

The slip of paper showed the right address. "I do. I'll have a car take me straight there from the airport."

"Good. I look forward to meeting you, Carson."

He hung up the phone, feeling a triumphant surge of adrenaline running through his veins. "Rebecca, book me the next available flight to Detroit!" he shouted and started gathering up everything he needed to leave.

When he looked up a few minutes later, Brooks was standing in the doorway with a frown on his face. His large frame filled the space; he was like an angry Viking. Carson was about to get it, he was certain. With Georgia absorbing his every thought, he'd forgotten that he'd left his brothers in the lion's den that morning.

"What the hell was all that about back at Sutton's? You walked out of a huge meeting. You left Graham and me dangling after the paternity test bombshell."

"I'm sorry," Carson said. He hadn't really considered that his brothers were probably upset about the news that their father was still a mystery. Graham had barely blinked, launching into an argument that would just secure a larger piece of the pie for Carson. "How did it go?"

Brooks shrugged. "A stalemate. With him dying, we don't have much time. And of course, there's still the matter of tracking down our father. How could you leave in the middle of all that? It was a crucial turning point for our plan."

Carson knew that, but in the moment, it simply hadn't mattered. "I just had to go. This was more important."

He didn't think it was possible, but Brooks's frown deepened. "She's just a woman, Carson. They come and go. We're talking about getting revenge for our mother. Making Sutton pay for how he treated her and abandoned you. How can some lady you're dating possibly be more important?"

Carson took a deep breath and sighed. Nothing he said would diffuse his brother's anger. It had taken Carson a while to get to this point, too. "Nothing we do to Sutton is going to change what happened to Mom. We can't change the past. We can't right the wrongs of thirty years ago. I've decided the future—my future with Georgia—is more important." He stood up and grabbed the baby blue bag from his desktop. "And she's not just a lady I'm dating, Brooks. At least, not for much longer."

"Is that what I think it is?" Brooks asked, his aqua eyes wide with surprise.

"Yep. The future starts today."

Georgia was helping put together a salad when a knock sounded at the front door. Sheila had dismissed her offer of a nice dinner out as a thank-you for taking her in, so she insisted on at least helping to cook.

"I'm in the middle of finishing up the pasta," Sheila said. "Can you get the door? It's probably just a package. I'm addicted to Amazon Prime."

"Sure thing." Georgia wiped her hands on a dish towel and trotted over to the front door. She flung it open, and stood frozen in shock when she found Carson on the doorstep instead of the delivery man.

"Hello, Georgia." He was wearing one of his best Armani suits and holding a bundle of bright pinkish-red roses in his hands.

How had he found her here? Georgia's gaze narrowed in suspicion as she glanced over her shoulder. The kitchen was miraculously empty, confirming what she thought to be true. Sheila had conspired against her and brought him here. She'd given Georgia no warning at all. She could've at least told her to change. Her hair was in a ponytail. She was wearing a pair of capri jeans and an oversized Detroit Lions T-shirt she'd bought at Walmart because she hadn't brought any clothes with her. She self-consciously ran her hand over her hair to smooth the flyaways.

"Are you going to say something?" he asked. His green eyes were pleading with her.

She wasn't going to give in that easily. She wanted to. Seeing him in that suit with those sad green eyes made her want to melt to the floor, but she wouldn't. Carson had a lot of groveling to do before she was going to forgive him for how he'd treated her. "I would, but it seems that everything I say or do is twisted and used against me somehow. It's probably better that I just let you do all the talking."

Carson nodded, his gaze dropping to the flowers in his hands. "That's fair. I deserve that. You're absolutely right. I took your well-intended advice and hard work for the company and turned them into something licentious. I should've trusted you the way you asked me to, and I didn't. I am very sorry for that. I realize now that I colored everything with my own hang-ups, and they had nothing to do with you. You didn't deserve any of the horrible things I said to you that night."

Georgia listened to him as he spilled his guts. He seemed genuine in his apology. But that wasn't nearly enough to heal what he'd broken.

"Sutton got everyone together yesterday and announced that he's dying. Of course, you already knew that." Carson looked at her, probably searching for some confirmation in her eyes. She kept a neutral expression. "I'm not sure he and I will ever be close, but I understand now what you meant about giving it a shot while I have the chance. We're far from good, but I'm open to the possibility, at least. That's a big step for me."

"Good for you. What about your brothers?" she asked in a flat tone. It would be hard for Carson to accept his father if his brothers felt different.

"Well, it turns out they're just my half brothers. Sutton is not their father."

Georgia nodded. This was also not news to her. She'd been right when she said Sutton was a jerk, but not a liar. "He told them that, but Graham wouldn't listen."

"I'm sure he did. Listen, I'm not sure what's going to happen with Sutton, or my brothers, or anything else there, but I know that I want you back in Chicago when it happens. The Newport Corporation needs you, Georgia. The plans for the charity gala have fallen apart since you left. The donation from Sutton needs to be put to good use and frankly, I need help. You're an integral part of the Newport family, and we need you. I want you there when we have the ribbon cutting because this only could've happened with you at my side."

Georgia felt her hopes start to crumble. Was that all he wanted from her? Public relations skills? He'd wasted a trip if that was all he had to offer her. "You've come an awfully long way just to offer me my job back, Carson. You could've done that over the phone." Not that she would've answered.

He winced slightly and shook his head. "No, I couldn't. And you know full well this is about more than just your job, Georgia."

"Then what *is* it about? Because that's all you've talked about."

"Okay. I know. Work is just easier to talk about for me." Carson swallowed hard and thrust the roses out to her. "These are for you. They're American Beauties. I thought that was the perfect rose for you."

She accepted the bundle of flowers and brought them up to her nose. They were amazingly fragrant and delicate with velvety petals. No one had ever given her flowers before. She hadn't even gotten a corsage at the prom because she didn't go. She never could've afforded the dress and everything that went with it. Since then, her relationships had been far too casual for a romantic gesture like flowers.

"Thank you," she said, unable to tear her eyes away from them.

"What I really came here to say…aside from apologizing…is that I miss you so much. Once you left, it was like I had this hole in my chest that I couldn't fill. I've always felt that way about not having my father in my life, like there was a part of me missing somehow. I'm sure you know how that feels, too, growing up without any family.

"After our fight," he continued, "I realized that those two feelings were different. In reality, I couldn't control my father and if he wanted to be in my life or not. But I was the reason you were gone, and I could do something about it. Blood doesn't always make a family. Sometimes it's more about who you choose. I don't just want you to be a part of the Newport Corporation family, Georgia. I want you to be a part of my family. We've both felt like we haven't really ever had one, or that we've lost it along the way. What I'm offering you is the chance to have a family, a real family, at last. With me."

Georgia clutched the roses in her hands as he spoke. Her chest grew tighter with every word. Was he really saying what it sounded like? That was impossible.

"I love you, Georgia. I'm stubborn and stupid and scared to death of this, and I know that I almost ruined it…maybe I have…but it doesn't change how I feel for you. I've spent my life being afraid of losing people because I wasn't worthy of their love. When I thought the same thing was happening with you, I reacted. I exploded. I pushed you away to protect myself, and it was absolutely the wrong thing to do.

"In the end, I was just as alone, just as heartbroken as if you'd left me, but I did it to myself. I don't want to make that same mistake twice. So this time," Carson said as he reached into his pocket, "I'm going to make it permanent."

When Carson pulled his hand from his inner breast pocket, there was a small, distinctively aqua-colored box in his hand. A Tiffany and Co. jewelry box by the looks of it. No one had ever given her jewelry, either, and since her mother had cleaned her out, the contents of that box were all the jewelry in the world that was hers. Or might be hers.

Georgia watched as Carson sank down onto one knee on Sheila's doorstep. "Georgia, I want us to start our own family here and now. You and me. I want us to put the past and all our pain behind us and start our lives together anew. If you'll agree to be my wife,

I promise to do everything I can to make you feel loved, valued, safe and special every day for the rest of your life."

Carson took the lid off the box to reveal a classic round Tiffany solitaire in a platinum band. She was no expert, but it had to be at least two or three carats. "I hope you like it. I wanted to go with something classic and traditional since neither of us have had much of that in our lives. You're beautiful and timeless and I wanted your ring to be the same."

"It's gorgeous," she said, although her words were muffled by her hand covering her mouth.

"Will you marry me, Georgia?" Carson held up the ring between his fingertips. The sunlight caught the large gem, and it sparkled with a thousand colors.

"Say yes, you fool!" a voice whispered harshly from the back of the house.

She didn't need Sheila's prompting to make up her mind. "Yes," she said, tossing the flowers onto the nearby table. "Not just yes, but hell yes."

Carson grinned wide and slipped the ring onto her finger. Squeezing her hand in his, he stood up and looked down at her with eyes that reflected the love and adoration she'd never expected to see. "I'm pleased by your enthusiasm," he said.

"You ain't seen nothing yet." Georgia smiled, wrapping her arms around his neck and bringing her lips to his.

* * * * *

Don't miss a single instalment of the
DYNASTIES: THE NEWPORTS
*Passion and chaos consume a Chicago
real estate empire*

SAYING YES TO THE BOSS
by Andrea Laurence

AN HEIR FOR THE BILLIONAIRE
by Kat Cantrell

CLAIMED BY THE COWBOY
by Sarah M. Anderson

HIS SECRET BABY BOMBSHELL
by Jules Bennett

BACK IN THE ENEMY'S BED
by Michelle Celmer

THE TEXAN'S ONE NIGHT STAND-OFF
by Charlene Sands

Available now from Mills & Boon Desire!

MILLS & BOON®

Desire

PASSIONATE AND DRAMATIC LOVE STORIES

A sneak peek at next month's titles...

In stores from 14th July 2016:

- **For Baby's Sake** – Janice Maynard *and*
  The CEO Daddy Next Door – Karen Booth

- **An Heir for the Billionaire** – Kat Cantrell *and*
  Waking Up with the Boss – Sheri WhiteFeather

- **Pregnant by the Maverick Millionaire** – Joss Wood *and*
  Contract Wedding, Expectant Bride – Yvonne Lindsay

MILLS & BOON®

Mills & Boon have been at the heart of romance since 1908... and while the fashions may have changed, one thing remains the same: from pulse-pounding passion to the gentlest caress, we're always known how to bring romance alive.

Now, we're delighted to present you with these irresistible illustrations, inspired by the vintage glamour of our covers. So indulge your wildest dreams and unleash your imagination as we present the most iconic Mills & Boon moments of the last century.

Visit **www.millsandboon.co.uk/ArtofRomance** to order yours!

MILLS & BOON®

Why not subscribe?
Never miss a title and save money too!

Here is what's available to you if you join the exclusive **Mills & Boon® Book Club** today:

* *Titles up to a month ahead of the shops*
* *Amazing discounts*
* *Free P&P*
* *Earn Bonus Book points that can be redeemed against other titles and gifts*
* *Choose from monthly or pre-paid plans*

Still want more?
Well, if you join today we'll even give you
50% OFF your first parcel!

So visit **www.millsandboon.co.uk/subscriptions**
or call **Customer Relations on 0844 844 1351***
to be a part of this exclusive Book Club!